# THE GOOD SISTER

ALSO BY JESS RYDER

*Lie to Me*

# THE GOOD SISTER

Jess Ryder

bookouture

Published by Bookouture
An imprint of StoryFire Ltd.
23 Sussex Road, Ickenham, UB10 8PN
United Kingdom
www.bookouture.com



ISBN: 978-1-78681-213-1
eBook ISBN: 978-1-78681-212-4

To all my ‘good sisters’.

# PROLOGUE

## August 1992

*Today, about a million people in the UK are descended from the Vikings. A finger deformity known as Dupuytren's disease is found in some people with Viking ancestry. This is possibly connected to the congenital condition of 'trigger thumbs'.*

He spread a blanket on the warm grass and laid the girls on their backs. Bending over to bathe them in his generous shadow, he carefully undid their pure white sleepsuits – so new they hadn't even been through the wash once. He stripped them down to their nappies to let them kick their long, slender legs. They looked so exquisite he could hardly breathe. He took their tiny hands in his and marvelled at the smallness of their fingers; gazed deeply into their bright blue eyes; stroked every inch of their soft pink skin, as yet unblemished by cuts and bruises. He smoothed the fragile wisps of auburn hair – the very same shade as his own – as they fluttered in the soft breeze. They were perfect. Genetic miracles of his own creation. Daddy's girls. His darlings. His warrior princesses both.

# CHAPTER ONE

## Now

*The Vikings came from Scandinavia, travelling very long distances from home to settle in other lands, including Britain, France, Ireland and as far as North America.*

It's three a.m. and he hasn't fallen asleep yet, not even for a few moments. His eyes are wide open, pupils fully dilated, and the room feels hot and airless. He lifts his head and looks through the monochrome gloom to the curtains, hanging heavy and motionless. What to do? If he gets out of bed to open the window, he'll need a pee. But then he'll be fully awake and might as well make a cup of tea. Watch a bit of telly. Check his emails. Read the latest threatening text.

That's the real reason he can't sleep. Nothing to do with the stuffy atmosphere, or the bottle of wine he drank with dinner. He eases himself out of bed, rising to his full, imposing height. He wraps a bath towel around his nakedness and, shutting the door behind him with a gentle click, pads barefoot down the stairs.

He creeps into the living room and gradually turns up the dimmer, catching his reflection in the patio doors and seeing a tall man with a decent set of abs, a strong straight nose, and bright blue eyes that contrast well against his full auburn beard. He's known as the Viking. In his fifties, and yet the female students still flutter around him, begging for 'feedback' on their mediocre essays. For years he revelled in his striking Nordic looks, but now they feel like a curse.

He goes to his briefcase and takes a small pay-as-you-go phone out of the inside pocket. He forgot to put it on charge at work and now there's hardly any battery left. He squints at the tiny screen, his stomach sinking as he reads the messages. So she's awake too.

*The deadline is almost up.*

*I mean it.*

Then a fifteen-minute gap.

*Are you ignoring me?*

Five minutes.

*Such a bad idea.*

Then nothing for an hour. Perhaps, like him, she went to bed. He imagines her tossing and turning between the sheets, unable to sleep with her brain on high alert for the bleep of his reply. She'll have taken his silence as enemy action, because that's what she always does.

*You have till the end of today.*

He wants to tell her to fuck off, but that will only make things worse. They need to sit down face-to-face and have a grown-up conversation; you can't discuss an issue as complicated and important as this by text message. Texts are short-form communications for making arrangements to meet, for apologies and reminders, expressions of affection or hurt. They're particularly useful for lies and deceptions, and he has exploited these particular functions for many years. But this is different; she's using her phone as a weapon. Not only is it irresponsible, it's undignified; all the players in this game are worth more than that.

He starts prowling the room, his feet slapping against the stone flooring. He won't be pushed into making a snap decision that will change lives forever. If he can't stop her completely, he should at least play for time. He picks up the phone again, his large fingers stumbling over the tiny keyboard as he types in the words, cursing as he automatically adds kisses then instantly deletes them. Like he feels any tiny morsel of affection for her right now.

*Let's talk this over.*

Her reply comes back almost instantly. *No more talking. Time for action.*

*Give me more time.*

*You know my terms. Agree to them or else.*

Or else. What is she, a kid? He knows she could cause colossal damage, but surely she'd never have the guts to follow through. Then again, she's at the end of her tether; people do terrible things when they're pushed to the limit. It doesn't bear thinking about, and yet he's thought of nothing else for weeks. He bangs the cluttered white wall with his forehead and a framed print shudders in sympathy. How did he let himself get into such a stupid mess?

Actually, enough of this. Time to be a man and take control. He sits on the arm of the sofa and turns to the phone again. Types. *Or else what?*

No response.

He stares at the screen for a couple of minutes, waiting and wondering what the silence means. She won't have given up and gone to bed, that's for sure. Is she trying to think of a suitably tough reply? Or has she finally come to her senses and realised there are other ways to solve this?

He stands up, his muscles tight and restless. The stale, over-heated air feels suffocating. At times like this, there's only one thing that has the power to relax him. An activity so demanding of his concentration that thinking of anything else is impossible. She's waiting for him in the garage. Ever faithful, ever willing. The winding lanes will be empty, the air sharp and fresh. It's been raining heavily and the tarmac will be slippery in parts. Poor riding conditions, but that's good. The greater the skill required, the easier to forget all this shit. He'll set himself a challenge to take the corners faster than he's ever dared. He'll ride up to Black Hill and watch the sunrise, then find a roadside café on the way back and have breakfast. His fingers start to tingle, his imagination already twisting the throttle.

He goes back to the bedroom, stealing yesterday's underwear and T-shirt from the floor. He tiptoes downstairs again to fetch his leathers from the hall cupboard, pulling on the tight, unrelenting trousers and zipping up the Marlon Brando jacket he's always being teased about. His boots are lying chilly in the porch and he puts them on, buckling the straps and stomping out of the house with his helmet and studded gauntlets tucked under his arm. The sky is dark, the stars shrouded in cloud, and the downpour has given way to a fine watery mist. As he crunches across the gravel, he can hear the trees dripping. He takes a deep breath, and fills his lungs with the innocence of a new day.

The garage door rattles as he pulls it up and over, the light coming on automatically to reveal the Bonneville in all her shiny black glory. Oh God, he loves this bike, the T100, an updated version of the 1960s classic he dreamed of owning when he was a teenager. Raised handlebars, a low-slung seat, flashy chrome pipes and eye-catching paintwork. She's even got retro scuff pads on the fuel tank. Okay, he admits it, he's what they call a 'born-again biker'. A middle-aged, middle-class man desperate to recapture the energy and freedom of youth. And the bike hasn't disappointed him; if anything, the sensations have been stronger, the thrills more addictive than when he was young.

The reimagined Bonneville has an electronic ignition and ABS, but she's still a powerful, challenging ride. Nothing beats the roar of liberation as you tear down an open road, the engine vibrating through your thighs, your body an echo chamber for the thunderous noise. The joy of complete oneness as you interlock with the machine, trusting your instinct to lean into the bend at the perfect angle and accelerate out at just the right moment. The freedom of visor-down, black-leather anonymity as you weave through the traffic to beat the lights, swearing at motorists who dare to block your way. And later, on the home run, your passion spent, easing off the throttle, gently on the back brake, feathering off as you bring her to a stop and take your hands off the bars. The thrilling possibility of death; the relief of still being alive. It's enough to turn a man to poetry.

He quietly wheels the bike to the end of the drive, then climbs on, fires up and speeds away. There are no street lamps or white markings here, making the road look and feel like a track. Oncoming traffic is extremely unlikely at this hour, so he takes up a confident position in the centre of the lane and accelerates. There are plenty of blind corners ahead to satisfy his lust, but in truth, he could drive this route with his eyes shut, navigate like a bat from the sound of the engine bouncing off the trees and hedgerows. He twists the bars and feels his way expertly around a sharp bend. This is all he wants to do, to ride and not think, to let his body be his brain.

He feels the wind wiping his face clean, the soft rainwater rinsing him out. He is a free man, his own master. But the sensation of happiness doesn't last long. He feels a vibration in his chest – it's his wretched phone, ringing from his top inside jacket pocket. Impossible to hear the ringtone above the rush of the engine, but he knows it's her. So now she wants to talk. Why did he bring it with him? Why didn't he put it back in its hiding place? The vibrations continue like an alien heartbeat, the insistent pulse of the enemy.

*Enough calls, enough texts. Enough accusations and demands and threats. Enough, enough, enough.* He takes his black-gloved hand off the bars and drags down the zip of his jacket, reaching in and extracting the phone. Letting out a triumphant, wolfish howl, he hurls it into the undergrowth and rides on, twisting like a ribbon around the bends. The feeling of freedom is so overwhelming and so sublime that for a split second he forgets he's riding a modern-day motorcycle with considerable poke.

It happens very fast, and yet slowly enough for him to know that there's nothing he can do to stop it. The road lurches suddenly to the right and he doesn't ease off, doesn't lean, his instincts deserting him along with the anti-lock braking system. A puddle of water forces itself beneath his tyres, and he skims over its surface like a polished black stone. He spins. He flies. Then hits the all-too-solid tree.

# CHAPTER TWO

*The Vikings believed that there was a misty, chilly world beneath the earth called Hel, the home of the dead.*

My client, an exhausted single mum with four kids, is changing her baby's nappy on the not-so-clean carpet, gripping his tiny ankles with one hand and cleaning his bum with the other. The room stinks of sickly-sweet poo and aloe vera wet wipes. She shouts out the information above his screams and I quickly type it in. I feel like a police interrogator, even though nobody's forced her to come here. She stuffs the dirty nappy in the basket under the buggy, where another child is drifting off to sleep, sucking on her dummy. The older two are at school, she tells me. Their father has done a bunk. The poor woman can't remember all the addresses she's had over the last five years.

She's typical of the people that use our services. Angry, tired, defeated. Either they don't have access to computers or they have trouble reading and writing. Often both. I compose complaints to landlords, or appeals against parking penalties, or desperate pleas to debt collection agencies. I go through their tenancy agreements, explain the terms and conditions of their hire purchase contracts and reveal the mess they've got themselves into. I fill in the incomprehensible forms that are designed to put them off and read them aloud before they sign. If they cry, I offer tissues and a plastic cup of water. I do my best to listen to their troubles –

aggressive exes, misbehaving teenagers, bouts of depression – but it's not supposed to be a counselling session. I've been sworn at more times than I can remember, but I've never had to press the panic button under the desk. More often than not, they're friendly and incredibly grateful.

There's a knock at the door, and before I can answer, my supervisor walks in. Jill comes round to my side of the desk, leaning forward so that her face is hidden from my client by the monitor. Her brows are stitched together in a worried frown.

'Josie, your boyfriend's here. He, er, needs to talk to you.' I look at her doubtfully. She must have got it wrong; Arun never visits me at work. 'He's in my office. I'll take over.' I stand up, still confused. 'Take your handbag, love, then you won't have to come back for it.'

That's when I realise it's serious.

I find Arun sitting nervously in Jill's office. He jumps up and closes the door behind me. The roller blinds are already pulled down so that none of my colleagues can peer through the glass. I feel like one of my clients; vulnerable and afraid, not really understanding why I'm here or what I'm supposed to do. He sits me down in the chair opposite and takes my hands, rubbing them as if they're cold. I can hear words, but they're refusing to form into a coherent sentence.

*Raining. Accident. Motorbike. Police.*

'I'm sorry,' he says. 'So sorry. I didn't want to be the one to tell you, but your mum thought it would be better coming from me.'

'Is she okay?' Stupid question. Of course she's not okay.

'She sounded calm on the phone, but you know Helen, it's hard to tell what's really going on inside.'

'I can't believe it,' I whisper. 'How can he be dead?'

My brain goes into free fall. All I can think is: today is Friday. We were supposed to be meeting friends this evening; I'll need to cancel. I'd promised Mum we'd go over for Sunday lunch because we hadn't seen them for weeks, due to social commitments that at the time seemed important and frankly more exciting, but now everything's changed and I'm never going to see my father, ever, ever again. My thoughts unstick with a jolt and the tears start to flow. Arun looks at me helplessly, as if I've just sprung a leak.

'There should be some hankies in the drawer.' He finds the box, pulling several tissues out in a flourish and passing them over. I take one and dab my eyes, leaving the rest nestling in my lap like a white origami chrysanthemum.

'When did it happen?'

'Not sure. A farm truck came across the accident at five o'clock this morning. Jerry was already… you know… There was nothing anyone could do.'

'Five in the morning?' Dad was never up and about so early. I suppose he could have been going into the department to prepare a lecture. He liked to leave everything to the last minute, but he tended to stay up all night rather than rise at dawn. What if the accident happened last night and he was lying there for hours, bleeding to death? But surely somebody would have come across him before that.

'Did you say a *farm truck* found him?'

'That's what Helen said.'

'What was a farm truck doing in Manchester city centre?'

He shrugs. 'Delivering something? Passing through? It's not relevant, is it?'

'Sounds odd, that's all. Where did the accident happen?'

'I don't know, sorry. You'll have to ask your mum…' He stands and reaches for my hand. 'Shall we get going? I said I'd bring you straight over. She shouldn't be on her own right now.'

I stare down at my Japanese tissue flower. A farm truck. Five in the morning. It doesn't make any sense.

We take a taxi to the house. As soon as Mum sees me, tears spill out of her eyes and roll down her cheeks. We fall into each other's arms, rocking and holding each other tightly, while Arun shuts the front door and squeezes past us. He takes off his suit jacket and hangs it up next to Dad's long winter coat, the one he used to take to conferences in eastern Europe. We used to tease him and say he looked like a Russian spy. Dad always loved to look the part. He was very handsome and knew it. But he was upfront about his vanity, so we kind of forgave him.

'I'll make some coffee,' Mum says, as we finally peel off each other.

'No, I'll make it.' Arun pushes us gently towards the living room. 'You two go and sit down.'

We head for the sofa and I cuddle into her shapeless beige jumper and grey jogging bottoms. Her skin is pale and feels papery. She looks terrible, as if she's been up all night.

'What time did the police come round?'

'About half eight, just as I was about to leave for work. As soon as I opened the door and saw them standing there, I knew what it was about. I always knew he'd kill himself one day.'

Something inside my stomach somersaults. 'But... but I thought it was an accident?'

'Sorry, darling, I meant riding that stupid bike. Every Friday night when he was on the motorway, I'd have my heart in my mouth waiting for him to get home. Why couldn't he take the train, like a normal middle-aged man? It wasn't as if he couldn't afford the fares. But no, he thought he was bloody James Dean. Pathetic!'

'You can't call him pathetic. He's dead.'

'I'm so angry with him, Josie. It was so unnecessary.'

'Anyone want a biscuit?' Arun enters with two steaming mugs of coffee, which he puts on the table in front of us. 'Or I could make sandwiches...'

'You're a star,' says Mum, forcing a small smile. 'But I'm too churned up to eat at the moment. You have something, Josie.'

'I'm churned up too,' I say.

'Of course. I didn't mean to imply...' She rests her elbows on her knees and leans forward with her head in her hands. 'I'm sorry... I'm sorry...' Arun pulls a face at me, as if to say, *Was that my fault?* I shake my head and he escapes back to the kitchen.

I stroke Mum's back for a few moments. This is probably not the right time, but I have to ask her some questions. Until I know the full story, this won't feel real. 'Mum... please, talk to me.' She pulls her hands away and sits upright.

'What?' She looks exhausted.

'Arun said a farm truck found him at five this morning. Do you know where?'

'Sorry, I... I couldn't really take it all in.' She waves at a package on the sideboard. 'They gave me a booklet – there's one for you if you want it. A family liaison officer is supposed to be getting in touch.'

I go over to the sideboard and pick up one of the booklets: *Information and advice for bereaved families and friends following death on the road in England and Wales*. A piece of paper is clipped to the front. It says, *Detective Sergeant Ravita Verma, Family Liaison, Derbyshire Police*. My heart leaps in a mad moment of hope and I swing round to Mum.

'Derbyshire? Do they know for certain it's him, or are they just going by the number plate on the bike? What if somebody stole it and went on a joy ride? We should ring his mobile, check with the department. He could be in the middle of a lecture – he could be *alive*!' I dive into my bag and take out my phone.

'Stop it, Josie. It's him. The police gave me a description. It's Jerry – without a doubt.'

My insides instantly drop again. I want to scream, I want to kick; I want to beat the furniture until I've no strength left. 'What the hell was he doing out in Derbyshire?'

'I expect he just went for a ride. He did that sometimes.'

'At five in the morning? On a work day?'

'Please, stop asking questions. What does it matter? He's gone, and he's never coming back.' She stands up, holding her forehead. 'I've got a headache. I need to lie down.' I watch her totter out of the room, her body bent forward, instantly aged by the shock.

But it *does* matter. Dad liked to take risks, but he wasn't stupid; he knew how to ride a motorcycle. And he had so much to live for, he would never have thrown it all away. Why was he out riding so far from family and home? Mum can put her head in the sand if she wants, but there's got to be an explanation.

# CHAPTER THREE

*Unlike the Christian concept of hell, Vikings did not consider the afterlife a place for moral judgement.*

We leave Mum to rest and call another Uber. As soon as I unlock the front door, reality hits me over the head and suddenly even a simple, ordinary action that I've done a thousand times seems impossible. I collapse at the threshold, feeling utterly defeated. Arun picks me up and staggers into the living room, tipping me onto the sofa. He fetches the duvet from our bedroom and wraps me up like a giant chrysalis.

'Can I get you anything?'

'No.' I reach for his hand. 'Thanks.'

He looks fidgety. 'I ought to call work, tell them I won't be in for the rest of the day. If you need me, I'll be in the bedroom.' He leaves, shutting the door quietly behind him. I turn my face to the cushion, sucking in the fabric. Everything is still and quiet. I can't remember ever feeling more alone.

Dad is dead. My father… is dead. No… He can't be. It doesn't *feel* like he's gone from the world. I've not seen him with my own eyes, I've just got other people's words to go on. What if it's all been some dreadful mistake? A case of identity fraud. It *does* happen. I'm filled with a sudden urge to try his number, and dip into my bag for my phone. I can feel my heart pounding as it rings out twice, then goes to voicemail. 'Hi, leave a message and

I'll get right back to you.' His voice is so warm and familiar, it's as if a tiny part of him is trapped in the handset. See? He's not dead, just busy. Typical Dad, going off the radar, not reporting in when he's supposed to. He often doesn't pick up, and he's always been hopeless at returning calls. No point in worrying. He'll be back when he's ready; in his Marlon Brando jacket, clutching a bottle of Scotch and a bunch of petrol-station flowers. 'What's up, princess? Look, I'm here! I'm fine!'

Except you're *not* fine, are you, Dad? You went and got yourself killed. I wish to Christ you'd never bought that fucking motorbike.

I toss the phone angrily into my bag. As it falls, I glimpse the booklet Mum insisted I took away with me and pull it out. I flick through the first few pages. *What happens now?* it says. Words swim before my eyes – *loved one*, *mortuary*, *post-mortem*, *tissue samples*, *coroner*, *inquest* – but it's like I'm reading in a foreign language. I know the vocabulary but can't understand the sentences. It's all too down-to-earth and practical. I'm not ready for this yet.

I shut the booklet and rest it in my lap, closing my eyes and summoning up an alternative image of my loved one. Not in his motorbike leathers, sprawled awkwardly across the tarmac, but lying on an ancient battlefield, a bloodied sword at his side. He has died an heroic Viking death, defending his land and people. Odin has sent the Valkyries to snatch his soul from his body, and, even now, they're flying over the rainbow bridge that connects the earth to Asgard, where the gods live. Viking warrior Jerry Macauliffe will take his place in the great hall of Valhalla, and spend the afterlife drinking and feasting in an endless party. That would suit him down to the ground. I hope those ancient stories he used to tell me turn out to be true. These silly thoughts comfort me for a while, but they don't stop the tears.

Arun emerges from the bedroom, takes one look at my ravaged face and reaches for the kettle. There's going to be a lot of tea-drinking over the next few days, I think. He sits on the edge of the sofa and strokes my hair while I sip listlessly. My eyes are smarting and my nose is so bunged it feels like I've suddenly come down with a bad cold.

Somehow, the rest of the day passes. We hug. We hold hands. I nibble the edges of a piece of toast but the crumbs stick in my throat, making me cough. We stare down at the rug or up at the pictures on the wall, every so often breaking the silence to say, 'I still can't believe it' or 'It doesn't feel real' or just 'Why?' As the light fades, Arun draws the curtains and turns on the heating. He orders in a Chinese, but most of it goes in the bin. I try to call Mum several times, but she doesn't answer. I contemplate ringing the family liaison officer to see if the police have any more information, but it's the evening now and I suspect she's finished her shift.

We go to bed, and to my surprise – even shame – I manage to sleep and don't dream about Dad. I wake up on Saturday morning forgetting for the briefest of moments what's happened. Then I remember; stuffing my fist into my mouth so that Arun won't be woken by the uncontrollable sobs.

I get up. Shower. Dress. Try Mum again, but she still doesn't pick up and I start to worry. It's not a problem if she doesn't want to talk, but I need to know she's okay. I text her instead and at last she replies. *Resting. Come over later if you want.*

Arun decides I need a cooked breakfast. I return to the sofa and watch while he bustles around the kitchen, peeling mushrooms and defrosting sausages. He gets the liquidiser down from the top cupboard and makes a smoothie with the last of the fruit and a floppy carrot. Tears roll down my cheeks as I watch him laying the table, putting out the mats we only use for guests and making sure the cutlery matches, my heart bursting with random memories of Dad. The flat always seemed to shrink when he came over. He towered over the furniture and had to duck out of the way of the light fitting.

'It's ready. Sit up,' Arun says, holding up a glass of orangey-brown sludge. The whole process has taken him so long, we've drifted into brunch. I move off the sofa and sit at the table. He puts a hot heaped plate down in front of me, but I can hardly see what's on it through the blur of tears.

'Come on now,' he says gently. 'You can't eat and cry at the same time.'

'I'm sorry. I was just thinking about…' I hesitate.

'About what?' He sits down opposite me and picks up his knife and fork.

'No, it's all right.' I cut into the egg, and the yolk seeps into the warm buttered toast. The bacon is overdone and the mushrooms are a bit gritty, but I'm not going to complain. I couldn't have got through the last twenty-four hours without Arun.

'We should go out.' He gestures at the window to remind me where *out* is. It's easy to forget here. We're on the fourth floor, with no lift. It's a quirky block, built in the thirties. There's a small patch of garden in front, which has recently been turned into a play area, the ill-kept grass replaced with brown cork chippings. In the evenings, teenagers emerge from the shadows and gather on the swings to smoke and drink cheap cider. It's not a place we can hang out, so if we need some green, we have to go further afield.

Arun must have had the same sequence of thoughts, because he suggests taking a bus to Regent's Park. 'We'll visit your mum afterwards,' he says.

We pick up our coats and leave the flat without doing the washing-up.

*

I thought the park would be safe territory, but of course it isn't. Dad took me here often when I was little, and there are memories lurking around every corner, waiting to pounce on me. Running around the open grassy area. Playing hide-and-seek in the rose garden. Feeding the ducks, queuing for ice creams in the summer. Dad always had pistachio and I had double chocolate chip. We never went to the zoo – he hated to see animals in cages, out of their natural environment. We used to imagine them breaking out and causing havoc. Lions in the garden, monkeys on the climbing frame, alligators in the pond, zebras on the zebra crossing. We thought it would be hilarious.

'Dad loved little kids,' I say, as we approach the open-air theatre he took me to many times as a child. 'He would have made a wonderful grandad…' I start to tremble, and Arun reaches out to steady me.

'Josie. There's no point tormenting yourself with what'll never be.'

'I know, I know…' I feel up my sleeve for a tissue. 'Let's go and see Mum.'

After a twenty-minute walk, most of it in thoughtful silence, we arrive at the house. I still have my own key, but it doesn't feel right to use it today, so I ring the bell. As we wait, I reflect on the fact that Dad will never answer the door again, and fight back yet another tear.

Mum looks relieved to see us. 'Brett and Lisa are here,' she whispers. 'They're already driving me mad.' As we follow Mum down the hallway, I brace myself for the shock of seeing Dad's living ghost. But as soon as I walk into the kitchen and see Brett leaning against the worktop, I realise how different the brothers look these days. Brett has Dad's height but stoops against it, and in recent years he's developed a paunch. They share the same wavy auburn hair, but Brett's is thinning and receding and his blue eyes lack Dad's wicked twinkle.

'Josie! How *are* you?' He doesn't wait for my reply. 'We're all still in shock.'

Lisa, Brett's second wife – ten years his junior – stops washing up and wipes her hands on a towel. 'It's so ghastly, I can't bear it,' she chimes in. 'Shall I make a fresh pot?'

Arun and I shake our heads. 'Not for me, thanks.' I walk past them into the conservatory and join Mum, who's parked herself in a chair by the window.

'I'm trying to persuade your mother to let me take care of things in Manchester,' Brett says, following me into the sunlight.

Mum's eyes flick up to him. 'And I've told you, I'd rather do it on my own.'

'Identifying a body is a very traumatic experience. You need company, Helen.'

Lisa walks in. 'Please let me come with you,' she says in a softer tone. 'You can't possibly do it by yourself, and besides, I'd like to say goodbye to Jerry too.'

'Well, you can't,' Mum retorts. Lisa's bottom lip starts to tremble, and she rushes back into the kitchen. There's a long, difficult silence.

'We'll go with you if you like,' Arun says, putting his hand on her shoulder. I nod in agreement, although the thought of seeing Dad's corpse drives a shudder through me. I'm not sure I'll be able to face it. Better to remember him alive, I think, than lying dead on a slab.

Brett purses his lips. 'I can liaise with the police, organise the death certificate and talk to the funeral directors. I'm retired now, I've got time on my hands – and he was my brother.'

'And *my* husband. I'm his legal next of kin, not you.'

'Can we please not fight over him?' I say. 'Isn't it bad enough that he's dead?'

Mum stares out of the window and Brett puffs a frustrated sigh. He goes to find Lisa. The clinking sounds of washing-up resume, punctuated by tense whispered conversation.

'Have the police said anything more about what happened?' asks Arun, after another pause.

'Not really. I've arranged to meet them at the mortuary on Monday afternoon.' Mum drops her voice and glances towards the kitchen. 'Don't tell Brett.'

'He's right about you needing company,' I whisper.

'Honestly, I'll be fine,' she replies, but she's not fooling anyone.

I crouch down and take her hands. 'No, I'm going to take you there, Mum. No arguments.'

# CHAPTER FOUR

*The Viking underworld was ruled by the goddess Hel, a beautiful woman from the waist upwards and a terrifying skeleton beneath. Her kingdom was guarded by a ferocious dog that let nobody escape.*

It takes so long to find the mortuary, tucked away in a labyrinth of hospital buildings, that we're fifteen minutes late for our appointment. Mum and I didn't say much in the car driving up, even though the journey took three hours. The steady, reasonable tones of Radio Four filled our silences. Every time I took my eyes off the road and glanced in her direction, she was staring out of the side window.

The mortuary is a single-storey brick building, with a strangely domestic feel, like the bottom half of a large Victorian terrace. There's a large bay at the front with frosted windows, and a covered driveway at the side. A young woman is standing at the foot of a ramp that leads to the entrance doors, stamping her feet against the morning chill.

'Mrs Macauliffe?' she says hopefully, stuffing her phone into her pocket and holding forth her hand. 'Detective Sergeant Ravita Verma. Please call me Ravi.'

'And I'm Helen. Sorry we're late.' Mum gestures towards me. 'This is my daughter, Josie.'

Ravi shakes my hand. 'Hello, Josie. I'm very sorry for your loss.' I offer her a small smile and we pause for a two-second silence. I've said that well-worn phrase to clients at work several times, but now I'm on the receiving end it feels a little hollow and pointless.

'Are you okay to go in straight away? The coroner's officer is expecting us.' We nod and follow her up the ramp. I grip Mum's sleeve as Ravi presses the bell and announces our arrival.

We're buzzed into a chilly entrance hall, our footsteps echoing as we cross the polished concrete floor.

'Sorry, the facilities aren't great here,' Ravi says. 'There's a waiting room where we can have a little chat. I can fill you in on the investigation so far, and there are a few routine questions I need to ask. Would you rather do that now, or after?'

'I'd rather get the identification over and done with, if you don't mind,' says Mum.

'Of course. No problem. I'll let them know you're ready.' She scuttles off through a pair of swing doors and returns a minute later with the coroner's officer, who introduces himself as Nick.

'Are you both viewing?' he asks.

'No, just me,' says Mum. I can tell by the way she's looking at him that she thinks he's too young to do a job like this.

'Fine. If you'd like to come this way…' He gestures to the swing doors.

'Actually, I've changed my mind,' I say, the words out of my mouth before I can stop them.

Mum turns round. 'Are you sure, Josie? You said you didn't…'

I draw in a breath. 'Yes, I'm sure.'

We're given the choice of viewing him through a window, but we choose to go in. The room is small, each wall lined with plain green curtains. The lighting is soft and the atmosphere very calm.

I hang back, acclimatising myself, but Mum walks straight up to the body and nods slowly.

'Yes, this is him,' she says, looking up at the coroner's officer. 'Jerome Macauliffe.'

'Thank you,' he replies. 'I'll leave you alone now. Take as long as you want.'

I take a couple of steps forward, still unsure. His skin is pale, the skin almost polished, his wavy hair untangled, his thick, luxurious beard carefully combed. He's never looked so neat and clean, and that thought makes me smile a little. My father, tamed and respectable at last.

I haven't seen a dead body before and I don't know what I was expecting. Someone who looked deeply asleep, perhaps? But that's not how he looks at all. It's the overwhelming stillness of him that seems most strange, most unlike him. Dad was always restless, always moving about, as if every seat was slightly uncomfortable, every conversation a little boring. He went to bed late, packing the hours with constant activity, unable to do just one thing at a time. When he went for walks, he listened to podcasts. When he read the papers, he played his old vinyls. He talked through every mouthful over dinner, marked essays in the bath. Even family holidays were exhausting – I was never allowed to lie on the beach doing nothing. He was always going away on conferences or field trips, researching for his next book or visiting his academic friends. Never stopping, hardly ever taking a break.

I edge closer and gaze at his handsome face, the strong chin tilted upwards, lips pressed together, neither smiling nor scowling. It's as if he's playing a game – 'Let's see how long I can hold my breath and make everyone think I'm dead.' Except he's not going to open his eyes and burst out laughing, not going to grab my hand and say, 'Hah! Got you there, princess!' He's quiet and still. So very, very still. And utterly empty. Like a beautifully sculpted vase.

Mum stands next to me and gently touches my arm. 'Shall we go?' she whispers. I nod, and she leads me out of the room.

Nick and Ravi are waiting for us in the corridor. They take us into another small room. A set of six upright chairs, their seats upholstered in brown plastic, hug the wall opposite a wooden mantelpiece. Dusty artificial flowers decorate the grate, and there's a low coffee table covered in small piles of leaflets about funeral services and benefits. I recognise a few of them from work.

'I need to give you your husband's possessions,' Nick says. 'You said on the phone that you didn't want his clothes or his motorcycle leathers.'

'That's right. Do whatever you normally do with them.' Mum glances at me for approval and I nod again.

'Right. Well… This was all that was found at the scene.' He passes a small plastic bag to Mum – it's transparent, like a police evidence bag, and I can see immediately that it only contains one thing. A small bunch of keys.

'That's it?' I say. 'No wallet? No phone?'

'No.' Nick shifts uncomfortably, as if he's somehow to blame. 'If you don't mind signing here, Mrs Macauliffe, to confirm receipt.' He hands over his clipboard and a pen.

'That's really odd,' I say.

'Not really.' Mum sighs. 'Jerry hated carting stuff around, you know that. When we went out, he used to make me carry his things in my handbag.'

'Yeah, but he was on his own, Mum, and a long way from home. It doesn't make any sense.' I gesture at her to show me the keys. 'Are those for the Manchester house?'

'I'm not sure. I expect so.'

'The Manchester house? What's that?' Ravi takes a slim brown folder and pen out of her briefcase. 'Mind if I make a few notes? Just background.'

'It's Jerry's bolthole,' says Mum. 'He stayed there in the week during term time, came home most weekends and for the holidays.'

'Do you know the address? Just for the record.'

'Fifteen Antrobus Street, Rusholme. Sorry, I can't remember the postcode. I never go there.'

Ravi writes it all down. 'Hmm, that must be about an hour's drive from the scene of the accident. Do you know what he was doing on the edge of the Peaks on Thursday night or during the early hours of Friday?'

'Out for a ride, I should think,' Mum replies. 'He did that sometimes. Took off without warning. He called it "putting the bike through its paces", but it was himself he was challenging.'

'Yes, well, we do have a lot of accidents involving men in their fifties.' Ravi scribbles a note. 'So he didn't actually tell you he was going for a ride?'

'No. Why would he?' There's a tinge of irritation in Mum's voice. 'I was at home, in London. Anyway, Jerry was very spontaneous, a free spirit…' I look away from her, thinking, that's a polite way to describe his complete lack of consideration about ever telling anyone where he was or what time he'd be back.

Ravi hesitates before speaking again. 'Sorry to bring this up, but… what about his mental health? Was he suffering from stress or depression? Problems at work? Personal life?'

Mum's expression hardens. 'Jerry wasn't suicidal, if that's what you're getting at.'

Ravi writes. 'I'm really sorry, but I have to ask.'

'He wasn't the type,' I add. 'And if he *was* depressed, you would have spotted the signs, wouldn't you, Mum?'

She bends down to put the evidence wallet in her bag, then lifts her head and looks Ravi straight in the eye. 'I'm a hundred per cent certain Jerry didn't take his own life.'

'Good, right, fine. Sorry, it's just something we have to consider. Obviously, it's very early days. We're appealing for witnesses. The crash-scene investigators are putting their report together and the bike has been taken away for examination – you know, to see if there was a mechanical fault.'

'So there was no other vehicle involved?' I ask, feeling suddenly anxious.

'All I can say at this stage is that no other vehicle was found at the scene and no third party reported the accident. It happened in a very quiet spot; there's no CCTV for several miles, unfortunately.'

'So it could have been a hit-and-run.'

'We can't say until we've examined all the evidence.' She registers the frustrated look on my face. 'I'm sorry to sound so vague. I don't want to say anything that turns out to be false information. But I promise you we're working very hard and will let you know more details as soon as we can.' Her eyes flick quickly across the pages of her notebook. 'As neither of you was there at the time, you won't be required to make a statement. Is there anything else you want to ask me?'

I nod. 'In the booklet we were given, it says you can give us the location of the accident so we can visit.'

'Oh, yes. If you write down your email address, I'll ping over the GPS coordinates.' She turns to an empty page in her book and passes it over with her pen. 'The investigators have finished now. You can visit whenever you like, but if you want me or another officer to go with you, we'll need twenty-four hours' notice.'

'I don't want to visit, thank you,' says Mum, stiffening. 'I can't stand it when people make those dreadful shrines at the roadside.'

'It's entirely up to you—'

'I know that,' she interrupts. 'Are we done? Only I'd like to go now.' She picks up her bag.

'Sorry,' I whisper to Ravi as soon as Mum leaves the room. 'She's just upset.'

'Don't worry, I understand.' Ravi gathers up her papers and stands. 'It's a difficult time for you all.'

I return to the entrance lobby, but Mum has already left the building. I find her outside, leaning against the rail of the disabled ramp, taking some deep breaths. 'You okay?' She locks her jaw and nods.

We stand side by side in silence, watching the cars trundling around the maze, driving into dead ends and reversing in tight spaces. 'I've always hated hospitals,' she says.

I nudge her gently and steer her towards the car. 'Shall we go to Antrobus Street this afternoon? You know, to pick up Dad's clothes and things. His phone, wallet, laptop and stuff must be there, and we can sort—'

'Not today… I can't face it.' She stops, removes her glasses and rubs her eyes. 'I just want to go home.'

'But we've come all this way. He might have left food out, stuff will go rotten…'

'It'll be okay for a few more days. I'll come back at the weekend.' She starts walking again, more briskly this time.

'But that's daft.' I hurry to catch up. 'We should at least check it over, make sure it's all locked up properly – switch off the heating, that kind of thing.'

'It can be done later. Or I can ask one of Jerry's colleagues to sort it. It doesn't matter.'

Mum walks up to the car, tugging at the door handle before I have a chance to unlock. I press the fob and it bleeps and flashes. She gets in and pulls the seat belt across her chest.

I walk around to the driver's side, feeling thwarted. I've never been to Antrobus Street. Dad called it his 'monastic cell'. I want to see how he lived when he was away from home. See what food he ate, what books he kept on his shelves. I want to wander around the house and feel his spirit. Bury my nose in his unwashed clothes…

I turn on the ignition and the dashboard lights up. 'I know it's been a tough day,' I say, driving out of the space, 'but it doesn't make sense to come all this way and then go straight back. It won't take long to drive into Manchester. What if I found you a nice café to wait in while I pop into the house? It won't take long.'

'You never give up, do you? Just like your father.' She sighs, as if determination is no longer a quality to be proud of. 'Tell you what. Drop me off at the nearest station and I'll make my own way back. Then you can go to the house, visit the crash site – do whatever you need to do…'

I pull out of the car park. 'No, no, I can't let you travel on your own in this state.'

'I'm not in a "state", Josie. I'm just tired and I want to go home. I've no problem with taking the train. That way we can both do what we want.' She takes out the evidence wallet and puts it in the glove compartment.

# CHAPTER FIVE

*As a sign of her important domestic status, the Viking wife carried the household keys on a chain, which was attached to her tunic. Some argue that their phallic shape symbolised the woman's control of her husband's manhood.*

Dad's tiny terrace sits in a long row of identical red-brick houses with plain, flat frontages and doors that open immediately onto the pavement. It's pretty bleak, a monastic cell indeed. Cars are parked nose to tail and there's not a tree or patch of grass in sight. Now I understand why he never invited us up – not once in ten years.

I squeeze into a space further down the street and walk back to number 15, past mean, narrow windows with grey net curtains and scuffed paintwork. I'm hit by a fresh wave of sadness as I think of Dad coming here after a long day's work, week in, week out. He must have felt lonely at times.

There was never any question of our moving up to Manchester to join him. The professorship was a great opportunity and we knew he had to take it, but Mum didn't want to leave her job and I was very settled at school. Uncle Brett warned Dad that once he left the London property market, he'd never get back in. So they bought this little house for next to nothing, not far from the city centre and a short bus ride to the university. Over the last year or so, Mum's been talking about early retirement; cashing in the two properties and buying a place in the countryside where she can grow veg and keep chickens. Dad poured scorn on her rural dream. He insisted he'd never retire, said he'd rather die than spend the rest of his life living like his brother – in other words, playing golf, going on cruises and watching daytime television.

I look up at the ugly exterior, trying to summon some feelings for the place. It served its purpose, that's the best I can say about it. Mum can do what she likes with the house now Dad's gone – she can do what she likes full stop. Maybe that's why she seems so angry. She got what she wanted, but at an unacceptable price.

There are two keys on the ring – a Yale and a deadlock. I try the deadlock first, but the key doesn't fit. It's completely the wrong shape. The Yale doesn't work either. I look up at the number on the door, wondering if I'm at the wrong house. But no, the brass figures clearly state I'm at number 15. That was what Mum told the sergeant, I'm sure of it. So why can't I get in?

I decide to take a look around the back. Could these keys be for the kitchen door? Perhaps Dad lost the front-door keys and never got round to having the locks changed – it wouldn't surprise me. I walk to the end of the row and turn the corner, finding a cobbled alleyway with back yards on either side. It's not wide enough for cars; littered with stray wheelie bins, rubbish, bits of broken furniture and a soggy mattress. I count the back windows until I get to number 15. There's a tatty wooden fence and a gate that's either locked or bolted on the inside. Not exactly top-level security, but getting in isn't going to be easy.

Fortunately, the alley is deserted. I look around for something to stand on and find a plastic crate. Carrying it over to the fence, I climb up and lean over the gate. No padlock, which is good. The bolt is rusty and stiff, but after a few grunts and groans I manage to pull it across. I open the gate and walk into the yard, which is unevenly paved with pink and yellow hexagonal slabs. Weeds are growing in the cracks and there's a rusty barbecue in the corner.

A couple of white plastic chairs are turning green with mould, used-up tea lights and candles in jam jars are scattered about and there's a large terracotta flowerpot full of worn-down stubs. I bend down, and a whiff of skunk shoots up my nostrils.

It looks, feels and smells studenty, not like the home of a university professor. I glance around me, trying to imagine Dad out here in the summer, soaking up the evening sun with a tumbler of whisky in one hand and a cigarette in the other, reading his latest political biography, acrobatic jazz sounds tumbling out of the window. It seems just about possible, at a push. But cooking a few sausages on that grimy barbecue? Not a chance. Mind you, it was probably there when he moved in and he never got round to taking it to the dump.

I try the keys in the back door, but they don't fit this either. Maybe Mum remembered the number wrong. I text her to ask and she replies immediately. *Definitely no. 15. Why? Something wrong?*

*No, just making sure.*

I notice that a window is slightly open in the brick extension that was probably once the coal shed. The glass is opaque and crinkled like waves – looks like a downstairs loo coming off the kitchen. I drag the crate over and stand on it, squeezing my hand through the gap and popping up the latch. The window creaks open. I hang my bag across my chest, lean over and peer inside. It's a whole bathroom, not just a toilet. I push, using all my arm strength, kicking my feet against the wall to propel me up and over the sill. There's a point of no return as my balance tips and I slide head first into the cold, hard bath beneath. I shuffle onto my hands and knees and climb out.

I don't know what sort of bathroom I was expecting to find, but it's certainly not this. The tub is ringed with dirt and the sealant around the edges is speckled with black mould. There's a damp patch on the ceiling, a rotting pink bath mat in the corner and the floor tiles are covered with hair, nail cuttings and screwed-up pieces of tissue. This is wrong. I walk out of the bathroom and into the kitchen. There are empty beer cans, bottles of wine and spirits on every surface, as if someone has had a party. The worktops are filthy and the laminate floor is thick with crumbs stuck into grease. An open bottle of milk is festering by the sink. There's not a clean mug in sight.

This can't be the right place. Dad was the first person to stick a dirty knife in the jam, but there's no way he would have lived like this. I must be in someone else's house and I'd better get out before they come home and call the police. I turn around, looking for the key to the back door, but it's not in the lock. With a flutter of panic, I realise I probably won't be able to climb back out of the window. There's no choice but to go out the front and hope to God nobody sees me.

I creep into the narrow hallway, glimpsing the front room through the open door. I stop at the threshold, my stomach tightening as I stare at the furniture. I know that sofa. Red leather with tartan cushions. It belonged to my grandmother. I recognise the coffee table too, although it's more scratched and stained than it looked in her sitting room. Other objects nudge at my memory – an uplighter we used to have in the dining room, a pine-framed mirror that once hung in Mum and Dad's bedroom. This *is* the right house. I start to feel sick and sweaty. Why are the curtains hanging off the rail? Why is the carpet so badly stained? Why are there no shelves lined with books, or pictures on the walls? This is the home of someone who's given up on life, who doesn't care.

Ravi's words echo in my head. *Was he suffering from stress or depression? Problems at work? Personal life?* Mum and I were so adamant that nothing was wrong, but if she was with me now and could see this… If the police came round…

God knows what it's like upstairs. Bracing myself, I go back into the hallway and slowly walk up. The stair carpet is worn and stained, frayed at the edges. There are greasy finger marks on the wall. I reach the landing and gaze around me. There are three rooms – two of the doors are open and the door to the front room is closed. I poke my head into the back bedroom first – it's long and thin, running over the kitchen. There's no bed in it, just a small desk and a load of suitcases and cardboard boxes. A storage area, nothing more. The middle room has a metal-framed double bed shoved in the corner, its mattress covered in brown stains. I can't bear to think how they got there. There's a large wooden wardrobe that I also vaguely remember, some laundry bags full of bedding, and more boxes, most of which are empty. Looks like he's not been using this room either.

I walk back onto the landing and stand before the door to the front bedroom, steeling myself for what I might find behind it. What if he's left a suicide note? My heart thumping out of my chest, I turn the handle and push the door open.

The curtains are drawn and the room is dark and smelly. I step into the gloom. The floor looks like an obstacle course – crumpled clothes, plates encrusted with smears of food, mugs and glasses, empty bottles… I feel along the wall for the light switch, but can't find it.

Then there's a blood-curdling scream and something hard and heavy hits me over the back of the head.

# CHAPTER SIX

*In the middle of the Viking longhouse was a fire, and at night the family sat around it together, sewing clothes, mending tools, playing games and telling stories of the past.*

Lights flash before my eyes and a violent pain sears through me. Groaning, I stagger forward onto my knees. My attacker leaps on me from behind, pushing me flat on the floor and straddling me.

'Who the fuck are you?' she shrieks. 'What are you doing in my fucking house?'

My brain is on fire, the world is spinning and it feels like an electric current is running through my neck and down my arms. I've only gone and broken into the wrong house! Jesus Christ, this woman must think I'm a burglar.

'Sorry, sorry,' I plead into the carpet. 'I made a mistake.'

She holds a hard, cold object against my ear like a gun, but I think it's a hairdryer or something. 'Move and I'll break your jaw.' She tightens her thigh grip around my chest. *She's going to call the police. I'll be done for breaking and entering, I could go to prison. How could I have been so dumb?*

'Who sent you?' she barks. 'Is this about the cash I owe BJ?'

'No! What? I think I'm at the wrong house.'

'So why didn't you fucking knock?'

'The key wouldn't work, so I had to break in… I didn't think anyone was living here, I'm really sorry. Please, let me go!'

Loosening her grip, she prods me in the back. 'Turn over. Slowly. No sudden movements, okay? Let's get a look at you.'

I feel so dizzy I can hardly lift my head, but I slowly roll onto my back. As the base of my skull hits the floor, I feel a fresh sharp pain and cry out. She's really thumped me; I might even be bleeding. Opening my eyes, I blink through the fuzziness.

She's about my age, dressed in black – leggings and a tight strappy top. She is tall and skinny, like me. Her long wavy hair is deep auburn, like mine. Her eyes are large and blue… like mine. My brain spins into confusion, refusing to compute what I'm seeing. She is staring back with exactly my expression – a mixture of wonder, bewilderment and horror. It's like looking in a mirror. A dark, cracked mirror.

'Who are you?' she whispers, staring down at me. 'What's your name?'

'Jo-Josie…' I stutter.

'Josie *what*?'

'Macauliffe …'

The hairdryer thuds to the floor. '*Macauliffe*?'

'Yes. What is it? Who are you?' I keep blinking, trying to make her come into focus.

'What did you say just now?' she asks.

'I… er, sorry, I… er, don't…'

'You said you got the wrong house. Whose house were you looking for?'

'Jerry Macauliffe's.'

'Yeah, this is his place…' She grabs the sides of my face and holds it up, her eyes drilling into me. 'Are we related or something?'

'I don't know,' I say. 'Who are you?'

'Valentina. Jerry's daughter.'

My brain spasms with pain. 'No, you can't be.'

'I think I know who I fucking am!' She lets go and my head thumps against the floor. 'That's why I live here.'

The pain in my head sharpens; I can't think straight, can't understand what she's saying. 'No, *I'm* his daughter...'

She puts her hand to her mouth. 'What?'

'I'm Jerry Macauliffe's daughter,' I repeat slowly.

'Oh fuck... I don't believe it. I don't fucking believe it.' Her bright blue eyes – my eyes, Dad's eyes – start to glisten with tears. 'Oh my God.' She leaps off me, backing into the wall with a horrified look on her face. 'This is crazy... this is fucking crazy.' She slides down to the floor.

'What do you mean?' My voice is trembling. Ridiculous, impossible thoughts are flying through my body, skimming the edges of sense.

'Look at us!' she cries. 'Our hair, our face, everything.'

'I know, but I don't understand.'

She throws back her head and groans deeply, as if a chasm is opening up within her. 'We're sisters,' she says.

She lifts me up and sits me on the bed, then fetches a cold flannel from the bathroom, placing it against the back of my head. The place she struck feels very tender and sore, but the pain and dizziness are fading.

'It's not bleeding,' she says. 'Just a bruise. Sorry about that.'

You could have knocked me out cold, I think, but I say, 'No, no, it's okay... you thought I was an intruder.'

'I heard you moving about downstairs. I thought you'd come to...' She stops, thinking better of it. 'Oh well, never mind... Fuck me... just look at you.'

We stare at each other for a few moments, registering the other's features and comparing them with our own image. We are not identical, but the likeness between us is undeniable. Our eyes are the exact same blue. Our noses are virtually the same length and width. Our mouths have the same bow shape and our upper teeth line up in the same way.

I know that Valentina's thinking the same. She's as shocked as I am. Just as angry and full of questions. Our throats are filling up with them; they're falling over each other as they fight to climb out of our mouths. But we don't seem able to speak.

It feels like we've fallen into each other's nightmare and can't get out. But we both know we're not dreaming. Everything is as real as can be. This little house, this room, this extraordinary moment. *She* is real. Just as I am real to her. But I don't even know where to start.

'I'm calling him,' Valentina says, breaking the charged silence. 'He's got to come over and explain himself.' She starts to rummage in the bedding.

I look at her, incredulous. 'But... but you can't...'

'I fucking can. He's not getting away with this.' She finds her mobile and scrolls down her contact list. A picture of Dad's smiling face fills the screen. Oh God. She doesn't know, she doesn't know...

I grab her arm. 'No, I mean you *can't*. It's not possible.'

'What do you mean? Get off.' She whips her arm away.

'You can't call him! He won't answer. He's... he's...' I hesitate.

'What? Tell me!'

'He had an accident last Friday. On his motorbike...'

'Stupid fucker,' she mutters. 'Where is he? In hospital?'

'No...' I take a deep breath. 'He died. He drove into a tree and died at the scene.'

'Oh...' She stares into her lap. 'Right...' There's a very long pause. She slowly puts the phone down as I stare at her, still not believing what I'm looking at, feeling helpless and angry.

'Does my mum know?' she says eventually.

'Your *mum*?' I stop. The thought that there would be another woman hadn't yet occurred to me. So Dad was having an affair. 'How would I know?' I say bitterly, and then, 'I can't take it all in. I'm sorry, I feel like my head's going to explode.'

'That makes two of us. I don't know about you, but I need a drink.'

'Yeah, some tea,' I say, starting to get slowly to my feet.

'No, I mean a drink drink. Vodka or gin, I don't care, anything. A big bottle.'

'I'm not sure that's such a great idea…'

'Please, Jodie – Josie, Jolene… Jesus Christ, I can't even remember your name.' She stands up. 'Have you got any cash? I'm cleaned out.'

I gesture weakly at my bag, which is still lying on the carpet. She passes it over and I take a twenty-pound note out of my purse. 'Here.'

She whips the cash from my hand, charges from the room and thunders down the stairs. The front door slams behind her and my veneer crumbles; I fall back onto the bed as my body convulses in painful, heaving sobs. This is all too much.

I lie there for a few minutes, waves of panic rising and subsiding. I know I can't stay here. I've got to escape before she comes back. I stand up, my body reeling as I try to find my balance. Clutching my bag, I totter towards the door and onto the landing. My legs wobbling, my head throbbing. Gripping the rail, I make my way downstairs, trying to move quickly without falling. As I reach the bottom step, the front door opens and Valentina whooshes back in.

'I was going to bring it up to you,' she says. 'Oh well, go into the front room and I'll see if I can find some glasses.'

I glance briefly at the front door – it's so tempting to run out, but it's too late. She'd only catch up with me in the street and there'd be a scene. No, I'm stuck here. I'm going to have to talk to her. I go into the sitting room and sit down on Grandma's old sofa – briefly thinking how shocked she'd be if she were still alive. How shocked I am. How shocked Mum's going to be, not to mention the rest of the family. And I don't know the half of it yet. How could he do this to us? How could he go and die and leave this mess behind?

Valentina comes back with a couple of not-so-clean-looking tumblers. She unscrews the bottle and pours us two generous shots of vodka.

'Cheers!' She knocks hers back, shuddering as the alcohol floods into her veins.

I hesitate, remembering the car parked down the street. I never drink and drive, not even if I'm under the limit, so if I succumb, there's no going back and I'll have to stay in Manchester tonight. I can't sleep here, even if she invites me. I'll have to call a taxi to take me to a hotel. Mustn't leave it too late. Better ring Arun to explain or he'll worry about what's happened to me. Anchoring myself to these small practical issues helps. Without them I feel I could drift out to sea and sink below the horizon.

There's a long, awkward pause.

'Drink up,' she prompts. 'You'll feel better, promise. And it'll dull the pain.'

Does she mean at the back of my head or in my heart? Hoping for both, I take a cautious sip.

Valentina looks at me directly. 'Okay, this is how we do it. We take it in turns. You ask me a question, then I ask you one.'

'Look, we don't have to do this straight away,' I say. 'We've both just had a terrible shock and I'm not feeling great.'

She pours herself a second glass and throws it back. 'Come on! You've got to be curious.'

'I... I don't know what I'm—'

'If you don't want to start the questions, I will.' She nods at the glass nestling in my hands. 'Go on. Drink!' I take another sip, longer this time. I'm trapped, so I might as well let the alcohol get to work. 'How old are you?'

'Twenty-four.'

Her eyebrows rise. 'Me too.'

'What? But that's… that's…' I stutter.

'Mental,' she finishes for me. 'When's your birthday?'

'August.'

'No way. Me too! What date?'

'Er… the thirteenth.' I can't believe this.

'Jesus, mine's the eighteenth! That's only five days' difference.' Valentina leans back against the sofa cushion. 'We're virtually twins.' We stare at each other, our minds drawing the same mad conclusion: what the hell was our father playing at? 'I was born in Camden,' she continues. 'How about you?'

'The same,' I gulp. 'The Royal Free Hospital.'

'That's insane, so was I!'

'God, it gets worse and worse,' I mutter.

'Must have taken some nifty footwork.' She laughs grimly. 'How did he explain that to the midwives? Unbelievable, eh?'

Totally despicable, I think, swigging the vodka back. Dad was full of chutzpah, but I never would have believed he'd go that far. The selfishness of it, the cruelty… it's unspeakable. I can see him now, dancing with Mum at their silver wedding party last year, drunkenly draped over her. He looked so happy with how his life had turned out. But if all that time he was still having a relationship with another woman… Flames of anger blacken the edges of the picture, and it disintegrates, turning to ash.

'I wonder if your mother knows he was married,' I say.

'Whoa, whoa, slow down! You saying he's *married* to your mum?' I nod. 'But he always said he didn't believe in marriage.

Fucking hypocrite. So she's the real wife and my mum's the mistress, which means you're the proper daughter and I'm the bastard. Hah! Thanks a bunch, Dad!' She slams her glass on the table and reaches for the bottle again. 'Okay. Next question. Do you still live in London?'

'Yes. They've been in the same house for as long as I can remember. I mean, they *were* in the same… Dad was… Mum's still there… Sorry, I'm getting my tenses mixed up.' I can feel the vodka swirling around my system, loosening the screws, easing the joints. 'Can I… can I ask you a question now?'

'Fire away.'

'Have your parents been together all this time, like a proper couple? I mean, did you think you were a normal family, or did he just turn up every so often? You know, to see you. Take you out, keep in touch.'

'Good question, sis.' Valentina pauses to consider. 'First, I'd say, what's normal? Did I have a normal upbringing? No, as it turns out, but it seemed normal at the time. I had a mummy called Sophie and a daddy called Jerry. No brothers or sisters, just me. He had to go away a lot. For his work – that's what I was told, anyway. We never saw any family on his side, which I guess was a bit strange, but he told me he'd had a big falling-out with them. We lived in this shitty flat in Cricklewood until I was fourteen, and then we moved to Derbyshire.'

'When he got the Manchester job,' I say, almost to myself.

'Yeah, I suppose so. We never really talked about his work.'

My mind starts to whirr. 'So you didn't all live here, in this house?'

'No! Mum hates cities. My grandparents died, left her a load of money, so she bought a cottage in the middle of fucking nowhere. The pattern changed then. Dad was at home during the week and away at weekends. Conferences. But, in fact, he must have been coming home to you.'

'Yes… And we thought he stayed here during the week.'

'Except he never did. He used to rent it out to students. I couldn't hack living out in the sticks, had no money, no job. Mum and I were fighting all the time; she chucked me out, so Dad said I could live here until I got myself sorted. Been here nearly three years…'

I realise I've finished my vodka as she leans in to top up the glass. We sit in silence for a few minutes, processing.

'He was a total shit, but I'm really, really sad he's dead,' Valentina says, licking the vodka from her lips. 'Because if he was alive right now, I'd attack him with a lot more than a fucking hairdryer.'

I can feel the alcohol igniting the anger in my stomach. 'Yeah, I think I'd join you…'

'Did he call you his Viking warrior princess?'

I sigh heavily. 'Yes.'

'There you have it – total bastard. Couldn't even give us different nicknames. He was obsessed with Vikings. Like a great big kid.' She reaches forward and clinks my glass. 'To our father, who art in hell. I suppose that's where liars and cheats go to.'

It hurts to hear her talk about him in this way, but I suppose she's right. 'Are we talking Viking hell, or Christian hell?' I say despite myself, the vodka burning through me.

'Who gives a fuck?' An angry laugh bursts out of her mouth. She fixes me with a defiant look. 'So what happens now, sis?'

# CHAPTER SEVEN

*The Vikings worshipped many gods, including a set of twins. Frey was the god of fertility, and his sister Freya was the goddess of love and death. She possessed magic powers that enabled her to predict the future and transform herself into different guises.*

Josie wouldn't stay over, in spite of my pleadings. I didn't want her to go. I could have stayed up all night getting to know her, and there were hundreds more questions I wanted to ask, but she'd suddenly had enough of me and left. Not that I blame her. There I was, her mirror image, staring back at her, the personification of all the hurt and anger she was feeling. She looked like she wanted to smash the glass.

Vodka always anaesthetises me, but it made my sister go all 'tired and emotional', as our dead father used to say. It was one of his favourite phrases; used to irritate the hell out of me when I was a kid. He'd take me on these long outings, driving for hours across the country to some ancient burial site full of old stones and grassy ditches, where he'd read aloud every single notice about how people lived hundreds of years ago, refuse to buy me an ice cream, and then moan because I got grumpy on the way home. Tired and emotional.

I go back upstairs to the bedroom. It's the only room I use since I found mice in the cutlery drawer. Spending the evening downstairs felt a bit weird, like I was sitting in someone else's house. Or a really shitty counsellor's consulting room. My eyes kept flicking into the corners, peripheral vision on high alert. 'Mice can't hurt you,' Dad says – sorry, *used* to say. 'They're more frightened of you than you are of them.' Like anyone could possibly know that. I always thought my father was a bit of a liar; just didn't realise the industrial scale he operated on.

My father is dead and my sister has been born. How fucking depressing and amazing is that?

It's not often I get visitors these days. Standing here now, in the full glare of the light, I can see how this bedroom must have looked to Josie. The wardrobe door is hanging off its hinges and there's so much stuff piled on the chair you wouldn't know a chair's there at all. The carpet is covered in stains from bottles I knocked over in the dark, and every surface is littered with dirty crockery and takeaway cartons. My clothes – I only wear black – are piled in a heap and look like the charred remains of a bonfire. Sweated alcohol fumes soak the air like a foul perfume. Did I disgust her or did she feel sorry for me? She was probably too shocked by my face to notice, and I *had* just smacked her over the head with a dryer.

I take off my clothes and climb into bed, putting my phone under the pillow; it's my best weapon and I need to keep myself safe. We swapped numbers before Josie left and I gave her Mum's name and address. I don't care if it causes more devastation; it's the least Mum deserves after what she's done to me. Lying to me my entire life. Keeping me in the dark. Putting me in a vulnerable position so that a stranger could crash into my universe and tell me that the father I loved had another daughter. A daughter who bears the Viking surname he was so proud of. Macauliffe, as in St Olaf, the renowned warrior and saint. The name I couldn't have because the job of wife had already been taken.

*My father is dead. My sister has been born. My father is dead and my sister has been born.* Got to keep saying it to make it real. *My father is dead and my sister has been born. My father is dead and* . . . I pull the duvet over my head and whisper it over and over in the dark.

My head emerges from the suffocating heat of my body and I breathe out. Maybe the witch doesn't know yet. She *would* have told me. Even though we haven't spoken for months and I haven't seen her for almost a year and my last text included the phrase *I never want to see you again*, she still would have told me. Surely. Even if it was only to make me feel bad about the way I've behaved recently. Which means she doesn't know that the love of her life is no more.

A huge weight falls *plop* onto my end of the seesaw and the balance tips in my favour. Power surges through me. For the first time in my life, I know something she doesn't. Oh. My. God.

I'm not going to tell her, either. I'm going to let her suffer. Yes, I know I sound like a heartless bitch. Any normal daughter would pick up the phone or rush over to the house to deliver the tragic news in person. I'm guessing that's what happened with the real Macauliffes. But I'm not a normal daughter and this is not a normal family. It's not a family at all, as it turns out; it's a couple of fucking liars playing mummies and daddies, and guess who got to play the baby?

What's going on right now at Wisteria Retreat, I wonder? I plant myself back into my old home life, imagining the scenario. It's Monday evening. Late. Dad was due home at around seven but he hasn't turned up. Mondays have always been special, treated like a homecoming. I expect Mum's feeling a tiny bit pissed off. She was so looking forward to seeing him, came back from the studio early, showered, put on fresh clothes and cooked one of his favourite meals.

But there's no sign of her beloved Viking. No roar of the Bonneville sweeping up the drive. No message from him either. She'll remind herself that none of this is unprecedented. Jerry does what he wants, when he wants, and she's always accepted that. He resents being chased or pinned down. Even so, she won't be able to stop herself leaving increasingly irritable messages on his mobile: *What time u getting here? Where r u? Y didn't you tell me u were going 2 b late? Call me asap!*

She won't sleep much tonight, listening for the sound of his key in the door, worrying that something's wrong. *That bloody motorbike.* Tomorrow morning, she might ring round the hospitals, maybe even call the police. She might have driven past the scene several times and not realised who the victim was. Somehow she'll find out, probably by chance. *What? He died last Friday? Are you kidding? He's been dead four days and I didn't even know?*

Yes, well, that's how it is when you're not the next of kin. When your lover's driving licence is registered at a different address. When you're a secret, you stay a secret. Nobody knows you need to be told. Mum's been skulking in the shadows for twenty-five years, and now she can stay there and rot. She had no part to play in Jerry's official life, so she can't expect to be involved in his official death either.

So where does that leave me? The other, unofficial daughter. The unwitting player in the game.

*My father is dead and my sister has been born.* Okay, she's a half-sister, but let's round up. Let's just call her my sister. *Hi, everyone, meet my sister. I'm spending the weekend with my sister. Sorry, my sister's calling. You like my shoes? I borrowed them off my sister. You must know my sister, she looks just like me. Hi, sis, how you doing?* Sounds odd. Like wearing a dress that doesn't fit very well, that's not my usual style.

But the funny thing is, and I promise I'm not lying here, deep down, I've always known I had a sister.

# CHAPTER EIGHT

*Vikings usually had one proper wife, but were allowed others if they wished. These women were 'thralls' (slaves) and had a very low status in the household.*

The hotel room is cramped and stuffy; there's no air con, and when I open the window, the noise is so loud I have to shut it again. I miss Arun and wish that he was lying next to me. We had a long, emotional conversation on the phone before I came to bed, and now I've gone beyond sleep. The back of my head is sore and tender. My brain won't let me rest. I'm feeling dehydrated and there's no bottled water in the fridge. This is a terrible hotel, but it's all I could get at eleven o'clock at night.

Sleep comes eventually in the small hours, but it's shallow and anxious. I dream of a tall woman, dressed head to toe in black, a veil across her face. She is both strange and familiar. Who is she? I follow her as she walks quickly; she knows I'm behind her and she's trying to get away from me. I fix my gaze on her back and by the time she enters a long street of flat-fronted houses, I'm only a few paces behind.

She stops by a door and produces an enormous silver key out of the air, slipping it into the lock and letting herself in. I creep inside, poking my head around the doorway to the living room, watching her as she walks slowly amongst the tatty furniture, looking up at the cobwebs, running her fingers over the dusty mantelpiece. I'm close behind her now, I've got her trapped.

I make a sudden move and hurl myself at her, pushing her backwards onto the carpet. I punch and scratch at her, straddling her body, pinning her down with my thighs. She lies beneath me, breathing hard. I tear off her black veil and she stares up at me, terrified. Of course it's Valentina's face I'm looking at. Or is it my own face and she has been chasing me? I wake up, face down on the mattress, tearing at the sheets and gasping for breath.

I have to tell Mum. She has to know; there's no way out of it. I can't keep this secret to myself; it's too big, too important. She'll help, she'll know what to do. She always makes everything all right. I take out my phone. But it's only seven a.m., too early to call. She may be sleeping and I don't want to wake her. Even if she's already up, I don't know what state she's in. I can't call her out of the blue and tell her something that will shatter her world forever. It would be an incredibly selfish thing to do. Why did I even think of it? I put the phone away.

I take a shower, then put on yesterday's underwear inside out and clean my teeth with my fingers. Gross. The buffet-style breakfast is revolting – stale cereal, unripe fruit, stewed coffee and slices of bread that won't brown no matter how many times I feed them through the toaster. I call Arun from the table, catching him on his way to the bus stop for work.

'How are you?' he says. For once, the question has real meaning. Our conversation last night ended with me in floods of tears. 'I couldn't sleep, I was so worried about you, Josie. I just can't get my head around it.'

'Tell me about it.' I put the phone under my chin and unwrap a pack of butter.

'Do you want me to come up and drive you home?'

'No, thanks, I'll be okay.' The butter is too hard to spread, so I attack the tub of jam instead.

'You shouldn't be driving right now. You're still in shock.'

'I'll take it slowly, promise. Have a good day. I'll see you tonight.'

'Take care,' he says. 'I love you.'

'Yeah, love you too.' I finish the call and put the phone away.

I spread strawberry jam over the warm, floppy slice of bread and take a half-hearted bite. The food sticks in my mouth and it takes two mouthfuls of cold coffee to swallow it down. Even if this were a five-star hotel, I wouldn't have an appetite. I'm feeling guilty about the conversation with Arun. I didn't reveal what I'm planning to do on the way home. He would have tried to stop me. Probably would have got straight on a train and bundled me into the boot of the car. But I have to do this. It's important.

An Uber takes me back to Antrobus Street. It's ten a.m. now and the curtains of Valentina's bedroom are still drawn. I decide not to ring the bell. She could be asleep, and anyway, I'm not sure I want to see her. It feels awkward, like I've slept with a stranger, the intimacy of the encounter too much in the cold light of day.

I get into the car and take out the address Valentina gave me last night. Wisteria Retreat, Brook Lane, near Allenshaw. I type the postcode into the satnav and it tells me I'm a forty-six-minute drive away. An acceptable daily commute to and from the university, especially given that Dad was used to London, where getting anywhere seems to take a least an hour. He wouldn't have minded; in fact he would have relished the ride back and forth each day, putting the bike through its paces.

As I turn onto the main road and head in a south-westerly direction out of the city, I take in the sights he would have seen each day. The dull parades of shops and endless terraced houses eventually give way to wider roads and higher speed limits. At one point I'm overtaken by a black-leathered biker on a shiny vintage machine, and for half a second my brain thinks it's Dad – or the ghost of him – riding past to lead the way. Foolishly I cling onto the image, watching the bike weave through the cars and trucks ahead, becoming smaller and smaller until it's a small black dot, then dipping over the horizon and vanishing forever.

The cityscape is well behind me now and the countryside is taking over. I don't know this part of England at all – Dad probably kept us well away deliberately. We are on the edge of the Peak District, known for its spectacular landscapes. I can imagine him roaring up and down the hills like a teenager, stopping at the top to smoke a fag. We did everything we could to persuade him to give up, but he wasn't interested. 'You've got to die of something,' he used to say.

As I drive through the twisting lanes, I feel as if I'm entering a force field. The atmosphere in the car is so charged, I can hardly breathe. I feel Dad's spirit pressing down on me, begging me not to do this, his wheedling voice drilling into my inner ear. *Come on, princess, slow down. It's not as bad as it looks. Let's talk this through, we can sort it out.* But I'm not listening. I don't care what he thinks any more, I don't have to do what he says. It's all right for him, he's dead; now the rest of us have to clear up his mess. I'm rigid with anger, as if I've swallowed a sword, its point digging deep into my stomach.

The road dips down and a sign warns me of a ford ahead. What does that mean? Is the water too deep for cars? Should I find another route? I glance at the map on the screen – looks like there's no other way. I drive on regardless, putting my foot on the accelerator as I approach the stream and driving through it, the water splashing the sides. Another sign tells me to test my brakes, but I don't bother. I follow the instructions, turning left at a small junction and driving down a narrow track, hedged on both sides.

According to the satnav, I'm less than half a mile away. I look left and right for the cottage, but there's no sign of any building. It must be hidden away somewhere, up a driveway. As the car slows to a crawl, my pulse rate quickens. I'm so near I can sense it. *Your destination is on the right.* No, it isn't. There's nothing here! I must have missed it. This is hopeless; I need to be on foot. Ahead, the road widens out slightly, so I pull up tight against the hedge, its spiky branches scraping the paintwork, and get out of the car.

The sun is shining, but it feels cold. I zip up my jacket and slip my bag over my shoulder. I start to walk back in the direction I came from, the cheerful breeze sweeping away the fug of last night's vodka, heightening my senses. The birdsong sounds as if it's coming through loudspeakers, the foliage is the brightest green I've ever seen and the air has never felt fresher. I'm a Viking warrior princess, preparing herself for battle.

# CHAPTER NINE

*Although Viking women's lives were largely domestic, there are records that also show them holding unusual jobs, such as rune carving and storytelling. They were forbidden to wear men's clothes, cut their hair short or carry weapons.*

I have to walk back several hundred metres before I find a gap in the hedge, just wide enough for a car to pass through. There's no sign announcing the cottage, but I know this is the place. I stride up the path, the tarmac soon giving way to sandy gravel. After fifty metres, the path opens up and I pass a large wooden garage. Another twenty metres or so beyond that is Wisteria Retreat, a detached stone cottage with square windows and a black slate roof. Retreat is the right name for it – it's completely invisible from the road, nestled amongst tall trees. I stop and gaze, my breath briefly stolen by its beauty. It's like something out of a picture book, with a gently sloping front lawn that leads down to a stream, fruit trees, a vegetable patch, and what looks like a chicken run. This is Mum's rural retirement dream – the dream Dad mocked and dismissed. Of course he did. He didn't need two homes in the country. And if he retired and left Manchester, what would have happened to his cosy country life here?

My heart starts to pound painfully and my throat dries. No going back now. My fingers fumble with the gate catch, the wrought iron creaking as I push it open. I walk up the flagstone path towards the front door, clutching my bag to my chest, propelling my legs forward on wobbly knees. *I can do this. I have a right to do this. I'm not letting her get away with it.*

There's no bell, just a large black iron knocker. I bang it twice and wait, my ears pricked, listening for the sound of her footsteps coming to the door. But there's only silence. I knock again, louder and more insistent. Still no response. This is not how I imagined it. For some ridiculous reason, it hadn't occurred to me that she wouldn't be at home, as if she'd received my telepathic message and was expecting me.

I take a few paces back, looking up at the windows for signs of life – a curtain twitching, a face peeping out. Where is she? It's Tuesday morning; she could be at work – Valentina told me she runs a pottery café in Allenshaw. But she'd only be at work if she didn't know…

A small porch juts out from the body of the building and I peer through its side window to see, amongst other male and female footwear, a large pair of walking boots, Dad's size 13s by the look of them. Three walking sticks lean against one corner and a large sack of kindling takes up the other. I'm suddenly overcome with an intense desire to go inside. What if the keys that were found on Dad's body fit this house? It would make sense. Dare I…?

I feel around in my handbag and take them out, holding them up to the sunlight. Two keys on a simple ring. The deadlock must be for the porch, the Yale for the front door within. I fill my lungs with air and push the larger key into the lock. It fits, and with some gentle easing, turns. Without really thinking, I push the door open and step into the porch.

The inner door, with its green paintwork and frosted window, beckons me forward. I've already proved my point, I don't need to check the other door, but the key's in my hand and before I know it I'm turning it in the lock. The door sticks at the bottom, but after a nudge it opens into a narrow hallway, paved with square stones. A large pine cupboard takes up most of one side, beyond which is a door leading into the sitting room. Another doorway on the right opens into a large kitchen-diner.

The house is so unlike my old parental home that for a few seconds I convince myself that Dad can't have been living here. There's been considerable refurbishment – walls knocked down to create a modern open-plan area, with white kitchen cabinets, gleaming granite worktops, and an island housing a butler sink with fancy taps. An open staircase in the far corner leads to the upper floor, and large glass doors reveal a stone patio behind the house. The walls are white and covered in art. Lino prints, woodland watercolours, abstract splodges, nude charcoal sketches… And there are pots everywhere. A curiously shaped vase on the dresser, brightly glazed flowerpots filled with herbs on the windowsill. A stunning fruit bowl on the country dining table. All artfully placed, as if for a magazine shoot.

I cross the hallway again and go into the sitting room: square and cosy-looking, with a wood-burning stove in the fireplace and two deep red sofas. More pots. Pots on every possible surface. And in case I thought I'd made a mistake, because my father couldn't possibly have felt at home somewhere so self-consciously designed, there are several framed photos of him on the walls. Most of them also featuring a blonde-haired woman who looks weirdly like my mother, only several years younger.

The bitch.

I pick up the pot nearest to me – a white vase with cracked glaze and fine fluted edges – and hurl it at her face. It smashes against the wall, scattering in jagged pieces across the ethnic rug. The release it gives me is euphoric – the sword in my stomach pulled out in one swipe. I reach for another pot – a candle holder this time – and throw it against the fireplace. Then a shallow bowl in the shape of a heart, which I send flying against another photo, which wobbles off its hook and crashes to the floor. Shaking violently, I pick it up. As I run my finger over the cut in the glass, a thin trail of blood smears the picture, but I can still see it clearly enough. Dad is in his holiday clothes – I recognise those yellow shorts – and he's cuddling a young girl, about eight years old: tall and skinny, with wavy auburn hair. My head spins with confusion. That's a photo of me. How dare Dad have a photo of me in this house? Then I remember: this isn't me, it's my sister.

I hear sounds. A car crunching on the gravel. Fuck. It's Sophie, she's back. I look around at the mess, the blood dripping from my hand onto the rug. My fingerprints and traces of my DNA will be everywhere. I stare at the crime scene for a couple of seconds, paralysed by my own stupidity. What have I done?

I stuff the photograph, frame and all, into my bag and head for the front door. My hand is on the latch when I realise that she'll see me as she walks up the path. Spinning round, I run back into the sitting room, but there's only a window there. I cross the hallway once more and go into the kitchen-diner. Bifold doors stretch across the back wall. Luckily, a tiny key is in the lock; I twist it open and slide back the heavy sheet of glass, stepping onto the patio. The garden is enclosed by a stone wall, but there's a small gate on the right-hand side, fastened by a loop of rope over the post. I flip it off and run around the side of the cottage, pressing my back against the wall as I edge forward, stopping at the corner and pressing my cheek against the cold stone. The garage, a separate building, is facing me. Should I run towards that now and hide around the side? Or should I wait till she's gone into the house?

The car engine has been switched off. I hear the opening and closing of the driver's door. The gate creaking open. Her boots on the flagstone path. Did I leave the front door open? I think I did. Shit… No more footsteps. She must be inside the cottage now.

How long will it take her to notice the damage? I have to take my chance now and run.

My legs feel heavy and weak, but I propel myself forward, belting down the driveway as if I'm running for my life, my skinny limbs flailing, my long auburn hair flying behind me like a sail. My large handbag, containing the framed picture, bangs against my side and my breasts bounce painfully as I thump against the uneven tarmac, splashing through shallow puddles, slipping on wet, mouldy leaves.

She's running after me. I can hear her calling: 'Valentina! Valentina! For God's sake, come back!' I don't turn round, don't stop. My side is killing me with a stitch and I can hardly breathe, but I force myself to run on. She shouts out again – 'Valentina! Please, come back!' – but her footsteps recede. She's given up the chase.

I keep going. I reach the road and hurtle towards the car, flinging open the door and hurling myself into the driver's seat. I shove the key into the ignition and fire up the engine, pulling away without looking behind me and accelerating forward. I have no idea where I'm going, but I don't care, I've just got to get as far away from there as possible. Blood is dripping onto the steering wheel, my hand has started to throb; a hard shard of glass is working its way up my arm and across my chest in the direction of my heart.

# CHAPTER TEN

*Viking justice took the form of trial by ordeal. Accused women had to pick stones out of boiling water. If they dropped them, they were found guilty. If they succeeded and their wounds healed, they were judged innocent.*

Somebody's banging on the door. It's the witch, no doubt, coming to tell me the news. I turn onto my front and put my hands against my ears. No way am I getting up to answer. What time is it, anyway? A shaft of sunlight is beaming through the gap in the curtains, heavy with motes of dust. I feel under the pillow for my phone. Two p.m. Shit. I slept right through the morning. *Bang, bang, bang.* She's very persistent. *Fuck off and leave me alone!*

I roll my tongue around in search of fluid, but my mouth feels gritty and tastes sour. Had a terrible night. Unsurprisingly. It's coming back to me now. I was expecting the dream about my sister, but I dreamt about Dr Bannister instead. I remember waking up in a sweat, screaming out and punching the darkness with my fists. I had to switch the light on to make sure I was alone, put some techno on at full volume to drown out the noise of my pain. The old bat from next door started banging on the wall. Well, I guess it *was* three in the morning.

And now there's more banging, I'm being assaulted on all sides. I kick off the duvet and pound my fists into the mattress. *No, no, no. Fuck off! Go away!*

She shouts through the letter box, her desperate tones climbing the stairs. 'Valentina! Open up. Please! I need to talk to you. It's important.'

*I'll decide what's important, not you.* I've got nothing to say to the witch. Words can't describe how I'm feeling right now. I'm not interested in her explanations, or self-justifications, or assurances that things aren't as bad as they seem.

'Valentina, I know you're there. Open up, or I'm coming in.' She has armed herself with the spare keys, by the sound of it.

'Hold on!' I shout, dragging myself to my feet. 'I'm coming!' I run across the landing and down the stairs, hoping to put the chain across before she opens the door, but she beats me to it.

'For God's sake, Valentina,' she cries, pushing the door into my face. She enters, letting it rattle shut behind her. 'Why wouldn't you answer? I've been screaming my head off out there.' She advances towards me, and I back away. I can feel her eyes boring into my puffy, tear-stained face and crumpled, slept-in clothes. 'Look at the state of you! Were you in bed?'

'So what if I was? I'm grieving!'

She stops. 'You know, don't you… about Jerry.'

'Yes.' I hug my arms to my chest. 'I know everything.'

She hesitates, searching my face for clues. 'What do you mean?'

'*Everything*, Mum. Every fucking disgusting thing.' I turn my back and march off to the kitchen. She follows me down the narrow hallway, standing at the door, unable to stop herself gasping at the rotting chaos. We face each other like animals trapped in a cage.

'How did you find out?' she asks, looking at me warily.

'About what? Dad's death, or the fact that the two of you have been lying to me my *entire* life?'

'Don't talk about it like that.' She holds out a hand. 'Come on, I know you're angry. I know it hurts. Let's go and sit down.'

I back away further, edging towards the bathroom. If the lock wasn't broken, I'd shut myself in and scream until she went away. 'Can you just go, please? I've nothing I want to say to you.'

'No, no, we have to talk. Tell me how you found out.'

'She came here.'

Her skin pales. 'Who?'

'Josie. My *sister*! It was fucking terrifying, like seeing my own ghost. She broke into my room, told me Dad was dead. Can you imagine how that felt? I nearly had a fucking heart attack.' I'm trembling all over, livid with anger. I want to punch her in the face, beat her to a pulp.

'I'm sorry. So, so, sorry… Please! Let's sit down and talk properly.'

'You've got five minutes,' I say. 'Then I want you out of my life forever.'

She turns round and walks back into the hallway. I have to stop myself from picking up a knife and stabbing her in the back. I follow her into the living room, letting her sink onto the sofa and taking a dining chair for myself, which I place directly opposite her, beyond touching distance. As far as I'm concerned, she's on trial.

'I'm really, really sorry you had to find out that way. Honestly, Valentina, I'm so sorry. It must have been devastating. I know how you must be feeling.'

'No, you don't …' I feel the tears pricking behind my eyes. Got to stay strong, can't let her wear me down. 'Just tell me what happened, Mum.'

She twists her hands together. I look down at her stubby fingers, the nails always cut short to work the clay, her palms stained pink with terracotta. I know those hands and that face so well, and yet she feels like a stranger to me. I know she was pretty when she was young; I've seen the photographs. She was one of Dad's students, eight years younger than him, only twenty when I was born; never came back after the long vacation for the third year. She didn't want to, she said; all she wanted to do was care for me. That was the romantic story they always told, with some vital pieces of information missed out.

'Jerry left the house very early on Friday morning, while I was still asleep. I didn't realise he'd gone until I woke up. It was so unlike him; he never left without saying goodbye. I assumed he'd had to go in to work early, but he'd left his stuff behind – wallet, laptop, even his phone. Idiot, I thought. I had no way of getting in touch with him, but as soon as the university switchboard opened, I rang. They said he hadn't turned up yet, didn't seem at all worried…' She looks up at me, her eyebrows raised in dismay.

'Go on.'

'But I felt uneasy all day. Jerry had been behaving really strangely these past few weeks; something was clearly bothering him, but he wouldn't talk about it. He said there were a few problems in the department, but I didn't really believe him. You know how chilled he was; he never stressed about work. I didn't hear from him all weekend, but I tried to stay calm. Kept hoping there'd be a simple explanation. I called the department again first thing yesterday morning and' – she exhales loudly – 'that's when they told me. He'd been dead all that time.' She searches up her sleeve for a tissue.

I pitch my voice hard. 'That was yesterday. It's Tuesday afternoon now. Why didn't you tell me straight away?'

She blows her nose. 'I was scared… I didn't know how to do it. I knew the time might come, if – *when* – he died… I knew I'd have to tell you the truth about his other family. But I never thought it would happen like this, not so soon, without warning. I was frightened of how you'd react. I know how you idolise him and I know how difficult things have been for you these past few years… I'm sorry, I'm so sorry… I should have come over straight away, but I was dealing with it too, you know? The shock. I went to the doctor's this morning to get some pills, and when I came back…' She pauses, shaking her head. 'I realised you must have found out.'

'What do you mean?'

'I saw you, Valentina. I know you trashed the cottage. All my best pots, destroyed. Twenty years of work – how *could* you?'

'I don't know what you're talking about.'

'If you wanted a photo of him, you should have just asked. Your blood is all over the carpet.'

'It wasn't me. I've been in bed all morning.' What is she on about? I can feel my hackles rising.

'Please, Valentina, don't play games with me. I ran after you, but you wouldn't stop. You didn't even turn around.'

I stand up, flinging the chair to one side. 'This is bullshit. You're blaming me for something I didn't do. As per fucking usual.'

'I understand you're angry, I get that. But please…' She rises and moves towards me, but I shrug her off.

'That wasn't me. It must have been Josie. We look fucking identical, by the way.'

She shakes her head. 'Josie wouldn't do a thing like that.'

'Oh, so you know my sister, do you?'

'I know enough about her to know she's not violent.'

I'm burning up, my voice shaking. 'Unlike me, is that what you're saying? She's the *good* one, is she? The perfect daughter? The daughter you wish you'd had?'

'Oh, don't be so ridiculous.' She looks at me, disgusted. 'You're twisting my words, like you always do. I don't care if you trashed the cottage, it doesn't matter. All I care about is you. I'm sorry. Your father loved you, *I* love you – we never meant to hurt you, Valentina. We just thought it was better that you didn't know.'

'I *did* know,' I snap back, playing my trump card. 'I knew all along.'

'No, you didn't.'

'I did! Those nightmares I've always had aren't nightmares, are they? They're memories!'

'No, they're not. That's not true. I promise you, that's *not* true.'

'Nobody believed me. Dr Bannister thought I was a freak!'

Now she's looking scared. 'Stop this, Valentina, now is not the time. Your father's dead, for God's sake! We shouldn't be screaming at each other. We should be facing this together.'

I back into the front window, pointing at the doorway. 'Get out. Go on, get out now. This is *over*.'

'Valentina, I'm begging you. Stay away from Josie and her mother. Forget about Dr Bannister. It was a long time ago; you've moved on, you've done so well – don't get dragged back there, for your own sake.'

'Please go.'

She sucks in a long breath and gathers herself together. I keep my finger pointing as she crosses the room, pausing at the threshold. 'You'll have to leave here, you know,' she says. 'This place belongs to Josie's mother now.'

'Jerry's wife, you mean.' My voice is cold. 'Say it, Mum, say it. Jerry's lawful wife.'

'I'll help you move out; we'll clear the place up. You can come back home. I know it won't be easy, but we'll work it out somehow. We need to stick together, Valentina. Listen to me. I love you, I'm only thinking of you. Please, please, stay away from the Macauliffes.'

I shove her into the hallway and push her out of the front door.

# CHAPTER ELEVEN

*The Vikings wore a lot of jewellery. They made brooches, pendants, finger rings, bangles, earrings and buckles out of copper, bronze, pewter, silver and gold. Jewellery was always decorated with twisting patterns and pictures of monsters and animals.*

As soon as I get home, I bathe the cut on my hand, apply a good splodge of antiseptic cream and stick on a large plaster. Returning to the sitting room, I take out the photo I stole from the cottage and remove the broken glass from the frame, wrapping it carefully in some newspaper. I don't want Arun to find it in the rubbish – he'll have a blue fit if I tell him what I did – so I take the package and frame down to the ground floor, putting them in the large wheelie bins that are parked behind the stairs.

I walk back up to level four and along the open corridor, pausing for a few moments to lean on the balcony and gaze at the lights twinkling in the early-evening darkness. The sounds of the city feel strangely comforting – police sirens, the rumble of traffic on the North Circular, takeaway delivery scooters. London will always be home to me. Even though I now know that Dad spent his weekdays living in the Derbyshire countryside, I still can't imagine him there. There was nothing of him in that house. No politics books, no piles of *Guardian*s and *New Internationalist*s. No ashtrays, no dirty socks shoved under the sofa cushions, no scruffy collection of bits and bobs that he'd take out of his pocket and leave on the hall table. No lingering smell of tobacco and red wine. If it wasn't for the pictures of him, I could have been persuaded that I'd gone to the wrong place.

The flat feels cold and I switch the heating on. Making myself a cup of tea, I take the stolen photo into the bedroom and sit on the bed with my legs crossed, staring at it. It's a closely cropped shot, so there's no scenery in the background, but on the back, in Dad's scrawl, it says *Bamburgh, July 2000*. He always wrote the location and date on the back of photos.

I'm finding it hard to believe it's not me in this picture. We often went to the Northumberland coast for holidays, and Bamburgh was our favourite beach. It's right opposite the island of Lindisfarne, where the Vikings first invaded. I gaze at the little girl's smiling face while I sip at my tea. The sun is shining, but she's clearly shivering in that pink swimsuit – I'm sure I had one almost the same. A large multicoloured towel is draped over her shoulders and her long red hair is flapping and tangling in the wind. There's a look of devilment in her eyes, and Dad is holding her tightly, as if he's trying to stop her from escaping. I peer in closer. Something is glinting on her chest – a tiny hammer-shaped blob. I gasp. She's wearing my Thor pendant. I remember never taking it off, not even at night. Especially not at night.

A memory strikes at the soft recesses of my brain. I'm seven, and I'm kneeling up on a chair, looking out of Mummy and Daddy's bedroom window at the front of the house. Waiting for Daddy to come home. He'd promised to be back in time for dinner but we had to eat without him. We're always eating without him. Often he doesn't come home until after bedtime, and Mummy has to do the story, which is never as good, because she reads from books. Daddy always makes stories up, and usually they're about Vikings. It's our special thing that Mummy can't share in because she doesn't have the Viking blood. Grandad's one too; he's got bent Viking fingers. So is Uncle Brett and my two cousins, Jake and Matthew.

I'm looking and looking, my eyes fixed on the street below. I know he'll come from the left side and it's making my neck ache. Mummy's calling me, saying it's time for bed, but I pretend not to hear. Then a black taxi turns the corner and stops outside the house. Daddy gets out. I bang my fist on the window, but he doesn't look up, just gives the driver something, picks up his case and walks up the front path.

I run out of the bedroom and bound down the stairs, my feet almost slipping on the hallway floor as I jump into his arms. He growls like a bear, kissing me on the check before putting me back down. '*Somebody*'s pleased to see me!' he says. Mummy comes out of the kitchen and stands there, waiting for her turn. She doesn't look happy.

'Sorry,' he says. 'Not my fault, problems with the trains.' She turns around and walks back to the kitchen.

'How was your raid?' I look around hopefully for a carrier bag of chocolate booty.

'A triumph!' He takes my hand and leads me into the sitting room, crouching down so that we're at the same height and he can look into my eyes. 'You should see the treasure we picked up!' he whispers. 'Gold and silver jewellery, iron helmets and battle shields, animal skins for the winter! We loaded up the longship and brought it all home. Buried it in a cave. I've left fifty warriors guarding it with their lives.' He reaches into his jacket pocket. 'Of course, I couldn't resist keeping a little something back for you.'

My heart skips as he pulls out a small gift bag, black with a swirly gold pattern. Inside is a necklace; a tiny silver hammer in the shape of a T threaded onto a black leather string. 'It's what's called an amulet,' he tells me. 'If you wear this, it will bring you good luck and ward off evil.'

'Wow!' It goes easily over my head, the hammer landing flat on my chest. I feel instantly safe – like someone has just cast a magic spell.

'Tell me, princess, which Viking god has a hammer?'

'Thor,' I answer proudly. 'The god of thunder.'

'That's my girl.' He stands up, shaking out his long legs. 'Right. Now I'd better make it up with Mummy.' He goes off to the kitchen. I pick up the pretty gift bag, smoothing it flat, and take it upstairs to my bedroom.

The memory skips forward to a few weeks later. I'm going to a party and there's a panic because Mummy has run out of wrapping paper. I remember the gift bag and go to fetch it. There's a slip of paper in the bottom of the bag. A receipt. *Jorvik Viking Centre*, it says at the top. That doesn't bother me. I'm nearly eight years old. I know Daddy didn't really go on a raid. It's the rest of it I don't understand.

*Thor Pendant £4.99*
*Thor Pendant £4.99*
*Total £9.98*

Why did he buy two?

Arun arrives home just after seven, which is very early for him. He's training to be a management consultant and they work him incredibly hard. They'd have him stay till ten, five nights a week, if they could.

'I'm so glad you got back safely,' he says, handing me a pizza box. 'You might need to warm it up a bit.'

'Let's just eat. I'm starving.'

He takes off his jacket, then washes his hands at the sink. 'I've been thinking about you non-stop. Feel really bad about not going up there with you.'

'You weren't to know what I was going to find.'

'But I'd have been there to support you. I could have driven you home.'

'I was okay. Just took it very slowly.' I look away, trying to banish the vision of myself throwing pots at the walls. What crime is that? Trespass? Criminal damage? She thought I was Valentina, although if she works out it was me, she could call the police. But would she dare?

I divide the pizza and burst open a packet of salad. We take our plates to the sofa and sit close together, picking up the slices with our fingers. It feels good to be home and to have him next to me. A drop of normality in a strange, tempestuous sea. I feel like I've been thrown off my ship and am battling against giant waves, each one higher and more menacing than the next. Without Arun to hold me up, I think I'd drown.

He fetches some kitchen towel and we wipe the spicy oil from the sides of our mouths. 'How did you hurt your hand?' he asks.

I feel my cheeks flaming. 'Oh, that. I broke a glass in the hotel. It's nothing. Just a scratch.'

'That's a big plaster for a scratch,' he murmurs, taking our plates and putting them on the counter.

'I don't know how I'm going to break the news to Mum,' I say quickly. 'Just the thought of telling her makes me feel sick. She'll be devastated, Arun. Utterly devastated. Dad wasn't just having a fling; he was living a parallel life! Like he was some double agent.'

Arun comes back to the sofa. 'Yes, it's completely mind-blowing. I'm still trying to take it in; God knows what it must be like for you. Unimaginable. I know Jerry was a one-off, larger than life, but I never thought for a moment... And you've got a *sister*... She's even the same age as you; that's just mental.'

'Honestly, if Dad hadn't died, I'd want to kill him. It's going to break Mum's heart.' Tears start to gather again and I swallow them down. 'It's already broken mine.'

Arun takes me in his arms, hugging me tightly, softly kissing the side of my neck. 'I know, hon. It's hard. So hard...' We stay there for a few moments, not talking, my chest heaving against his.

I pull away, rubbing at my eyes. 'I've been thinking. The clues were there... I just didn't spot them. Over the years, he made a few slips, said odd things that didn't really make sense – I'm starting to piece it together. He was away from home so often, even when I was little, long before he got the Manchester job. I don't know why Mum didn't put her foot down. She didn't seem to notice, or care – she was always so wrapped up in her own career. He put on this big act, pretended that he was chaotic, a free spirit, doing everything on the spur of the moment, but in fact he was running a military operation. He *had* to be. It wouldn't have worked otherwise. He must have had two phones. Two email accounts. Two Christmases, two birthdays, two summer holidays, two anniversaries. No wonder he was always complaining about being strapped for cash. But *why* did he do it? That's what I want to know. Why wasn't one wife and daughter enough?'

Arun shrugs. 'It's natural to want to ask questions, but you've got to be careful, Josie, or you'll drive yourself mad. Only Jerry has the answers, and he's gone.'

'Yeah, he's got away with it. Left behind the biggest pile of shit for me to clear up.'

'If you want me to come with you when you tell Helen, I will.' He bites his lip. 'It's going to be very hard to take time off work this week; you're not allowed compassionate leave for a non-family member... We could go over there tomorrow evening, perhaps?'

'Maybe… She's still in shock about his death; I don't want to push her over the edge.'

'You've got to tell her, Josie. You can't keep something as huge as this a secret. She has a right to—'

'Yes, I know that,' I reply, a little abruptly. 'But it's been a secret for twenty-five years; it can wait a few more days.' I get up and go to the sink, turning on the hot tap for the washing-up.

'Let me,' says Arun. 'You go and rest.'

'Thanks, love.' I dry my hands and go into our bedroom, kicking off my shoes and lying on top of the duvet. There's a sharp pain behind my eyes and my head feels thick with blood. My phone pings. It's a text. I hope it's not from Valentina. She's already texted me three times today and I haven't answered yet. I should answer her. But I have this feeling that once a conversation gets going, it's never going to stop.

I pick up my phone. The text isn't from her; it's from a number I don't recognise, and it's very long. I scroll down, squinting at the tiny screen, the pain in my head tightening its grip.

*Dear Josie, I'm extremely sorry you had to find out the way you did. No doubt you are feeling very angry, but I want you to know that your father loved both his families very much. Please, I beg you, do not tell your mother. She doesn't need that burden. Also, please stay away from Valentina. With respect, Sophie.*

My stomach flips over and over. I think I'm going to throw up. I read the words again, trying to understand what she's really saying. It doesn't read like a threat, and yet there is something sinister in the politeness of her tone. Who is she really trying to protect – my mother, or herself? And should I do as I'm told?

# CHAPTER TWELVE

*Every summer Vikings gathered together in one place for a 'thing', where they exchanged news, made new laws, judged crimes and settled arguments.*

I don't show the text to Arun because I know what his response will be. He'll want me to go straight over to Mum's and tell her everything. I flop onto my back and gaze at the bedroom ceiling, tracing the fresh cracks in the plaster made by the people above us. Arun will demand instant action – he can't bear uncertainty of any kind – but I need to think everything through carefully.

If I tell Mum, I risk destroying her peace of mind. If I keep my mouth shut, I'm colluding in the secret. I feel like I'm lying on the sea floor, tangled in a net. The water is thick and murky, and no matter how hard I look, I can't find a way out. It would be easy to cut myself free – all I have to do is tell the truth. The problem is, I don't know what the truth is yet. I don't know *why* Dad led this double life. Because he liked danger and excitement? Because he couldn't make up his mind? Or was he tangled up too?

I go back to Sophie's text. I understand why she doesn't want Mum to find out, but why does she want me to stay away from Valentina? I find that a bit insulting, like I'm going to do her harm. She's been deceived just as much as I have, so there's no reason to blame her. Anyway, it's Valentina that's been texting me, not the other way around. There's too much to think about and I'm too tired to make any decisions tonight. I turn onto my side and close my eyes. Maybe in the morning everything will become clear.

The night feels endless. I lie in the darkness, listening to Arun's gentle snoring, feeling envious of his peacefulness. I hover anxiously at the threshold of sleep, begging to be let in, my limbs aching with tiredness. It's not until the small hours that I feel myself tumbling over the edge, falling helplessly into strange, vivid dreams.

When I wake, it's late and Arun has already left for work. I get up and shower, scrubbing my skin till it hurts. My plaster falls off in the hot water, so I apply more antiseptic cream and re-dress the wound. Feeling a lot better, I go into the kitchen to make some breakfast. But my mouth is dry and I can't manage more than a spoonful of cereal. I drink a large glass of water instead, leaning against the kitchen island and staring out of the window at the tops of trees. This is almost my favourite time of year. Everything is slowly coming into leaf; within a few weeks the houses and office blocks will be hidden from view and all we'll be able to see is green.

Jill has given me the week off as compassionate leave. Yesterday, a sympathy card arrived in the post, signed by all my colleagues. *Take as long as you need*, Jill wrote in her message. I've no idea how long that might be. Weeks? Months? Years? Maybe it's not a good idea to mope around the flat on my own. Maybe I should go back to work – concentrate on other people's problems instead of obsessing over my own. But I know I'm in no fit state to be of help.

It's not just my father's death that I'm grieving. Other things have died too: my trust in Dad, my understanding of the man he was, the influence he had on my life. My love for him has fallen into a coma and I don't know if it's ever going to wake up. I walk over to the window and rest my head on the cool glass. Do I want to put my mother through what I'm suffering now? It's Dad I'd like to punish, not her.

My phone tells me I've got a text. It's from Valentina – again. Perhaps Sophie should tell her daughter to leave *me* alone, if she doesn't want us to be in touch.

*My mum knows u broke her pots btw. Respect! How r u? I feel like shit.*

I quickly tap in a reply. *Me 2. Yr mum told me to keep away from u. Why?*

*Hates me. Ignore her.*

*And she warned me not to tell my mum. Why???*

*Scared.*

*Who of? My family??*

*Dunno. Do what u want – bitch deserves what she gets.*

I stop it there. This isn't helping; it's just invoking stronger, more violent emotions. Something snapped inside me yesterday when I threw those pots at the walls. It wasn't me, it was somebody else, somebody unable to control their anger, who actively wanted to cause harm. I don't want to be reminded of that girl, I need to push her into the shadows and make her stand with her face against the wall.

The day drags by. I clean out the fridge. I go to the supermarket and drift through the aisles, picking up things I don't want or already have. When I put them on the conveyer belt, I go into meltdown and walk off without a word of explanation. Lunch is a couple of stale cheese biscuits and the watery dregs of a carton of cottage cheese.

Mum rings me in the afternoon, the sight of her name on my phone screen making me start with fear. 'You didn't call me yesterday,' she says, her tone rueful. 'How did you get on at the house? Did you pick up his stuff?'

In all the chaos, I hadn't thought about how I was going to get over that problem. 'The keys didn't fit,' I tell her, which is actually the truth. 'They must be for his office at work or something.'

'But they were house keys,' she replies. 'Did you try properly? Maybe they were just stiff. There's often a knack.'

I don't respond. 'How are you?'

'Up and down, you know how it is… I want to get on with organising the funeral, but the coroner won't release the body until she's seen the toxicology report.'

'I'm sure there's nothing to worry about.'

There's a long pause. 'Do you want to come over?' Her voice sounds hopeful.

I hesitate. 'Er, sorry, but I'm not feeling great. I think I need to rest. Is that okay?'

'Of course, darling. Come over whenever you want. How about lunch on Saturday? Bring Arun.'

'Yes, will do… I'll call you tomorrow, okay? Take care.'

This is unbearable. I should be helping her do all those things you have to do when somebody dies. I can't keep avoiding her; she'll be really hurt if she thinks I don't care. And I care so much, that's the problem. It hasn't always been easy between us. I love her like anyone loves their mother, but my father was the one I went to when I had a problem; he was the one whose opinion I really cared about. Mum always seemed more interested in her work, and made me feel like it was my job to fit in around it. I was a daddy's girl, through and through. But everything has changed. It's Mum that matters now, and Arun's right. I've got to tell her. No matter how important Sophie thinks it is that I don't.

I pace around the flat, rehearsing various speeches, but I can't find the right starting point. Do I lead into it gently or do I go in at the climax and work back? Maybe doing it face to face will be too traumatic – Mum hates big emotional scenes. I spend two hours composing an email, then delete it. That's the coward's way, I can't do that. I find a piece of paper and write two lists, outlining the possible consequences of telling and not telling, a kind of emotional flow chart. The page quickly fills with underlining and ringing-round, arrows and question marks. Only one factor sticks out. If I *don't* tell her, Mum's world doesn't change. Mine has changed forever, I can't help that. But as far as she's concerned, there's a choice.

I manage to get through the rest of the week without seeing Mum, limiting our contact to brief calls and neutral texts. She sounds okay on the phone, but not her usual sharp self. Dad's body still hasn't been released and I think she's run out of jobs to do. It doesn't feel great, avoiding physical contact, but acting isn't something that comes naturally to me, and I need time to prepare my role.

Saturday lunchtime arrives all too quickly. At least Arun will be with me, I keep thinking to myself. I feel sick with nerves in case she asks an awkward question and I slip up.

'Please promise me you won't say anything,' I tell Arun as we drive down the Finchley Road towards St John's Wood. 'No matter how much she goes on about what a wonderful husband Dad was, just bite your tongue.'

'Yes, yes, I know. But I really hate lying like this.'

'We're not lying, we're being considerate. Dad's only been dead for a week and she's still in shock.'

'For sure. But she's stronger than you think. Helen's an extremely capable woman; she's not a teenager.'

There are no spaces outside the house, so we have to park further down the street. 'Let's not argue,' I say, getting out. 'We've decided not to tell her and that's that.'

'Okay, but she has to know the truth eventually, Josie.' He points the key fob at the car and the lights wink in agreement.

'Not today,' I insist.

The sun is shining and all the cars are covered in a fine layer of city dust. I trail my fingers in it as we head towards the house, thinking of all the times I walked along this street on my way back from school or from the tube. We've always lived here. Even though I moved out three years ago and love our little rented flat, I still struggle not to think of it as home, and can't bear to relinquish my door key.

I haven't brought it with me today so I ring the bell. Mum takes a long time to answer. Her hair is unwashed and she's got no make-up on. 'Oh,' she says. 'Am I expecting you?'

'You invited us for lunch.'

'What, today?' She blinks at us, puzzled.

'It doesn't matter,' says Arun brightly. 'We can go out.'

She shakes her head emphatically. 'No... no...' We pause uncertainly on the doorstep, not knowing whether to come in or run away.

'Have you got any food, Mum? Perhaps we could rustle something up for you.'

'That would be great,' she says, relieved. 'Please, come in.'

We follow her through to the back of the house, its warm, non-matching tattiness revealing yet again the fact that Dad loathed DIY. He and Mum were always too busy to hire workmen, so things never got done – evidenced by the hole in the landing ceiling that's been there for as long as I can remember. I think of the romantically named Wisteria Retreat, refurbished to within an inch of its secret life. Which was the real Jerry Macauliffe, I wonder, as I open the fridge and take out possible ingredients for pasta or a stir-fry.

Arun starts washing up the mound of dirty dishes and a suspicious number of used wine glasses, while I chop some limp celery and overripe tomatoes. Mum sits in the chair by the window, gazing into the middle distance, barely responding to our trivial chatter about work, and even the bloody weather. I'm desperately trying to make sure we don't stray into dangerous territory, and every time Arun opens his mouth to say something, I cut in with yet another banality. Surely he can see that she's in no fit state to hear any shocking revelations today.

I find some more vegetables in the freezer and produce a passable sauce, which I pour over some pasta shells. We sit at the kitchen table and she pushes her food around the plate, hardly eating a mouthful. I think of the hundreds of meals we've eaten here, just Mum and me. She never seemed the slightest bit bothered that Dad was away so much. I used to think she almost preferred it. But today, his absence is palpable. I can tell that she's thinking about him constantly – missing him terribly.

After lunch, we take our coffee into the sitting room. I read the sympathy cards, which have engulfed the mantelpiece and sideboard and are overflowing onto the top of the piano. It looks like Christmas without the tree and tinsel. Strange that I've received only one card and Mum has over fifty. I guess it's a generation thing.

'I've made a decision about the funeral,' she says, resting her mug on the coffee table. 'I'm not bringing him back to London; it's too expensive and I can't see the point. Not for a cremation.' Her voice is so brittle it sounds as if it might snap. 'So we'll do it in Manchester. Just immediate family – the three of us and Brett and Lisa. No friends or work colleagues, no hymns or prayers.'

I look up from my coffee. 'Really? Are you sure about that?'

'Yes, positive.'

Arun leans forward. 'But, Helen… isn't that a bit austere? Lots of people are going to want to say goodbye to him.'

'They can do it in their own way. I don't want a fuss, I can't bear it. I know I won't be able to cope.'

'But Jerry was such a popular figure, a real character—' Arun continues, but I silence him with a stare. Maybe she's right. A quiet funeral is a good thing. More controlled. Less chance of anything coming out of the woodwork.

'It's your decision, Mum,' I say. 'We'll do whatever you want.'

# CHAPTER THIRTEEN

*Vikings were essentially pirates. They travelled far from home, making well-planned and violent attacks on communities. Surprise was one of their most powerful weapons.*

I drag the large black suitcase out from the cupboard under the stairs and take it up to my room. It's a cheap old thing made of cardboard, the covering frayed at the edges from being bumped up and down steps and thrown carelessly onto luggage carousels. Not that I'm much of a traveller; I can't pretend this case has seen the world. A school trip to Italy when I nearly got sunstroke from tramping over ancient ruins. The French exchange when I fell out with my partner so badly I was sent home early. Five days on the Red Sea Riviera with a married guy having a nervous breakdown. Happy days…

There's not enough clear space on the floor, so I put the case on the bed. The zip sticks, and when I wrench it, the teeth start to come apart at the other end. It's unlikely to survive the journey, but it's the largest suitcase I have, so it will have to do. I'm not just taking clothes; there's all my other shit. Important documents, a few books that have been with me so long I can't bear to throw them away, the laptop Dad bought me when I signed up for that access course. It's still going, amazingly; lasted a lot longer than I did at the college.

The wardrobe is already empty, and there's hardly anything in the drawers. All my clothes are in that dirty pile. If I was sensible, I'd wash everything first – I don't think there's a washing machine where I'm going – but I can't be arsed and there's no time to wait for it to dry. I go over to the mound and scoop up as much as I can in my arms. As I carry the stale-smelling items over to the bed, knickers and socks drop onto the carpet. I bend over to pick them up and others drop instead. I repeat the pantomime, the frustration making me cry. Can't seem to do the simplest thing at the moment without blubbing. Not the simplest fucking thing.

I stare down at the crumpled mass of jeans, leggings, Ts, shirts, what my mother would call 'tunic tops' and some vintage stuff I wear for parties. Black, black, black. I could attend a funeral every day of the week. Not Dad's, though. Can't go there. Not allowed. Josie's made that very clear to me, on the grounds that it would upset her mother. We must be invisible; the wife and daughter that never were.

The cremation's taking place today. Close family only. The irony of those words twists like a knife in my heart. I don't want to go anyway, although it's tempting to show up in a fabulous black dress and a lace veil; oh so tempting to burst into the chapel and throw myself over his coffin like a flag. Who is this mysterious wailing stranger? they'd wonder. Hands fly to mouths, the vicar stops in the middle of his eulogy. Cats and pigeons come to mind. Worms and cans. Boxes and curious Greek women.

The suitcase is soon filled. I zip it up, then discover a few things under the bed – a pair of flip-flops, a favourite silky scarf, yet another pair of black leggings – and stuff them in too. Done. I heave the case off the bed and trundle it to the top of the stairs, looking around for a few seconds to make my silent goodbyes to the place I've called home for the past few years. I don't feel particularly fond of it – not the house itself. But it's been a welcome refuge from the witch. If it hadn't been for Dad, I'd have been on the streets. But there are thousands of sentences I could begin with that phrase. He was a complete crock of shite, but I don't know how I'm going to manage without him.

I go downstairs, thumping the heavy case behind me like a third leg. There's not much worth taking from the bathroom, but I hold a few tubes and bottles up to the light, gagging at the mouldy slime that's collected on their bottoms. A chewed toothbrush, a nearly empty tube of toothpaste and a nearly full bottle of anti-frizz shampoo are the only things that make the cut – I push them into the outside zipper compartment.

No room for any kitchen equipment or my collection of DVDs. That's okay. I'm not much of a cook – what am I saying; I *never* cook – and any film I want to watch again I can stream. Surprising how little you can manage with if you really try. I do one last scout of the downstairs rooms, making sure I've left nothing crucial behind. Got to stop dithering and get out. I'm booked onto a train that leaves in forty-five minutes. Bye-bye, Manchester. Hello, London. Back to where it all began.

It is early evening by the time I arrive at Euston station. I walk around the corner to the tube station, going underground and resurfacing at Finchley Road. I check the text from Zoheb. *L out of station then 100m on L.* As I set off, weaving my way through the throng, the heavy case does a sudden twist and falls over, wrenching my wrist. I trudge on up the hill, my lungs bursting with polluted air. Zoheb didn't mention a hill, and no way is this a hundred metres. If I'd known it was this far I'd have jumped on a bus.

At last I can see my new home, a few staggers ahead. Its sign is still swinging from the wall; it's weather-beaten and faded, but

I can just about make out a pair of crossed keys against a black background. The whole of the ground floor is boarded up with metal sheets. I take out my phone and scroll back to some earlier texts with Zoheb. The entrance to the pub, apparently, is at the side, and involves going down an alleyway. I pick a path over litter and small puddles, arriving outside a large reinforced door. *Bang loud* is chalked on the front, so I put my case down and do just that. Several times.

While I wait for someone to answer, I look up at the windows. Some are broken, the holes stuffed with rags, and one is half curtained with what looks like an African tablecloth. Either nobody's in or they can't be arsed to come downstairs. I bang until my fist hurts. I try ringing Zoheb, but he doesn't pick up. I text him: *Am here where the fuck r u?* Still nothing.

What am I supposed to do now? Sit on my suitcase in this dodgy alleyway and wait to get mugged? Just as I'm making a list of everything I would lose, I hear footsteps and the sound of a key turning. Then the door opens and Zoheb's head peeps round.

'Why didn't you answer?'

'Soz… I was asleep.' He lets out an ugly yawn to prove it.

It's been ten years since I last saw Zoheb in the flesh. We were in the same top set for maths and English in Year 9. Like me, he was clever, and like me, he went to great lengths to hide the fact. But he couldn't hide the fact that he was gay; tough when you're a Muslim and your school is rife with homophobia. He got bullied a lot and I was one of the few kids that would speak to him. When I was dragged 'up north', he made an effort to keep in touch via Facebook, and he's always the first person to send me a birthday message.

Zoheb has had a rough time with his family. His parents had their hearts set on him becoming an accountant, but he flunked his exams and works on a zero-hours contract putting up temporary staging for gigs. I have to say, I'm a bit shocked when I see him. He looks a lot worse in real life than he does in his Facebook party photos. His skin is puckered with acne scars and his greasy black hair could do with a wash.

'Is there a secret password or something?' I say. 'Only I'd quite like to come in.'

He opens the door wider. I pick up the case again, hoping he might take it off me. He doesn't.

'Electrics have fused,' he explains, flicking on his lighter and shining a path down a bare corridor. I follow him into the old pub kitchen. Everything useful or valuable has been stripped out and the room is empty, apart from a skanky cooker and a battered fridge-freezer, which look as if they came off a skip. Two taps are sticking out of the wall, a large bucket beneath them.

'You *can* cook here,' Zoheb says, 'but you'll probably get food poisoning. And don't come in here at night unless you like rats.'

'There are rats? Seriously?'

'In the cellar mainly, but if you leave food out they'll find their way in. The council don't collect the rubbish so you have to get rid of it yourself.' I shudder. Mice in Antrobus Street; now rats. We had them running around the garden at Mum's because she insisted on having an organic compost heap, even though Dad warned her what would happen. Rats are fucking evil. They'll gnaw through anything and I hate their long, thin tails.

Making a note to self never to go into the kitchen, day or night, I follow Zoheb into the old saloon bar and he shines his lighter flame over the dismal scene. The furniture has been removed and the shelves behind the counter are empty and thick with dust. We cross the floor and push through a glass door labelled *Snug*, our feet squelching on the greasy carpet.

'We use this space to hang out,' Zoheb tells me. The door to the outside is covered in metal sheeting, so we have to make our way back through the saloon to get upstairs. There are two large function rooms up here, and another small bar, which is packed with junk. In each room, plywood partitions have been erected to form rows of cubicles, which look a bit like temporary toilets. The windows are all blocked, so there's no natural light. Zoheb's in one room, I'm in the other. It's not divided along gender lines, he explains – just first come, first served.

'Most of the guys that live here are cool. We get the odd weirdo, but they tend not to stay long.'

Next, he shows me the ladies' toilets. The shower turns out to be a garden hose that has been run from one of the hot taps and flung over the door of a cubicle, where the loo has been ripped out and replaced with a tray. The room smells damp and is wet underfoot.

'How many people sharing?' I ask.

'Sixteen, which is pretty luxurious. Some places have double that and only one shower.'

'Hot water?'

'Most of the time.'

'Luxury,' I murmur. It's no better than a squat – actually, it's worse than some squats I've visited in Manchester. I've got to pay five hundred quid a month to live here, and I can be evicted with only forty-eight hours' notice. It's shit, but as I've got no job, I'll never get a proper tenancy. I posted several requests for accommodation in London and Zoheb was the only friend that replied. He told me about the girl who was leaving and offered to get me her place. I took an online 'quiz', had a quick telephone interview and tomorrow I go into the office to sign the contract.

'No guests allowed, no overnight visitors. Parties are banned,' Zoheb says. 'The inspectors can let themselves in at any time of the day or night; if you're caught doing anything they don't like, they'll throw you out and you'll lose your deposit.'

Shit. I'd forgotten about the deposit. That'll have to go on the credit card. Dodgy electrics, no proper kitchen, no refuse collection and rats in the cellar. Five hundred a month? I must be insane. I could rent a three-bed terrace in Salford for that money. But I can't go back, I have to be here.

'Gemma's left you her mattress and fairy lights. They run on a battery, so you're lucky.' Zoheb extinguishes his lighter, bends down and flicks a switch at the end of a line of stars. The lights twinkle, illuminating the pale wooden walls, which are covered in bits of torn posters, doodles and cheesy quotes scrawled in coloured felt pen. *Happiness is the spiritual experience of living every minute with love, grace and gratitude.*

I dump the case on the narrow, thin mattress. 'I'll unpack later. Shall we go for a beer?'

He gives me a sheepish look. 'I'm, er, meeting someone tonight, so sorry, can't hang out. If you need to eat, the Chicken Cottage two doors down is the cheapest.'

My spirits sink even further. 'No worries, I'll sort myself out. I just need a key to the front door.'

'You'll get that tomorrow, when you sign the contract. We're not allowed to lend or copy keys; they're really strict about that. You were only allowed here tonight because you're moving in. We're like bodyguards, we have to keep out squatters.'

'Yeah, but what about this evening? How am I going to get in and out?'

'You could ask around, see if anyone's staying in, though to be honest, we spend as little time here as possible. And you'll need to buy a padlock for your room, 'cos stuff gets nicked all the time.'

'You're really selling this to me, you know?'

He shrugs. 'I never said it was a palace. But it's cheap for this part of London and you can leave when you like.'

'It'll do for now,' I reply. 'I'm not planning on being here long.'

Zoheb leaves me to settle in while he goes to tart himself up for his date. I unzip the case and look around for somewhere to store things. Looks like the suitcase is going to have to be my wardrobe, chest of drawers and bedside table rolled into one. Good job I'm not fussy about creases. I take out my sleeping bag and hug it to my chest like a teddy, taking comfort in the nostalgic smells of sweat, beer, weed and curry. This is my festival sleeping bag, with its broken zip and crusty mud stains. Come to think of it, living here is not much better than camping. Yeah, I can do this.

I stare at the graffiti-covered walls. *Happiness often sneaks in through a door you didn't know you left open.* I won't be leaving any doors open here, that's for sure.

My phone pings, making me jump. I pull the handset from my back jeans pocket and swipe into my text feed. The message comes from a private number. It's short and to the point.

*I'm watching you.*

# CHAPTER FOURTEEN

*The Vikings conducted elaborate funeral rituals to prevent the dead from rising again. These included binding the big toes together and driving needles into the soles of the feet.*

Five of us sit in the shiny black funeral car: me, Arun, Mum, Uncle Brett and Aunt Lisa. As we follow the hearse – Dad's coffin adorned by a single bouquet of white lilies – our bland, awkward conversation stops and starts along with the heavy Manchester traffic. It's Thursday, the last day before the Easter break, and everyone seems to be leaving the city early. Fine weather is forecast for the weekend, or so Uncle Brett told us during one of our particularly long silences. I have a vague memory that we'd planned to go to Brighton with some friends, but can't remember the details. Hopefully Arun has cancelled.

It's been three weeks since Dad's death and I'm still struggling with simple, everyday activities. I'm back at work. Jill, my supervisor, is being very understanding, but I feel bad because my mind isn't fully on the job and I keep making stupid mistakes. Clients say things that trigger random memories. Before I know it, I'm crying and they're comforting me, rather than the other way around. It's normal, everyone tells me. It's just how it is.

As the car crawls along like a shiny black slug, I study my fellow mourners. Uncle Brett is wearing a black suit, white shirt and thin black tie, and Lisa is in a black trouser suit with a grey blouse. Mum specifically asked us not to wear black because she finds it depressing, but they refused to take notice, adopting a superior attitude towards my purple coat and her dark red mac. Mum's gripping her handbag and looking away from the rest of us, her forehead leaning against the window. She still doesn't know.

The secret lies between us like an impermeable membrane. I want to comfort her but she feels out of reach, on the other side of a great emotional divide. Over the past couple of weeks I've avoided being alone with her, which is really bad of me. We've never been super close, not like some of my friends are with their mothers, and not like I was with Dad. She was never the parent I turned to in a crisis, but I've never felt like we don't love each other or don't get on. Now when I'm with her, I feel tongue-tied and awkward. I'm sure she's noticed, but typically she hasn't said anything – assuming, I guess, that it's the grief that's making me clam up. Arun is getting increasingly unhappy about the deception. I've promised him I'll tell her once we've got over the funeral, but I'm still not convinced it's the right thing to do.

'I don't blame Jerry for riding a motorbike,' says Lisa, her thin, whiny voice drilling into my thoughts. 'I mean, the whole country's becoming gridlocked, you can't move.'

My stomach is fluttering with anxiety. I texted Valentina, begging her not to turn up today, but what if she takes no notice? She could be waiting for us outside the crematorium, preparing for a showdown. The last couple of nights, I've hardly slept for worrying. Sophie knows she has to stay away, but I'm not sure I can trust Valentina. People can be unpredictable when they're angry and upset. After what I did at the cottage, I know that better than anyone.

We creep in single file past roadworks already deserted for the holidays. Brett looks at his watch for the tenth time. 'This is ridiculous. We'll miss our slot at this rate.'

'It doesn't matter,' murmurs Mum, not looking away from the window. 'We only need five minutes.' Lisa rolls her eyes in despair and Brett tuts disapprovingly.

'We should have given him a Viking funeral,' Lisa says suddenly. 'Put him in a barge, set fire to it and let him sail down the Manchester Ship Canal. He would have loved that.'

'No, he wouldn't,' I retort. 'Burning valuable boats is a myth created by Hollywood. I'm surprised you didn't know that.' Lisa quivers with indignation and Mum quietly sniggers under her breath.

Brett ignores the exchange, twisting round to draw back the glass hatch separating us from the driver. 'Isn't there a short cut you can take?'

'Not that will get us there any quicker, sir,' is the reply. 'It's the Easter getaway.'

I'd love to get away too. I'm too hot in this coat and my bladder is bursting with the bucket of coffee I drank at the motorway service station. I open my window, and polluted city air wafts in, mixing with all our complicated feelings – towards the dead man in the car in front of us, towards each other, towards ourselves …

We eventually arrive at the crematorium ten minutes later, the hearse almost zooming up to the entrance. I look around anxiously, but thankfully there's no sign of Valentina. Arun and I exchange a relieved glance.

The coffin is snatched out of the back and loaded onto a trolley. Our small, tight-lipped gang follows behind. We fit easily onto the front row, but Brett and Lisa choose to sit behind, so they can whisper and exchange exasperated glances, no doubt.

Once the coffin is loaded on the plinth, the funeral director, a kindly-looking man with a polished bald head, coughs for our attention and tells us what we already know: that we have come to pay our respects and farewells to Jerome Henry Macauliffe, loving husband of Helen and devoted father to Josie. He looks to my mother, hoping perhaps for a last-minute change of heart – a eulogy, a prayer – but she simply nods at him to press the button. We're asked to stand as tinny canned music plays (contrary to her express instructions) and green velvet curtains close around the coffin. The mechanism clunks and Mum suddenly grips my arm, holding it so tightly I can feel her nails digging through my sleeve. I place my hand on hers and we stare at the curtains for a few seconds, as if waiting for them to burst into flames.

'Right, I suppose that's it,' says Uncle Brett, his voice catching with emotion. Ugly tears stream down my aunt's cheeks as she hands him a tissue from her handbag. We troop out silently, my mother still holding on to me with Arun supporting her on the other side. Everyone looks shaken and tearful. I want to cry too, but the tears won't fall.

As we emerge from the crematorium, everything looks different, as if the world has put on new clothes while we've been inside. The sun has come out from behind the puffy white clouds and bathed our surroundings in bright light, the air zinging with spring freshness. It looks too cheerful, at odds with the drawn expressions on the faces of the new batch of mourners that have already gathered for the next funeral. They seem curious to see so few of us, assuming, I guess, that our deceased was very old or extremely unpopular. I want to explain that there were dozens of people who wanted to say goodbye to Dad, but Mum didn't want them there. It was a dismal, wretched send-off, but after what he did, I kind of feel it was what he deserved.

'Will the undertakers take us back to where we left our car, or do we have to get a taxi?' asks Lisa.

'I'm sure we can get them to drop you off,' Arun replies. 'I'll have a word.' He scampers off in search of the driver.

Mum suddenly looks weak and makes for a bench. Lisa follows her, sitting down and enveloping her sister-in-law in an unwanted cuddle. She thinks she's Mum's best mate, always popping round for a chat, inviting her to go on shopping trips or pamper weekends, but I know the friendship isn't fully reciprocated. As a relative newcomer, Lisa has tried hard to push her way into the centre of the family. She was always organising jolly foursomes, including several weekend breaks abroad, which Dad loved but Mum secretly hated. Oh well, I think, watching her freeze in Lisa's tear-stricken embrace, at least Mum won't have to endure that any more.

I turn back to Brett, who clears his throat as if about to make an announcement. 'So… the coroner decided it was accidental death,' he says. 'That's a relief. I knew all along it wasn't suicide, but it's good that it's official. Puts everyone's minds at rest…'

'Yes,' I agree, wondering why he's chosen to bring this up now.

'Your father wouldn't have taken his own life, no matter what trouble he was in,' Brett continues. 'Not that he *was* in any trouble, you understand. If he had been, I would have known. Take it from me, I knew Jerry better than anyone. *Anyone.*' He edges closer to me, so close I can smell coffee on his breath. I'm drawn back to visits to his house when I was a child, Sunday lunches in winter and barbecues in the summer, taking me to one side before we left and pressing a pound coin into my palm. It was one of his rituals and he meant it as a little treat, but I always felt slightly uncomfortable, as if I was being paid to keep some unknown secret.

'If you have any problems, talk to me first and I'll deal with it. Got that?' He gives me a clumsy hug and I feel myself instinctively stiffen against him. 'I'm always here for you,' he whispers against my cheek.

'Thanks.'

Brett releases his hold, then stands back, admiring me like I'm something he's just made. 'You've always been a good girl, Josie.

Your dad was very proud of you. His easy-care daughter, that's what he always called you, remember?'

'Yup.' I used to take it as a compliment, but now I wonder if it was simply a comparison.

Arun comes over to rescue me. 'We can get a lift back to the city centre,' he says. 'Ready to go now?'

'Absolutely,' Brett says. He immediately walks over to Mum and Aunt Lisa.

'I'm sorry, can I use the loo first? I'm bursting.'

'Okay, but hurry up.' Arun goes towards the car.

I dash to the toilets around the back of the crematorium, locking myself in the cubicle. I replay the uncomfortable conversation with Uncle Brett. He's such a creep. As if I'd ever go to him if I had a problem… Now that Dad's dead, he thinks he can airbrush out all the negative things and pretend he was some kind of saint.

I walk back into the sunshine, shaking my damp fingers. The light is fierce and I stop, closing my eyes for a second, pressing down on my forehead as yet another headache begins. When I open them, I see a woman standing alone on the edge of the driveway, silhouetted by the sun. I'm sure she wasn't there a moment ago. She's dressed from head to foot in black, wearing a floppy sixties hat and dark shades. It's impossible to see her features from this distance, or tell her age. Is she here for the next funeral? If so, she's late. Everyone else has filed in and I can hear 'My Way' playing through the chapel walls. She's standing still. Maybe I'm imagining it, but I think she's looking at me. I stop and give her a long stare. Even though she's wearing dark glasses, I know she's staring back.

Who is she? Should I go and talk to her? I glance towards the waiting car. Arun is standing by the open door. 'Come on!' he calls, tapping the roof impatiently.

'Sorry.' As I walk towards him, I can feel her eyes burning into the side of my face.

Arun tuts. 'You're keeping everyone waiting.'

'Sorry.' My knees start to feel like jelly. Maybe it's Sophie, come to say her last secret goodbye. Or maybe she has nothing to do with us at all. I want to talk to her, but then Mum will see and ask questions, and Brett will get involved and there'll be a scene.

'Are you okay, babe?' Arun's dark eyebrows dip. 'You're as white as a sheet.'

'I'm just a bit upset, that's all.' He nods and gets back in the car. I slip in beside him, apologising again to everyone. The car sweeps around in a semicircle, then rejoins the drive. The woman stands her ground, doesn't flinch as the car brushes past. I take her in greedily, trying to imprint her features on my brain. Not a young woman, but not old either. In her forties, perhaps. High cheekbones, a straight nose, fiery red lipstick. Could there have been a third woman in Dad's life? I look out of the back window as we drive slowly away. She turns to watch our departure, raising her arm in an insolent wave.

# CHAPTER FIFTEEN

*The Vikings wrote using picture symbols called runes. These were used to mark ownership and on memorial stones for the dead. Runes were also used for writing magic spells and curses.*

The limo drops us off outside our anonymous, city-centre hotel. We walk into the foyer and stand in an awkward group. The place is noisy, with people checking in and out, wheeling luggage around our legs and standing between us. None of us knows what to do next. Usually after a funeral there's at least one drink to toast the departed, but nothing's been arranged. Mum looks worn and fidgety, like she's at the end of her tether and just wants to go home.

'It's like Piccadilly Circus,' says Brett. 'We can't stay here. I'll check out the lunchtime menu. Mind you, if it's anything like the breakfast…' He goes off, muttering to himself.

Brett is clearly sulking because Dad didn't get the appropriate send-off. Apparently, he's trying to organise a memorial at the university, so that his academic colleagues can give eulogies and students can make tearful tributes to his teaching skills. He wants photos of Dad looping on a giant screen to live jazz music. He wants beautiful poems and funny anecdotes. In short, he wants a show. But it's not about celebrating Dad's life; it's about basking in the reflected glory and everyone knowing that he's the big brother. Brett is Mr Ordinary, always has been. But does he know all Dad's secrets? I still can't decide.

Arun breaks into my thoughts. 'What do you want to do now, Josie? Have some lunch, then push off?'

I throw a glance towards Mum, who's still being petted by Lisa. 'No, let's just go.'

'Hope you don't mind,' says Arun, interrupting. 'We're going to head off now, before the holiday traffic gets going.'

'Good idea.' Mum looks towards Brett, who's threading his way back through the throng, brandishing a menu. 'I don't want to hang around either.'

Lisa hugs me goodbye. 'Are you still going to visit the crash scene on the way back?' she asks quietly.

'Yes, that's the plan.' Mum has already made it very clear that she doesn't want to go, and I haven't tried to persuade her.

'Good for you,' Lisa says, squeezing me. 'I'm sure it'll give you closure.' I try not to wince visibly at the crass phrase. 'We'll get Helen back to London in one piece, don't worry.'

Feeling a bit guilty for leaving Mum in their clutches, Arun and I make our exit. We get into the car and I punch in the GPS coordinates the police gave me. As we head out of Manchester, I don't tell him that I've driven this way before. The cut on my hand has healed, but I can still remember every second of that awful visit to the cottage. And the bloodied photo of Dad and Valentina that I stole is still hiding in my bag.

'Did you see that woman at the crematorium?' I say, once we're out of the city centre.

'No.' Arun quickly takes his eyes off the road. 'What woman?'

'She was there when we came out. You must have noticed. She was lurking like a black widow spider.'

Arun laughs. 'I didn't see anyone. Are you sure you didn't imagine her?'

'Yes! She was standing on the path, staring at me like she knew who I was.'

He shrugs. 'No… Maybe it was Sophie.'

'I don't think so. I texted her to say she shouldn't come, and she replied saying she had no intention of turning up. I think it was someone else.'

'Like who?'

'Another mistress crawling out of the woodwork.' I shudder involuntarily.

'Surely not!' he scoffs. 'Jerry wouldn't have had the time, or the energy. He was a two-woman man, through and through.'

'Don't say that. It's not funny, Arun. I'm serious. There was something really weird about her. I think she even waved at me. In a sort of mocking way. It was horrible.'

He puts his foot down as we hit the dual carriageway. 'You're being paranoid. She could easily have been there for another funeral – he wasn't the only one being cremated today.'

'I'm not imagining it. She was there to say goodbye to Dad. I felt her trying to threaten me.'

'Oh, Josie.' He sighs. 'I know this has been a terrible shock, but you've got to stop feeling so vulnerable. Not every woman in Manchester was having an affair with your father. Even if she was some old flame, why would she want to threaten you?'

Tears gather in my nose and I sniff them up angrily. 'I don't know… Nothing's how I thought it was. My whole life has been turned inside out. I don't know what's real and what's not any more.'

'You should get some help,' he says. 'Grief counselling.' I give a non-committal grunt in reply.

After about forty minutes, the satnav directs us off the A road and we enter a network of narrow lanes with hedges on either side. The closer we get, the sicker I feel in my stomach. We are deep in enemy territory now – a few miles from Sophie's cottage. Dad must have known these roads like the back of his hand, and he would have treated them with respect. He would have known where to slow down and where to keep to the nearside edge, where the blind corners and hidden entrances were. He liked to push the boundaries, but he wasn't a maniac.

Why was he out so early that morning, and why he was driving so fast? Nearly twenty miles an hour over the speed limit, the coroner said in his report. In the dark, in wet weather – it was crazy. Was he in a temper? Had he and Sophie had a row? Perhaps he was on his way to meet someone. My mind briefly shoots back to the woman at the cemetery. Did I imagine that wave, or was she just adjusting her hat?

As we follow the directions, I try to see the surroundings through Dad's eyes, to feel the road beneath me as if I were on the bike, twisting the throttle and leaning into the bends. The engine roars in my ears as we approach a sharp corner.

I only ever went on the Bonneville once. Dad stuck me on the back and we rode up to Epping Forest, a well-known bikers' trail. The helmet was stuffy and uncomfortable and I was so terrified we were going to crash, I don't think I took a breath the whole way. When we stopped at a refreshment shack in the forest, I leapt off the bike and refused to get back on. I made him order me a taxi to the nearest train station and went home alone. He laughed at me for being such a wimp, said that if I was afraid to die, I must be afraid to live too.

*Your destination is on the left.* Arun screeches to a halt, and I lurch forward against the seat belt. I slam my hand on the dashboard. 'For God's sake!'

'Sorry. I wasn't expecting that.'

My heart drops back into my chest. 'You can't park here, it's not safe.'

We drive on until we find a muddy patch of ground next to a farm gate. Arun parks up and turns off the engine. I can almost hear my heart thudding in the silence.

'Still sure you want to do this?' he says eventually.

'Yup. It's important. I don't know why, but it is.'

'Come on, then.' He removes his seat belt, but I put my hand on his arm.

'Actually – do you mind if I do this alone?'

He stops. 'Of course not. I'll wait here. Take as long as you need.'

'Thanks, hon.' I lean across and kiss him on the cheek. 'I couldn't have got through this without you.'

I get out of the car and walk back to the bend. There's no pavement and I have to press myself against the hedge when a car drives past. I stand with my hands in my jacket pockets, surveying the forlorn, abandoned scene. All that's left of the crash investigation is a piece of red and white accident tape that's got snagged in a bush. The grass is flattened where the bank dips down, and I can almost see the ghost of the Bonneville, lying on its side with its wheels spinning.

I say a silent, godless prayer to whoever might be listening. Not my father; he's long gone from here. The field mice, the birds, maybe a hedgehog or two if they've woken up yet. It's Easter; they must have done. I laugh quietly to myself. I'm such a city girl; I know nothing about nature. I try to think of Dad living here, tramping the lanes in a wax jacket and muddy boots, perhaps even walking a dog, but the image won't solidify. He was a committed city dweller too. At least that was what he always said… Another lie. But it's nothing compared to all the others.

There's no shrine here. No burning candles or messages of grief. Just a solitary bouquet of red roses leaning against the tree trunk. I bend down and pick it up, the thorns pricking my palms beneath the flimsy tissue paper. The roses are fresh, some of them still in bud, their scent heady and expensive. A small piece of card is attached to a ribbon that twists around the base of the stalks. On it is a brief typed message. My pulse quickens as I read. *A Viking would rather die than reveal his darkest secret.*

How utterly, utterly disgusting. Who wrote this? I look around as if expecting the culprit to walk out of the shadows. It can't be Sophie; she wants to keep under the radar. Besides, she already knows Dad's secret is out. No… somebody else left these roses, and I've a strong feeling that the message is meant for me. A picture of the woman at the cemetery floods my inner eye. I can see her as clearly as if she were standing next to me now. I feel her malevolent spirit goading me to respond.

With a sudden rush of anger, I rip off the card and hurl the bouquet into the ditch.

# CHAPTER SIXTEEN

*The Vikings played a game called hnefatafl on a chequered board. White pieces were placed in the middle and surrounded by black pieces. There were more black pieces than white. The object of the game was for the white king to escape to the edge of the board.*

I've got several days of leave left, but decide to return to work straight after the Easter break. Now that the funeral's over, things have to return to normal. They aren't normal, of course. They've been changed forever, but I can't keep thinking about that or I'll go mad.

My afternoon's schedule of appointments stares back at me from the computer screen. Most of the names are new to me, but there are a couple I recognise – our regulars. They come for some human contact. Without organisations like ours, they'd have nobody to talk to. Loneliness is a huge problem, especially among older people. I always wonder what's happened to their families; spouses, children, siblings, cousins – why don't they help?

There's a knock and Jill pops her head around the door. 'How was the funeral?' She smiles at me gently.

'Extremely quiet… not my father's style, but it was what my mother wanted.'

'Well, I always say funerals are for the living, not the dead.' She pauses, looking me up and down, taking in the bags under my eyes and my listless hair. 'You sure you're okay to be here?'

'Yeah, honestly, I'm fine. I got through the morning and there's a full afternoon ahead. You need me.'

'That's true… If you find you're struggling, though, just say and I'll take over.' I assure her again that I'll be okay and she finally gives up.

My two o'clock – a new client called Freya Thorburg – is ten minutes late. She sounds Scandinavian, but that's okay; her English will probably be better than mine. I'm cross that she's not here yet. Punctuality is really important. We're not allowed to overrun, so I'll have to end the session regardless of when she turns up. *If* she turns up. I drum my fingers impatiently on the desk, rehearsing my stern face and silently practising the standard speech we're supposed to make. I've reached the bit about this being a partnership requiring mutual respect when the door opens and she walks in without knocking.

'Sorry,' she says airily. 'I've been walking round and round and I couldn't find the entrance.'

It's Valentina. What is she doing here? I look up at her, startled afresh at the sight of my face in hers. She's dressed from head to toe in black – tight skinny trousers, a short black jacket over a long black shirt. Big black boots with ugly thick heels. Her bright blue eyes sear into me like a laser, making thousands of little hairs all over my body stand instantly on end.

'What are you doing here?' I gasp. 'You gave a false name.'

'Yeah, a Viking one. Did you like it? I thought you'd guess straight away.'

'Well, I didn't. Valentina, this isn't approp—'

'Do I sit here?' She lands in the chair in front of the desk. 'I didn't want to give my real name, I thought you might refuse to see me.' She looks at me reprovingly. 'You haven't been replying to my texts.'

I sigh. 'I've been busy… how did you know where I worked?'

'You told me.'

'Did I?' I have no memory of doing that. 'You shouldn't be here,' I say stiffly. 'These appointments are for members of the public – people with problems.'

'Oh, I've got problems! Fucking hundreds of them.' She catches my irritable expression and pouts. 'Come on, please don't be cross. I was desperate to see you. There's no one else I can turn to.'

'You came down from Manchester just to—'

'No, no, I left Antrobus Street last Thursday, the day of the funeral. It felt kind of fitting, you know? Leaving at the same time as Dad.'

'I wish you'd told me you were coming. If my supervisor finds out you're here, she'll…' I abandon the rest of the sentence. The truth is, Jill would probably be cool about it, but she doesn't know I have a sister, or that Dad had a secret second family, and I don't want to tell her. Not until I've told Mum, at least. 'Look… we can't talk now, not here. I'm supposed to be interviewing clients.'

She bounces forward and stands up. 'You finish at five thirty, right? I'll wait for you outside, we can go for a drink. There's something I need to talk to you about. It's really important. What do you say, sis?'

*Don't keep calling me sis*, I think, but what I say is, 'Um… all right… yeah…'

'Excellent. Laters!' She swings round, her wild hair crackling as she swaggers out of the room.

I drop my head onto the desk and breathe in deeply, sucking the oxygen into my lungs. My chest hurts. I can't take much more of these shocks that keep coming like giant waves, pushing me under again and again, with no time to come up for air. What does she want from me? She can't just waltz in here under a false name and expect us to be best friends. Why, why, why did I say yes to meeting after work? I'm such a coward.

*Calm down*, I tell myself. *You don't have to meet her if you don't want to.* I could tell Jill I'm not feeling well – it wouldn't even be a lie – and go home early. Escape before Valentina catches me. The idea is extremely tempting, but I know my conscience won't let me do it. It would be cowardly and rude. She'll be standing outside waiting and waiting; she'll be really hurt if I stand her up. I can't stay away from work indefinitely because I'm scared she might come back. And there's no reason to be scared. She's my sister.

My last client, a poor old chap who's been ripped off by his builder, leaves just before five thirty. I go back to my office to collect my jacket. The room overlooks the street; I can't resist standing at the edge of the window frame and taking a peek through the vertical blinds. My stomach dips as I see Valentina standing in a doorway on the other side of the road, shoulders hunched, hands shoved into the pockets of her black silky bomber jacket. The weather's fine today, but her body language suggests she's frozen to the bone; as if being cold has become a habit.

I retreat from the window. This feels wrong, like I'm betraying somebody. Yet another part of me is skipping with excitement. It's natural to feel curious about her, isn't it? When Dad wasn't with me, he was with her. I want to understand how their relationship worked; whether he taught her the same games, told her the same bedtime stories, took her on the same trips. Was he strict about homework and staying out late? Did he lecture her about boys wanting 'only one thing'? I want to know if we've been leading parallel lives.

Because if we *have*, how come we've turned out so differently? Valentina is my opposite – wild, daring, spontaneous, unrestrained. She doesn't seem to give a toss about authority or having anyone's approval. I feel staid and sensible beside her. A boring young fogey. The easy-care daughter – as exciting as one of Dad's non-iron shirts.

But not for much longer. Valentina has triggered something inside me. From the moment we met I started to change; to see the world differently, to feel emotions more strongly than ever before. I've already acted on those feelings once. The old Josie would never have broken into somebody else's cottage and smashed up their stuff. I'm not proud of what I did, but I'm not ashamed either. I don't care that I broke the law, although the fact that I don't care frightens me. Thrills me, even. Maybe, through getting to know my sister, I'll discover another side of me. The question is, do I dare take the next step?

*Come on. One drink can't hurt, can it?*

'Yay! You came!' she cries as I cross the street to meet her. 'I had a horrible feeling you were going to blow me out.'

'No, I wouldn't do that.'

'So, where's the best boozer?'

There's a pub around the corner, but that's where people from work tend to hang out, so I take her to another one further away. As we walk down the street, she loops her arm into mine, firing questions at me about my job – how long have I worked there, what's my boss like? She even asks how much I get paid.

'I've never had a proper job,' she says proudly. 'Not unless you count bar work. I tried working in a call centre but I only lasted three days. The customers were so rude.'

'We get some difficult clients sometimes,' I admit.

'Yeah, but I bet you never lose your temper or throw things.' She fixes me with a pointed look, then roars with laughter in exactly the same way Dad used to.

'I couldn't stop myself. I was so angry.'

'Yeah, well, you had a right.' She raises her hand and we do an awkward high-five.

Valentina makes a beeline for a table in the corner, while I go to the bar and buy the drinks. I have a white wine spritzer and she has a pint of strong lager.

'And one of those big bags of posh crisps,' she shouts out. As soon as I bring the tray over, she grabs the bag and opens it with her teeth. 'This is the first thing I've eaten today, I've been that busy.'

'Doing what?'

'Applying for jobs I'll never get in a million years.' She lifts her glass. 'To the Viking, the lying, cheating bastard!' she cackles.

I wince. 'Are you okay? You seem a bit… well… wired.' Actually, I think she might be high. Her pupils are dilated and she can't sit still.

'I'm shitting myself, to be honest.' She looks around furtively, then leans forward, her hair dusting the table. 'I've been getting these hate texts. I don't know who it is or how they got my number, but it's totally creeping me out.'

'What do they say?'

She digs her phone out of her bag and passes it to me. 'See for yourself. They started on the day of Dad's funeral, virtually the moment I arrived in London. I thought maybe you were getting them too.'

'No…' I murmur, reading the messages. They're nasty and childish, vaguely threatening. *I'm watching you… I know where you are… You won't get away from me…* 'These could just be random. Kids mucking about.'

'No, they're not. Read the next one.' Valentina points at the screen. 'This is the latest, it came today. *Go back to Manchester.* That's not random, that's specific. They know I'm here. Probably know exactly where I'm staying. It's fucking scary. Every time I go out, I get this feeling I'm being followed.' She shivers.

I pass the phone back. 'Have you fallen out with anyone in Manchester?'

'Loads of times. I know some really dodgy types,' she says with a hint of street pride. 'When you broke in, I thought this guy BJ had sent someone round. I owe him.'

'Maybe he went to the house, realised you'd moved out and now he's trying to spook you.'

'Nah… They wouldn't bother stalking me. They'd just find me and beat me up.' She stares into her empty glass. 'Shall we have another? I'd get them in, but until I find a new job…'

'Same again?' I stand up. 'If I were you, I'd get a new number.'

'Guess I'll have to.' She calls after me, 'Bring back a menu!'

I go up to the bar. While the barman pours her pint, I text Arun to say that something's come up and I'm going to be home a bit later than usual. I glance back at Valentina. She's scrolling through her messages. A thought occurs to me. I return with our drinks and a menu tucked under my arm.

'Something strange happened to me too,' I tell her. 'Maybe it's even connected.'

'Oh yeah?' Valentina whips the menu out from under my arm and starts devouring the words.

'This strange woman turned up at the funeral. She didn't say or do anything, just kept staring at me.'

'You sure it wasn't my mum?'

'I don't think so… She promised she wouldn't come. Then, afterwards, I went to the crash site and somebody had left a bouquet of red roses and there was this message.' I open my bag and take out the crumpled card. 'What do you think it means?'

She holds it between the tips of her fingers like it's a piece of evidence and reads aloud: '"A Viking would rather die than reveal his darkest secret." What a twat.' She throws it onto the table and returns to the menu.

'I have this feeling it was the woman at the funeral who wrote it.' I scoop up the card and tuck it away. I don't know why, but I need to hold on to it. 'She's basically saying Dad killed himself.'

'Yeah, but he didn't, did he? And his secret's already out, so who gives a shit?'

'I know, but… listen, Valentina,' I press, trying to get her away from the menu. 'Right at the beginning, the police asked if it could have been suicide. We said absolutely not, but now I'm wondering…'

'Hmm… I can't decide whether to have a starter…'

'Maybe there's more to it. Maybe it's this woman who's sending you these texts?'

She flicks her hair back dismissively. 'But how would she know my number?'

'I don't know. Maybe they were having an affair or something and she got it off Dad's phone,' I say, making it up as I go along. 'I'm just guessing, I might be wrong.'

'Rib-eye or the salmon – what do you think?'

'Valentina, I'm serious.'

She laughs. 'So am I. Oh, let's go mad, it's not every day you go out with your long-lost sister, is it?'

Somehow I find myself going back to the bar and ordering her the most expensive thing on the menu. I choose a starter for myself, on the basis that I'll be eating later with Arun, although in my heart I know I'm here for the long haul. I've also got a feeling I'm going to be paying for both of us.

I return to our table, determined to make more normal conversation. 'So, how come you've moved down to London?'

'Oh, I'd done with Manchester,' she says airily. 'It was time to move on.'

'So where are you living now?'

'In a derelict pub on Finchley Road. It's a live-in guardian set-up. Really disgusting. You have to see it to believe it.'

'Finchley Road is pretty long. Whereabouts?'

'Near the tube station.'

'Oh, you mean the Crossed Keys? That used to be a really rough pub. I pass it every day on the bus; it's only about a mile from my flat.'

'Yes,' she says, 'I know. I chose it especially because it was close to you.'

'Right…' A strange, uncomfortable feeling starts to build in my stomach. 'How do you know where I live?'

'You told me. Don't you remember?'

'Oh. Right… yes.' I know we swapped phone numbers and emails, but I don't think I gave her my address.

'It's great to be back home,' Valentina says, picking up her pint. 'And so close to where we were born. It feels amazing, like a rebirth. Finding you is the one good thing that's come out of this tragedy. A new beginning for both of us. Cheers, sis!'

'Yes, cheers,' I reply, raising my glass and clinking. Our identical blue eyes lock for a second; I wish I could read the thoughts that are whirring in her brain. Why is she here? What does she want?

Fifteen minutes pass, during which Valentina regales me with humorous tales of how she hates 'up north' and how boring it was living 'in the middle of fucking nowhere'. Then our food arrives. Her steak is huge, making my starter of three prawns look positively anorexic. The waitress asks if she wants mayo, ketchup or mustard.

'Bring the lot, to be on the safe side,' she declares. But Valentina doesn't seem to be on the safe side of anything to me.

# CHAPTER SEVENTEEN

*Odin was the chief of the Viking gods. He owned two ravens, called Huginn (Thought) and Muninn (Memory). He sent them out every day to find out what was happening in the world.*

I switch off the fairy lights and lie face down on the grubby mattress. The alcohol is dancing through my body, grabbing me by the hand and dragging me into the well of sleep. I close my eyes and the room spins. I know the dream will come again tonight. It's fidgeting in the shadows, waiting to make its entrance. For once, I want to bring it on.

The scar at the back of my head itches in sympathy. I fight my way through my hair to locate it just above the base of my skull. Gently I stroke the thin raised line, where the skin feels silky. As I drift out of consciousness, I feel the wound reopening, the flesh being parted, my fingers excavating the memories. I pull up deep-rooted images and shake off the dusty earth of the past. I hear birdsong and the distant chatter of grown-ups; smell freshly cut grass and scented flowers. The afternoon sun bears down on my face and I squint at the cloudless sky.

I'm four years old, playing in a strange garden. I've never been here before. 'Come on, I'll show you the tree house,' says the little girl who looks like me. She leads me down the stepping-stone path and we stand beneath the large oak tree, craning our necks back, looking up into its branches. Sap drips onto my head and glues itself to my hair. Green acorns nestle beneath our feet. 'Come on, let's go up!'

I'm not sure. My fingers pick nervously at the rough bark. I look up at the jumble of wooden planks – it's a longship, a longship sailing on a sea of leaves. It looks dangerous up there, like it could fall apart at the slightest touch.

The girl starts climbing, giggling and shouting at me to follow. I peer upwards at the white knickers beneath her dress, her pale legs sticking out like lolly sticks. My feet wobble on the rope ladder as I climb, up and up, my hands gripping the rungs, my cheeks brushing the sappy leaves. She pulls me up through the hole and we fall onto the wooden floor, gazing about us in delight. It's even lovelier than I imagined. 'This can be our castle!' she cries, dancing around the dinky furniture, pointing everything out. There's a fluffy red rug on the floor and squashy coloured cushions scattered about. Bright blue, yellow and green, like the colours in my paint box.

She shows me the toy box. It looks like an old wooden treasure chest, and it's exactly like the one in my bedroom at home. I open the lid and take out a soft rag doll. Her limbs are long and floppy, and she's wearing a long green tunic, tied at the waist with a red cord. Her yellow woollen hair hangs in two braided plaits, and there's a woven band wrapped round her forehead. She's a Viking doll. I have one just like this at home, only her dress is yellow and her hair is black. 'She's mine,' the girl says, 'but you can play with her for a little bit if you like.'

I hold the doll in my arms and stroke her hair. She smells of damp wood and there are tiny green flecks on the edge of her tunic. The little girl who looks just like me watches as I move the doll's arms and legs around, making her dance. Then I lie her on her back and rock her to sleep.

'That's enough. I want her back now,' the girl says. But I don't want to give the doll up yet. She's happy lying in my arms. 'I said give her back.' The girl scowls at me. I don't like her any more; she's mean. She grabs at the doll's leg, but I hold on all the tighter.

Neither of us will give up. We tug back and forth, digging our nails into the doll's woollen flesh. She starts to drag me into a circle, spinning me into a fighting dance. We gather speed with every revolution, sparks flying from our heels, our long red hair shooting behind us like flames from a Catherine wheel. Still I hold on. Objects flash before my eyes – their shapes and colours blurring into a rainbow swirl of light. The force is building and the oak tree is shaking, hundreds of acorns tumbling to the ground. With a loud groan, the tree house wrenches free and takes off, hurtling through the sky.

And then she lets me go.

I wake up in a sweat, cramped in my little wooden coffin, feeling a desperate urge for space and air. I sit up and wriggle out of my sleeping bag, tripping over stuff to get to the door. Pulling the bolt across, I open up and listen. Soft snoring is coming from one of the cubicles, but everyone else is either sleeping silently or not sleeping here at all. I go to the bare window and try to open it, but they're all nailed shut. It's the middle of the night, but I can hear cars and trucks roaring past like it's the rush hour.

Pulling away from the window, I go to the bathroom and splash some cold water on my face. I knew the dream would scare me, but I had to go there again; had to check. And I was right. My reflection stares at me through the greasy mirror, her eyes glittering dangerously. She leans forward, her sour breath clouding the glass. *Your sister tried to kill you*, she says.

When I wake again, I feel like a different person. Lighter and cleaner, as if all the poison has been flushed out of my body. I can hear noises coming from the makeshift shower room. I've no idea what time it is, but I have an urge to get outside.

First things first. Mustn't forget my daily ritual. I heave myself up, scrabbling around for my black felt pen. I've drawn a headstone on the chipboard wall, right next to my head. *RIP The Viking*, it says, next to a drawing of him in battle gear, wielding a broadsword. I add another stroke to the tally – that makes four weeks and three days since he died. The fact is indisputable, and yet I still can't really believe I'll never see him again.

Do I miss him? Desperately. After Mum chucked me out and I moved into Antrobus Street, we stopped functioning as a family, but Dad tried to stay in touch. He would zoom up on his bike without warning and take me to the Irish boozer on the corner. Once he'd softened me up with a couple of pints, he'd start quizzing me about jobs and boyfriends, the dodgy characters I was hanging out with and whether I was taking my medication. The evening would usually end with chicken kebab and extra chilli sauce, a large portion of chips and a massive screaming row in the street. I'd accuse of him of harassment and he'd accuse me of wrecking my life.

Poor man, I was such a disappointment, such a worry. I know I kept him awake at night. But no matter how bad I was, he never let on that there was an alternative daughter out there, a new, improved model – sane, loving, well behaved; achieving in all the ways I wasn't. Why didn't he just dump me in landfill and give all his love and energy to her? I would have done it like a shot. Now that he's dead, I can't ask him why he never gave up on me. Why he refused to believe the sad but obvious truth that I'm broken and beyond repair.

I plant a kiss on the lying bastard's badly drawn face.

Everyone seems to want a shower this morning, so I skip the queue and go in search of breakfast instead. Eating out is compulsory here. I'm not keeping any food in my cubicle, not even a box of cereal, because I know the vermin will sniff it out. I lock the door with the padlock I bought on Zoheb's recommendation, and sling my other new purchase – a small padded backpack for my laptop – over my shoulder. No way am I ever leaving my most valuable possession here. My cellmates seem harmless enough: white middle-class hippies (with the honourable exception of Zoheb) with rich parents or low-paid jobs, passionate about recycling and the sharing economy. Which would be fine if they had anything worth sharing. I was only there five minutes before someone sniffed the laptop out and asked if they could take it to Costa and check their emails. Yeah, right… I know the type. I met enough of them in Manchester. You lend them something and they break it, or lose it, or leave it unattended and surprise, surprise, it gets nicked.

The thundering traffic hits me as soon as I open the door. I sprint down the road to what has quickly become my favourite café. The prices are cheaper than the fancy places, although still insane compared to up north, and the free Wi-Fi actually works. I collect my coffee and croissant from the end of the counter and take it over to the table by the window.

I'm in a good mood today. As I tear off a piece of croissant and dunk it into my coffee, I think back over yesterday evening. The encounter went well. Josie wasn't thrilled about my turning up out of the blue, Dad style, but she didn't blow me out. We even had a few laughs together. I know these are early days, but I feel like she's warming to me. Mustn't push it, though, or she'll get scared and back off. It's really important that I keep my patience and don't lose control. It would be a shame to mess things up when I'm so damn close.

I imagine Dad sitting opposite me, frowning at my battle tactics. Yeah, I know, Vikings were not known for making friends with their enemies – they just went out and attacked them. The poor fuckers were always at a disadvantage because they had families, homes and crops to protect, whereas the raiders were miles away from their loved ones and weren't afraid of dying.

The coffee tastes more bitter than usual. I rip open a packet of brown sugar and sprinkle it into the mug. Am *I* afraid of dying? Hard to say. I've tried it several times but never got very far. People have always insisted on saving me. Mum, girls at school, an ex-boyfriend, even total strangers. And Dad, of course. He pulled me out of the gutter and stuck his fingers down my throat, and twice he smashed his way into the bathroom and took me to A & E. At the time I cursed him, but later, when it was all over, I was relieved. He'd proved that he still loved me, and that made me feel that perhaps life was worth living after all. That's the strange thing about my condition – sometimes you're full of hope and joy, and the world seems like the most amazing, beautiful place. Then one tiny thing goes wrong and you're thrown back into your own steaming black pit of hell.

Thoughts, thoughts, thoughts. I can't stop them flying around my brain. I take another bite of croissant and wash it down, burning the roof of my mouth.

My phone pings under the table. A text from my sister, perhaps, saying how much she enjoyed seeing me last night? I bend down to remove the phone from the charger, unlocking the screen with a swipe. But no. It's from my curiously named nemesis: Private Number.

*Nice croissant?*

What the fuck? I swing around, my eyes darting across the café. Where is she? Or he? They've got to be right here! Two women are chatting intently over their coffees; a young guy is eating scrambled eggs and studying his tablet. A couple of older men in high-vis jackets are waiting for takeouts. Can't be any of them. I swivel back and glare out of the window. Commuters are marching left to right on their way down to the station; nobody seems to be hanging around. I weave my gaze through the busy traffic to the other side of the road, but the only person standing still is a mother with a pushchair at the bus stop.

My fingers are shaking as I type a reply. *Show yourself, perv.*

A response comes instantly. *Not possible.* Not possible… Why not possible? Are they not here, then? Are they watching me remotely? I peer at the laptop screen. Maybe they've got control of my webcam.

I slam the lid shut and text them again. *Who r u?*

*Wouldn't you like to know?*

That stupid, smart-arse reply's going to get us nowhere. I type again. *Why r u doing this?*

There's a pause. They're thinking about it. They want to tell me, I can sense it. Come on, come on, you fucker, explain yourself! Let's get it all out in the open. But nothing happens. They've managed to resist the temptation. Okay, let's try a more direct approach.

*Is this anything to do with my dad?*

No answer. I'll take that as a yes. I pause, remembering Josie's theory about the roses and Dad's 'darkest secret'. Is this the same person? My fingers fly across the tiny keyboard. *R u the one that knows his darkest secret?*

Silence. I glare at the screen. Come on! Spill the beans. Where's the fun in keeping it to yourself? A few seconds pass, then at last, a reply.

*Go back to Manchester.*

*Why should I?*

*Because you'll regret it if you don't.*

My response is swift. *I'm not afraid of you.*

*No? You should be.*

# CHAPTER EIGHTEEN

*Vikings carried their wealth in plain silver rings, worn on their arms. When they needed to buy goods, they hacked off pieces of silver, which were weighed and used as coins.*

It's Saturday morning, and Mum has asked me to come over to the house. I'm on the bus, wedged between the stairs and a protruding pushchair, grinding my way down the Finchley Road. We live just over a mile from the nearest tube. When we took on the tenancy of the flat, I thought it wouldn't matter; even fantasised that I'd walk to and from the station, but I never do. Either I'm running late in the mornings or I'm too tired after work.

I've known this road all my life. It feels comfortingly familiar, even though the landscape is forever changing. Old blocks of flats, pubs and office buildings keep being pulled down to make way for luxury apartments. Why anyone would want to pay two million pounds to live on one of the busiest roads in London, I don't understand, but the apartments are always sold before they're finished. Often there are delays while locals protest about planning and the strain on local amenities. Vacant properties soon fall into disrepair, their gardens used for illegal tipping, or they're quickly demolished and then left for years. In between the tired shopping parades and glossy apartment blocks, large patches of ground litter the sides of the road like bombsites. It's as if the city's at war with itself.

The bus passes the old Crossed Keys pub, where Valentina claims she's living now. It looks empty, the ground floor covered in rusty metal sheeting. There are banners strung across the upper level, informing would-be intruders that the place is guarded by live-in security. To keep out squatters, I guess. She couldn't stay in Antrobus Street, and I'm glad she moved out without being asked, but I feel bad that she's living somewhere so disgusting. Why didn't she just find somewhere else in Manchester? Rent is far cheaper there and she must have a network of friends. I feel uncomfortable about her being so close by, especially as Mum doesn't know of her existence yet.

I get off the bus by St John's Wood tube station and walk the rest of the way to Mum's on foot. Arun has been pushing me to tell her today. 'The time's right,' he said. 'The funeral's over, she's come to terms with Jerry's death. There's nothing stopping you now.' Nothing except my gut instinct. Telling her feels unnecessary and cruel. Dad's deceptions are over now, so what's the point of upsetting her? 'I'm going to see how she is first,' I told him this morning over breakfast. 'Test the temperature of the water before I dive straight in.' Am I just being a coward? Pretending I'm considering her feelings when in fact I'm more worried about my own? Oh God, I wish I could make up my mind.

I ring the doorbell, then let myself in with my key. 'Hello! It's me!' My eyes are drawn to a row of bulging black bin bags lined up against the wall of the hallway. I take off my jacket and hang it over the end of the banister.

Mum pads down the stairs, carrying a cardboard box. 'What's in those bags?' I ask, unable to keep the suspicion out of my voice.

'I've been sorting stuff out, that's all.'

'Dad's stuff?'

'Mostly. We've needed a clear-out for a long time.'

I kneel down and undo the knot of the first bag, digging out items of clothing: jumpers, cords, shirts, pairs of baggy shorts, underwear, socks… His red summer trousers, his 'Never Mind the Bollocks' T-shirt, the rough woollen waistcoat he bought in Peru.

'Mum! How could you?' I hold up a short-sleeved shirt covered in saxophones that he always wore to jazz concerts.

'The refugees need them.' She folds her arms across her chest and looks at the floor.

'But it's too soon! What if you regret it later? Don't you want to keep some things to remember him by?'

'I don't need objects. It's all stored up here,' she says, tapping the side of her head. 'Take what you want. I'll make some coffee.'

She walks past me and goes into the kitchen. I sink back onto my heels, the shirt still crumpled in my hand. I don't know what to do. Arun will go crazy if I turn up with a load of bin liners. There's not enough room in the wardrobe for our own clothes, let alone Dad's, and we've no storage at the flat. What does this say about Mum's state of mind? It feels like she's accepted the reality of Dad's death and is starting to move on. No doubt Arun would think it's a sign that she's ready to hear the truth, but, actually, it might set her back.

I look down at the sad heap of clothes; they look as if Dad has only just stepped out of them. They are all that's left of him: traces of his DNA on the insides of his collars, strands of hair caught in the jumper fibres, his smell lingering in the creases. If I tell Mum now, she might go crazy and rip him to pieces. I may feel angry and disillusioned, but I don't want that to happen. Allowing myself a final fond stroke, I put the saxophone shirt back and reknot the bag.

After lunch, we load up Mum's car and drop the bin liners and three boxes of old books at the nearest charity shop. She insists on giving me a lift home, even though the Saturday-afternoon traffic is terrible and it takes longer than it would have done to walk.

'Thanks, darling, you've been such a help,' she says as we draw up outside our block. 'I suppose I'm going to have to tackle Antrobus Street next.'

'I'll do it,' I reply quickly, remembering the state of the place. 'Arun and I will go up there one weekend.'

'But you said the keys didn't work. I've hunted high and low for spares, but I can't find any.'

'Don't worry, we'll get a locksmith onto it.' Or I'll ask Valentina if she's still got her keys, I think to myself.

'Thanks, darling, there's no hurry. I can't put it on the market until probate comes through, and that will take months.'

I invite her in for a cup of tea, but to my relief, she refuses. Arun's at home, and I'm frightened that he might let something slip, or even tell her about Jerry himself. Feeling tired and stressed, I climb the stairs to the fourth floor and let myself in.

And thank God Mum *didn't* say yes to tea, because Valentina is sitting on the sofa with Arun.

'Yay!' she cries, holding up a bottle of beer. 'My long-lost sister returns! I'd nearly given up.'

My heart is racing, like I've narrowly avoided an accident. 'Arun! Why didn't you tell me?'

'I did,' he says, getting up. 'I sent you a text.'

'Me too,' Valentina adds.

I silently curse myself for not checking. 'So, how come you're here?'

'I went for a walk, trying to get to know the area, and suddenly I realised I was right outside your block. Thought I'd just say hello… Luckily, your lovely boyfriend was in.' She smiles at Arun appreciatively.

He bustles into the kitchen area, mouthing 'sorry' as he passes. 'Beer or wine?'

'It's a bit early for either, isn't it?' The words freeze on my breath.

'Sorry, that's my fault,' Valentina insists. 'Arun asked me if I'd like a drink and I thought he meant booze.'

I force a smile, taking my jacket off. 'So, how's the job hunt going?'

'Hmm, nothing yet. I keep applying for things online but don't hear anything back. I'm not sure the jobs are even real.'

'There's always work available; it depends what you're prepared to do.'

'Oh, I'll do *anything*.' She grins, winking in Arun's direction. Is she flirting with him?

Arun leans against the kitchen island and takes a swig of beer. 'I said Valentina should try the O2 Centre; there are loads of bars and restaurants in there and it's only a few yards from where she's staying.'

'Good idea,' I agree. 'By the way, Valentina, do you still have the keys to Antrobus Street?'

'Er, think so… not sure… Why? Thinking of moving in?' She laughs.

'I need to go and sort the place out. So it can go on the market.'

'Oh… did Dad leave it to you in his will, then?'

'No. I don't want my mum to see the mess it's in, that's all. I don't know what's happening with the will. I doubt he made one. I expect everything will go to my mother.'

'Yeah… guess so,' says Valentina, looking wistful. She finishes the bottle and puts it on the table. 'Well, thanks for the "hand-crafted" beer. Local brewery, too. Very fancy.'

'Want another?' Arun gestures towards the fridge. I shoot him a private look. He clearly hasn't got the message. How obvious do I have to be that I'm not thrilled about her being here?

'No, I'm good. Josie looks tired, I think she needs a rest. Anyway, I need to get back. Application forms await!' She pulls a sorry-for-herself face and stands up. 'If I find that key, I'll pop it in. Or we could meet up. Sometime this week?'

'Yes, maybe…'

'I'll text ya.' She pulls on her silky black bomber jacket. 'Nice flat… amazing views… I'd give anything to live in a place like this.'

I walk her into the hallway and open the front door. 'Let me know when you find that key.'

'Will do.' She loiters on the threshold. 'I'm still getting those weird texts and it's getting worse – I think there might be spyware on my phone. This person knows exactly where I am and what I'm doing. Like they knew I was eating a croissant, for fuck's sake. I looked it all up on the net. It's not just your phone conversations they can listen to; they can turn your speaker on remotely and hear what people are saying in the room. They can turn your webcam on and watch you!'

'Oh my God, that's awful,' I say, thinking she's got to be exaggerating. Surely you can't upload spyware without having access to the handset. 'Perhaps you should buy a new SIM and change your number.'

'Yeah, I really want to do that. Trouble is, I'm at the limit of my overdraft. Dad always helped out with the old cash flow, but now…' She pauses hopefully.

'I don't have much on me, I'm afraid,' I say, feeling awkward.

'Whatever you've got will do for now. Please,' Valentina presses. 'I'll give it you back the moment I get paid, promise.'

Reluctantly I go to my bag. I'm reminded of being accosted by a girl at King's Cross station once. She was in floods of tears, claiming she'd been mugged, lost her bag, purse, credit cards, train ticket, everything. Like an idiot, I believed her and gave her forty quid. She took down my address and promised she'd post a cheque for the money as soon as she got home. Of course, I never heard from her again.

But this is different; this is my sister. I take out my purse and hand Valentina a crisp twenty-pound note, fresh from the cashpoint.

'Thanks… I don't suppose…' She gives me a sheepish smile. 'It's just that twenty quid won't be enough. I *will* pay it back.'

'How much do you need, then?'

She puffs out her cheeks. 'Good question. As much as you're able to lend me… what have you got on you?'

With a sinking feeling, I go back to my purse and take out another four twenties. Valentina takes them off me and gives me a fierce hug in return. 'Thanks! You're a lifesaver. I'd be lost without you, sis!'

I wave her out of the door, shutting it behind me with a sigh.

'Did I do the wrong thing?' asks Arun as I come back into the living room. 'I couldn't really turn her away. I'm sorry, hon.'

'It was a near miss, her seeing Mum, that's all.' I sit down wearily on the sofa. 'And, no, I didn't manage to tell her. Can I have that drink now? Wine – whatever colour we've got.'

He takes a bottle of white out of the fridge and twists off the cap. 'I see what you mean about the likeness. Even with all that make-up she wears, you can still see it. Incredible. Anyone would mistake you for twins.'

'Yes… you'd think our mothers would have had some impact, but no, Dad dominated. As ever.'

'You should wear your hair down like that,' he says, pouring my wine.

'It gets in the way.' My fingers instinctively go to my ponytail and I tighten the band.

'I know, but it looks really cool. Women pay a fortune for that look.'

'What look?'

'You know… wild… unpredictable… like she could eat you for breakfast.'

I glance at him sternly. 'Do you fancy my sister?'

'No!' He blushes, walking towards me, glass in hand. 'I mean, she looks like you, so obviously I find her attractive, but only because I find *you* attractive. I wouldn't otherwise… she's not my type… I don't mean *you're* not—'

'Stop!' I hold my hand out for my drink.

# CHAPTER NINETEEN

*Viking women used a combination of magic charms and herbal medicine to prevent illness and heal the sick. The herbs they used included ground ivy, mayweed, wormwood and opium poppy.*

'Here you go.' I give Zoheb two twenty-pound notes in return for the tabs he got me. 'Sorry for the delay.'

'Ta.' He gestures at me to join him on his mattress. I sit down gratefully and watch while he rolls a joint way too loosely. He's never been good with his hands. I remember him crying in metalwork because he couldn't work a hacksaw. No wonder he got bullied.

'Here, let me,' I say. 'You'll have us coughing to death.'

It's Saturday evening and this is how low I've stooped for entertainment. The rest of Josie's money burns in my pocket. The beer I had at her flat has given me a taste for more, not of the craft variety, just some bog-standard tins from the nearest supermarket. But once I start, I can't stop, and I don't want to blow all her cash on drink. Got to pace myself. Eke it out. I won't be seeing any more money from the Bank of Jerry, that's for sure.

I light up and take the first drag, drawing the smoke into the bottom of my lungs. 'This place is disgusting,' I say. 'It's a complete scam. Needs exposing.'

'Yeah, I know,' he agrees, taking the joint from between my fingertips. 'I don't get why you've come back to London. Isn't

Manchester supposed to be really cheap, like, and have loads of cool clubs?'

'I told you, I've come to be with my sister. Now that Dad's gone, she's all I've got.'

He coughs, inexpertly. 'Why don't you go and stay with her?'

'I haven't been invited. Anyway, we're only just getting to know each other… Don't hog it, Zo.' He passes the joint back. 'I didn't plan on living in a derelict pub on the M1; it was all there was on offer. And I really want to be as close to Josie as I can.'

Zoheb picks at a crusty stain of something on his jeans. 'I know this place is a fucking dump,' he says, 'but the transport links are amazing.'

'What are you, an estate agent?'

'Seriously, Vee. The Heath's only one stop on the Overground. We should go there when the weather warms up, when it's sunny. Have a picnic or something. Get wasted.'

'Yeah, maybe.' I watch a trail of smoke climb the cubicle wall and disappear over the edge like a cat. I don't plunge into the story about the last time I went to Hampstead Heath, although the words are gathering in the back of my throat, hopeful for a rare outing. It's the kind of thing people confess to when they're high. I glance at my old friend, leaning back against the wall with his eyes closed. He might already know. There would have been gossip at school when I suddenly disappeared during the middle of the term, never to return. And it might have been linked to stories in the local press about a gay couple rescuing a teenage girl from the Men's Pond. If I remind him, he'll feel bad for mentioning the location. Unless he remembers it only too well and was trying to suck the story out of me. I'm not falling for that trick.

*

I don't know what happens to Sunday; it sneaks past me when I'm not looking and suddenly it's Monday morning. Every day seems much like another when you don't have a job, but I think my weekend unawareness comes from my childhood. Weekends have a chequered history in my so-called family. Until I was fourteen, they were *everything*. Dad would pop round a couple of times during the week, sometimes just for coffee, occasionally to eat, but he very rarely stayed the night. At the weekend, however, he was around a lot and slept in Mum's bed, and oh what a fuss she made of him.

Then we moved up north and the arrangement flipped. Suddenly, it was the week that was special, because Dad was with us all the time, and it was the weekends that were ignored. My mother retrained as a ceramicist and opened her pottery café, running workshops in the back studio, while her minions (including me till I got myself sacked) served tea in Sophie Lane mugs and slices of cake on Sophie Lane plates. I don't know why I'm thinking of her in the past tense– she's not dead. Wishful thinking, I suppose. Anyway, weekends when I was a teenager were shit. There was no public transport, Dad was away, and Mum was always too exhausted after work to give me lifts.

As I lie in bed, picking over the dung heap of memories, a crazy idea starts to develop in my head. The more I think about it, the more compelled I feel to put it into action, so I get up and dress without bothering to wash. Ignoring the need for a caffeine fix, I leave the building and cross the busy road, stepping into Psychoanalysis Land – a maze of classy back streets on the edges of Hampstead. I decide to take a roundabout route, passing the house where Sigmund Freud once lived – in fact, only for a year, but it's clearly considered significant enough to warrant a museum – and the private girls' school where Josie probably went, although I don't know for sure. Must ask her when we next meet. There are so many gaps yet to fill.

I pause outside its impressive red-brick frontage, imagining all the current Josies diligently working inside. I was at the sink comp in Hendon – it was the only place that would take me with my behavioural record. We didn't have anything to do with the posh girls, but I saw them on the bus, in their plaid skirts and thick green tights, banging their cello cases against my legs. Never once saw my doppelgänger, though. Maybe she walked home, or was collected by car, or stayed after school to practise netball. I can just see Josie playing netball – with her height, she would have been a natural goalkeeper. I hated all sport; my main after-school activity was detention. Enough about schools, I think. I'll process my pitiful education another day.

Turning left at the next corner, I walk in the direction of the hospital. At least I *think* it's the right direction. When I was fourteen, I got lost every time and turned up late for my sessions. There was this research project going on and the school referred me to take part. Just a few workshops after school, playing games, chatting and filling in questionnaires. The organisers were very vague about the purpose of the research, but it had something to do with highly intelligent teenagers who exhibited challenging behaviour. In other words, naughty kids who ought to know better. I was the perfect candidate and that's how I met Dr Bannister.

Obligingly, the building is sitting exactly where I'd left it in my memory. I can feel my pulse quickening, my body heating up. A hole of hunger opens in my stomach. All signs of stress, I know that. I calmly take note of my symptoms and concentrate on my breathing. In through the nose and out through the mouth. Nice deep breaths. All techniques I learnt here, ironically.

I walk up the driveway to the entrance. A few people are standing outside in their dressing gowns, snatching a quick fag, and I decide to join them. The first puff of the day almost knocks me backwards, but the rest of the cigarette tastes dry and dull. I throw the half-smoked stub on the ground and grind it beneath the heel of my boot. Yes, I should have put it out in the sand bucket and then thrown it into the metal bin provided, but life's too short. You really appreciate that when you visit a hospital.

I pass through the revolving door and enter the reception. It's been refurbished since I was last here. The place was scruffy and welcoming then, but now everything is smooth, anonymous grey. They've gone very hi-tech. There are lots of information screens and machines for logging in to your appointment, but they're clearly so difficult to use they have to have people standing by to help. Dad would have found that very amusing, and I allow myself the briefest moment wishing he was with me.

As I make my way through the maze of corridors to the back staircase, I feel an urgency in my feet, making me want to take two steps at a time. I quickly reach the fifth floor, turning right after the lifts and finding myself in the same sludge-grey corridor, leading to the same reinforced glass double doors. And the same arrangement of chairs along three sides of the room, with a long desk in front of the consulting rooms.

I pause, shuffling myself into the past. I remember every detail of Dr Bannister's room. The shelves lined with books with incomprehensible titles, the leather chair behind the desk, the arrangement of armchairs and coffee table. I can picture myself refusing to sit down, wandering about the room, picking up objects and being asked to put them back. Once I tried to smash a glass paperweight, hoping that the butterfly inside would break free and fly out of the window. But I only managed to chip it.

'Have you brought your letter?' asks the receptionist, pulling me back sharply into the present. I stare at her blankly. 'Your appointment letter.' She tuts. 'Name?'

'I don't have an appointment,' I say. 'I just want to talk to Dr Bannister.'

She scrutinises my features, then looks down at her list. 'Are you a patient?'

'Not any more.'

'Then I'm sorry, I can't help you. You need a referral from your GP.'

'But it's urgent.'

'You still have to see your GP first.'

'I only need a few minutes.' I glance towards the doors of the consulting rooms, wondering which to burst through first.

'Dr Bannister isn't here today,' she says firmly.

'You sure?'

'Positive.'

I hesitate, trying to decide whether the woman's lying to me. Maybe I should sit down and wait until the doors open and the doctors emerge. There are a few people sitting here, clutching their letters and looking nervous.

'I'll wait.' I march over to the nearest seat and sit down, stretching out my legs and folding my arms defiantly.

I turn to my fellow patients. 'I'd be careful if I were you. You could end up being more fucked up than you were to start with.' They instantly look down at the laps. 'It happened to me.'

'You really need to leave right now,' the receptionist says, getting to her feet.

Ignoring her, I roll up my sleeves and display the insides of my arms, etched with thin silvery scars. 'I didn't start doing all this until *after* Dr Bannister. So if that's who you're all waiting to see…'

'I've already told you, the doctor isn't on duty today,' says the receptionist, her mouth twitching with irritation. 'Please leave or I'll find someone to escort you.'

I jump up from my seat and stride over to the desk. 'Are you threatening me?'

'Are you threatening *me*?' She picks up the phone.

'Oh why don't you all go fuck yourselves?' I turn on my heel and storm out.

# CHAPTER TWENTY

*Vikings lived in extended family units, comprising several husband-and-wife couples, with one member of each couple related by blood to the group. Arguments were inevitable and were often settled with violence.*

Ever since Valentina's impromptu visit last Friday, there's been a strange atmosphere in the flat. It's as if the ghost of her is still here, hiding under the bed, eavesdropping on our conversations and muttering 'fuck off' when we mention her name. Arun is clearly fascinated by her, in a twisted kind of way. I think he's excited by the fact that she looks like me physically, yet in every other way is my complete opposite. I think he's also a bit scared of her.

I want to stop talking about what Valentina really wants, and when I'm going to pluck up the courage to tell Mum about Dad's secret, and have a romantic evening together for a change. We haven't made love for weeks – my fault, I've been feeling so out of it – and Arun's reaction to Valentina (there I go again) has made me realise that he's probably been feeling a bit frustrated.

It's Wednesday evening. I leave work early and stop off at Waitrose to buy some luxury ready-meals, a decent bottle of red and a large slab of nutty aphrodisiac chocolate. I lay the table with a cloth, our best mats, candles and two enormous wine glasses. While the lasagne is heating in the oven, I go into the bedroom and change out of my work clothes. I put on a pair of jeans and a tight-fitting top, then remove my hairband and let my hair fall in soft waves around my face. Arun's right, it *does* suit me. After applying a little more lipstick than usual, I return to the kitchen and wait for his return, my stomach fluttering with anticipation.

He comes through the door a few minutes later, shouting out a brief hello, then walks straight into the bedroom. I immediately rise and go to see him, lingering seductively in the doorway as I watch him unbuttoning his shirt.

'Did you have a good day?' I ask, hoping he'll look up and notice that I've made an effort.

'So-so,' he replies, throwing the shirt into the laundry basket and taking a football top out of the drawer. My spirits take a nosedive as I realise my mistake.

'You playing football tonight?' My words are edged with disappointment.

He pulls the red silky top over his head and starts removing his trousers. 'Same as every Wednesday.'

'Do you have to go? I've bought a really nice lasagne; it's already in the oven.'

'I'll heat it up when I get back.'

'But I want us to have some "us" time tonight.' I can hear my voice turning thin and brittle. 'I know I've not been paying you much attention recently and I want to make up for it.'

He looks at me reproachfully. 'Don't make me give up my football; it's the highlight of my week.'

'Fine!' I snap. 'Suit yourself.' I march back to the kitchen and blow out the candles, gathering up the cutlery and almost breaking the wine glasses as I slam them back on the shelf.

Arun comes to the doorway, holding his kit bag. 'Look, Jos, I don't want to fall out with you. I won't be long. We'll talk when I get back. Leave me the dishes.' He gives me one of his lopsided smiles, which usually melts my heart, but not tonight. I stare at my feet, refusing to answer, leaving him no choice but to turn on his heel and leave the flat.

*Well, that went well,* I mutter to myself. I turn off the oven and slump into a chair, feeling cross and defeated. I should have remembered about football. Then again, he might have stayed at home for once.

Arun is on my side, deep down I know that, but I don't feel he really understands what I'm going through. His family works very differently to mine. He broke away when he went to uni, but the rest of them live on top of each other. His brother works for his dad's electrical business and his mum looks after his sister's kids while she's at work. They're always in and out of each other's houses and seem very happy to do everything together. It would be totally impossible for Arun's father to run a secret second family – the idea is absurd.

I rise and stand in my favourite place by the window, gazing out at the twilight cityscape. Mum and I are a pathetic excuse for a family compared to Arun's, but it's all I've got and I need to protect it. The overwhelming question is: would telling her the truth be an act of kindness or cruelty? That's what I can't decide. I need help. The only other family I've got are Brett and Lisa. The strained conversation I had with my uncle at the funeral sweeps into my thoughts. *Any problems, talk to me first and I'll deal with it.* Maybe, for once, I should take him at his word.

In the morning, I ring work and ask Jill if I can take a day's leave. 'Sorry it's such short notice. There are some family things I need to attend to.'

'Are you okay, Josie? Don't be afraid to admit you're struggling,' she replies. 'This has hit you very hard and I'm concerned about you. Have you thought about bereavement counselling?'

'Honestly, I'll be fine. I've just got a few things to sort out.'

I catch my usual bus down the Finchley Road towards the tube station. As we pass the Crossed Keys pub, a shiver runs through me as I realise how physically close I must be to Valentina. It's only just gone nine; she's probably still asleep. Even so, I look around cautiously as I get off at the bus stop, worried that I'll see a flash of auburn hair hurtling towards me, a voice shouting, 'Sis! Sis!' I keep my head down as I wait impatiently at the traffic lights, dashing across the road as soon as the cars stop and running into the station.

Brett and Lisa live on the outskirts of Uxbridge, at the end of the Metropolitan line. The trains that pull in on the south-side platform are heaving with commuters, but those heading north have far fewer passengers.

The carriage I am in virtually empties at Wembley, and by the time we reach the end of the line, nearly an hour later, I'm the only one left. As I leave the station, the noticeably fresher air punches into my lungs and I instantly feel healthier. It's a short bus ride out of the town centre, and by half past ten I'm walking down the leafy suburban street towards Brett and Lisa's house.

Number 73 Kilworth Avenue is a large semi-detached property, built in the thirties and covered in ugly brown pebble-dash. Brett has lived here forever – well, as long as I can remember – and has always hosted Macauliffe family events. My cousins, Jake and Matthew, are quite a lot older than me; they used to tease me and exclude me from their boisterous games. Their mother, Brett's first wife, sadly died in her thirties, and he married Lisa not long afterwards.

The doorbell rings out a tune I remember from childhood, and after a few seconds, the door opens and Uncle Brett, dressed in casual trousers and a red sweater, steps back in surprise.

'Josie!'

'Hello, sorry I didn't call in advance. It was a spur-of-the-moment thing.'

He shouts up the stairs. 'Guess who's here! It's Josie!'

'Hang on!' shouts Lisa. 'I'll be right down.'

Brett turns back to me. 'Everything okay? No more bad news, I hope.' He sees a shadow flit across my face. 'Now what? Oh God… You'd better come in and sit down.'

I follow him into the large rectangular sitting room that runs from front to back. Nothing has changed much. The same magnolia walls. The same cream leather sofas, the same pine furniture. The seat cushion farts as I sit down.

'Tea? Coffee? Glass of water?'

'No, thanks.'

'Right…' He sits in the armchair and rubs his face nervously. 'Don't start yet. Lisa will be down in a moment.'

While we wait, I study Dad's big brother, marvelling at how alike and yet unlike they are. Brett is a safe, toned-down version of Dad. He doesn't have the hipster beard or the biking leathers; he wears checked shirts from Marks & Spencer and drives a Ford Mondeo. Brett likes classical music; Dad loved experimental jazz. And, as far as I know, Brett has only ever had one wife at a time.

As if on cue, Lisa enters. 'What's up? Is Helen okay? I saw her the other day – she seemed very lost. We all are.' She pauses to look at me. 'We still can't believe he's really gone, can we, Brett?'

'No. I keep wondering why he hasn't called, then I remember.' Brett's blue-grey eyes moisten and he sniffs the tears back. 'We were very close, you know.'

'So what's wrong, Josie?' says Lisa, sitting down next to me. 'It must be serious for you to turn up unexpectedly like this.'

'Go on,' says Brett, gripping the arms of the chair.

I clear my throat. 'Did you know that Jerry had a mistress?'

'Oh my God…' Lisa puts her hand to her mouth.

'A mistress?' Brett gulps. 'What do you mean?'

'I suppose that's what you'd call her,' I continue, watching his expression very closely. 'But she was more than that. She was another wife, basically. They were together for over twenty-five years and they have a daughter called Valentina. She's my age; we were born in the same week. Sophie, the other wife, lives in Derbyshire, very close to where Dad crashed. That's where Dad's really been living these past ten years – during the week, I mean. The little house he bought in Manchester was just a cover, Valentina was living in it. That's how I found out.'

There's a very long pause.

'Oh dear…' Brett draws in a troubled breath. 'Oh dear, oh dear, oh dear.' He covers his face with his hands.

'You poor thing! Come here.' My aunt lurches forward and envelops me in her arms, patting my back. I almost gag on her heavy floral perfume.

'I'm okay,' I say, pulling away. 'It was a terrible shock at first, but I'm coming to terms with it.'

Brett removes his hands and turns to me. 'Are you absolutely sure of your facts?'

'Totally. I've had contact with Sophie by text and I've met Valentina several times now.'

'Several times? Why?' Brett looks at me as if I'm mad.

'She's moved to London… She wants us to be like, well, like proper sisters.'

'That would be a very bad idea,' he says immediately. 'If I were you, Josie, I'd give them both a very wide berth. You can't trust people like that.'

'It's not Valentina's fault. She was completely in the dark.'

'Even so, you mustn't have anything to do with her,' insists Brett. 'She's not part of our family and never will be. Isn't that right, Lisa?' She nods vehemently. 'If that girl starts sniffing around for money, you tell me, okay?' My cheeks redden as I think of the hundred pounds I've already lent her, knowing full well that she'll never pay me back.

'It's Mum I'm more worried about,' I say. 'She doesn't know yet. I don't know how to tell her. I don't know if I *should* tell her... What do you think?'

'No, don't tell her. Absolutely not,' he says, shifting uncomfortably on the leather cushion. 'There's no point. It's all over now and it's not like this Sophie woman is mentioned in the will. Or the wretched daughter, for that matter. We mustn't tell Helen, don't you agree, Lisa?'

Lisa tosses her head. 'I'm sorry, sweetheart, but no, I don't agree. You know how fond I am of Helen, we're like sisters. The last thing I want to do is hurt her, but she *has* to know; this is too important to sweep under the rug. There have been enough lies and secrets in this family as it is; the truth has to come out.'

'No, Lisa,' Brett protests. 'I won't have her told.'

'It's not up to you,' she snaps. 'The secret's out now – you can't control it. If Josie wants to tell her, she can.'

Brett huffs and folds his arms sulkily.

'Arun thinks she should know,' I say, trying to defuse the conflict.

'And he's right.' Lisa nods. 'Enough's enough.'

We pause to think our own thoughts. I feel myself leaning towards Lisa's point of view. Why *should* we let him get away with it? His mistress and daughter helpfully retired to the shadows, his reputation as a faithful husband and loving father preserved intact. I look out of the window at the back garden – the scene of so many happy family events, and where he must have told a thousand lies. My world has changed, and yet everything outside looks the same, frozen in time: the chequered patio, the stepping-stone path, the stretch of lawn and the tall oak tree at the bottom. Dad used to chase me and my cousins around it, roaring at the top of his voice and shouting in his made-up Viking language. Strange to think that there was another little daughter living not so far away, who was probably playing on her own and wondering why her daddy wasn't there. He didn't just cheat on Mum, he cheated all of us.

'So what are you doing to do, Josie?' asks Brett, pulling his jumper down over his bulging stomach.

'I think I'm probably going to tell Mum, as soon I can pluck up the courage. I've no idea how she's going to react – badly, I expect. I just needed to find out if you already knew.'

'We didn't, did we, Lisa?'

'No,' she says evenly. 'We didn't.'

The air is crackling with tension. I don't know whether it's because they actually had known about Dad's other family and this is a well-worn argument between them, or whether they're in shock and can't agree about whether to tell Mum. I seem to have lost all sense of judgement recently. I believe everything and nothing. After what Dad did, I feel like I can't trust anyone, and yet I'm also desperate for the truth.

'Anyway, it's good that you know now,' I say, also trying to keep my voice level. 'Because Mum might need some support – especially from you, Lisa,' I add deliberately. 'I'm sure she'd appreciate it.'

'You know you can count on me,' she says. 'It's going to be a terrible shock.' She looks from me to Brett, then back. 'But you must tell her soon, Josie. Before somebody else does.'

# CHAPTER TWENTY-ONE

*Brewing mead was an important part of a Viking woman's household duties, along with cooking, sewing and childcare. This alcoholic beverage made from honey was drunk in great quantities.*

'Fuck me, if it isn't my long-lost sister!' Valentina cries, answering my phone call. I'm standing outside the Crossed Keys, the phone pressed firmly against my ear as I try to shut out the traffic. 'Where are you?'

'Right outside the pub. Are you in?'

'Yeah, great! Go down the side alley and I'll meet you at the door. You can have the grand tour.'

Tiptoeing between the piles of rubbish and what look like pools of urine, I find my way to the entrance and stand nervously by a large black door, trying my best not to look conspicuous. This alleyway hugs the railway line and is well known as a haunt of drug users and alcoholics.

I wasn't planning to see her – the idea slid into my head on the way back from Brett and Lisa's and refused to go away. I'm feeling angry and rebellious. I still think Brett was lying to me. And he was so mean about Valentina, behaving as if she's to blame. She didn't ask to be born on the wrong side of the frigging blanket. His attitude is positively medieval. Not part of our family? She's as much a Macauliffe as I am, whether Brett likes it or not. He has no right to tell me not to have anything to do with her.

Valentina opens the door with a flourish. 'Ta-da! What a lovely surprise!' She stares thoughtfully at my relative-visiting clothes – a knee-length skirt with embroidery around the hem, a white shirt with a lacy collar, navy linen jacket and ballet-pump-style shoes. 'Hmm, you're not exactly dressed for a building site. But never mind, come in, come in!'

I step inside and follow her down the gloomy corridor. She scurries along like a tarantula, in black skinny jeans and a tight black long-sleeved top, waving her thin arms from side to side.

'On our left is the kitchen of death,' she announces. Her hand pauses on the doorknob. 'You haven't got a rat phobia, have you?'

'You've got *rats*?' I step back a few paces.

''Fraid so. Big ones too, the size of cats, some of them. They're shy, though, they'll run away as soon as we go in.'

'Let's not bother. You should get the council to get rid of them. Every borough has a pest control service, you know; I can send you the contact details.'

'No point, they'd only come back.' We turn towards the stairs. 'I'll show you my room, only keep your voice down, 'cos we're not supposed to have visitors.'

'Why not?' I lower my voice as we climb.

'Dunno. It's the rules.' She stops and holds her nose. 'So-called bathroom on your right. I wouldn't bother…'

The smell of mould and blocked drains fills my nostrils. 'I don't know how you can bear it.'

'It's better than the streets… here we go…'

She leads me into what must have once been an upstairs function room. I might even have gone to a gig here when I was a teenager. The room has been stripped of furniture and a row of wooden cubicles sits in the middle. 'So, what is this, personal storage?'

Valentina laughs. 'These are the bedrooms.' She takes some keys from her back pocket and frees the padlock from the door at the far end. 'Welcome to my dear little home.'

My eyes flick over a single mattress on the floor, a torn, muddy sleeping bag, a battered suitcase bulging with clothes. The plywood walls are covered in graffiti, felt-pen drawings, frayed posters and random bits of paper. It smells of cosmetics and sweat. 'I'm sorry,' I say, 'I don't mean to be rude, but it's Third World.'

'Not that bad, but I know what you mean.' She scoops a strand of hair off her face and grins. 'Anyway, I'm going to move out as soon as I get a job.' She sits on the bed and pats the sleeping bag for me to join her. Not wanting to appear squeamish, I sit down.

'Well, this is fun,' she says after a pause. 'You're my first illegal visitor.'

'Am I? Oh.' I stretch my legs out and stare at my pumps. 'So you haven't bought a new phone yet, then?'

'What? Oh. No, not yet. Working on it.'

'Any more nasty texts?'

She shakes her head. 'Not since the weekend. So, why are you here? Why aren't you at work?'

'I took the day off… went to see my aunt and uncle.'

'Very dutiful of you.'

'We were deciding whether or not to tell my mum about Dad's…' I hesitate, not sure how to phrase the rest of my sentence.

'It's okay, I get that you're the proper daughter and I'm the aberration.'

'Don't say that, it makes me feel bad.'

'But it's true, isn't it?'

'Of course it's not. You're just as valid, just as important.'

'So, what did you decide? Are you going to tell her or not?'

I breathe out heavily. 'I'm not sure. I keep changing my mind; it's driving me mad.'

She moves her head from side to side and makes considering noises. 'I say, if you're not sure, do nothing. Once you've told her, you can't take it back.'

'That's true...'

'It'll be like throwing a burning match into a firework factory. *Whoosh!*'

'Yes, that's what I'm worried about.'

She leaps up. 'Don't think about it now. Shall we get out of this stinking hellhole? I could do with a drink.'

'Me too. It's been a tough day.'

Valentina rummages around in the suitcase and takes out a large-toothed comb, wincing as she drags it through her tangled hair. 'Shall we go to Camden tonight? There's this DJ on at the Queen's Head. He plays Afrobeat, it's great for dancing. You like dancing?'

Tonight? I frown. I was thinking of a quick drink, then straight home for an evening in front of the telly with Arun. 'Love it. But tonight's not good. Arun will be expecting me...'

'He won't mind, surely?'

'And I'm not really dressed appropriately.' I hold out my skirt.

'Borrow something of mine.' She crouches down and dives back into the case. 'You're the same as me, yeah? Size eight?'

'Yes, but... I don't think...' My mind is searching frantically for excuses. I don't want to go dancing, I don't feel like dancing. But it's too late now, she's got me trapped.

She throws a pair of black satin jeans onto the bed. 'Try these. I've got a sparkly top somewhere that goes really well... *if* I can find it... Ah, here.'

I stare down at the dark clothes arranged on the mattress like a shadow. 'Why don't we wait till the weekend? I've got work tomorrow and—'

'This guy's only on tonight; honest, he's amazing. I saw him at Bestival.' She gives me an endearing look. 'I can't go on my own and you're pretty much the only person I know in London. Come on, it'll be *fun.* Otherwise all I'll do is lie here waiting for the ceiling to fall down, listening out for the rats.'

'Okay,' I say, picking up the clothes. 'I'll go and change.'

Valentina wasn't exaggerating about the disgusting bathroom facilities. I do the fastest costume change I can manage and emerge looking like Olivia Newton-John at the end of *Grease*. I clutch my own clothes to my stomach. This is so not me. 'Do I look okay?' I ask doubtfully.

'Fucking gorgeous!' She slips the sparkly top off my shoulder. 'That's better. Now, why don't you leave your sensible stuff here; you don't want to carry it around. I'll bring it next time we meet.'

'Okay… thanks…' I lay the clothes in a neat pile in the corner of the room, thinking, What am I doing? Arun would have a fit if he saw me looking like this. But another part of me is starting to feel excited. I haven't been out since Dad's accident, and a dance will help release the tension that's been building up over the past weeks.

Valentina grins at me. 'Now all you need is some eyeliner.' She makes me kneel on the mattress while she fills in my brows, then draws heavy black lines under my eyes and across my lids, finishing with swooping Amy Winehouse flicks. 'There you go! Valentina Mark Two,' she declares, thrusting a hand mirror beneath my nose. I stare at the strange girl looking back at me. Her blue eyes are really intense, her expression defiant and moody. It's kind of scary, but I like it.

She slips her arm into mine as we walk to the bus stop. It's still early, and the street is thronged with commuters on their way home. The Camden bus arrives and we clamber up the stairs, grabbing the front seats like teenagers. I chew my lip, tasting the blood-coloured lipstick Valentina insisted on applying, and think of how it might have been if we'd grown up in the same family. Ready-made playmates and best friends. We might have fought occasionally, but deep down there would have been such a tight bond between us.

'I hate the thought of you living in that dump,' I say, as the bus turns left towards Camden High Street. 'The housing crisis in London is beyond a joke.'

'I'm going to move out as soon as I find a job, but it's not so much the rent that's the problem as the deposit.' She stretches out her legs, resting her boots on the window shelf. 'Dad used to help me out when I got into difficulties, but now he's gone…' She lets the rest of the sentence disappear into a sad silence.

'What about your mum? Can't she lend you the money?'

'You must be joking! Honestly, sis, she doesn't give a shit about me.'

'You'll be okay once you've found a job,' I say uselessly. 'I'm sure something will turn up.'

'Yeah, hope so.' She leans her head on my bony shoulder. 'I feel so much more positive about the future now I've found you.'

We go to a pub first to 'pre-drink', starting off with a glass of wine, then moving on to sickly-sweet Jägermeister. When Valentina orders shots of tequila, I raise my hand in protest.

'Not for me,' I say, already feeling a bit spacey. 'I need to pace myself.'

'But we'll never afford the drinks in the gig – this is Happy Hour; make the most of it.' She slams the shot glass in front of me. 'That's an order.' I swallow it down and my body instantly tingles, like I'm thawing in front of a log fire.

Before I know it, I've drunk three tequilas and a flaming aftershock. Warmly lubricated, we slither down the street like a couple of black eels, holding onto each other for support and giggling at the slightest thing.

'If Uncle Brett could see me now…' I say, as I catch sight of my alien reflection in a shop window. 'He'd be so furious.'

'Fuck Uncle Brett!' she shrieks. I pull a disgusted face and we collapse laughing.

It's a cool club with an amazing atmosphere, seriously good music and a brilliant DJ. We buy a bottle of water each and head straight onto the dance floor. Within seconds I've succumbed to the insistent African rhythm, letting it invade my body and become my heartbeat. I stick out my bum and bend my knees, hands slapping thighs, feet pounding the floor. Sweat trickles down my back and between my breasts, sliding the skinny top from my shoulders, sticking my skin to the satin jeans. I gyrate on the spot, my red hair flying like sparks of flame off a wheel. Valentina's clothes are like a mask, hiding my boring, sensible, everyday self. I feel liberated. Even when I lose my balance and fall over, I don't care, laughing it off as Valentina picks me up. Because this isn't Josie dancing, it's someone else, a crazy, exotic stranger I've never met before.

Then, out of nowhere, the alcohol hits me like a truck. My vision slows right down and there's a riot raging in my belly. I spin round, looking for Valentina, but she's on the other side of the dance floor, grinding her hips into some guy.

Staggering into the loos, I steady myself against the washbasin. Red and green tiles fracture into twirling patterns, and I feel like I'm in a giant kaleidoscope. The cubicles are all occupied. I bang on the doors – 'Can you hurry up, please? I feel sick.' My head is thumping like a kid going mad on a drum kit. I lift my head and try to focus on my sweaty face. I look terrible. My hair is a mess and Valentina's thickly drawn eyeliner is dribbling down my cheeks. I bang the doors again. 'Please! I don't want to throw up out here!'

'Piss off!' says a voice from the middle cubicle.

I need some fresh air. I lurch out of the toilets and head for the exit. Where is Valentina? I stumble through the door and find myself on some kind of terrace, packed with smokers. The cold air hits me in the stomach and I buckle forward. This is not good. I really don't want to throw up over people's shoes… I lift my head and try to take some deep breaths, willing the alcohol to stay put. Closing my eyes, I let the world spin free.

'Josie! There you are! I thought I'd lost you.' Valentina shakes me by the shoulders. 'You okay? You look fucked!' I cling to her, groaning. 'Come on, let's get you home. Are you on Uber?'

I nod. 'Phone… bag… somewhere…'

'Leave it to me.' She leads me through the maze of bodies and out through a side entrance. It only takes a couple of minutes for the car to arrive. 'Don't let the driver see you're pissed,' she whispers, waving at it to stop. She opens the back door, resting her hand protectively on my head as she guides me into the back seat. I feel like I've just been arrested.

Valentina chats away to the driver as we weave clumsily through the back streets, the evil alcohol sloshing around my stomach. I sit stock still, not daring to open my mouth, fixing my gaze on the bald patch on the top of his head. *Nearly there*, I keep saying in my head, *nearly there*. At last the taxi swings into our street and parks up near the playground. Valentina helps out and leads me towards the entrance.

'I don't think I can make it up the stairs,' I groan.

'Yes, you can.' She puts one arm around my shoulder and, grabbing me by the waist with the other, heaves me up, one step at a time. We slowly make it to the fourth floor, creeping along the balcony to the front door of my flat. The bedroom curtains are drawn and the light's off. 'Key?' she says.

'Bag… inside pocket.' I put my finger to my lips. 'Shh… don't wake Arun… he'll kill me…' Valentina laughs softly as she opens the front door. As soon as we enter the hallway, I lurch into the bathroom and finally empty my guts.

# CHAPTER TWENTY-TWO

*Viking men were promiscuous before, during and after marriage. They could purchase a 'bed slave' for up to twelve ore (the value of 489 yards of homespun cloth).*

I squeeze open the door and tiptoe into the dark bedroom. Arun is lying on his side, snoring softly, a tousle of jet-black hair poking out from the top of the duvet. Wobbling across the room, I make it round to the other side of the bed. I undo my jeans and ease them over my hips, taking my briefs with them. My head reels as I remove the rest of my clothes, then climb carefully into bed.

The sheet is cold, but Arun is radiating an inviting heat. I edge across and snuggle up to his back, curving my body into the crook of his bent legs. We fit like pieces of a jigsaw. I nuzzle into his shoulder blades and he stirs slightly, murmuring in his sleep.

I hear the alcohol singing in my head, making me want to touch every part of him. Legs, arse, stomach, cock… my fingers are trembling. I'm opening up, becoming wet, my nipples sharp with expectation. The feeling is so intense, I might have to pull away. But I can't. His body is so warm, his flesh so yielding. I sweep my hand down his back and across his perfect buttocks, then over his hips, my fingers burrowing to find him. He's in that delicious state between soft and hard, ready to respond to my fingertips. I hold him firmly but not tightly and gently start to stroke him, up and down, up and down. He stirs again.

'Mmm… mmm…'

'Shh…' He is huge and hard now. He pulls my hand away and turns over, falling onto me. He buries his head in my chest and starts to suck my nipples greedily. I let my hair fall across my face, raising my pelvis and pressing it against him. He shoves my legs apart and opens me up, pushing himself into me. I gasp, my stomach lurching.

The booze is egging me on like a bad angel. He arches his back, eyes closed in ecstasy as he builds up his rhythm. He's in his own world; I'm just the body beneath him. His body shudders as he comes, grunting like an animal and falling heavily onto my chest.

'Fucking hell, that was good,' he says, panting into my neck. I feel my desire subside like a pot that's been taken off the gas. He rolls off me and switches on the bedside lamp.

I lie completely still, like a bird playing dead. He turns back, freezing as he stares at my naked body, his mouth gaping open in a silent scream. 'What the fuck! Valentina! What the fuck! Jesus Christ!'

'Shh… you'll wake her.'

He covers his face, shaking his head. 'Oh God, oh shit… this didn't happen, this didn't happen.'

I lean up onto my elbows. 'Oh yes it did. Don't tell me you didn't know it was me.'

'It was pitch dark, I was asleep! You… you bitch.' He grabs the edge of the duvet and flings it at me. 'Cover yourself up, for God's sake.'

'You didn't feel very asleep to me.'

'What the fuck are you doing in my bed?' He stands up and starts to hyperventilate.

'There was nowhere else for me to go, so I just crept in. Look, I didn't mean it to happen. I was just snuggling up. You started it.'

'No, *you* started it.' He looks around wildly, as if my sister might be hiding behind the curtains. 'Where's Josie?'

'Conked out on the sofa, pissed out of her skull. Keep your voice down or you'll wake her. We don't want that, do we? It would be really embarrassing if she came in right now.'

He walks around to my side of the bed. 'Get dressed. Then get out!' he spits, gathering up my clothes and throwing them in my face. 'Leave us alone; don't you dare come round here ever again, understand? Don't you ever contact her or... or...' He stands there, naked and shaking, like a frightened little boy.

'Or what?' I look at him defiantly. 'Or *what*, Arun?'

'Just go!'

'Or you'll tell Josie you "accidentally" fucked me?' I slowly put on my bra. 'How do you think that's going to go down? You're going to admit that you were so caught up in your own orgasm you didn't realise it wasn't her?' I step into my knickers and pull them up. 'It's an easy mistake to make. I mean, if that's how you usually do it – in the dark, no talking, humping and grunting away... I'm really surprised you didn't feel my belly stud.'

'Shut up! Shut up!' He picks up his shirt and holds it against himself. 'I know what you're doing. I'm not stupid. You're trying to blackmail me. You had all this planned.'

'I didn't, actually.' I lie back, wriggling into my jeans. 'Come on, you know we fancy each other. You think I'm a slutty version of Josie. When I came over the other day, you couldn't put your tongue away – you were coming on to me the whole time.'

'That's so not true.'

'I think the evidence is against you.' I sit back up and pull my top over my head. 'Look, it happened. We shouldn't have done it but we did. We couldn't help ourselves. I promise not to tell if you don't.' I stand and pick up my boots.

'You're such an evil bitch. If Josie knew...'

'She'd be devastated, so we mustn't tell her. Go back to bed and try to sleep. I'll see you soon.' I go to kiss him but he smacks my hand away. I knew he would.

'Get out before I hurt you,' he says, his eyes full of hate.

'Save that for next time.' I grin. Bending down, I turn off the bedside light and leave him alone in the dark.

It's a long walk home, but I don't care. I feel wired. Powerful. Immune from danger. I stride down the Finchley Road, my confident step beating a rhythm against the endless groan of the night traffic. My heart is racing. Fear and excitement are exactly the same; it's all about how you interpret the bodily sensations. Tonight I choose to be excited.

The cold air finishes the job of sobering me up, and by the time I reach the pub, my senses are sharp and my head's clear. Checking to make sure nobody's about to leap out from behind me, I unlock the heavy door and let myself in. It's late, but I don't bother to creep around. Many of my fellow guardians will still be up, and I can hear laughter and guitar music coming from the snug. Every night's like a lock-in here. I decide not to go and join them, climbing the stairs and going straight to the front function room, where my wooden cell awaits.

I remove the padlock and enter, switching on the fairy lights and kicking off my boots at the same time. I collapse onto the mattress. It feels a lot thinner and harder than my sister's cosy bed. Fucking hell, what a night… Turning onto my back, I gaze up at the high ceiling, with its ornate cornice and a plaster rose in the centre. It feels as far away as heaven. Do I feel guilty? No. Do I feel ashamed? Not at all.

The risk was too high to ignore, the dare too outrageous to resist. I can be such a bad girl when the mood takes me. It seems to come naturally. I know I won't even regret it when I wake up. The taste of danger always lingers in my mouth. Maybe later, perhaps, if it all goes wrong… Things usually *do* go wrong in the end, but for now, I feel in control. Glorious. I've a feeling Arun's going to keep our little secret safe, and, as my sister herself seems to believe, what you don't know can't hurt you.

# CHAPTER TWENTY-THREE

*Viking warriors often spent long periods of time away from home. Their wives ran the household in their absence and organised celebrations on their return. Sometimes they commissioned poems that praised their husbands' courage in battle.*

I groan and smother myself with the pillow. Except it's not a pillow, it's a cushion, and I'm not in bed, I'm lying on the sofa. My head is pounding and my stomach feels stretched and raw. What time is it? Images from last night rotate before my inner eye: staggering up the stairs, Valentina holding back my hair as I vomited into the toilet bowl, crawling out of the bathroom on my hands and knees and collapsing on the carpet, while the universe went into a rapid spin. I felt like I was going to die. I *wanted* to die...

It was a great night, but I'm paying for it now. Don't know how I ended up on the sofa. I suppose Valentina must have laid me down and covered me with our TV-watching blanket. Where is she? My head weighs a ton, but I lift it carefully, expecting to see her on the floor or cuddled up in the armchair. She's not here. Must have gone home... What time is it? It's daylight, but it feels early. I ease myself into a sitting position, then slowly stand. I sway for a couple of seconds, as if I'm on a rolling ship, then find my balance. Shuffling over to the kitchen area, I squint at the clock on the cooker, trying to focus on the small illuminated figures: 08:11. Shit, I should be on my way to work. But no ... no, it's 06:11.

Only six o'clock, phew. Even so, I won't make it in to work today. I'll have to call in sick. Must ring Jill, I think. But not now. Later. Maybe after I've had a sleep I'll feel better. It's pretty despicable, calling in sick with a hangover. If I get some sleep and take a load of ibuprofen, I might manage to get in for this afternoon.

I run the tap and take a glass off the shelf. The cold water hits my bloodstream, giving me instant brain freeze. I know we've got some Nurofen somewhere. I pull open the drawers and rummage around until I find a partly used sheet of capsules. Digging two tablets out of their foil casing, I pop them into my mouth and wash them down.

What I really want to do is get into bed. Mustn't wake Arun, though. Can't face a telling-off right now. I cross the corridor and lean against the bedroom door, gently pushing down the handle as I open it.

'Oh,' I say. 'Oh. You're awake.' He's lying with his head propped against an upright pillow, hands clasped behind his head, staring into space. 'You haven't been awake all night, have you?' I croak, my throat coated in crushed glass. 'I'm really sorry. I mean, *really* sorry.'

'Why are you dressed like that?'

'What? Oh, these are Valentina's. We went to a gig in Camden… did too much dancing. I didn't mean to get so drunk. It was ever so hot and I kept getting thirsty…' I make my way around the bed and climb in. 'Did we wake you up?'

'No.'

'Good.' I move across, nestling into his chest. He puts his arm around me, but there's no warmth in his cuddle. 'Are you cross with me?'

'No.'

'Are you sure? I wouldn't blame you.'

'You should drink water if you're thirsty.'

'Yeah, I know. It was stupid. On a work night too. If Valentina hadn't taken care of me, I could be lying in the gutter.'

He removes his arm and slides down the bed, turning away from me and drawing his knees up. 'Do you mind if we don't talk about her for once? I need to sleep,' he says. I take off my clothes and retrieve my pyjamas from under the pillow. As I put them on, I feel a strange, intangible distance opening up between us. I can't explain it.

I sleep very fitfully, but I don't think Arun sleeps at all. His breathing never deepens and there's a stiffness to his body, as if he's holding something in. At half seven, the alarm goes off, jolting me out of an odd, dancing dream.

His side of the bed is already empty. I can hear the shower pump whirring away in the bathroom. I'll make him some breakfast, I think. Eggs and bacon. Mushrooms, if we've got any. Grilled tomatoes. Coffee, toast. The thought of eating anything myself makes my stomach churn, but it won't stop me cooking. At least I hope it won't. I press my fingers against my temples; my brain is still swollen and tender and my mouth feels like the proverbial parrot's cage. Sitting up, I gingerly swing my legs round and stand. I feel a bit wobbly, but I'm okay. Unhooking my dressing gown from the back of the door, I slip it on and pad into the kitchen.

My movements are slow and heavy; every sound I make echoes through my head. I've only just managed to switch on the grill and fill the kettle when Arun comes in, already dressed in his work suit.

'What are you doing?' he asks.

'Cooking breakfast.'

'Why?' He looks at me, bewildered.

'To say sorry. For last night.'

'Please stop talking about last night.' He looks exhausted and stressed. 'I'll just have a cup of tea.'

Sighing, I turn off the grill and throw a tea bag into a mug. 'I think I just needed to let go of some stress. After the shock of Dad's death, finding out about Sophie and Valentina, the issues of telling Mum…'

'Josie!' He holds up a hand to stop me. 'I just want to say one thing. Please, please, I'm begging you, please don't have any more to do with Valentina.'

'I know she's a bit, well, off the scale,' I admit, pouring boiling water into his mug. 'I felt really uncomfortable about the whole thing, but she's okay, you know. She's just a bit… lost. Her heart's in the right place.'

'No, it's not. She doesn't care about you, she's just playing games.'

I open the fridge and take out the milk, my stomach rolling at the smell of the food. 'What do you mean? What games?'

'I don't trust her, that's all, and I'd really like you to stop seeing her.'

'Don't you start; you're as bad as Brett and Lisa!'

He frowns at me. 'What do you mean?'

I slam down the milk carton. 'I went to see them yesterday, told them about Dad. They pretended they didn't know, but I'm sure they did. Brett gave me a lecture about steering clear of Valentina. Why does everyone think they can tell me what to do all of a sudden?'

'I'm not telling you what to do.'

'Yes, you are!' My angry tones beat against the side of my head. 'It's up to me whether I see her or not. She's *my* sister.'

'Half-sister,' he corrects. 'And so what if she is? You can't be friends with her and carry on not telling your mum. It won't work. It'll end badly. And you'll be the one that gets hurt.'

'Oh, leave me alone. Stop nagging me.'

'I'm serious, Josie. Valentina is bad news. If you care about us, you'll stay away from her.'

He leaves the flat a few minutes later, without saying goodbye. I take his tea and sit down, putting my elbows on the table and hugging the mug in both hands. Why is he being like this? Just because we went dancing together on the spur of the moment. Okay, maybe I should have left it to the weekend, maybe I should have come home and cooked dinner like I usually do, sat with him watching box sets and flicking through Facebook. Maybe I should have been the dutiful little wife – although excuse me, we're not actually married. My head starts to thud again. I feel terrible, I can do without this.

I call the office and make a feeble excuse about eating something that's disagreed with me. It feels bad, lying to Jill, especially when she's been so kind to me since Dad's death, but I can't bear to tell her I've got the mother of all hangovers. I take a long shower, scrubbing off the black eyeliner and washing last night's excesses out of my hair. When I look in the bathroom mirror, I smile with relief. I look and feel like me again, not some poor copy of Valentina.

Going back to the bedroom, I dress in a simple pair of joggers and a white T-shirt, throwing my borrowed clothes into the laundry basket. I will have to get my other clothes back at some point. And then there's the key to Antrobus Street; I forgot to ask Valentina for it yesterday. Already there are physical connections between us – items borrowed and lent. Unfinished business. Conversations still to be had. I can't suddenly stop seeing her; I don't *want* to stop seeing her. Besides, she has no plans to go away.

True to form, she texts me shortly after ten am. *R u still alive? xxx*

*Just about*, I reply. Then, *Tx 4 looking after me last nite.*

*No probs. What sisters r 4. xxx*

I make myself a slice of dry toast, then take some more ibuprofen and lie down again on top of the bed. As I feel myself finally drifting off to sleep, my phone pings again.

*Want 2 meet 4 a drink 2nite? xxx*

I bite my lip. One, I'm never going to drink alcohol ever again, and two, Arun will go mental if I see Valentina again so soon. I lift my head and tap out a reply. *Sorry. Busy.*

*Tomorrow then?*

Oh dear, this is getting tricky. I don't want to be rude or make her feel rejected, especially after she was so lovely last night. But I don't want to fall out with Arun over her either. I'm feeling irritated with him because he's being an arse about this, but on the other hand… He's right about the difficulties of being friends with Valentina while Mum still doesn't know she exists. It almost makes me like Dad.

*Sorry*, I reply. *Arun and I going away for wknd.*

*Boo! Where?*

*Brighton.* It's the first place that comes into my head. We have some friends that have recently moved down there.

*Lucky u. Have a gt time. Bring me back some rock! C u v soon love. xxx*

Then a final text. *Still getting those hate texts btw. xxx*

I put the phone down on the bed and roll into my usual sleeping position. Is Arun right about her playing games? Did she drop in that killer line at the end to make me feel bad? But the threats are real, I've seen them on her phone… I don't know what to think. It's all so confusing…

After some much-needed sleep, I go for a walk around the local cemetery. It's a strange place to choose for a stroll, but it's the only green space around here, unless I trudge all the way to the Heath.

I like its peacefulness. People walk their dogs along the neat gravel paths and small children learn to ride their bikes. There are several benches, positioned in both sun and shade, and, in late summer, blackberries grow profusely around the graves, aided by the rich natural compost. This is probably where Dad would have been buried if Mum had wanted him brought back to London. It feels like he died yesterday, and years ago. So much has happened, so many things have changed.

I sink onto a bench in the turning circle by the old chapel. The pain in my head has dulled now but my stomach still feels sore. It's late afternoon, and although it's nearly May, the air feels chilly. I must talk to Arun properly this evening, I think. Something's wrong and I've got to get to the bottom of it.

He arrives back from work earlier than expected – usually he stays for a drink on Fridays. I take it as a sign that he wants to make up, and I greet him with a hug and a kiss.

'This is a nice surprise,' I say.

He releases me, then goes into the bedroom. 'I'm going straight back out again.' He bends down and pulls a small suitcase from under the bed.

I follow him and stand in the doorway. 'What's going on?'

'I've been invited to Bobby's stag weekend.'

'Bobby…?'

'Bobby from the contracts team.' He starts removing shirts from their hangers. 'I must have mentioned him before.'

'I don't think so.' There are dozens of guys where Arun works, most of them about his age and half of them getting married. 'You're going *now*?'

'Yup. Somebody dropped out at the last minute. We're driving up to Leamington Spa this evening. There's go-karting, shooting, paintballing, the usual, you know. Boys' stuff. You don't mind, do you?'

'Well… no, but I thought we were going to—' I bluster.

'We could probably do with a break from each other, don't you think?' He opens the drawer and takes out some underwear. 'It's been so intense these past few weeks.'

'You can say that again.'

'I'll be back on Sunday afternoon. Right… toothbrush, shaver… oh, yes, swimmers. There's an indoor pool, apparently.'

'Lucky you,' I say coolly as he brushes past me on the way to the bathroom. My spirits sink as I think of the lonely weekend stretching ahead. I lied to Valentina because I thought Arun would want us to spend it together, but he seems desperate to avoid me. Just because I let my hair down for once. Irritation pricks my skin. What's his problem?

# CHAPTER TWENTY-FOUR

*The Vikings were terrified of the draugr, or 'dead walkers', who rose from their graves to guard their treasure or avenge past enemies. They possessed supernatural powers and were extremely violent.*

The dream comes back again. Usually I wake up at the worst bit, when I'm flying through the air and crashing into the tree-house wall, but tonight it takes me all the way to the end. I'm lying on the floor and my sister is bending over me, her blue eyes as big as plates. She has blood all over her hands and she's screaming, 'Daddy! Daddy!' Suddenly everything goes into double vision, like looking in a distorted fairground mirror, and there are two Daddies and two Josies – or maybe it's two Valentinas? Everyone's shouting and crying and I can't work out who is real and who's the reflection.

Gradually the noise begins to fade and I start to feel calmer and lighter. So light that I float out of my body and up to the ceiling. I waft around, looking down on myself. A pool of blood is seeping out from the back of my head and I'm lying completely still, like when we play sleeping lions. And then I realise that if I don't get back into my body, I'm going to die. I start to panic, flapping my arms and legs in mid-air. I try to cry out to the others below, *Pull me down! Pull me down!* But the words are silent and nobody hears me.

I sit bolt upright, gasping for air and drenched in sweat. I reach for my bottle of water and pour half of it over my head. My eyes blink in shock as the cold liquid runs down my face, dripping off my chin and into my cleavage. I pat myself dry with the end of the sleeping bag, then reach for my cigarettes. We're not allowed to smoke inside – health and safety – but nobody takes any notice. I light up and inhale deeply. The tip of the fag burns like a glow worm, comforting me in the darkness. For all its nightmarish qualities, the dream feels more real than ever. How did I ever let Dr Bannister convince me it was a figment of my imagination? I must have been mad.

I remember every one of those sessions in full, high-definition detail. The psychological research project was borough-wide. There were about eight high-achieving troublemakers in my group, all from other schools. We began with a workshop, during which we were supposed to get to know each other. This mainly involved throwing a ball around a circle and playing word-association games. We also attempted some simple trust exercises, but they had to be abandoned before somebody got hurt.

After a break (pieces of fruit and bottled water), we had to sit at desks and fill in a questionnaire, ticking boxes in response to various statements. *I feel nervous or anxious. People annoy me. I feel bored and restless. I think about harming myself. All the time? Some of the time? Hardly ever? Never?* My 'all the time' score was the highest of any kid on the research project, which put me straight through to the next round. I'd already worked out that would happen, which is why I'd exaggerated the intensity of my feelings. I was very competitive, even when it came to being mentally ill.

The most troubled and interesting among us were given individual follow-up sessions with the doctors. They would take place at the hospital, as part of their normal clinics, and last an hour. I managed to wangle an eleven a.m. slot so that I could take the whole morning off school. For me, it was a bit of a laugh, but Mum took it way too seriously. She was ashamed that I was seeing a shrink, like it reflected badly on her as a mother, and made me promise not to tell the grandparents, or even Dad. She fled to work and I took myself to the hospital, waiting on the seats outside the consulting rooms with all the other nutters, feeling rather special and important. I was fourteen and I thought I knew it all.

A little after eleven, I was called in. Disappointingly, there was no psychiatrist's couch, and after pacing about, I was persuaded to sit in a chair. To begin with, I decided to pretend that I didn't want to talk. Dr Bannister didn't seem to mind, just looked calmly out of the window at the birds flying past and the tops of the trees swaying in the wind. It was like we were playing a game, to see who was going to crack first. And annoyingly, it was me.

'Psychiatrists are interested in dreams, aren't they?' I said. I'd watched a documentary about Freud on YouTube. 'Do you want to know about my recurring dream?'

'Only if you want to tell me,' said Dr Bannister, still looking out of the window. So I launched into my well-rehearsed and graphic account of the tree-house fight. The doctor's ears pricked up when I mentioned that the other little girl in my dream looked exactly like me, and even started to take notes.

'Are you always the same girl, or do you swap?'

'Oh, I'm always the victim.'

'You say this is a recurring dream – how often do you get it?'

'A lot,' I replied, adding, 'especially when I'm stressed.'

'How often is a lot? Every night? Twice a week? Once a month?'

'I don't know exactly, I don't keep a record. Once every few weeks, I guess. I've had it for years and years. I think it must be a suppressed memory.'

'Why?'

'Because I have this scar.' I stood up and waltzed across the room, lifting my hair and presenting the back of my head. 'It's hard to see, but it's there. You have to feel it. Go on.'

'No, thank you. I believe you... Please sit down.'

I returned to my seat, feeling excited that at last someone was actually listening to me. 'I'm pretty sure I got this in some tree house somewhere. But my dad says I got it falling off a climbing frame in the park.'

'And you don't think you did?'

I shrugged. 'All I remember is waking up in the hospital with a head injury. Everything else before that is a blank.'

'Why do you think your father would lie to you?'

'Because he doesn't want me to know I have a twin sister.'

'Right... Can we just backtrack here? You think you have a twin sister?'

'No,' I answered steadily. 'I *know* I have a twin sister.'

Dr Bannister wrote a note and looked it at for a few seconds. 'Were you born a twin? Was your mother pregnant with twins but only you survived?'

'I don't think so. Anyway, that doesn't make sense. In my memory she's about four years old. Of course, she'll be fourteen now, like me.'

'I see... yes... so where do you think she is at this moment?'

'No idea. Dead? Adopted? I've asked Mum hundreds of times, but she keeps telling me I'm imagining her. And Dad says it's a case of psychological projection, whatever that means. In other words, he thinks I've got a screw loose. He can talk. He thinks he's a fucking Viking!'

Dr Bannister bristled at that. I came to learn that psychiatrists don't like people making amateur diagnoses. 'Well, I think that's enough for one day. You've done really well, Valentina. Everything you've told me has been extremely illuminating.'

I grinned from ear to ear like I'd been given a gold star. I thought the doctor was giving my theory full consideration, but in fact I was scoring top marks for 'Do you think your patient is totally out of their mind?'

It's still the middle of the night. Everyone else around me is asleep and I daren't go down to the kitchen for a cup of tea, not at this dead hour. I lie back on my pillow and attempt one of my breathing exercises, but my lungs feel sticky and I end up having a coughing fit. Maybe I should try some mindfulness. Lots of people say it's really helpful for controlling mood swings, but they always say it in such a superior way, it puts me off. I don't want to be fully in my mind, I want to be out of it. I want oblivion. Unfortunately, I can't afford oblivion at the moment.

I lounge about with my thoughts until half six and then get up. Half past bloody six on a Saturday morning and I'm up and dressed. Anyone would think I had a job to go to. With a bit of luck, one of the cafés on the Finchley Road will be open – I don't care which one, as long as they serve hot, sweet black coffee. I padlock my cell and go downstairs, letting myself out. Some poor fucker is sleeping in the alleyway, encased in pieces of cardboard. There but for the grace of a God I don't believe in…

As my bad luck would have it, none of the cafés on either side of the tube station have their shutters up. The morning air is sharp, so I take shelter in the station ticket hall – studying the timetable and route map, spinning the carousel of greetings cards in the newsagent's, leaning against the tiled wall. I think of Josie and Arun, snug in their king-size bed in their boutique Brighton hotel, Arun's secret lying between them like a venomous snake.

I know I shouldn't have done it, but I genuinely couldn't help it. It's part of who I am. There's a dark monster inside me that

I can't control. He makes me court danger, take huge risks, do things I later regret. People get hurt. I lose friends and bits of family. They think I don't care, but I do. I'd stop the monster if I could. Because what nobody realises is it's me he hurts the most.

I cross the ticket hall and stare into the shop that does key-cutting and shoe repairs. Was Josie telling the truth last night, when she said they were going away for the weekend? She didn't mention it before. What if she's lying because she doesn't want to see me? What if she's only pretending to like me? The thoughts bite into me.

No… she wouldn't do that.

Would she?

Perhaps I should go and check.

I leave the station and start walking up the lovely Finchley Road, filling my lungs with traffic fumes. Fortunately, the air feels fresher after the junction at the top of the long hill, when most of the vehicles veer off left to join the M1. I grab a coffee from a just-opened Costa and carry it between scalding fingers, stopping every few metres to take a sip.

Josie and Arun's flat is in a block down a leafy side road. I take the stairs up to the fourth floor and walk along the outer balcony, slowing my pace and tiptoeing as I get closer to their flat. The bedroom curtains are drawn and there are no lights on. I crouch down under the window and listen for sounds of life: doors opening, conversation, music playing, a toilet flushing. But I can't hear a thing. Either they're away, as Josie said, or they'll still asleep.

I can't stay here and risk being seen. I'll have to find somewhere to hide, so I can keep watch. I walk back to the dark, windowless stairwell and light a cigarette. Can't be caught here either. Shit… I plonk my way down the steps, feeling a bit stupid because I haven't resolved the issue one way or another. There are wheelie bins on the ground floor, tucked under the stairs, one for general waste and another for recycling. I could hide there, perhaps. Then if Josie or Arun come down the stairs, I'll definitely see them. Unless they come down to put their rubbish out, in which case they'll definitely see me too.

This is hopeless. I'm being an idiot. Why am I always so suspicious? Josie has no reason to lie to me. She's not a lying kind of person. Cut her open and you'll see goodness all the way through. We are black and white, yin and yang, form and shadow. She is the girl I want to be, yet am afraid of becoming.

Throwing my cigarette stub on the floor, I march quickly out of the block and jog down the road. My phone buzzes in my back pocket and I take it out. It's another text from Private Number.

*You've no reason to be here. Get away from the flat.*

I gasp, sweeping around and looking behind me. It's happened again. Everywhere I go, they know. But how? There's nobody here. The street is quiet and empty. Not even a net curtain is twitching. I bend over, the phone trembling in my hand like a grenade. I want to throw it behind me and run. It pings again.

*I won't warn you again. Leave now, or you'll be sorry.*

My sweaty fingers stick on the letters as I type. *Why are you threatening me?*

*I'm not. I'm trying to protect you.*

Yeah, like fuck, I think. Instead, I type, *From what?*

*A repetition of the past.*

My brain jolts. What past? I could think of a thousand things I don't want to repeat. What do they mean? It's like they're inside my head, vandalising my memories. A procession of faces flashes before me: friends I've pissed off, boyfriends I've cheated on, strangers I've scammed, doctors I've attacked, even kids I fought in the playground. Maybe this is nothing to do with Dad's darkest fucking secret.

Another message jumps onto the screen.

*You're giving me no choice…*

Then another.

*I'm very close.*

I spin around, my eyes darting in every direction. *Who are you?* Where *are you?*

The phone pings a final time.

*Run, Valentina, run.*

I take off up the hill, thundering along the pavement, dodging lamp posts and letter boxes, looking this way and that. My legs feel heavy and my lungs are bursting. I can't see for the hair flapping across my face. Is someone running after me? My heart is thumping so loudly I can't hear anything else. Daren't look back – got to keep going. It's like someone's planted a bomb and it's about to go off in my face.

Now I'm on a random side road. I don't know how I got here, haven't a clue where I am. Please let it not be a dead end. A stitch is stabbing into my side, forcing me to slow down. I stagger onwards, bent double, breathing hard through my nose. I turn a corner and suddenly I'm at the top of the street and the busy Finchley Road is ahead of me. Nobody will attack me out here. Thank God. I'm safe.

I make it to the pedestrian crossing and press the button. WAIT lights up in green as an endless stream of traffic shoots past. A black figure on a shiny vintage bike roars towards me; the rider is wearing an old-style helmet and a full beard. Behind him, a dark saloon car is accelerating towards the junction.

Then I realise it's aiming right at me.

# CHAPTER TWENTY-FIVE

*Every Viking had to own a sword, axe, spear and bow, plus three dozen arrows. He also carried a wooden shield, in the middle of which was an iron boss – useful for forcing one's enemies to the ground.*

I've woken up in a sour mood. Why did Arun rush off last night, with barely so much as a discussion about the stag do? It's so unlike him. Usually we plan our weekends well in advance. I know we hadn't booked anything in for this weekend, but I was looking forward to having some time with him. Everything's been so hectic and traumatic since Dad died, we've hardly had a chance to catch our breath.

With nobody to share a traditional cooked Saturday breakfast with, I settle for a couple of slices of toast. It's still early – much earlier than I usually get up at the weekend. I try to imagine Arun in the hotel in Leamington Spa, helping himself to rubbery scrambled eggs and watery tomatoes from the buffet. He didn't text me when he arrived last night. I hope he's okay. I reach for my phone and press his tiny image on my contacts list. The phone rings out, then goes to voicemail. That's not unusual. He probably can't hear it ringing above the boisterous gaggle of his fellow stags. Even so, his failure to pick up is irritating; he should know that I'd be expecting to speak to him. Actually, he should be the one calling me.

He's not lying to me, is he? The thought strikes me in the guts and a sick feeling nestles in the pit of my stomach. I put down my half-eaten toast. I don't have any reason to feel suspicious, but he was in a very strange mood last night, dashing in and out of the flat in about five minutes, rattling on about some work mate I've never even heard of. The more I think about it, the odder it seems: to go away on a stag weekend at such short notice, even if somebody did drop out. And these things cost a fortune... Would I be crazy to check up on him?

I scroll further through my list of contacts, looking for his work colleagues. There's a guy called Ned we see from time to time; I get on well with his girlfriend. Ned might well be on the weekend too. If I call him, I could just say I've been trying to call Arun and not getting any answer – pretend to be worried about him. I take a deep breath and press dial.

'Josie?' His voice sounds like thick soup – I've obviously woken him up.

'Hi, Ned. Sorry to call you so early,' I chirp. 'I thought you'd all be up by now, you know, for the paintballing or whatever.'

'Paintballing?'

'Oh. Sorry. Aren't you on the stag weekend with Arun?'

'Wha'? Er, no... What stag weekend?'

My hand starts to sweat around the phone. 'Oh, one of the guys at work... Bobby.'

There's a long pause on the other end. 'Oh right, yeah, Bobby, I remember...' he says eventually.

I swallow hard as I realise that Ned is a better friend than he is a liar. 'Oh well, never mind,' I say brightly, trying to sound as if I've fallen for it. 'Sorry if I've woken you up.'

'No, it's okay. Needed to get up anyway... Take care, Josie.' The line clicks into silence.

The bastard. The shit. Why is he doing this? Haven't I been put through enough lately? I start pacing about, curling my hands into fists. So who's he seeing? How long has it been going on? My brain goes into overdrive as I think back over the past few months, reassessing every time he stayed out late or didn't pick up when I called. What about his Wednesday football? *Don't make me give up my football; it's the highlight of my week.* I bet it fucking is. Maybe that's another lie. I grab my phone and start searching for his football club on the net, but I'm so angry I can't remember its name.

Suddenly the flat feels tiny, its walls closing in on me. I can hardly breathe. Running into the hallway, I grab my jacket and bag and slip on my shoes. Then, taking my key off the rack of hooks, I march out, slamming the door behind me.

I don't know where I'm going, just that I have to get away. My whole body feels charged, like an electric current is flooding through me, making my fingertips burn. I run down the concrete steps and burst onto the front path. What should I do? Go and see Mum? No… too difficult. Call a friend, perhaps. As I stride along towards the Finchley Road, I try to think of who I might ring. Nobody springs to mind. I don't want to be one of those sobbing women that hijacks their friend's weekend, getting pissed and stuffing chocolate cake into my mouth, wailing, 'I think my boyfriend's cheating on me and I don't know what to do!' It's all so demeaning.

No. I'll do something more constructive. Buy a load of expensive clothes. Get my hair done, have a manicure, pedicure – the works. By the time he gets home tomorrow, I'll be looking so gorgeous he'll regret it. What am I saying? Do I want to fight to get him back? No way. If he thinks he can treat me like Dad treated Mum, he's got another think coming. How can he do this to me? Especially right now, when all this shit is happening in my life.

As I turn the corner, growing angrier and more indignant with every step, I see flashing blue lights ahead. A couple of ambulances have pulled onto the pavement by the junction with the Finchley Road. A police car is there too, and a small crowd has gathered. It looks like there's been a road accident. My fury evaporates as I worry that someone's been badly hurt, and I slow my pace. I don't want to be a rubbernecker, but it's my only route to the bus stop.

A policeman is unrolling a reel of plastic tape. He ties one end around a small tree and then looks around for somewhere to attach the other. Behind him, the traffic is stacking up and people are beeping their horns with the usual London impatience. Another police officer is trying her best to protect the scene. 'There's nothing to see,' she shouts. 'Everything's under control.' Paramedics are gathered around a body in the middle of the road and I can just make out a leg clad in black leather. It's a biker.

'What's happened?' I ask a guy holding on to a small, anxious dog.

'Hit-and-run, apparently. Disgusting, isn't it? A pedestrian got caught up in it too. I think she's okay, though.' He points to a crumpled figure wrapped in a foil blanket, sitting on a low wall by the traffic lights.

'Oh my God!' I burst through the tape.

'Stay back!' warns the police officer, coming towards me.

'That's my sister over there! Please let me go to her.' She nods, letting me pass. I rush over and crouch down. 'It's me! Are you okay?' Valentina lifts her head and pushes back her hair. 'What happened?'

'I was waiting at the lights when this car just shot up and went on the pavement, then swerved off… The motorbike was in the way…' She shivers. 'Poor fucker. Is he dead?'

'Hope not.' I pull the foil blanket across her chest. 'You're shaking. Are you hurt?'

'Just my knees and elbows. I flung myself out of the way just in time.'

'Jesus, you could easily have been killed.'

'Yeah, he had a fucking good try…'

'So what happened, did he jump the lights?'

'No!' She gives me an incredulous look. 'Don't you understand? I was the target.' I let out a nervous laugh. 'I'm not joking. It was for real.'

'No… that can't be right. It must have been a boy racer – they're terrible around here. Rich kids with sports cars…'

She glares at me. 'It was an ordinary car and it drove straight at me.'

'Did you see the driver?'

'No… it all happened too quickly.'

'Well, don't worry about it too much.' I sit next to her, putting my arm around her shoulders. 'Honestly, I'm sure nobody deliberately tried to mow you down. That kind of thing doesn't happen in real life.'

'It does in mine,' she retorts. 'Someone's out for my blood.'

'Don't say that to the police, they'll think you're a bit… you know…'

'I'm not mad.' She dips into her back pocket and pulls out her phone, handing it to me. 'See for yourself.'

I reluctantly read the messages. Their tone is a lot more threatening than the previous ones, and when I get to the last text – *Run, Valentina, run* – a chill goes through me. 'Oh… see what you mean. No wonder you were scared. Perhaps you should mention it.'

'No way! What if it's a gangster from Manchester?' She lowers her voice. 'I owe a shitload of money.'

I sigh. 'Well, it's up to you…' I scroll through the messages again. *Get away from the flat.* Do they mean my place? Oh God, what has she got herself mixed up in? 'Valentina? Were you at my flat earlier?'

'No! Anyway, aren't you supposed to be in Brighton?' Her bright eyes flash a warning.

'It got cancelled. Arun's gone on a stag weekend.' No need to go into that right now, I think, giving the handset back.

There's activity in the road. I look over at the motorcyclist and briefly see an image of Dad in my head. The paramedics have lifted the guy onto a stretcher and are wheeling him carefully towards one of the ambulances. He raises a black-leather arm. That's hopeful, that's a really good sign. The back doors close and the ambulance moves off, its siren blaring as it forces its way through the heavy queue of traffic to turn right.

One of the remaining paramedics walks up to us and says, 'How are you feeling, love? Shall we pop you over to A and E?'

'No, I'm okay,' Valentina says. 'Don't much like hospitals.'

'Hmm…' He crouches down. 'Why don't we go to the ambulance and I'll check you over.'

I wait while the paramedic cleans her wounds and applies large white plasters to her knees and elbows. She emerges from the ambulance, gives them back the foil blanket and hobbles over to me heroically.

A police officer comes across. 'How're you doing?' Valentina shivers theatrically. 'Well, I won't trouble you any more now. I've got your details. I'll give you a ring later and we can arrange for you to make a witness statement. In the meantime, if you remember any more details about the car or the driver, please get in touch straight away.' He hands her a small card, then walks back to his colleague.

'Fuck that,' she says as soon as he's out of earshot. 'I gave him a false number.'

'Do you want to come back to my place?' I ask.

'Please.'

She grabs my arm and we hobble slowly down the road. I've no idea whether she's right about what happened, but she seems quite shaken – her shiny armour scraped and dented.

'Hang on, sis.' She stops and takes out her phone again, removing the back panel. I watch as she digs her nails under the SIM card and flicks it free. 'Should have done this long ago.' Taking out her lighter, she holds the tiny chip up to the flame and lets it burn black.

# CHAPTER TWENTY-SIX

*Unusually for the times, Viking women were allowed to own and inherit property. The dividing line between men's and women's responsibilities lay at the doorway to the house. Men were in charge of everything outdoors and the women took responsibility for everything indoors.*

Valentina installs herself on the sofa while I make a cup of tea. 'I'm so glad your trip to Brighton was cancelled,' she says, rolling up her jeans and peering at her plasters.

'Yes, me too,' I say, busying myself with the kettle. She still hasn't explained what she was doing around here. Somehow I just don't see Valentina as an early-morning jogger. I have a strong suspicion that she didn't believe my excuses and came to check me out. Hard to criticise her for that when I did exactly the same with Arun.

'So how come Arun's gone to a stag weekend?' she asks, examining her elbows now.

'Somebody dropped out at the last minute, so he took their place.'

'That was lucky.' She takes a mug off me. 'Bit bad abandoning you, though. I wouldn't stand for that.'

'Oh, I don't mind.' I can feel my face flushing – my lies must look so obvious. But fortunately Valentina doesn't continue on the Brighton theme. I sit in the armchair and drink my tea. 'You need a new SIM card. We could go and buy one this afternoon. If you're up to it, that is.'

She flicks her hair behind her shoulder. 'I'd love to, but I can't afford it.'

I can't help but frown. 'What about that hundred quid I lent you?'

'It all went on food and stuff,' she says. 'I need a new phone, but pay-as-you-go is insanely expensive, and nobody will give me a contract with my credit rating.'

'Just get a new SIM for your old contract.'

'It was in Dad's name, he paid all the bills. If I try to change things, they'll find out that my beloved father and benefactor is no more.'

'Oh, yes… hadn't thought of that.' I look down into my mug.

'Never mind, it's over now. I'm free and phoneless. Whoop!' she adds sarcastically.

'No, you've got to have a phone; nobody can manage without one these days. I'll help you,' I find myself saying without really thinking. 'It'll have to be a cheap SIM-only contract; I think you can get the basic level for about ten pounds a month.'

She sits up, almost spilling her tea. 'Really? You'd do that for me?' Her eyes shine with tears. 'You'd really do that for me?'

'Of course. You can have the account put in your name when you start earning. Just don't go over the call limit.'

'I won't, Brownie promise!' She holds up her fingers.

I look at her doubtfully. 'You were in the Brownies?'

'Only for three weeks. They chucked me out for attacking another girl with the giant toadstool.'

'No way, you just made that up,' I laugh.

'No, it's true! I was expelled from everywhere. I went to two different primary schools and three secondary schools. I'm a fucking nightmare.'

'No, you're not.'

'Oh, I am,' she insists, swinging her legs round and standing up. 'Shall we go shopping, then?'

There's a small phone shop in St John's Wood – they sort of know me, and there aren't the long queues you get in Oxford Street – so I suggest we go there on the bus. Valentina gets a bit wobbly as we reach the junction with the main road, but I steer her quickly past the scene. There's no sign of the accident apart from a free-standing board appealing for witnesses.

As we sit on the bus, I find myself mulling over the morning's strange events. Did somebody *really* try to run Valentina over? It seems unlikely, and yet those texts were pretty vicious. She's obviously been mixing with some nasty criminals in Manchester. Drug dealers, I expect – very bad people to owe money to. I glance across at her curled form on the opposite seat, eyes closed, boots on the upholstery. She looks childlike and vulnerable. But she's got herself into this mess. I've got enough to worry about without taking on her problems as well.

Unzipping the inside pocket of my bag, I take out the piece of card I found at Dad's crash site and reread it for what feels like the hundredth time. It's like a cryptic clue in a crossword. On the surface, its meaning is clear. Someone – probably the person that wrote this message, who was possibly the woman at the funeral – threatened to expose Dad's secret family. He crashed into a tree because he couldn't face our finding out. But the more I stare at the words, the more I see deeper, different possibilities. What if the darkest secret is something we can't even imagine? And what if his death wasn't suicide, and not an accident either?

I quickly put the card away. I'm letting Valentina's sense of the melodramatic infect me. Putting two and two together and coming up with a hundred and four. 'Wake up,' I say, nudging her leg. 'We get off at the next stop.'

It doesn't take long to set Valentina up with a new SIM-only contract in my name. She's only got 200 minutes on it and a very limited data allowance, but she assures me that'll be plenty. 'I'll only use it for finding a job,' she says. 'And calling you, of course.' She takes my arm as we walk back to the main road. 'So this is your 'hood, is it?'

I laugh. 'I suppose you could call it that. I was brought up on that side street.' I point over the road to Melrose Gardens. 'And my old primary school is round the corner, in that direction.'

She pauses, looking around, as if imagining me walking along the pavement in my school uniform, book bag in one hand and plastic lunch box in the other. 'Does your mum still live in the same house?'

'Yes.'

'Will you show me? Please? Just the outside. I want to see where Dad lived when he wasn't with us.'

I hesitate. 'I don't think that's a very good idea. What if my mum saw you? It's too risky.'

'We'll go on the other side and walk straight past. Come on, you've seen where I grew up. It's only fair…'

She squeezes my upper arm and drags me across the road. I don't know why I'm allowing her to do this. If Mum sees us, it'll be catastrophic. I shouldn't really have come anywhere near the house – what was I thinking? We turn down Melrose Gardens, a leafy street full of large, elegant houses, most of them now converted into flats.

'Which number?' she asks.

'Hold on. Let me go and see if her car's there. If it's not, I'll wave and you can join me, okay?'

'Suppose so…' She rolls her eyes.

I carry on down the street, almost hoping to see Mum's dark grey Prius parked up outside the house. But there's no sign of it.

I raise my arm and signal to Valentina. She immediately scampers towards me, her knee injury briefly forgotten. Her blue eyes pop out on stalks as she takes in the large Victorian terrace before us.

'Fuck me, it's enormous! How much is it worth?'

'I don't know. A lot.' I daren't tell her that it probably runs into the millions.

'And it all belongs to your mum now?'

'Yeah… There may still be a mortgage, but maybe that'll be paid off.'

'Wow,' she says, open-mouthed. 'I'd love to go inside.'

'I've got a key, so … we'd have to be super quick. I mean, I've no idea where my mum is; she could come back at any…' I stop myself. What am I doing? This is madness. I'm letting Valentina infect me. And yet I know that I want to show her around. I want to show her what Jerry Macauliffe's *real* home looked like, not the pretend show home he shared with Sophie. I secretly want Valentina to imagine him in his natural habitat.

'Come on then, what are we waiting for?' She pulls me up the front steps. I take my key ring out of my bag and nervously open the door. We rush in and the alarm immediately goes off. 'Oh fuck! We've been caught!' she cries, dancing around. I punch in the code and the noise stops.

'Quick tour. Don't disturb anything.' We run through the downstairs – the front room, where Dad played the piano; the kitchen, where he didn't do much at all; the conservatory, where he languished with a glass of red and chatted to Mum while she cooked. I take her upstairs, pointing out the hole in the landing ceiling and the chipped paintwork on the banisters.

We go into his study in the small bedroom, where my heart starts to hurt because his desk has been tidied. Then we pop our heads into my old bedroom. The walls are still painted dark blue with lime green in the alcoves, but all the posters have gone and the shelves are empty. We don't bother with the second floor – it's a spare bedroom mainly used for storage – and Valentina doesn't seem very interested in the bathroom. Our last stop is Mum and Dad's bedroom, which overlooks the front of the house. It feels quite bad to be coming in here, because this is Mum's private space. I go to the window to check that the car hasn't turned up, while Valentina walks around the bed, staring at the pillows.

'I never really thought about where he was sleeping when he wasn't with us,' she says.

'Well, I thought he was living in Antrobus Street,' I remind her. I cross back to the door. 'We should go now.'

'Can we see the garden? Please?'

I sigh. 'Okay, but we've got to be really quick. We're pushing our luck as it is.' We go back downstairs and into the kitchen. I take the key from the cutlery drawer and unlock the back door. Valentina follows me down the cobbled side path and into the garden. 'Don't go any further,' I say, keeping my voice down. 'Don't want the neighbours to see us.'

'I thought it would be bigger,' she says.

'Most gardens around here are tiny.'

'Hmm… I was expecting a tree house.'

'Sorry, no tree.' I gesture at the high brick wall at the end of the small lawn. 'Why did you think there'd be a tree house?'

She shrugs her shoulders. 'Oh, I just have this memory of us playing in one when we were little.'

'You and me? But we didn't know each other then.'

'That's the thing, you see, I think we did. At least, we met, maybe only the once. Dad brought us together.' She looks around, disappointed. 'I'd got it into my head that it was here…'

'My aunt and uncle used to have a tree house in their garden,' I say. 'They took it down years ago – my cousins still haven't forgiven them!' I tug at her sleeve. 'We should go.'

She turns to me, her face suddenly alight. 'Your aunt and uncle – are they my aunt and uncle too?'

'Well, yes… Brett is Dad's older brother. I told you I went to see them.'

She gasps, lifting her hand to her mouth. 'Does he look like him?'

'Not much, not these days. I think he used to.' I hop from one foot to the other. 'Please, we need to go.'

'The two daddies,' she whispers to herself. 'The two daddies in my dream.'

I've no idea what she's going on about, but she needs to shift her arse now. 'Sorry, Valentina, we've got to get out of here. I'm feeling really nervous.' I reach forward and take her hand, pulling her back down the path, through the house and out of the front door.

# CHAPTER TWENTY-SEVEN

*If a Viking man wanted to divorce his wife, he simply announced his intention in front of a group of witnesses. Wives could divorce their husbands in the same way.*

As we run down the front path, I can hear the beep of the alarm setting. The sound seems to continue in my head, placing me on high alert. Josie is trying to hurry me away from the scene, but my legs refuse to keep pace. I can't process information of this magnitude and run at the same time.

'Slow down! My knee's hurting…' I stagger to a halt.

Josie looms over me, hands on hips. 'Please, Valentina… I want to get away from here. My mum could drive around the corner at any moment.'

'Just chill for a second, will you? It's okay. We got away with it.'

'I won't feel relaxed until we're on the bus.' Josie looks around shiftily. 'I should never have agreed to take you there. It was stupid.'

I straighten up and rest my weight against a lamp post. 'Sometimes, sis, you just have to live a little, you know? Jesus, anyone would think I'd asked you to rob a bank.'

After a few moments, we continue our escape and reach the safety of the main road, taking refuge in the bus shelter. The illuminated display tells us our bus will arrive in three minutes, which seems very quick to me, but makes my sister groan in frustration. I perch on the bench and she stands in front of me, hiding me from the road. If she was *that* worried about being caught, why did she agree to it in the first place? But I don't say anything. I want these few minutes for thinking.

I have an uncle. His name is Brett. And this uncle once had a tree house at the bottom of his garden. I can see it now. A home-made affair. Rough wooden planks nailed horizontally together with pegs and bolts joining overlapping pieces. A longship, tossed into the air during a thunderstorm and caught high in the branches of the tree. It lists to one side as if permanently stuck on a wave of green. I'm standing on the ground, looking upwards. The rope ladder swings before my nose. The other little girl puts her foot on the bottom rung. *Come on, let's go up.*

For many years, I sewed my dreams together out of the ragbag of Dad's Viking tales. Fearless seafarers and warriors, one-eyed Odin with his eight-legged horse and Thor with his hammer that bashed the clouds together. They thrilled and terrified me at the same time. But the tree-house dream was different. It was very specific and the details were always the same. I wanted it to look like a longship on the inside, but it wouldn't obey my wishes. It carried on looking like an ordinary playhouse, with coloured cushions and a fluffy rug. There were no barrels of mead or piles of weapons. No hairy warriors straining at the oars. The other little girl in the dream – who Dr Bannister insisted was me – was always there, no matter how hard I tried to get rid of her. She climbed the ladder ahead of me and pranced around, showing everything off like it all belonged to her. But now I know it wasn't her tree house at all; it was her uncle's. *Our* uncle's. And it wasn't a dream, it was a memory.

'About time,' says Josie, tapping my shoulder. The bus draws up at the kerb and we climb aboard, trundling northwards on this awful road I can't seem to get away from.

How many times did Josie and I play together? I wonder. Maybe it was only that one time. Why did Dad do it? For a dare, perhaps. My father loved doing dangerous things. Or maybe he wanted – *needed*, even – to see us standing side by side. To make him feel complete for once. Or perhaps to check whether we still looked like twins in the flesh. Whatever his motive, he took a massive risk and it all went horribly wrong: his daughters fought and one nearly died. 'We almost lost you,' said Mum, when I woke up in the hospital. Sometimes I think she wished they had.

I gaze out of the window as we pass the Victorian apartment blocks, my fingers straying to the hidden scar on the back of my head. Should I show Josie my battle wound? No, I don't think so. Everyone else in this strange, fractured family has secrets – this is mine.

'Do you want to go home or back to my place?' she asks, pulling me away from my thoughts.

'I'll come back with you, if that's okay.'

The bus stops right outside the Crossed Keys, unloading and reloading identical-looking passengers, and I think briefly of the revolting wooden cell that lies behind the boarded-up windows. I don't know how I'm going to find the money for next month's rent. Josie and Arun probably pay more than double that for their one-bedroom flat, but it's more than twice as nice, and there's two of them, *and* they've both got proper jobs.

I steal a glance at her, her face clean of make-up, hair tied back in a smug ponytail, jogging up and down contentedly as the bus trudges up the hill. Being brought up in that huge house in one of the best parts of London, going to some fancy private school and getting top marks in her exams… she's had it so fucking easy compared to me. How come we ended up this way round? I hate bleating, but it's just not fair. The ghost of my father whispers in my head: *Life can't always be fair, Valentina…* I accept that's true, but why does the unfairness never come out in my favour?

'Are you okay?' Josie asks, pressing the bell for our stop. 'You've hardly said a word since we left the house.'

'Just tired, that's all.' I follow her off the bus. 'I nearly got run over today, remember?'

'Of course. You're probably still in shock. We'll have a quiet night in. I'll cook. You can stay the night, if you like.'

She 'rustles up' some tuna pasta and we curl up on the sofa together, armed with the remote control and her Netflix subscription. There aren't many series she hasn't already watched with Arun, and most of her movie suggestions I reject for being too girlie.

'Hey, look, there's this Russian Viking film that came out last year,' I say scrolling through the international list. 'We've *got* to watch that.'

She wrinkles her nose. 'It'll be violent and incomprehensible.'

'So? We can imagine we're watching it with Dad and point out all the historical inaccuracies. You must have done that, surely, when you were a kid?'

'Yes, but we're not kids any more, are we?'

I see the two of us spinning around the ship in the sky, fighting to the death over a rag doll. 'No, sis,' I reply. 'No… we're not.'

We compromise on a Hollywood drama starring Meryl Streep, which is as boring as fuck, but I don't care. I'm enjoying the novelty of performing sisterhood. We lean into each other, stretching our long legs out and resting them on the coffee table. Our feet look as if they come from the same four-legged animal. We both have bony, flat toes, the littlest one curving slightly inwards to its neighbours. We sip wine; we make popcorn and take it in turns to hold the bowl. It feels almost normal. Like we've known each other all our lives.

I spend the night on the sofa, wrapped in the spare duvet, advising myself not to even think about tomorrow. But, inevitably, it's all I think about as I lie in the dark, listening to the night sounds. The drama is winding up like a spring. Arun will come back from his 'stag weekend' – if Josie believes that, she'll believe anything – and I need to decide whether to be here to greet him. I've no doubt that he ran away for the weekend. It's tempting to stick around to see how he reacts when he walks through the door and finds me here.

He won't tell her he fucked me, will he? Some men are compulsive confessors. Just can't keep their mouths shut. I've had it before; it's never worth it, causes far more damage than was done in the first place. I shift position, turning over and pressing my nose into the back of the sofa. I really hope he doesn't play the 'oh poor guilty me' card, because if he does, I'll come out as the main villain, Josie will never speak to me again, and it'll wreck all my plans. Which would be such a shame, because we're getting on so well…

It's about half four the next afternoon. Josie is tapping away on Facebook, pretending not to worry about where Arun's got to, and I'm sitting cross-legged on the floor, scrubbing my chipped nails with remover. Usually I just bung on another layer, but Josie doesn't have black in her collection of colours, so I'm going naked for a change. I hold my hand up to the light and frown at the result. I look like an alien, with extra-long pointy fingers.

We both glance up when we hear the sound of a key turning in the front door. 'He's here!' she says, over-brightly. I can smell her nervousness as he enters the living room.

'Valentina!' He scowls. 'What are you doing here?'

'She's been keeping me company.' Josie lifts the laptop off her thighs and lays it on the floor, then stands and walks over to him, kissing him on the mouth. 'Tea?' She's playing it cool, I'll give her that. I watch her flip the lid off the kettle to check the water level and press the 'on' switch. 'Poor Valentina was nearly run over yesterday.'

'Was that you?' I say under my breath.

'I wish.'

Luckily Josie can't hear us under the roar of the kettle. She searches in the cupboard for clean mugs. 'Did you have a good time?'

'Yes, great, thanks.'

'What was it, paintballing and go-karting? Sounds fun,' I say. 'Show us the photos, Arun.'

'I didn't take any.' He checks that Josie's not looking our way and shoots me a death stare.

'Really?' I arch my eyebrows. 'You know what they say... Sorry, no pics, didn't happen.'

'I didn't want my phone to get broken, okay? I left it in my room.' Not a bad excuse, I think. I wonder how long it took him to prepare that.

Arun takes his drink and goes into the bedroom, muttering something about being up all night and needing to rest.

Josie smiles at me apologetically as she goes back to her laptop. 'I don't know why he's being like this,' she says quietly.

I don't tell her that I do.

We resume our gentle Sunday-afternoon tasks. I dig out bits of black varnish from my cuticles and Josie catches up with her friends' Facebook feeds. She doesn't seem to want me to go. In fact she asks me if I want to stay another night and I instantly say yes. I don't know why – for the hell of it, I suppose. I think she wants to use me as a human shield, protecting her from Arun. Or maybe I'm a weapon to beat him with. It's hard to know for sure. I don't know anything about either of them, not really, and I haven't a clue how their relationship works. I've just dive-bombed in and fucked it up.

The evening passes slowly, and when Arun still doesn't emerge, Josie weakens and joins him in the bedroom. I tidy up the day's debris and wash the dirty crockery, pausing with my hands in the water as I listen to their conversation on the other side of the wall. They're deliberately speaking quietly so I can't make out any words, but the tone is unmistakable. If I wasn't in the next room, they'd be screaming at each other. I dry my hands and go into the hallway, positioning myself between the bathroom and the bedroom door.

'Why are you so against her?' Josie is saying.

'Because she's a scheming little bitch.'

'You can't say that without giving a reason.'

'I just *know*, okay?'

'Sorry, that's not good enough.'

'Jesus Christ, you're so fucking naïve sometimes.'

I hear footsteps approaching and quickly jump into the bathroom, shutting the door behind me and turning on the light. I scrape my long, messy hair behind my ears and study my features in the mirror. Relaxing the tension in my jaw, I smile with my mouth and eyes. It's like casting a spell. If I can meet the world with my sister's innocent face, nobody will see the darkness that hides beneath.

# CHAPTER TWENTY-EIGHT

*In Viking society, although slaves were sexual property, it was forbidden to give unwanted attention to a free woman. One story tells of a man being fined two ounces of gold for kissing a woman four times against her will.*

I don't know what time Valentina left, but when I get up on Monday morning, she's not here and it doesn't look like she slept on the sofa. Perhaps she heard us arguing about her last night and made an embarrassed escape. I feel bad about her running off without saying goodbye. I knew her presence would cause problems; I shouldn't have asked her to stay. I only did it to annoy Arun, and it definitely worked.

He got up while I was still asleep and left the flat without my knowing. I wander around in my dressing gown, feeling like I've misplaced something precious. Suddenly, out of nowhere, we seem to be in trouble. We're standing on an eroding cliff, the ground shifting beneath our feet. Maybe it's been happening for a while, but I've not seen the warning signs to stay away from the edge. I know I've been very preoccupied lately, but the circumstances have been extreme. It's hardly surprising that I haven't given him much attention. I thought he understood, that he was on my side. He's been so supportive since Dad died and I found out about his secret family; he even accepted my decision not to tell Mum. So why has he changed? His negative attitude towards

Valentina is just weird, and when I try to talk to him, he won't look me in the eye.

We stutter through the week. He comes home late every evening and leaves early the following morning, claiming he's got a lot on at work. Somehow, I don't believe him any more than I believed the stag weekend. Valentina texts several times a day, asking my opinion about various jobs she's seen advertised, thanking me for the new phone and generally sending oodles of sisterly love. She and her fellow guardians have decided to hold a party this coming Saturday, even though it's totally against the rules of their contract, and she's desperate for me and Arun to go. *Pleeeease!* she texts. *I won't know anyone if you don't come.* I haven't mentioned the party to him. There's no point; I know he'll refuse to attend. A party in a rat-infested derelict pub is not his kind of thing. It's not my kind of thing either, but the more Arun shuts me out, the more inclined I am to go.

When Saturday comes around, Arun gets up early and goes to the gym, comes back for a quick shower, then dresses in smartish clothes. He tells me he's going to meet an old school friend I've never heard of before in Covent Garden.

'I might make an evening of it,' he informs me, just before he walks out of the door. 'Don't wait up.'

'What's going on, Arun?' I say. 'Are you seeing someone else?'

His olive skin instantly darkens. 'No! Of course not.'

'Only you're behaving like someone who's having an affair.'

'That's ridiculous,' he replies hotly. 'When you've had enough of Valentina, let me know.' Ah… so he's jealous. Feeling too weary to get into another argument, I let him go. But his aggressive attitude solidifies my decision. I'm going to the party, so there.

I spend hours deciding what to wear. All my clothes look too sensible, but there's not enough time to buy something new. In the end, I opt for my staple red dress. It's sleeveless, with a boat-shaped neck and a shiny thin belt – the sort of thing you'd wear to a corporate function or dinner in an expensive restaurant rather than a squat party, but I know it suits my figure. I select a small matching bag and put on the highest heels I possess, then parade around the bedroom, catching sideways glimpses of myself in the wardrobe mirror. I will never look as sexy or as confident as Valentina, but I'll do.

The taxi drops me off outside the pub. I send a text to say I've arrived, then walk down the windswept alleyway.

'Yay! Sis! You made it!' Valentina bursts out of the door, throwing her skinny arms around me and sticking several lipstick kisses on my cheek. I follow her into the pub. The corridor is dingy but I can still see she looks gorgeous, dressed as always in her signature black. Tight shorts and fishnet stockings show off her long legs; a thin vest clings to her taut breasts, over which she's draped a vintage see-through shirt. Her face is heavily made up: deathly-pale foundation, red lips, black lids fading to silver under her brows, false lashes and a thick smudge of liner beneath her intensely blue eyes. We look like the 'before and after' in some makeover programme.

Valentina drags me into what was once the saloon bar. 'So? What do you think? I did all this.' She waves at a few fairy lights strung across the empty shelves and some candles stuck into melted wax on the counter. 'Looks fucking cool, doesn't it?'

I nod weakly. The windows are boarded up with metal sheets that glint eerily in the candlelight. If this was a Halloween party, it would be the perfect location, but tonight it looks shabby and a bit creepy. I arrived as late as I could and there are already lots of people here, huddled in small groups with their backs turned away from us, swigging beer or clutching bottles of wine. Several people are smoking joints, and the air is thickening with the sweet, cloying smell. I can't help thinking about fire hazards and the lack of proper escapes.

'You should have worn those satin jeans I lent you,' she says, studying my boring dress.

I blush. 'Oh, yes, I didn't think.' Come to think of it, I haven't seen Valentina's clothes since that night I came home drunk. I make a mental note to look for them when I get home and give them back to her. Surely Arun wouldn't have got rid of them?

Techno punches out from the other bar like a raised fist, making the walls and floorboards shudder. The building feels like it could fall down at any moment. Valentina shouts in my ear. 'Come on. Let's get you shit-faced.'

'Actually, I don't want to drink tonight. After last time…'

'One or two won't hurt you.' She runs behind the bar and retrieves a bottle of white wine and two glasses. 'Wine from plastic cups is just gross. These are like gold dust,' she says, adding, 'Guard it with your life.' She unscrews the cap and holds it between her teeth as she fills both glasses to the brim. We clink and say cheers. 'I'm going to take this back to my secret hiding place, okay? Just tell me when you want a top-up.' She goes back behind the bar, leaving me alone in the dark, noisy room of strangers.

As the first sip makes its way down to my stomach, I remember that I didn't manage to eat before coming out – I was in such a panic about deciding what to wear. I glance around, hoping to see a bowl of crisps or some peanuts, but it seems to be a food-free zone.

'Yay! The lads are here!' shouts Valentina, lifting her arms and waving them furiously above her head. 'Tosh! Joey! Get your arses over here!' Two guys standing in the doorway shout something back and start to cut their way through the crowd like explorers in the Amazon.

'I thought you didn't know anyone in London.'

'I don't! They're from home. Come down especially to see me.' She flicks her hand, as if cracking a whip. 'Whoop! Whoop! Make way for the Mancs boys! Tosh! What took you so long, knobhead? I was expecting you hours ago.'

'Had a few roadies on the way and got fucking lost, didn't we?' Tosh picks Valentina up and twirls her around, letting his hands slide down the sides of her breasts as he puts her back down. He's tall and built, Mediterranean-looking, wearing jeans and a checked shirt, the sleeves rolled up to the elbows, revealing densely inked tattoos on both arms. 'You didn't say the pub was a fucking building site.'

'Yeah,' says the other one, who I assume must be Joey. 'Should have brought our hard hats, like!' He laughs loudly at his own joke. He's shorter than Tosh, but is just as muscled and has even more tattoos. A blue-black serpent coils around his neck, its head resting on the front of his chest. His head is shaved and he's wearing a ring through his stubby round nose.

'There'd better be plenty of booze in those backpacks,' says Valentina.

'No worries, we're sorted, everything you asked for.' Tosh gives her a conspiratorial wink.

'Meet my long-lost twin!' Valentina grabs me by the arm and pulls me forward. 'Didn't believe me, did you, you daft prick? You're seeing double and you're not even pissed. Hah!'

'Well, fuck me…' Tosh looks me up and down and I can feel his eyes burning through my dress. 'Double trouble.'

'Hardly,' I say.

'You're not *real* twins, like?'

'No. We're half-sisters. Same father.'

His dark, bushy eyebrows rise. 'Ah… the Viking.'

I step back in surprise. 'You knew him?'

'Yeah, had a fight with him once. Gave me a black eye.' He snaps his fingers. 'Respect!'

'Really? That doesn't sound like my—'

'I was fucked up at the time, that's the only reason he got away with it!' Tosh laughs. He swings the rucksack off his back and unzips it, taking out a four-pack. Joey grabs one can and Valentina another. Joey pulls back the tab and the beer, shaken with travelling, fizzes over the top, dripping down the sides of the can and onto the floor.

Tosh turns to me. 'Want one, Twinny?'

'I'm okay, thanks.' I gesture to my wine glass, still three-quarters full. 'I don't take alcohol very well, so I try not to mix drinks.'

As soon as the words leave my mouth, I feel like a complete idiot. Tosh belts out a laugh and Joey smirks into his can. I feel my cheeks going hot and red, hoping they won't show up in the darkness. What am I, a schoolgirl?

Joey turns to Valentina. 'Where's a good place to dump our stuff?'

'In my room. Come, I'll show you… You'll look after Tosh, won't you, sis?' Before I can reply, she leads Joey through the growing throng, leaving the two of us staring at each other. Is she trying to set us up? Tosh crouches down on his haunches and starts expertly rolling a joint. I find myself watching him, not knowing what else to do. I'm not such a goody-goody that I've never smoked weed before, but the couple of times I tried it I threw up, so I no longer bother. I don't do other stuff either.

Tosh licks the edge of the paper and looks up at me. I know what's coming next; it almost feels like a test. He'll offer me the joint and I'll feel pressurised to take a puff. But the wine is already making me feel a bit light-headed; I daren't risk it.

'Think I'll check out the music,' I shout down at him.

'Fair enough.' He stands up and reaches into his back pocket for his lighter. Holding my glass in front of me like a precious object, I weave my way through the crowd towards the door marked *Snug*. To my relief, Tosh doesn't attempt to follow me.

The snug is certainly that. There must be fifty people dancing in here, their sweaty faces flashing pink, blue and green under the lights. As they jerk about, enslaved to the insistent beat, they seem to merge into one pulsating, many-headed monster. I find a hiding place in the corner, camouflaging myself against the peeling red wallpaper. The loud, incessant techno pummels my ribcage. It's so hot and cramped and smoky, my throat is tightening and I'm finding it hard to breathe. I gulp back my wine to quench my thirst, even though I know it won't help. The glass is soon empty, but I don't want to lose it. Unzipping my shoulder bag, I drop it in and close it up.

For a few minutes, I enjoy the anonymity, dissecting the monster into individual characters. Most of the dancers are clearly off their faces, popping pills and washing them down with large bottles of water. A few guys have taken off their tops and are parading their smooth, waxed chests, tight abs glossy with sweat. Couples are kissing, hands going everywhere, hips grinding against hips. Some guy reaches out and tries to drag me into the crowd, but I pull my hand away and shrink back into the shadows. I'd do anything for a glass of water. The heat is sapping my energy; my armpits and the back of my neck feel sticky. I'm finding it harder and harder not to move as the music beats through my body.

'*There* you are!' cries Valentina, coming towards me. 'I've been looking for you everywhere!' Her eyes are wild and staring, her cheeks flushed pink like a doll. She's no longer wearing her black see-through shirt and her bare arms are glistening. 'Great party, eh? Fuck knows where all these people have come from; word must have got around. It's mental upstairs. Bodies everywhere. I keep falling over people. Come on, let's dance, you know you want to.'

I let her pull me onto the floor, and we raise our arms above our heads, twisting our bodies in response to the sounds. She grins at me and I grin back. My muscles start to relax and my limbs loosen. We twirl around each other, making patterns with our hands, our eyes locked in a secret pact. She stands in front of me and we play the mirror game. I copy her movements, then we swap and she takes the lead. We try to catch each other out, speeding up and making complicated moves, but we remain in perfect sync. I am she and she is me. Sisters. Almost twins.

The guys – Tosh and Joey – find us, and after watching us for a few minutes, decide to barge their way into the sweaty pit. There are an insane number of bodies pressed against each other and we become separated by a surge from the DJ's end. I feel myself being tossed around in the waves of sound.

'It's like being in a fucking tsunami!' shouts Valentina when we finally manage to manoeuvre our way back into a foursome. The guys try to copy our mirror dance but they haven't a clue. Valentina mocks them and they exchange cheerful insults. 'I know, I'll show Joey and you show Tosh,' she shouts above the din. Tosh pushes in front of me, standing so close that it's impossible to see what he's doing with his hands or feet.

'This isn't going to work,' I tell him, pulling a face.

'Nah,' he agrees. 'Want a drink?'

I nod. 'Valentina's got a secret stash of wine behind the bar.'

'She'll be lucky if it's still there.' I open my shoulder bag and take out my empty wine glass. 'Hah! Nice one!' He takes it off me and disappears.

I cast around for Valentina, but her mirror game with Joey has turned into a semi-smooch. I laugh to myself, threading my way to the edge of the floor and finding a small gap by the wall between two groups of drinkers. God knows what time it is. God knows what Arun's doing tonight. I dip into my bag again and check my phone. It's just gone midnight. I've had no missed calls. No texts. Then again, I haven't been in touch with him either. Didn't even leave him a note. What is happening to us? I close my eyes. I can't think about that right now. Let me have one night off, at least.

Tosh's tall frame suddenly appears at my side. 'Here, Twinny, get that down your neck,' he says, handing over my refilled glass. 'Then we can have some fun.'

# CHAPTER TWENTY-NINE

*The Vikings routinely used slave girls for sex. An eyewitness describes a girl walking over a path of male hands to board a ship, where she was given a cup of intoxicating drink before lying with her masters.*

'Eurrgh…' My eyes are stuck together with gunge. The air smells sour – stale booze, tobacco, weed… Blindly I start to explore my surroundings. The sheet feels worn and gritty, the mattress hard and thin. Ah… I know where I am. I run my fingers across my stomach and over my breasts, then down my thighs. I'm stark naked. I prise open my eyes with my fingers and try to sit up, but it's as if an invisible force is pushing me back onto the pillow. My tongue is furry and there's a strange taste in the back of my mouth.

'You're awake – at last.' The voice seems to come out of nowhere. I open my eyes again and frown tightly, trying to stop my brain from bursting out of my skull. 'Want some water?' I nod to whoever's speaking and a figure swims into view, leaning over me – a fractured mirror image of myself. I lean forward and she helps me take a sip from a plastic cup.

'You're going to have one hell of a hangover!' she says cheerfully, perching next to me.

The sleeping bag slips from my breasts and I reach up to cover them. 'Where are my clothes? I don't remember taking them off.'

'Maybe you didn't.'

'Shit… Did you have to…? I'm so sorry. Did I throw up all over myself?'

'No, don't think so…' She pauses. 'Are you serious? Do you *really* not remember what you did last night?'

'No.' I feel so odd, out of my body. 'What time is it?' Valentina shrugs. 'Can you pass me my clothes, please?'

She kicks around with her bare feet, finally picking up my bra with her toes. 'Here you go.' I take it off her, suddenly aware of how overwashed and shapeless it looks. Valentina gets down on her hands and knees. 'Can't see your pants anywhere. Hmm … I suppose they might have been taken as a souvenir.'

I put my bra on blind beneath the cover. 'A souvenir? What do you mean?'

She raises her head. 'You don't have to pretend to me, you know. We're sisters. We keep each other's secrets.'

'I don't have a secret.' As I shift around, the tops of my thighs seem to stick together. 'Are your friends still here? I've forgotten their names…'

'Tosh and Joey? They left at about four, went on to another party. Don't worry, you'll never see them again. Nobody's going to grass you up.' Valentina is crawling around the floor, picking up bits of rubbish and hurling them into the corner.

'What do you mean?'

'Come on, stop being so coy. Is this your dress?' She holds up a crumpled red rag. I snatch it off her and try to put it on, but it's been ripped from top to bottom.

'Oh God… Look, it's ruined!'

'Hmm, shame… I'm not judging you,' Valentina continues. 'Not for one second. It's about time you let go and followed your own impulses. Arun's got too much control over you. The booze relaxed you, lowered your inhibitions, and you went for it. Good for you. I'm impressed.' I stare at her in horror. 'Don't look at me like that. It's only a bit of sex!'

'What do you mean? I had sex with someone? Who?'

She grins. 'Tosh… and Joey.'

'No… no…'

'That's what the boys said. Apparently, you were well up for it.'

'No. That's impossible. It didn't happen. I know it didn't happen!'

I close my eyes and roll into a ball, shutting her and everything else out. But I can't stop the picture that starts to form in my head. *Arms held high, red cloth wrapped around my face, the sensation of somebody pulling, pulling, then a loud tear as I burst free, gasping for air.* I snap my eyes open and stare at Valentina, bewildered.

'I was drunk, I tried to take my dress off without undoing the zip and it tore. That's all!'

'It doesn't matter,' she says. 'It happened, so what? Accept it and move on. Nobody died, okay? And Arun need never—'

I cut in angrily. 'I *didn't* have sex with anyone last night!'

'Are you sure about that? You said you couldn't remember.'

'I think I'd know, no matter how drunk I was!'

'Yeah, well, whatever you say… I'll back you up, no matter what.'

I can't stay here any longer. Valentina's messing with my mind. I have to get away, get home, have a shower – clean my teeth. I feel so grubby, my skin is crawling and I can't get rid of this strange taste in my mouth.

'I need something else to wear,' I say, throwing the dress back on the floor. 'What about the clothes I left here when we went to that gig? You know, the skirt and jacket, a cream shirt, I think…'

Valentina grimaces. 'Oh *those*. I spilt curry all over them the other day so I took them to the dry cleaner's. Forgot to pick them up. They're still there and they're closed today. Soz. You'll have to borrow something of mine. Again.' She throws open the suitcase and rummages around, bringing out some black leggings and a long black jumper.

Feeling vaguely annoyed, I wriggle into the leggings under the cover and pull the jumper over my head. My shoes are lying askew at the end of the bed. I put them on the floor and push my feet in.

'Now I just need my bag.' I cast my eyes around vaguely.

'Not here,' says Valentina, holding out open palms. 'Shit. I hope you didn't leave it downstairs.'

'No, I wouldn't do that. I'm always really careful… It must be here somewhere.' I lift up the sleeping bag and toss it aside, baulking as I catch sight of a large damp stain on the sheet. Another image starts to form behind my eyes, but I push it away. 'I need my bag! There was a load of cash in it, my Oyster…'

'You brought a load of cash to the party?' Valentina sounds incredulous. 'I'm sorry, but that's really dumb.'

'Maybe I left it in the bar.'

'Forget it. It's like Aleppo down there.'

'It's still worth looking. You never know.'

Valentina lets out an ironic laugh. 'I admire your trust in human nature.' She stands up. 'I'll go and look, you're in no fit state. What's it like?'

'Black, with a red trim.'

As soon as she's gone, I roll up, burying my head in the dark well between my knees. My body starts to rock back and forth. *I can feel the techno beat thud-thudding through my brain, coloured lights flashing before my eyes. Dribbles of sweat are running down my back. The room is spinning round and round and I can't keep up with it. My legs collapse under me like a folding chair and someone catches me, scooping me up and throwing me over their shoulder, fireman-style. The blood rushes to my head as I hang over their back, strong, cloying aftershave swooping up my nose. I feel the strap slipping off my shoulder as I'm carried through the crowds, my fingers hopelessly grabbing the air as the bag drops to the ground.*

'No luck!' I jerk my head up and the image cuts out. Valentina's back, with something in her hand. 'Is this your phone? I found it just outside the cubicle.'

I reach out and take it. 'Yeah, think so…' My fingers fumble with the side buttons.

'It's dead,' she says helpfully.

'What about my bag?'

Valentina shakes her head. 'Sorry. But if you put temptation people's way…'

Tears prick behind my eyes. How could I have been so stupid? I can only remember having two glasses of wine. Okay, so they were bucket-sized and I hadn't eaten, but I still shouldn't have got *that* wasted. I have to get out of this hellhole. Now.

'Can I borrow some money for a cab?'

'Of course!' She digs out her purse from its hiding place behind her bed. 'Shit, I've only got three quid; that won't be enough, will it? Will Arun be in? He can pay at the other end, can't he? Or do you want me to call him, ask him to pick you up in the car?'

'No!' That's the last thing I want. Cold reality starts to dawn. Arun will be frantic because I didn't come home. He'll have been up all night, texting and leaving messages on my phone. He might even have called the police. How am I going to explain the state I'm in? How am I going to tell him what happened when I don't even know myself?

'I'll walk.'

'Really? It's a long way. Are you sure you're up to it? Let me call Arun—'

'I said no! I want to walk.'

She follows me downstairs and opens the door. I step into the filthy alleyway, strewn with cans and bottles from last night.

'Take care, Josie. If you need me, you know where to find me.'

'I'm fine. Honestly, I'm fine. Nothing bad happened.'

She shrugs. 'Whatever you say, sis.'

I drag my body up the hill, every step a monumental effort. My legs are aching and my bare heels are rubbing painfully against the back of my party shoes. It's Sunday morning, but it looks like the weekday rush hour. The noise is deafening, the fumes choking. Every time I see a black cab, I have to fight the urge to flag it down. I need this walk to get my thoughts straight before I see Arun.

*I'm so sorry, I drank more than I realised, it was really stupid of me. I was sick all over my clothes and Valentina had to lend me some. I fell asleep in her room and when I woke up I couldn't find my bag. I think somebody must have nicked it. I wanted to call you to let you know I was safe, but my phone ran out of juice.*

That's the truth, isn't it? It's got to be the truth. There's got to be another explanation for the stickiness on my thighs and the stain on the mattress. I would never have sex with anyone else, and never, never with two men at the same time. I should have had more control over my drinking; I should have kept a closer eye on my belongings. No, actually, I should never have gone there in the first place.

I reach a bus shelter and sit on the bench to rest my aching limbs, closing my eyes and letting the sounds of the traffic rush through my ears. Another image suddenly flashes across my inner eye – *my body falling and landing like a dead weight. Everything feels so heavy, and I can't move. Sit up. Sit up! I feel hands running over my thighs and stomach, squeezing my breasts. I'm being dragged up, my arms wrenching out of their sockets, my back arching as I lurch forward like a broken doll. Raise your arms. Higher. My dress is pulled up and over my head. I feel exposed. A hand presses down on my shoulder and I shove it off, shouting out—*

'Get off me!'

'Sorry, love!' I blink open my eyes. My chest is heaving, breaths coming short and fast. A woman is sitting next to me on the bench, a kind, worried look on her face. 'I was only trying to help. I thought you were having an asthma attack.'

'No, I'm fine… just… I'm fine… thanks. Sorry, I didn't mean…'

'That's quite all right. You don't look well. Is there somebody I can call?'

'No, I'm really fine.' I stand up, too fast, almost losing my balance. 'Thanks.'

My legs feel wobbly, but I carry on up the hill, head down, eyes glued to the pavement. I hug the shadows of imposing Victorian mansion blocks, trying to make myself invisible. Fifteen minutes and I'll be home. Fifteen minutes in which to work out what really happened last night. Strange, hazy images are prowling around my brain, waiting for another chance to attack. I won't be able to hold them off forever. As the terrifying truth falls into place, I realise that what really happened and what I'm going to tell Arun are two entirely different things.

# CHAPTER THIRTY

*Contrary to popular myth, Vikings were not filthy ruffians. They were extremely clean and cared about their appearance. Artefacts found at archaeological sites include combs, razors, tweezers and ear spoons.*

'Where the hell have you been?' cries Arun, opening the front door. His face is a mixture of worry and anger and I start to shake inside. 'I've been texting and ringing all night. I was about to call the police!'

'Sorry… my phone died…' I ease off my shoes and edge towards the bathroom like a frightened child, trying not to catch his disapproving eye.

'Are those Valentina's clothes?'

'Yes…' I mumble. 'There was a bit of a gathering at her place and… er… I got a bit drunk. I spilt wine all over my dress.'

'God, just look at you. You look…' He struggles to find a suitably damning adjective. 'I told you – I *begged* you – not to see Valentina. Why won't you listen?'

'Please leave me alone. I don't feel very well and I need a shower.' I rush into the bathroom, slamming the door against him. How am I going to get through this?

My head feels like somebody's attacking it with power tools. I start to undress, but the effort of it makes me dizzy. A wave of nausea rises in my stomach and I throw up last night's alcohol into the toilet bowl. Sitting on the edge of the bath, I close my eyes and put my head between my legs.

But I can't hide from the flashes from last night that burst out of nowhere. *I can't breathe. My face is surrounded with a suffocating red cloth. I want to pull the dress back down but my arms are so heavy I can't lift them. He tugs and tugs until the fabric rips in my ears and he wrenches it free. I feel myself being pushed backwards and hitting something hard. Hands all over my body, fingers pulling at the top of my knickers …*

Stop it! Stop it! I fall forward onto my hands and knees, then curl into a frightened ball. The floor is cold and hard. I feel so dirty; I'm sure I stink of sex. I lift my thumping head and tear off the alien clothes. There are no bruises on my body, but I feel branded. The smell of their aftershave, of wine, lager, weed, their disgusting spunk, clings to my hair. It's disgusting… *I'm* disgusting…

Reaching up, I turn on the shower full blast and spin the dial to its hottest setting. I crawl into the cubicle and let the needles of water drill into my skull. My skin won't come clean, won't smell fresh. I take the pumice stone and scrub my flesh red and raw. Desperate to get rid of the smell, I smother myself with fragrant shower gel. As it foams and spreads, my hands turn rough and large; they grab my arse and breasts, pushing my thighs apart. I drop the bottle and sink into the corner, wrapping my arms over my head, sobbing helplessly as the water runs cold.

Arun bangs on the door. 'Josie? What are you doing in there?' I ignore him. 'Are you okay? Answer me!'

'Leave me be!'

Getting slowly to my feet, I turn off the shower and step out of the cubicle. I reach for a towel and wrap it around me. I'm shivering. My wet hair hangs wretched and tangled about my face; my blotchy skin tingles with pain. I can't face Arun like this. I'll have to stay locked in.

He knocks on the door again, more gently this time. 'Josie… speak to me. What's wrong?'

'Nothing,' I lie.

There's a pause. 'Okay… Look, I'm going for a run. See you later.' I shudder with relief as I hear the front door opening and closing. At last I'm alone.

I come out of the bathroom and run into the bedroom, dressing quickly in the oldest, most unattractive clothes I can find – a pair of saggy jogging bottoms and a large T-shirt. I try not to catch my reflection in the wardrobe mirror. Drawing the curtains, I climb into bed and pull the duvet over my wet hair. I feel numb. Detached from myself. It didn't happen. The images inside my head are fake – a nightmare, not a memory. I would never do a thing like that. It *didn't, didn't* happen.

*Oh, but it did, Josie*, a sinister voice says.

I'm exhausted, my mind refusing to stop picking at fragments from last night. Every time I feel myself dropping off, hands thrust through the darkness and paw over my body. I have to shake myself awake to escape.

Why is my system feeling so fuzzy and churned up? I only remember having a couple of glasses of wine. I throw off the duvet and slowly sit up. Maybe some food will help. Or water. Yes, I should flush the bad alcohol through my system. I totter into the kitchen and force myself to drink three large glasses from the tap.

Where is Arun? He's been gone for ages. Not that I can bear to face him. I'm frightened that he'll read my thoughts; that he'll look into my eyes and see sex scenes playing on the screen inside my head. My secrets have been turned inside out and I am totally exposed. Dressed, and yet naked. Last night's smells and stains still there for all to see; their fingerprints forever pressed into my flesh.

I should leave before he comes back and finds me like this. But where can I go? I can't tell any of my friends – they all love Arun, they'd be horrified and appalled by my behaviour. I can't confide in Mum, either. She thinks he's wonderful, perfect son-in-law material. And she's the last person I should talk to about infidelity and betrayal. I drain the third glass of water and stare into the middle distance. No, there's no one.

Arun doesn't return home till early evening. God knows what he was doing all that time, but I'm sure he wasn't running. He's not sweaty or breathless and he doesn't bother with the charade of a shower. I don't ask him where he's been or if he was with anyone. It feels like it's none of my business. Anyway, if I start asking questions, so might he. Can't risk that. So I mumble something about not feeling well and go to bed.

At last I sink into a heavy sleep. When I wake, it's early morning – half five. I turn over and reach my hand out for Arun, but find only empty space. The sheet feels fresh. I don't think he slept here last night. Turning on the bedside lamp, I sit up and stare about the room for evidence. The pillow is undented; there's no discarded underwear on the floor. Relief and panic simultaneously flood my senses.

He must be sleeping on the sofa. I carefully creep out of the bedroom and tiptoe towards the living room. The door is slightly ajar and I push it open, trying not to let the hinges squeak. The room is empty. It looks like he *was* sleeping on the sofa, but he's not here now. I stare into the gloom, wondering how we have let this happen. I start to feel angry. Unless he really *can* read my mind, he thinks I just went out on the piss, overdid it, and didn't turn up till the next morning. Stupid and a bit inconsiderate, but not a crime. So why is he punishing me when he doesn't actually know that I've done something wrong? What would he do if he *did* know?

I cross the room and sit down, hugging the abandoned duvet to my chest. He's been acting strangely for the past ten days, ever since I went to that gig with Valentina. Something happened overnight; it was like a fuse blowing. At first I thought all we had to do was flip the trip switch back up and everything would start working again. But I'm starting to think it won't be that easy. He's been avoiding me, shutting me out. I'm sure he lied about the stag weekend. That's why I went to the party in the first place – so if you trace it back, it's kind of his fault that I got off my face and lost control.

The word 'party' presses a button in my brain, and suddenly I'm engulfed by a roar of techno music. I put my hands over my face and scream, shaking my head violently to make the sounds fall out. What am I going to do? This torture can't go on. I have to stop it somehow; I have to take back control.

Panting for breath, I run back to the bedroom and draw the curtains. Early-morning sunshine covers the furniture like a cloth. I need light and air. I'm rotting in here. I fling open the wardrobe and stare at the row of disembodied images of myself: Work Josie, Casual Josie, Holiday Josie… I take out a crisp white shirt and a smart navy suit, laying them on the bed. It's Monday, so I'll go to the office. I'll be Work Josie; calm, efficient, compassionate. I'll act normal and busy myself all day.

Once I've dressed, I dig out an old purse and slip my bank cards inside. At least I wasn't stupid enough to take them to the party. Finally, I take the spare keys from the rack by the front door and put them in my everyday handbag. If I concentrate really hard, I can do it. I've got the props and costume; all I have to do now is be the character.

*

But I'm not fooling anyone. I arrive at the office very early, just as Jill is opening up. She greets me warmly and asks how my weekend was. I almost burst into tears.

'Sorry, Josie,' she stumbles. 'I didn't mean to… What is it? Is something wrong?'

'No, not at all. I'm fine…' I rummage in my bag for a tissue. 'Sorry. Just not sleeping very well.'

'Oh dear.' She lingers in the doorway of my room. 'Did you see that bereavement counsellor I recommended?'

'Not yet.' Turning on the computer, I shuffle into my chair and pretend to look for something in the desk drawer. Jill doesn't move. I sense her maternal instincts coming to the fore – caring, but also curious. She knows I'm hiding something, but fortunately she decides not to press any further. 'Well, if you need to talk any time, you know where to find me…'

'Thanks,' I say.

My first appointment isn't for another hour, so I catch up with some emails and check my schedule. There are a few clients' names that I recognise, so I look up their files and familiarise myself with their cases. I try to focus on their problems, and make notes about other things I could suggest that might help them. It helps to put my own issues into perspective. I'm not homeless, I'm not unemployed, I'm not in thousands of pounds' worth of debt and I'm not being beaten up by my boyfriend.

At ten to nine, I take my client list and a few relevant folders and go to the interview room I've been allocated for the morning. All the computers are networked, so I switch on the desktop and drop into the swivel chair. *Come on, you can do this. It's only listening to people and filling in a few forms.*

The first three clients are fine. One is being evicted by her landlord, the second is having problems with Family Credit. The third is well known to us – he has mental-health issues and sees us as the next port of call after his GP and A & E. I listen. I offer up suggestions. I write notes. I feel just about okay.

My twelve o'clock is a young woman called Kerry-Jo. She's only two years older than me, but she's got a drug problem and she looks about forty. She tells me she has a young daughter who's been put into care; her social worker is refusing to let her see her until she's proved herself to be clean for three months. It's supposed to be an incentive, but to Kerry-Jo it feels like a punishment, and she uses to dull the pain.

'And what about her father? Is he on the scene?' I say, already sure of the answer.

'You're kidding,' she says. 'He was a one-nighter, you know. I went to this party and next thing I know I'm waking up in a strange bed with some guy I don't even remember meeting and I'm knocked up.' My insides turn over. 'It's okay, though, 'cos I love her. She's like the best thing that ever happened to me, you know? So I'm thinking…'

Her voice fades out as a queasy feeling rises from my stomach. What if *I'm* pregnant? I won't even know whose it is– Tosh or Joey's. I can't be pregnant. I'm on the pill. But I was sick when I got home. What if I vomited Saturday's pill up? Oh God, what if their sperm are still swimming about inside me? What if they've got chlamydia, what if they're HIV positive? Fear surges in my bowels.

'So? What do you think?' says Kerry-Jo, one leg jogging up and down nervously. 'Do I say, like, I want a new social worker? I mean, is that allowed?'

'Sorry, I don't feel very well.' I stand up, pushing my chair back so violently it topples over, and run out of the room.

Jill finds me in the ladies'. It seems that Kerry-Jo, bless her, went to fetch someone. 'Josie, love,' she says, bending over me, 'whatever's the matter? You know you can tell me anything…'

It all spills out. I tell her about the party, getting drunk, waking up naked with no memory of what happened. Losing my bag. The feelings of shame and anger that I could have been so stupid. The vile pictures that keep coming back to me – things my brain can't accept I did.

We sit side by side on the floor and she tears off sheets of toilet paper to mop up my tears. 'Do you know what I think happened?' she says cautiously. 'I think you might have been raped.'

I stare at her, bewildered. 'But in these flashbacks, I'm not fighting back. I'm letting it happen.'

'Hmm… letting it happen because you weren't physically capable of stopping it is not consenting. Could you have been drugged? Did someone bring you a drink you didn't see being poured?'

My stomach flips and I suddenly feel very sick. 'Yes… I remember being in the dance room and this guy, Tosh, turning up with a glass of wine. The rest is a blank.'

'Did the wine taste strange at all?'

'I don't think so. I can't remember. But when I woke up, it was like the worst hangover I've ever had. And these memory blanks are really frightening.'

'We need to get you to a sexual assault referral centre,' Jill says.

'No, I c-c-can't, I'm—'

She grabs my hands and makes me look her in the eyes. 'Listen to me, Josie, this wasn't your fault. It sounds like you were deliberately drugged, but even if you were just very drunk, it makes no difference. You were incapable of giving consent, which means – very simply – that this was rape.'

'But they said I was up for it.'

'Of course they did.'

'And there's no proof. I… I washed it all away.'

'The doctors at the centre can examine you if you want that; the earlier you go, the better. They'll run tests, give you information and advice about what to do next.'

'I don't want to go to the police.'

'Nobody will push you into doing anything you don't want to do. And nobody will judge you.'

'Arun will judge me, I know he will. He'll hate me for being so stupid. He mustn't find out. Ever!'

She helps me to my feet. 'Would you like me to book you an appointment? I think it would be good to get yourself checked out at least.' I shake my head. She steps back, momentarily defeated, then tries one more sally. 'Think of it this way, Josie. If a client came to you with the same story, what would be your advice?' She pauses, waiting for my reaction. 'You'd encourage them to seek help, yes? You'd tell them about the expert, specialist support out there.' I nod. She's right, of course, but now I realise it's easy to dole out advice when it's not happening to you. 'At least talk to someone,' Jill continues. 'The Rape Crisis Line is very good, and available twenty-four hours.'

'I'll think about it.' But I know I won't; the idea of going through it all over again horrifies me.

'Please do. Now let me call you a taxi to take you home. Will you be all right on your own?'

'Yes…' But I won't be all right. I know I won't.

# CHAPTER THIRTY-ONE

*The Vikings believed they had a religious obligation to offer hospitality to strangers. 'Do not abuse a guest, or drive him out the door. Instead, do well for the wretched.' (Hávamál, Old Norse poem)*

I'm fourteen again, sitting in my usual chair in Dr Bannister's consulting room. We're well into our session, so my guard is fully down. It's taken several weeks for me to relax and open up about my feelings, but now I can't stop.

'My biggest problem is that I have a very weak identity,' I say. I've been researching psychological disorders on line and think I've found the one I match most closely. 'I'm not in charge of myself, I don't feel responsible for my actions – does that make sense? It's like I'm the narrator telling the story of Valentina. I can see what a mess she's making of her life but I can't do anything about it.'

Dr Bannister is looking out of the window and doesn't seem to be listening. I start to feel cross. What's wrong? Have my problems suddenly become dull and ordinary? Until now, I've been made to feel like I'm a fascinating and unusual case. Extra sessions have been arranged and I've even begun to look forward to them. We've become friends; had some really enlightening conversations about family, school and life in general, and I've been able to dig pretty deep into my emotions. Finally I've found someone who really understands me and wants to help.

I've even accepted that I don't actually have a living sister somewhere out there, but that she's my 'shadow self'. We've had lots of deep chats about the positive and negative sides of our personalities and the importance of integrating them into one whole human being. In these six or seven weeks, I've made enormous progress.

But today the doctor is either worried about something else, or tired, or just plain bored. If there's one thing guaranteed to wind me up, it's being shut out. So I decide to conduct a little test. I do this at home sometimes, when Mum and Dad are being all lovey-dovey and ignoring me. I say things like 'I'm going to shave my head and become a nun', or 'I tried heroin today, it was amazing'.

'I keep having these fantasies about drowning myself,' I say quietly. I pause, peeping from the corner of my eye for a reaction. Nothing. Not a word, not a quiver of interest. What is going on? I've just admitted to wanting to commit suicide and it hasn't even registered. The pause becomes thick and heavy; the room starts to fill it up with it. It's choking me, but the doctor hasn't even noticed.

Hot coals of anger burn in my stomach. Blood from everywhere is rushing into my head, leaving my fingers and toes tingling. 'I just said, I want to kill myself,' I say, this time with a bite.

'No you don't, Valentina. You're trying to shock me into paying attention.' Dr Bannister turns around. 'I'm sorry, you caught me out. I wasn't listening properly. I was trying to work out how to give you some news I suspect you won't like very much.'

Everything inside jolts, like I've just done an emergency stop. 'What do you mean? What news?'

'I'm afraid this has to be our last session. We can't meet any more.'

'Why not?'

'I've come to the end of my time on this project, that's all.'

My mouth goes candyfloss dry. 'No, no, you can't do this.'

'You've had more time than was originally allocated as it is, and now I have other commitments to attend to. Sorry, but that's how it is.'

I run over, sinking to my knees. 'You can't turn me away, it's not fair. I need this. You're the only one who cares about me; we're close, there's something between us. You feel it too, I know you do – why are you doing this?'

'Please try not to take it personally. I understand your needs, so I've arranged for someone else to take over. She's an extremely experienced therapist; I'm sure you'll get on very well.'

'I don't want someone else,' I rail. 'I want you. Only you! I love you!'

Dr Bannister freezes for a few seconds, then says, with a coldness that cuts right through me, 'No you don't. You think you do, but you don't. Please get up. Don't make this any more difficult than it already is.'

My legs trembling, I rise to my feet and back away. 'Don't abandon me. Please, don't abandon me…'

'I'm not abandoning you; I just can't treat you any more. Calm down. Come on… don't let the emotions control you. Breathe deeply, like I taught you.'

But I can't breathe at all. Anger is filling my lungs, and my heart has bolted away from me. There's so much feeling inside, I feel like I'm about to combust.

'You can't do this to me. I won't let you!'

'I'm afraid I need you to go now, Valentina. Dr Fried, your new therapist, will be in touch about your next appointment.'

'Don't fucking bother,' I shout. 'I'll be dead and it'll be all your fault!'

'No, no, stop that—'

But before I can be caught, I run out of the room. I rush through reception, bang through the swing doors, leap down the stairs and escape from the hospital. I run and I run – down the hill and around the corner, my instincts driving me towards open space.

The pavement twists and then climbs again. I follow it blindly, and find myself on the Heath. I dart across through the car park and crash onto the path, helter-skeltering around dog-walkers and mums with pushchairs, gaining momentum as I hurtle down into the dip.

And there it is. A large pond, glimmering darkly before me. I wasn't looking for it; I'd forgotten it was there. It's as if some strange magic has drawn me here. I stop at the edge and stare in wonder at the flat expanse of sludgy green. Everyone else fades away and I'm the only one here. It's *my* pond. It exists for me, for this moment.

*I keep having these fantasies about drowning myself.*

It wasn't even true; I just said it to cause a stir. But now the fantasy I conjured, almost as a joke, has transformed into reality. It's a sign from the gods. Odin is challenging me to make good my word. At that moment, everything crystallises. I'm no longer the spectator of my own drama; I am truly myself: the loving and the hateful, the generous and the selfish, the frightened and the brave – the warrior princess who would rather die than face dishonour.

I fling myself into the freezing water.

Somebody's pounding on my door. 'Valentina! Valentina! Are you there?' The memory cuts to black and I drag myself back to the here and now.

'Zoheb?' I roll off the bed and pull the bolt across. 'What's up?'

He bursts into my cubicle, his limbs jerking about like he's just been given an electric shock. 'Have you seen the email?'

'No. What email?'

'We're all being evicted! We've got twenty-four hours to get out, and if we don't, they'll call the police and we'll be charged with trespassing!'

'Fuck. How come?'

'Breach of contract. Somebody grassed on us over the party. If I find out who it was…'

I put my hand on his shoulder. 'Hey, calm down. It could be anyone. The agency phone number is plastered all over the banners outside.'

Zoheb tears at his hair. 'Where am I going to go? I can't go back home! I'll be on the streets.'

'It'll be okay.' I give him a motherly hug. 'You'll find somewhere else. Another property. Somewhere nicer.'

'No, we'll be blacklisted – you wait – and we'll never get our deposits back.' He pulls away from me. 'I *knew* it was a shit idea to have that party. It's your fault – everything was going okay until you turned up.'

'Oh, thanks for the solidarity, Zo! Yeah, it was my idea, but I seem to remember you were all up for it. Everyone invited heaps of friends, so don't suddenly blame me.'

He smashes his fist against the wall and the plywood wobbles. 'Twenty-four hours. It's not long enough. I bet it's not even legal.'

There are noises downstairs. Some of the other guardians have turned up. One of them, a German girl called Astrid, marches in and bangs on all the cubicles like she's a prison warder. She pokes her head around my open door.

'You heard the news?' We nod. 'Guardians' meeting in the big bar. Five minutes, *ja*? Everybody be there!' She wags her finger at us. 'Five minutes!'

'Yeah, we'll be there,' says Zoheb. Astrid marches off in search of more people to boss about. 'Come on, we've got to fight this. It's not fair. If we stand united…'

'You go ahead, I'll be down in a mo.'

He leaves and I let the news sink in. It feels okay – if anything, it's a relief that it's over. I'm not going to take part in their little protest meeting. They'll only turn on me if I do – the new girl from up north, the outsider. Even Zoheb thinks I'm to blame, and he's my friend. Oh well, that's how it goes. It always seems to turn out like this. People start off thinking I'm really cool and daring. They admire me because I'm prepared to push the boundaries and break the rules, but as soon as it goes wrong, they back off big-time.

I drag my old suitcase onto the mattress and open the lid. Might as well start packing. Not that it's going to take twenty-four hours, but the sooner I get out of this shithole, the better. It's served its purpose. And thankfully, I've got somewhere else to go.

'Valentina!' Josie stands on the threshold, damp tea towel in hand. Her eyes flicker over me, landing nervously on the large suitcase at my side. 'What's up?'

'I've been evicted.'

'Oh my God!'

'Sorry. I couldn't think of anywhere else to go.'

'Right… well…' She opens the door more widely, stepping back as I shuffle gratefully in.

We go into the living room and she offers me a cup of tea. I collapse on the sofa and take off my boots. The room is warm, bathed in evening sun. Josie busies herself in the kitchen area, filling the kettle, drying some mugs, sniffing the milk bottle.

'I wasn't sure you'd be in,' I say, massaging the balls of my feet. 'I was expecting to sit on your doorstep for a couple of hours.'

'I've been off work.' Her voice is flat, and when she brings over my mug, there's a dullness in those familiar blue eyes. 'Here.' She sits, facing me.

'Is it okay if I stay here for a few days? Obviously I'm going to look for somewhere else as soon as I get my deposit back – *if* I get it back.'

'I thought having the party might be against the terms of your licence,' she says. The mention of last Saturday seems to take her somewhere else briefly. I attempt a slurp at my tea, but it's too hot, so I rest it on the coffee table.

'Valentina…' she ventures.

'Yes?'

'Can I ask you something?'

'You can ask me anything, sis.'

She crumples up her mouth. 'Last Saturday… you know… when we were dancing with Tosh and Joey, and Tosh went to get me a drink…'

I give her an uncomprehending look. 'Yeah… what about it?'

'Do you think he might have put something in it?'

My eyes widen. 'You think one of my friends spiked your drink? You think they'd dare do that to my sister?'

She looks down at her hands, which are twisting nervously in her lap. 'I don't know. I keep getting these flashbacks. Horrible, violent images. I felt really sick on Sunday; it was more than just a hangover… It all points towards me being drugged.'

'Nah. You were cutting loose, that's all. Now you're feeling guilty so your brain is trying to deny it.'

'No, that's not true. I would never have had sex with those guys voluntarily.'

*Charming*, I think. *I've had sex with both of them in my time.* But I don't react, just nod thoughtfully. 'Joey's a bit manky, I grant you,' I say. 'But Tosh is buff! Honest, he doesn't have to drug a girl to get her into bed, and you have to admit, you were hitting on him all night. The way you two were dancing… I mean, you were virtually having sex there and then.'

'No, we weren't,' she replies firmly. 'Okay, maybe I was a little bit flirty, but I did not consent to having sex with either of them. I was drugged, I wasn't capable of consenting.'

I raise my eyebrows. Now we've come to the nub of it. 'Oh… you're saying they *raped* you?'

She nods.

'Fucking hell, Josie, that's a pretty serious accusation.'

'I know, I know… but I've been thinking about it and I've talked to somebody at Rape Crisis, and it's the only explanation that makes sense.'

'It doesn't make sense to me,' I huff.

She turns to me with a hurt-puppy look on her face. 'I thought you'd be more supportive…'

'I *am* being supportive.' I leap off the sofa and go over to her, crouching down and taking her hands. 'I'm trying to save you a load of grief and humiliation. If I thought you'd been raped, I'd cut their pricks off myself… Look, I know what it's like to step out of your comfort zone and do dangerous stuff. It gives you an incredible hit, but then later you come back down to earth, and sometimes, well, you wish you hadn't done it. I do it all the time, I know how scary it feels.'

'That's not how it was, Valentina,' she snaps. 'I think I was raped.'

I stand up, backing away. 'Okay… okay… Have you been to the police?'

'No, not yet.'

'Think carefully about what you'll be putting yourself through. For a start, it happened nearly a week ago, so there won't be any evidence. And if you tell the police you were at a party where people were openly taking drugs, you'll get zero sympathy.'

She purses his lips. 'Apparently there's more awareness of date rape nowadays.'

'Honestly, sis, don't go down that road, it's not worth it; there's no way they'll prosecute. Arun will find out and God knows how he'll react.' I pause, peering into her face. 'You haven't told him, have you?'

'No… I want to, but…'

'Don't. He won't believe you, I know what guys are like, especially when there's no proof. I'm sorry, sis. That's how it is. Don't risk it. It could be the end of your relationship.'

'Yeah… That's what worries me.' She sighs, her eyes starting to fill with tears.

There's the sound of a key turning in the front door. Josie looks up, startled. 'Shit, that's him.' She takes a tissue from her sleeve and dabs her eyes furiously. I stand up and try to look casual.

'What's that old suitcase doing in the—' Arun stops as soon as he sees me.

I beam across a smile. 'Hi. I've been thrown out my gaff. My kind, sweet sister says I can stay here.' He doesn't even attempt to hide the appalled look on his face.

'She's got nowhere else to go,' Josie says stiffly, rising and hurrying into the kitchen area.

'But don't you think…'

I walk over, brushing his arm as I pass. 'Careful,' I mouth. His glare is a sharp cocktail of loathing, anger and a large splash of fear.

# CHAPTER THIRTY-TWO

*The Vikings valued courage above all other qualities. Not simply physical courage in battle, but moral courage – standing up for what you believe in and doing what you know in your heart is right.*

Valentina gives me an embarrassed smile. 'Tell you what, why don't I leave you alone so you can have a talk.'

'No, there's no need…' I start, but she walks back to the hallway and picks up her bag.

'I'm gasping for a fag anyway. I won't go far, I'll be on the balcony.' She opens the door and walks out, leaving it slightly ajar.

I turn immediately to Arun. 'Why were you so rude?'

'I didn't say a thing!'

'You didn't need to. It was totally obvious you were really pissed off.'

Arun crosses to the window and leans his hands on the sill, looking away from me. 'I don't want her staying here, Josie.'

'I get that, but why?'

'I don't like her. She's got a screw loose, she's dangerous. She's been trying to worm her way into your life from the start.'

'No, she hasn't.'

'You think she's your friend, but she's not – she's using you!'

'Now you're being ridiculous.'

He heaves an enormous sigh. 'I'm not. Trust me, Josie, I'm not.'

I walk over to him and hug him from behind. He stiffens beneath my touch. 'I'm sorry you don't like her, but she's my sister. What could I do? I couldn't turn her away. I'll make sure she only stays for a few days.'

Arun swings round to face me. 'She's got no job and no money; how's she going to find somewhere? We'll never get rid of her. She's got us exactly where she wants us.'

'Oh, stop it, you're making things really difficult!'

'I can't do this. I give in, she's won.' He marches off towards the bedroom.

'What do you mean?' I follow him, horrified as I see him pulling a suitcase out from under the bed. 'What are you doing?'

'I'm leaving.'

'What? Stop it! Stop it!'

He flings open the wardrobe door and starts ripping shirts off their hangers.

'Please don't go, let's talk. We'll reach a compromise. I'll tell her she can only stay for three nights.'

He folds the shirts roughly and throws them into the case. 'It's her or me, Josie. You can't have us both.'

'Why not?'

'I can't explain, you just have to trust me. We've been together for five years; you've known Valentina for five minutes. Think about it!' He goes over to the chest of drawers and takes out all his underwear and T-shirts, tossing them into the case.

'But there's this connection with Dad – she's my flesh and blood.'

'So what? It doesn't mean a thing.'

'Well, it does to me…' I sink onto the bed, watching him dart around the room, gathering up his stuff – shoes, trainers, headphones. Why is he so angry? Has he found out about Saturday? Perhaps somebody we know saw me with Tosh and Joey. Did

Valentina tell him? No, she wouldn't do that, and I'm sure I didn't know anyone else at the party; they weren't our crowd. Anyway, if he knew, he'd come out with it straight away. He'd accuse me, wouldn't he? No, he can't possibly know. And telling him now would be the worst thing; it would finish us completely.

The suitcase is virtually full now, piled high with his belongings. He pulls over the lid and zips it shut, leaning on the top and pausing to catch his breath.

'What's wrong, Arun? Please, please tell me. Whatever it is, we can deal with it.'

'I'm sorry, Josie,' he says tearfully. 'I'm really sorry… I love you, but I can't stay here right now, not with her. It's impossible. I want to be with you, honestly I do, but not if she's in our lives. It's up to you. You have to decide.' He lifts the case off the bed and trundles it out of the bedroom, pausing only to remove a couple of jackets from their pegs by the front door.

I don't shout after him, or follow him onto the walkway. I remain in the narrow hallway, paralysed, all the energy sucked out of me. I don't understand how we've gone from a happy, normal couple to two strangers unable to communicate, so far apart emotionally that we can't bear to share the same space. It's as if we've been cyber-attacked, our systems corrupted and disabled, poison injected into our veins. We didn't see it coming, we weren't properly protected, and now everything's wrecked and we don't have the skills to put it right. We are broken. Possibly forever. I slide my back against the wall and collapse in a heap on the carpet. Is this my fault? What did I do wrong?

Valentina comes back into the flat and crouches at my side. 'Josie, are you okay? I saw Arun going off with a suitcase. What's happened?'

I lift my head weakly. 'He's left me.'

'Did you tell him about …?'

'No. I don't understand it. Something's wrong, but he won't explain… And he's really unhappy about you being here.'

'He's jealous, that's all, sis.' She strokes my hair. 'He hates me because he wants you all to himself. He's been controlling you for years, but you've been so under his spell, you've got used to it.'

'No, you're wrong. Arun's not like that.'

'When you're inside the relationship, you can't see it, but I picked up on it straight away. He realised I was a threat so he tried to turn you against me. That's what these bastards do. They dress it up as love, but it's just abuse. Anyway, it didn't work – we're strong, we're sisters… Viking warrior princesses, remember?' She pulls me to my feet. 'I'm just glad I came along and set you free.'

'Sorry, Valentina, but you're wrong. Arun and I were fine until…' I stop myself. *Until you came along*, I want to say. 'Until Dad died and everything came out. I think he's found it very unsettling.'

'Exactly! Because you were finally challenging his power over you.' She folds me into her arms. 'Come on, don't be down. I know it feels bad right now, but in a few days' time you'll be thanking me.'

'You don't understand, Valentina. I love Arun. We were happy, we'd been talking about getting married. This is wrong, it shouldn't be happening, it's all a mistake…'

'Shh… don't torment yourself. He walked out on you, so that's his loss, okay? Stupid fucker. You deserve better, Josie, believe me. You don't need Arun.'

I stagger into the kitchen area and open the fridge, grabbing a bottle of white wine. Alcohol is the last thing I need right now, I know that, but I can't stop myself twisting open the lid and pouring two large glasses. I hand one to Valentina and down the other in a single gulp. The wine is so cold it stings my teeth. I refill the glass straight away and walk around the island to the sofa, the liquid sloshing over my fingers as I thump myself down next to her.

She puts her arm around me. 'You should have brought the bottle over,' she says, 'I've a feeling we're going to need it.'

We sit together in silence for a few minutes. I don't understand how it has come to this. How my long-term boyfriend could have walked out and my short-term sister have slipped into his place. I poke about in my mind, picking at the threads that have tangled themselves into this knot. There must be a way to untie it.

'No more secrets from now on,' I say suddenly. 'I'm going to tell Mum. I'm going to drive over to her place tonight and tell her everything. Arun was right all along. She has a right to know and I'm not going to be the keeper of my father's dirty secrets any longer. Enough!'

Valentina sits up with a start. 'I don't think that's a very good idea. You've drunk too much for a start…'

'Then I'll go on the bus. Or take a taxi.'

'No, no, you can't turn up pissed and dump all that shit on her. It's not fair.'

'It happened to me!' I knock back my glass.

'Yeah, I know, me too, and it was horrible, remember?'

'I'm still going to tell her tonight.'

'Please don't.' Valentina grips my arm. 'You'll spoil things. We're supposed to be celebrating.' She stands up and fetches the bottle.

'Celebrating what?'

'Your freedom.' She refills her glass.

'What are you talking about? My life's completely screwed up.'

'No, it's not, it's just changed, that's all. For the better. *You're* changing. Becoming a new person…'

'I don't want to be a new person!' I shout. 'I want to get my life back on track, and the first thing to do is tell my mother the truth!' I stand up and go over to my phone, but Valentina lunges forward and snatches it off the counter. 'Hey! What are you doing? Give it back.' I hold out my hand.

She traps it in the crook of her arm, shaking her head. 'If you tell your mother, she'll turn you against me. She'll say we can't be sisters any more.'

'You don't know that.'

'Then what will happen to me? I'll have nowhere to go and nobody to turn to.'

'Look, I'm not saying it's going to be easy; this is all very complicated, but we'll work something out.'

'Don't abandon me, sis,' she pleads. 'You're all I've got.'

'Who said anything about abandoning you? Please give me my phone back.'

She steps away. 'You don't understand. I need you. Now that our dad's gone, there's nobody else to look out for me. Nobody else to stop me doing bad stuff.'

'What bad stuff? What do you mean?'

'If I told you, you'd hate me forever. It's bad. Really bad… But I'm not a bad person, sis. I don't want the bad things to happen, they just do – I can't stop myself. You think I'm lively and funny, always up for a dare, but you don't know the real me. You don't understand the pain I suffer inside all the fucking time, the terrifying darkness I live in every single day.'

'Valentina, you're scaring me. Give me my phone back.' My tone is insistent. 'Now.' She slowly unwraps her arms and lets me take it off her.

'Don't abandon me, sis! I don't know what I'll do if I lose you.'

'Trust me, it's going to be okay.'

Her eyes are flickering wildly. 'Don't tell her we're close, don't tell her I'm living here. Please!'

*You're not living here*, I think to myself. *I don't even want you staying.* What is wrong with her? She's really starting to worry me.

'Look, I'm just going to give her a call and arrange a time to talk. I'll take it slowly. I probably won't mention that we've got to know each other, not at first, anyway.'

'Don't mention it ever.'

'Leave it to me, I know what to do. I'll just call her now, yeah?'

I go into the bedroom and shut the door. Shit… Why did I say she could stay? I sit on the bed and nervously dial Mum's landline. After a couple of rings, it goes to voicemail. Of course, it's Thursday. She works in the rehab clinic on Thursdays. I call her mobile instead, hoping she won't have switched it off. Luckily, it rings. I wait for her to pick up. *Come on! Answer before I lose my nerve.*

'Josie? I'm a bit busy right now, can I call you back?'

'Sorry, but I need to talk to you. It's really, really important.'

'What's wrong? You sound strange.'

I start to cry, my words stuttering through the tears. 'Everyone's been… been lying to us, Mum… for years and years. But I know… I know the truth now and I can't keep it in any longer.'

There's a slight pause. 'The truth about what?'

'I can't… can't tell you on the phone. We need to meet…' Another pause. 'Mum, are you still there?'

'Just try to keep calm,' she says. 'I'll call in on my way home. I'll be there within the hour, okay?'

The call ends and all the emotion I've been holding inside me for the last couple of months floods out. I'm going to tell her everything. It's going to be fine. Mum will fix things. She always knows how to fix things.

There's just one problem. I need to get rid of Valentina before she arrives.

# CHAPTER THIRTY-THREE

*Living truthfully was an important part of the Viking moral and religious code. Lying was strictly forbidden – with one important exception: if you were being lied to.*

'How can you treat me like this? I've only just moved in, and now you're chucking me out!' Valentina is standing in front of me, hands on hips, chin jutting forward.

'I'm not chucking you out,' I reply, trying to sound calm. 'I just need you not to be here for a short while.'

'You said you were going to fix a time to talk. I thought that meant like in a couple of days, not fucking now!'

'I didn't have much choice. She said she'd come over straight away, and I couldn't think of a reason to say no.'

She folds her arms defiantly. 'I'm not going. She'll just have to meet me.'

God, I could really do without this. 'Come on, Valentina, five minutes ago you were begging me not to tell her about you.'

'Why are you spoiling everything?' she cries. 'It's not fair. I wanted it just to be the two of us.'

'I know, I'm sorry, but I have to talk to her before I lose my nerve. She can't meet you tonight. It would be terrible – utterly shocking for her.'

'Yeah, I'm the aberration, the love-child monster.' She makes a cross of her fingers. 'Get thee gone, witch!'

'I didn't mean it like that. Please, be reasonable. All I'm asking is that you give us some time, an hour or so.'

'What am I supposed to do? Hide in the wardrobe? Disappear in a puff of smoke?'

'No, I was thinking you could go to the pub, actually.'

She tosses back her hair. 'I don't have any cash.'

I walk over to my bag and rummage around for my purse. 'I'll give you some. Get yourself something to eat. The King's Head is just around the corner. If you don't fancy the pub, there are plenty of cafés on the Finchley Road that stay open late.' I open the purse. Shit. I've only got a couple of quid in change. I whip out my debit card. I know it's stupid, but I don't have much choice. 'You'd better take this. The pin is zero eight nine two, the month and year of our birthdays, easy to remember.'

'Huh.' She snatches the card off me and sticks it in the back of her jeans.

I pick up her jacket and hand it to her. 'I'll text you as soon as she's gone, then you can come straight back.'

'Whatever.' Valentina storms out, slamming the door behind her.

Part of me wants to rush after her and tell her not to bother coming back. How dare she talk to me like that? But I haven't got time to think about it now. Mum will be here soon. I've got to clear away any signs of Valentina's presence. I drag her heavy suitcase into the sitting room and hide it in the corner by the bookshelves, then cover it with an old throw. I wash her wine glass and put it back on the shelf. I feel like a criminal, covering up the traces of a crime.

I adjust the lighting – turn off the overhead light and switch on the side lamps. I draw the curtains and plump up the cushions. Perched on the edge of the sofa, my heart pumping the blood around my body at an alarming speed, I practise my lines. The words in my head sound clear and strong, but I've no idea what's going to happen when I speak them out loud.

The doorbell rings and I start with fright. She's here. At least, I hope it's her and not Valentina returning. I stand and walk quickly to the front door, peering through the spyhole to see Mum's familiar shape.

'Thanks for coming over,' I say, opening up to let her in.

'I was so worried, I finished the session early. What's the matter, darling?'

'It's a very long story. Take your coat off, Mum. Let's go and sit down.'

I steer her into the living room and settle her on the sofa. And then, after a couple of stuttering false starts, I tell her the truth… Well, most of it.

'I'm sorry,' she says. 'I'm finding this very hard to take in… He was living with this woman, Sophie, in some village, yes? Near where he crashed. Right… And the daughter, this Valentina, was living in the house *we* bought with *our* savings…' Mum is pacing around the room, breathing heavily in between words, gesticulating with both hands like she's trying to push the facts into her brain. 'So for the past *ten* years, since you were fourteen, in fact—'

'Yes, but obviously it'd been going on for a lot longer than that,' I interrupt, keeping my voice low and gentle. 'Because Valentina and I were born just a few days apart, in the same hospital.'

'I know, you said. It's beyond appalling, it's… it's unspeakable…' She leans on the back of the armchair and swallows hard. 'Let's get this straight: did Jerry move up north to be with them, or did they move to be with him?'

'I don't know, does it matter?'

'Yes, it matters! I need to understand this.'

'Um, well, all I know is, Valentina's grandparents died and left her mother loads of money. She wanted to get out of London so she bought a house in Derbyshire. Maybe – and I'm just guessing here – Dad took the job in Manchester to… er, to carry on, or make it easier… I don't know. Ever since I found out, I've been trying to get my head around it and it still doesn't make sense.'

She shakes her head in disbelief. 'Why didn't you tell me straight away, Josie?'

I look into my lap. 'You were grieving and I didn't want to make it worse. I was worried that you wouldn't cope.'

'I'm not a child!'

'I didn't mean that, but Dad had just died and you were very—'

'I needed to know the truth, Josie.' She leans off the chair and starts pacing again, the anger giving her fresh energy. 'Who else knows? Arun, of course. What about Brett and Lisa?' She sees a shadow cross my face. 'Oh great, so they do.'

'I'm so sorry, Mum, but I didn't know what to do. I went to see them because I needed some advice. Brett was upset…'

'No, I bet he's known all along. He always covered up for his little brother, right from when they were kids.'

'I don't know, he seemed totally shocked.' My mind whizzes back to the day I went to see them. I remember the looks on their faces. Brett was embarrassed, and Lisa was furious. If they *did* already know, it was an incredible acting job, but then the ability to lie and pretend seems to run in the family.

'I don't buy it,' continues Mum. 'Brett must have known. Jerry told him everything – everything! No wonder he's always behaved like he's got something over me, the nasty little creep.' She exhales a puff of hatred. 'I expect he told you to keep your mouth shut.'

'Yes, he did, but Lisa thought I should tell you. And so did Arun; he kept on at me, but I couldn't make up my mind. I was so scared of hurting you.'

Her eyes flash at me. 'So I'm the silly fool, the fragile little wife who has to be kept in the dark for fear she'll do something stupid. Is that how you all see me, Josie? Some pathetic, weak woman, totally in love with her husband, who could go over the edge at the drop of a hat? You have no idea. No idea how strong I am, not a bloody clue about what I've done for you. All the sacrifices I've made so you can have a stable, happy life.'

'Look, I know it's been difficult at times and I really appreciate everything—'

'No, you don't, Josie, you actually don't. You always preferred your father, right from when you were a baby. You cried every time he left the house and you sulked until he came home. He filled your head with all that stupid Viking stuff and the two of you shut me out. I wasn't part of your little gang, I wasn't *fun.* I was just boring ordinary Mummy who looked after the house and went to work and took care of you while he was away.'

Her words cut deep. He *was* my favourite. I tried not to let it show, but it must have been obvious. 'Why are you turning against me, Mum? We're both victims here. I'm just as upset and angry with him as—'

'No, you're not,' she says, raising her hand. 'I promise you you're not. You didn't tell me because you wanted to protect him. Even though he's dead and I can't get to him, more's the pity. You didn't want the truth out in the open, because then everyone would have to accept what a lying, cheating shit your father was. And everyone would know that he never really loved you, or me, or his other family for that matter. He was just a selfish bastard who didn't *love* anyone but himself.'

I know what she's doing. Lashing out at me because she can't hurt him. I stand up and walk over to her, feeling my courage growing. 'Yes, I know that, Mum. I'm not as naïve as you think. My feelings towards Dad are very complicated. I'm incredibly angry, and hurt and upset, but I also love him and miss him. I know I shouldn't, but I do. I don't know what stopped me telling you… just cowardice, I think.' I hold out my hands towards her. 'I never meant to insult you. And I finally realised I was making a mistake, which is why I've told you now. I didn't want you to find out the way I did. It was really shocking… just barging in on my sister like that.'

'Half-sister,' she snaps. 'She's your half-sister.'

'I know, but honestly, she could be my twin. It's so weird…' I pause, thinking about Valentina sitting in a nearby pub, her suitcase hiding in the corner. This has gone so badly, I can't possibly tell Mum about her now. It would be the final straw.

Mum turns and stares at me. 'You're not still in touch with her, are you? Because that would be a really, really stupid idea.'

I hesitate. 'No… of course not.' My cheeks flame and I turn my face away from the light. It's a lie I'm going to have to turn into a truth. I've got to cut all ties with my sister as soon as possible.

'Thank God for that,' Mum says. 'Do not have *anything* to do with her – or her mother. Keep well away from them. Promise me, Josie.' She grabs me by the arms, her eyes full of fear. 'Promise!'

# CHAPTER THIRTY-FOUR

*A Viking witch practised seiðr magic with her spindle and distaff, weaving spells into goatskins and the threads of her family's clothing, and taking revenge on the powerful using the skills of sorcery.*

It's fucking cold out here in the dark, banished from the warmth and comfort of Josie's flat. I am the freak, the outcast; my very existence heaps shame upon others and I must be kept hidden. They wouldn't let me eat my takeaway in the pub. Didn't allow me to drink my own booze, either. Got some fat bastard in a bomber jacket to escort me off the premises.

So now I'm walking 'home', kicking the polystyrene box before me, necking out of the bottle and letting the wine drip off my chin like blood from a cut throat. I wipe my mouth with the back of my hand and let out a loud belch. The bottle is almost empty. If I'm not careful, there won't be any left for sis. Shame…

She thinks she is the true warrior princess and I'm the bastard child, the young pretender. But there are two sides to every secret – I am hers and she is mine. We have a deadly symmetry. Secrets are the devil's work, for sure. They grow invisibly under each other, like layers of fresh skin. They multiply like worms. Cut one wriggling secret in half and suddenly you have two. Do the same again and you have four, eight, sixteen – and so it goes on until you have a plague.

I have my very own special secret, of course. Feeling around in the forest at the back of my head, I find it. Here is the scar my sister gave me – so slight an event in her childhood that she doesn't even remember doing it. I trace its raised line with the tip of my finger, then dig at the edges until I feel the pain of the past. This is what she did because she didn't want to share. Well, sis, I don't want to share either. I want you all to myself. I drain the bottle and hurl it onto the path, shivering deliciously as the glass smashes into hundreds of pieces.

I bend down and pick up a large shard, tucking it into my back pocket. The urge to cut is strong tonight. More powerful and insistent than it's been for a long time. The insides of my arms are itching like crazy. I hug myself protectively. Later, later… all in good time…

The apartment block with its four rows of white-edged balconies looms before me. A few lights shine out from the flats, like dots on a screen. She must be up there by now. The legitimate wife, the rightful widow, the official mother of the proper daughter. Viking royalty, no less. I walk into the play area and sit down on a swing, pushing off with my feet and creaking back and forth, back and forth. How is the conversation going up there? Is there shock and horror? Weeping and wailing? Kisses and embraces? I feel my ears heating up as they chew me over. *You're not to have anything to do with the bastard child… But, Mother, I'm all she has, the only one left who cares… Even so, daughter, she's not one of us, she cannot be part of our family.*

Maybe, in time, when the tears are dry and we've all 'come to terms', I'll be brought out of the wilderness and welcomed into the Macauliffe fold. Welcomed is probably too strong a word. I'll be tolerated, but never fully accepted. The guest who's difficult to introduce, who volunteers to sit astride the table leg and eat off the odd plate; who collects the dirty dishes and busies herself in the kitchen with the washing-up. Grateful to be included, content to not quite belong. So what's new? I've always been an embarrassment, a problem that just won't go away.

I hear a door opening above and glance up to see a figure walking along the balcony. It must be her. I jump off the swing and hotfoot it to the entrance, crouching behind a bush. She's coming down the stairs, her smart heels bouncing off the concrete. The double doors swing open and she emerges, pausing to steady herself and take a breath. We're very close to each other but she has no idea that I'm here.

She walks on down the path, past the swings and the small slide. I wait a few seconds then creep after her. Digging into her bag, she takes out a key fob and points it like a magic wand. A smart grey Prius ten metres away twinkles in response. She walks towards it – maybe there's a slight wobble in her step – and I follow. As she flips back the wing mirror and opens the driver's door, light from the street lamp catches her face.

I let out a small gasp and stagger back. She looks around for a brief second, then gets into the car, shutting the door. I can't breathe… I cannot fucking breathe… I clasp my chest and sink to the ground. She turns on the headlights, then the car reverses out of the space and glides silently away like a phantom.

*No, no, no, this can't be.*

I have to talk to Josie. I rise slowly to my feet and stumble back to the building, feeling so weak it takes all my strength to push open the swing doors. My legs are so heavy I can barely get them up the stairs. This doesn't compute, doesn't make any sense. I grip the metal stair rail as I climb, frightened that my head is going to spin off my shoulders and send me flying. Somehow I make it to the top and almost crawl along the balcony, finally making it to Josie's front door. I pound on it with my fist.

She opens up, her face pricked with irritation. 'I thought I told you to wait until I texted.'

'Let me in,' I pant, staggering past her. 'Shit, my chest hurts… can't breathe.'

'Valentina, what the hell? What's wrong?'

I head for the living room, but suddenly I don't know where I am. My brain has gone into spasm. I can't think, can't calculate. All those conversations… Except they *weren't* conversations. They were cross-examinations.

*Tell me more about your father. What's his name?*

*Jerry. Short for Jerome. Jerome Henry Macauliffe.*

*And he's definitely your father.*

*Yeah! I'm the spitting image of him. We have Viking blood running through our veins.*

*Does he live with you?*

*Sometimes.*

*Where is he when he's not with you?*

*Dunno. In hotels, I think. He goes away all the time for work.*

*What sort of work does he do?*

*He's like this massively important lecturer who travels all over the world… Does it matter? Can we talk about me now?*

I remember sitting in the armchair opposite her desk, bleating my little heart out about how much my father loved me. I showed her the Viking pendant I always wore around my neck. I brought in the Viking book I'd made when I was a kid, full of interesting facts he'd taught me, illustrated with my own drawings. She looked through it really carefully, as if examining a very important document, like it was telling her all about my life.

'Valentina? What's wrong?' Josie tugs at me. 'Have you just taken something?'

'No! Fuck off.' I shake myself free and slosh some wine into the nearest glass.

'Look, I've just had one of the most difficult conversations ever. I don't need you to start swearing at me,' she says in a teacher voice. 'I know you were unhappy about leaving the flat, but—'

I scream into her face, 'Just shut the fuck up!' and hurl the glass at her head. She ducks and cries out as it shatters against the wall behind her. There's a second of thrilling silence as streaks of red wine drip down the white paint.

'Valentina!' she gasps, staring at the pieces of glass at her feet. 'What the hell are you doing? Calm down!'

But I don't want to calm down. I want to rage. I snatch another glass off the shelves and pour myself more wine. 'Your mum's a psychiatrist, is she?'

'Yes. A consultant psychiatrist, actually. How do you know that?'

'She uses her maiden name for work, right?'

'Yes. So what?'

Raising my glass, I shout, 'To Dr Bannister! The evil bitch who wrecked my whole fucking life.' I down the wine in one go, then smash the glass onto the floor.

Josie gazes at me, mouth open. 'What on earth do you mean? You don't even know her.'

Wild howls of laughter vomit out of my mouth. 'Oh yes I do! I know her and she knows me. She knows *exactly* who I am; she's known for *years*!'

My sister moves towards me. 'Valentina, stop this, you're talking rubbish.'

I shove her back onto the broken glass. 'You don't have a clue, do you? Not a fucking clue!' I prod her in the chest. 'She *treated* me' – prod – 'she *pretended* she was my friend' – prod – 'she acted like she *cared*.'

'No, no – you've got it wrong. She didn't know – I told her about you just now and she was really shocked.'

I give her another hard push and she staggers backwards, steadying herself on the arm of the sofa. 'She was lying to you, you stupid tosser!' Mad energy is flowing through my veins like an electric current. I charge crazily around the room, tearing at my hair, pushing over chairs and anything else that dares to stand in my way, flinging objects off the shelves – books, picture, ornaments – now I see, now I understand, now it all makes sense.

Josie is cowering against the wall, hands over her ears as the contents of the room crash and smash around her. 'Valentina, please stop! Talk to me! Tell me the truth.'

I run over and grip her shoulders. 'You want to know the truth, do you? You really want to know? Okay, I'll tell you. When I was little, I was sure I had a sister who looked just like me. I used to dream about you all the time. In my dream, we were in a tree house and we had a fight, and you hurt me. You gave me *this*.' I grab her wrist and twist it round to the back of my head.

'What are you doing? Let me go!'

'Feel it! Go on! Feel the scar… Go on…'

Josie starts to squeal. 'Stop it.'

'You nearly killed me.'

'No, I didn't!' She jerks her hand free.

'Yes, you did, but you were so young you don't remember. Other people know what happened. Our dead father, for sure. Our uncle too, I expect. Maybe my mum, who knows? Probably. She was in on everything. But I was told I was imagining you, making it all up. And then, when I was fourteen, I met Dr Bannister. I told her about my dream and she was fascinated. But as I talked to her, she started to work out who I was. And more to the point, who my father was.'

'No, no, it can't be true… My mother wouldn't—'

I pin her against the wall. 'Get it into your stupid thick head. I'm the only one that's telling the truth… the *only* one! You can't trust anyone else. Just me – just your sister. Okay?'

She nods, her eyes staring wildly. 'Yes… yes… go on.'

'Dr Bannister found out I was her cheating husband's bastard kid. She wanted me out of the way. She didn't give a toss if I went and topped myself… no, no, I understand now, she *wanted* me to do it. She *wanted* me dead. And she knew how to make it happen. It was so easy – all she had to do was make me feel like she cared, then abandon me, just like that, no warning, no reason. She knew I'd try to kill myself. Job done! Good riddance. Murder without having to lift a finger!'

'Don't say that. She wouldn't… she couldn't…'

'But she *did!* That's exactly what she did.' I push my forehead against hers, spitting into her face. 'When are you going to wake up? Your mother's a *liar*! She lied to you tonight, just as she's been lying to you for ten years. They've all been lying to us, sis! Mums, Dad, aunts, uncles – they've lied to us our whole fucking lives!'

She cries out like a wounded animal and slides to the floor, burying her face in her hands and sobbing. I stand over her, panting for breath, trying to feel a drop of sympathy as her world crashes down around her. Poor sis… all these years, she's led such a calm, happy life with her clever mummy and daddy with their professional careers and fat salaries, living in their million-pound house, going to her posh private school so she didn't have to mix with the lowlife at the scummy comp, jolly time at uni, decent job, gorgeous boyfriend. The beloved only child, the princess, sole heir to the throne, surrounded by love and adoration. Now look at her. She's no better than me.

But I don't want her all defeated and sorry for herself. She's no use to me like this. No use at all.

I wrench her up by her armpits and smash her against the wall, lifting my hand and slapping her hard around the face. 'Shut up! Stop crying!'

She flinches, then stares back at me, her eyes wide and liquid.

'It's time to face the truth, dear sister! They don't love us, they don't give a fuck – they think they can do what they want. Because we're nothing to them, we're nobody, just a couple of stupid girls who don't count. They think they can lie through their teeth and keep their filthy secrets and it doesn't matter – as long as we don't know, we can't be hurt. But we know now, we've found them out, we know what utter fucking shitty bastards they all really are. Yeah? You understand?' I shake her.

'Yes… you're right. I see it now.'

'So we mustn't fall apart, because that's what the fuckers want. They want us to be sad and weak and suicidal, 'cos then we can't fight back. But we mustn't let them get away with it. We've got to be warriors, right? We've got to attack. Make them pay for what they've done. We've got to get angry!'

'I *am* angry,' she says, her voice low and trembling. 'I *am.* I'm really angry.'

'Good girl… that's it…' I stroke the red slash I've made on her cheek. 'Don't fight it; let it flood right through you. Let it build, let it grow. Feel the fury running through your veins.'

'Yes, I can feel it. I can feel it rising.' She pushes me away roughly and I stagger backwards.

'Yeah, that's what I want to see. Give in to it. Let it fill you up and take you over. Tell me how angry you are. Go on, say it!'

'I'm fucking angry.' Her voice is growing stronger. She walks forward, picks up a china candlestick and throws it with all her might across the room. 'I'm fucking angry!' she shouts as it hits the table and smashes to the floor.

'That's it. Say it again. Louder. Scream the words in my face!'

She throws back her head and roars. 'I hate them all! I'm fucking, fucking, *fucking angry*!'

# CHAPTER THIRTY-FIVE

*The Viking warriors known as berserkers were notorious for their ferocity and fearlessness in battle. They drugged themselves with poisonous red toadstools and fought without protective clothing.*

At last the flat is dark and totally quiet. I get up and dress without switching the lights on. My fingers fumble blindly with the buttons on my shirt, which in turn catches in the zip of my skirt. I rip it free, not caring, and tuck it into my waistband. The jacket goes on next. I don't bother with tights or socks, slipping my bare feet into a pair of flat ballet pumps and creeping out of the room. I shut the door quietly behind me and grope around in the darkness for the key rack by the door. Lifting the keys carefully, so as not to let them jingle, I slip them into my jacket pocket. I squeeze the handle and open the front door, then step onto the balcony and close it behind me with the tiniest of clicks.

It's late. Gone two a.m. I hold out my hand and feel heavy rain. The night air is cold, but my febrile state cannot be cooled or dampened. It's important not to disturb anyone, so I don't press the switch for the walkway lighting, choosing instead to edge my way past the front doors. There are no lights on in the neighbours' flats, no sounds of music playing. The silence is eerie, as if the block has been abandoned. I glance upwards at the city sky, illuminating my way with its dull, polluted glow.

As I skip down the steps, adrenalin courses through my veins. I splash through the puddles of the children's playground and run down the middle of the road, past the rows of sleeping cars. My ears are pricked, my night vision focused on the distant target. A fox screams somewhere close by and I send a wolf howl in response. I am wild and angry. My heart is pumping Viking blood through my body. I am a berserker.

Berserkers worshipped the cult of Odin; they were shape-strong and invincible. They wore bears' pelts into battle to transform themselves into ferocious animals with supernatural strength. They gnawed the iron rims of their shields. They drank and drugged themselves into a trance-like state known as *hamask*, where nothing could touch them. They terrified the enemy into submission because they knew no fear.

My feet are soon drenched, slipping and sloshing around in my boat-like pumps, the earth hard and stony beneath their flimsy soles. But I don't feel any pain. The rain soaks into my skull, and my hair, which is fastened tight behind my head, drips like a long rat's tail down my back.

Up the hill to the top of the street, then down again. Onto the main road, where the cars and trucks and express coaches flash past in a ground-level thunderstorm. I march on, furious and determined, my pace quickening to the drum of my pulse. But I have to control the anger, bottle it up and stuff in the cork. There's a long way to go yet; I mustn't spend all my energy now.

Looking to my left, I see the shape of a bus in the distance. I dash across the first lane and stand in the centre of the road, buffeted by the wind of the cars whipping past on either side. Jumping up and down impatiently, I spot a small gap in the traffic and dart across, pursued by a blast of horns, waving my arm frantically to flag down the night bus.

The driver doesn't even glance at me as I press the card against the ticket reader and bound up the stairs. I sit down, my clothes dripping all over the upholstery, and press my forehead against the rain-spattered window, trying to make out where we are. But all I can see is a watery nightscape: white headlights and red tail lights merging with the dissolving glow of street lamps. The bus lurches forward like a drunken beggar. I feel hot, but I'm shivering. I bite into the metal pole and listen out for the stops.

St John's Wood station. Here we are. I scramble down the stairs and leap off, landing heavily on the slippery pavement. The tube is closed for the night and there are very few people around. Nobody is looking at me, and I feel invisible. The rain has washed me away, as the sea wipes out pictures in the sand. I turn down the side road and steadily make my way to the house.

The anger that I've corked up is heating and expanding. I don't know what I'm going to say. Maybe we are beyond words. All these years of being lied to, of being tricked and deceived, are over. Mum and Dad can't work against me any more, spinning their evil *seiðr* magic. My sister and I have found them out and exposed all their secrets. We won't let them wrap an enchanted goatskin around our heads, altering our vision, manipulating our minds. It's our turn to be the witches and work our magic on everyone else.

I stand before the house and take a deep breath. The front tiled path is slippery and I almost fall as I move towards the front door. Taking the keys out of my pocket, I find the right one and ease it into the lock. The door rattles as I push it forward. I close it quietly behind me, then slip off my pumps and wipe my bare feet on the rough, bristly mat.

The staircase is ahead of me, looming out of the darkness. Stretching my arms out, I edge blindly towards the bottom step, then hold the banister and climb up to the first floor. The house creaks, as if turning in its sleep. Her bedroom door is slightly ajar. I lift it off its hinges so that it doesn't squeak as I walk in.

She's on her back, snuffling through her nose, her chest rising and falling in a natural rhythm, chin pointed upwards. Funny how she keeps to her side of the bed, as if hoping my father might still sneak in beside her. As I stare at her sleeping form, I imagine his ghost lying there. His thick auburn hair on the pillow, his broad shoulders and hairy naked chest, his strong, bearded features just visible in the gloom.

Vikings had swords, bows and arrows, but they would attack their enemy with whatever came to hand: sticks, stones, planks of wood, metal cooking pots. They shamed their honour with curses and insults; took their victim's trousers down before they stabbed them in the guts.

I climb onto the bed and straddle her. She stirs and blearily opens her eyes.

'Josie? What are you—'

'Gaze upon your destiny. I have come to stop the lying maggot mouth in your foul swine's head.' I take my father's pillow and push it into her face.

I channel all my superhuman strength into my hands, pressing them down and holding them there. She kicks; she tries to move her head. She reaches up and tears at my neck, but I shove her off with my knees. I keep the pillow there until all she can do is twitch. And then, even the twitching stops.

# CHAPTER THIRTY-SIX

*Viking laws were not written down, but were passed down orally through the generations. When there was a trial, the law sayers spoke the law to the assembled throng, who discussed the case and gave their verdict.*

I pretend to sleep, hoping that if I lie there long enough with my eyes closed, my brain will be fooled. But instead it gets to its devious nightly work. Disgusting, violent images fester in a sea of memories, gathering momentum as they form a giant wave. I turn and swim desperately away, but I can feel their power as they chase me down, roaring and shouting like sea warriors. The wave builds and builds until it strikes from behind, tossing me in the air and then dragging me under. Down and down I sink into the murky, swirling water, spinning blind and helpless towards the bottom. I lie there for an age, tossed by storms, lost and forgotten. If I'm ever washed up on the shore, it will be as flotsam and jetsam – unidentifiable bones and pieces of rag.

Succumbing to the night terrors seems to work, because eventually a peaceful sleep takes over and carries me through to morning. As soon as I wake, my ears reach for sounds of company. The flat seems quiet, but I get up and do a proper recce. Thank God, I'm alone. I go to the bathroom and wash my face, pressing a hot flannel into the puffy bags beneath my eyes. There's no point in showering yet. The work I have to do today will make me sweaty.

I poke about in the drawers for some soft, comforting clothes and pull on a pair of leggings and a thin blue top. Then I drag my hair into a ponytail, drape a thin scarf around my neck and slip on a pair of flip-flops. The air in the living room is thick with yesterday's revelations, so I open the windows as wide as they'll go and wave them out. It's a sunny day; last night's heavy rain has cleansed and purified everything. That's what I'm going to do here. I'm going to wash and scrub and polish.

There's no time for breakfast, not even a cup of tea. I'm sick to death of tea. And alcohol. From now on I'm going to drink only water. Flipping on the tap, I fill a large tumbler and swallow it in one go. The coldness burns my head. Right. Let's get to work. I bend down and open the cupboard under the sink, taking out a bucket, a bottle of bleach and a pair of cracked rubber gloves.

Maybe I should dust and hoover first – suck up all the stray hairs and dead skin cells. Yes, got to do this in the right order or it'll be a waste of time. I find a duster in the drawer and swoosh it over all the surfaces, starting in the bedroom. I lift every little trinket from the windowsill and clean underneath before putting them back in exactly the same position. I dust the photo frames and the bedside lamps, stand on a chair and clean the top of the wardrobe. I lift the jewellery box and put it on the bed so that I can do the chest of drawers in large sweeps.

The temptation to paw over things is irresistible. I open the jewellery box and run my fingers through the tangle of necklaces and bangles, sparkly earrings and glittery hair slides. Underneath the heap, I glimpse a small silver hammer. I pull it out, shaking it free from the knot of chains and beads. I ease the leather lace over my head and the hammer nestles in the well at the base of my neck. I turn to look at myself in the wardrobe mirror, smiling approvingly at my reflection. There was a time when I never took off my Thor pendant. Maybe that's what went wrong. I stopped wearing it and lost my protection from evil spirits. Well, I'm safe now…

I shut the jewellery box and return it to its rightful place. Mustn't keep stopping like this, there's too much to do. The dusting complete, I get out the hoover and attack the carpet, dragging out boxes and bags from under the bed and shoving the tube into all the awkward corners.

Moving into the bathroom, I clean the floor first, making sure I find every stray hair. Then I fetch the bleach. I douse every surface liberally, then scrub at them with a brush. The ammonia makes my eyes sting, and I start to cough. Suddenly I hear a door slam. Who's that? I poke my head anxiously out of the bathroom. But there's nobody here. A draught is blowing through the flat and the door to the living room has shut.

I touch the Thor pendant. It's okay, the charm is working.

Now to the kitchen and sitting area. I take out the broom and sweep up all the broken glass and china, wrapping the pieces in newspaper and putting them in the bin. Then I put the photos and ornaments back on the shelves. Dragging the sofa away from the wall, I hoover behind and under, picking up crumpled sweet wrappers and hair grips, stale peanuts and a single dusty sock – Arun's by the look of it. They all go into the bin. I hoover the sofa cushions, and shake out the rug. I bleach the surface of the low coffee table and the dining table. I scrub the dirty finger marks off the backs of the upright chairs and rub at stains on the seats.

Finally I set upon the kitchen units. Here I can use the bleach without fear, and soon everything is drenched in its killer fluid. The smell makes my head swim and I have to run onto the balcony to gulp in some fresh air. I empty the contents of the hoover bag into a bin liner, then take all the rubbish down to the wheelie bins at the bottom of the stairs. Returning to the flat, I lean against the front door and let out a long sigh of relief. I've finished. I've done it. The past is gone and there's not a trace of anything or anyone left.

It's about half two when the doorbell rings, its insistent tone making me jump. I drag my weary limbs to the door, stopping to peer through the spyhole. Two people are standing there. A man in a suit, and a woman in a dark uniform.

Police.

I open up immediately. 'I'm Detective Constable Jonathan Harris,' the man says, holding up a badge. 'Are you Miss Josie Macauliffe?'

'Yes,' I answer, gripping the door frame. 'Why are you here? What's happened?'

'It's not very easy to talk on the doorstep. Do you mind if we come in?'

I take them into the living room. 'What is it? Is it bad news?'

DC Harris looks at me kindly. 'Shall we all sit down?'

'Yes, er, sorry… please…' I back onto the sofa, while he takes the armchair.

'Shall I make some tea?' asks the policewoman, walking into the kitchen area.

'No. No, I'm okay.' She moves away, pulling up an upright chair and sitting down. 'Can you please just tell me why you're here?'

'I'm afraid it *is* bad news,' he says. 'I'm very sorry, but…' *Just say it. Say it!* 'Your mother, Helen, was found dead at her home this afternoon.'

My stomach lurches and my heart leaps into my mouth. 'What? No… no… this can't be happening. No, please, no—'

'I'm very sorry, this must be a terrible shock for you. I believe you lost your father only a couple of months ago.'

'Yes. I'm sorry, I don't understand. What do you mean "found dead"?'

DC Harris pulls out a small notebook and glances at it. 'Lena Paszek, your mother's cleaner, found her in bed earlier this afternoon. She was very distraught and called us straight away. I gather she's worked for your family for many years; she seemed to know a lot about you. She gave us your details as the next of kin.'

'Yes, of course… What was it, a heart attack?'

'We don't know yet. As with all sudden deaths, there will have to be a post-mortem. I'm sorry, I know this can be very upsetting.'

'No, I understand… We need to know…' The tears start to fall, and I wipe my cheek with the back of my hand.

'Are you sure you don't want that cup of tea?' the policewoman says. 'Or a glass of water?'

I shake my head. 'No, thanks, I'm fine.'

The detective leans forward. 'Is there anyone we can call, another relative? A friend? Someone who can come and be with you?'

'No, I'm okay. There are people I can… I'll sort it. Thanks.'

'We'll need you to identify the body, but that can wait until after the post-mortem. We'll be in touch as soon as there's anything more to tell you.' He pauses, exchanging a glance with the female officer. 'Can you just tell me when you last saw your mother?'

'Last night,' I reply. 'She popped round for a chat, left at about ten, I think. Maybe a bit later, I'm not sure.'

'And then she went home?'

'Yes.'

'Did she seem unwell to you? Was she complaining of anything?'

'No, she seemed okay. A bit stressed with work and stuff.'

'Would you say she was depressed at all?'

'Not really. She was still upset over my father's death, and various things had come out that she wasn't too happy about, but… I don't think it was enough to kill herself.'

'Thank you, that's very helpful. Would you like my officer to stay with you?'

'No, honestly, I'd rather be alone.'

He hands over a card. 'This is my direct number if you want to contact me. We'll be in touch again once we've got the post-mortem results. Do you have a mobile number?'

'Yes.' He puts it straight into his phone.

'Now, if you're sure you're all right, we'll leave you in peace.'

'Please.'

He nods at the officer, who immediately stands up. 'We'll see ourselves out.'

As soon as they're gone, I run into the bathroom and throw up into the beautifully clean toilet. When I've emptied my stomach, I lean on the side of the bath and pull myself upright.

I study my pale, dishevelled features in the mirror. Who is this woman staring back at me? I've never looked or felt less like myself. My fingers tighten around Thor's hammer and I draw in its magic powers. I can do this. All I have to do is hold my nerve.

# CHAPTER THIRTY-SEVEN

*Women in Norse sagas often acted as inciters. The goading scene is a classic in Viking stories. The men were goaded to act when otherwise they would have been content to do nothing.*

I cross over the Finchley Road and weave my way through the streets of huge, imposing houses to Golder's Hill Park. This was once heathland, but it has long since been tamed and brought to order; the grass is kept short and the paths are trimmed. There's a small free zoo, which of course Dad disapproved of. Whenever we came here, crowds of small children would gather outside the cages, trying to catch sight of the animals, mostly birds, which were either asleep or hiding. 'They should be free to stretch their wings,' he'd declare, running ahead of me and flapping his arms. I smile quietly as I conjure the mental footage of the two of us hurtling down this very path, threatening to take off into the air and fly over the trees.

No flying today; I'm so tired I can barely walk. I pause by the walled garden and find a wooden bench. It's still damp from last night's rain, but I sit on it regardless. My head is bursting with everything that's happened over the last twenty-four hours, and I can't see how my thoughts will ever come to rest. I feel utterly changed on the inside, and although it's shocking and alarming, it's also exciting. It's as if I've been in a cage, too, for all my life and the door has finally been opened. I'm free. I can go anywhere now. I can do what I like.

I go back to the path and climb to the top of the hill where the bandstand is, gazing down at the bright sward of English green. I probably won't stay in the UK. I might travel to South America, or maybe Japan. I want to go somewhere with a different culture, where I can't speak the language. How liberating that would be, not to be able to explain myself or answer questions. To let my own tongue fall into disuse so that eventually even my memories would sound foreign and incomprehensible.

Leaving the park by the opposite gate, I walk down the hill towards the Heath. I've been on my feet all day and my legs are aching, but I have to keep going. This is my farewell tour and there are places I need to say a proper goodbye to.

I've always loved Hampstead Heath. I love the wide promenade that leads down from the main road, like the arterial vein of a giant leaf, canopied with trees and always slightly damp underfoot. One minute you're tramping along with the Sunday crowds – lovesick couples, cumbersome families, dog-walkers, impatient joggers – and the air is alive with all the languages of the world; then you take a side track and suddenly you're on your own in an enchanted, overgrown labyrinth. It's as if the trees have cast a spell on everyone else and made them disappear. I'm forever getting lost here. The scenery seems to shift when nobody's paying attention, the landmarks mischievously changing places.

I leave the main path as soon as I can, taking a left turn into the woods and walking until I come to a small sun-dappled glade. There's an old dead tree stump lying on the ground, flowers growing through its holes. I couldn't have found my way here deliberately, but I recognise this place. Dad and I played loads of Viking games here. They were just ordinary kids' games like chase and hide-and-seek, but he always gave them a twist. Straggly branches reach out and grab my fingertips, dragging me back in time.

It's summer, and the two of us are on a Viking adventure. We've already sailed our longship across the sea, and after encountering lots of obstacles and dangers, we've finally reached the woods where the fierce and terrifying dragon Fafnir lives. I am Sigurd the warrior and Dad is the dragon. I close my eyes and count while Fafnir goes to hide in his lair. Then, raising my sword and holding my shield before me, I prowl about, looking for my prey.

Suddenly Fafnir leaps out at me with a loud roar and chases me through the trees. But I turn and attack him bravely with my incredibly strong sword, cutting out his heart. I make a pretend fire out of twigs and leaves and roast the heart over the flames. The dragon's blood drips onto my hand, giving me superhuman powers.

'Listen, Sigurd!' says Dad. 'Listen to the birds. What are they saying?'

We stay still and silent, looking up at the sky and peering into the bushes.

'They're warning me that my friend is in fact my enemy,' I say, knowing the story of Sigurd and the evil Regin. 'I must flee this place before he finds me.'

'Quick, quick,' says Dad, standing up. 'Pick up your enchanted sword and go!' And then he decides he wants to be the dragon again, so he comes back to life and chases me all the way back to the car park.

Those beautiful memories have been spoilt now. Because on other days, he was having the same adventures with his other Viking warrior princess. Running around the same trees and hiding behind the same bushes. Filling her head with the same violent stories and talking to the same birds. Or maybe other magic trickery was at work and he was here with both of us at the same time, only we never realised it. When we thought he was hiding, he had in fact slipped into a parallel universe and was helping his other daughter to roast a dragon's heart.

I start to feel angry again. This was supposed to be a coming-to-terms so I can move forward, but it's making everything worse. The sun has dipped behind the trees and there's a new chill in the air. I was going to look for the ponds, but I think I'd better turn back.

It's dark when I reach the flat. There are no lights on in the hallway and the internal doors are closed. No sounds are coming from beyond. I am alone. I gaze at the empty sitting room. Everything looks so tidy and smells so clean – it's as if last night never happened. Perhaps it didn't. Perhaps it was all one long, complicated nightmare…

The doorbell buzzes, twice – three times. Who can that be? I sit up and rise slowly to my feet. I open the front door and my aunt almost falls across the threshold. Her face is tear-stained and her eyes sore with crying.

'Josie! Josie! Oh my God!'

'Lisa? What the hell's the matter?' I catch her before she hits the floor and steer her into the sitting room. 'Here. Sit down.' I lower her onto the sofa.

'I feel so awful, I can't bear it, can't bear it,' she wails, her chest heaving up and down. 'My heart is going to break.'

I sit next to her. 'What? What?'

She stops and stares at me, panting. 'You… don't know?'

'Don't know what?'

'But the police said they'd called round! Hours ago! I was waiting for you to ring. I couldn't stand it any longer, I had to come…'

'I'm sorry, but I don't know what you're talking about.'

'Helen!' she splutters.

'What about her?'

'Oh God, oh God…' She starts to hyperventilate.

'Lisa,' I say firmly. 'Get a grip. What's happened to Helen?'

'She's dead!'

The words ring out across the room like a gunshot. My brain goes into free fall and for a second I can't remember what 'dead' means. Then it hits. I feel all the blood draining away from my extremities, a terrible sinking feeling in the bottom of my stomach, a vast hole opening up inside and the rest of me crumbling into it.

'They won't say how… I don't think they know yet, but I think…' She clasps my hands. 'Maybe it was an overdose? I'm so sorry… I thought… The police told me they'd told you…' Her words sound as if they're coming from a very long way away, at the other end of a large, empty space. 'We were supposed to be meeting for lunch but she didn't turn up. I thought she'd forgotten, so I went round…'

I fold over, unable to take in what she's saying. There's no room inside my head for anything other than those two words: 'she's dead'. *First my father, now my mother. Dead. Gone from me. Why? Why?*

'There was a police car outside the house,' she carries on. 'An officer was guarding the door. He wouldn't tell me anything, wouldn't let me in. Then I saw the cleaner; she was in floods of tears. She said' – she heaves another breath – 'she said that Helen was… She'd found her in bed, couldn't wake her up. Poor woman…'

She runs out of words and starts to cry again. But my eyes are dry. The anger that Valentina whipped up in me last night starts to bubble up again. How dare Mum kill herself? How dare she do that to me? After everything that's happened. After Dad, after all their lies… How dare she run away and leave me on my own?

'Did you tell her about…?' Lisa asks, flinching before I can even reply.

'Yes. Last night.'

She lets out a wail. 'I knew it. It's all my fault, all my fault.'

'No, it's not. It was my decision.'

'But I started it. And it's worse than that. It's my fault that Jerry killed himself.' She chokes up ugly sobs of self-pity. 'I'm so sorry, Josie. I feel terrible.'

I feel my hackles rising. 'Stop, Lisa. I don't want to hear about Dad.'

'But I can't keep it in any longer.'

I'm feeling so angry I could throttle her. 'Shut up! I don't want to know. Not now. Not ever. I've had enough, okay? I can't take it all in.'

But she won't stop. No, she's going to make me listen.

'Jerry and I flirted with each other for years,' she says, trying to steady her voice. 'But nothing ever happened because he wouldn't betray his brother. Brett told me about his secret family, and it excited me. Brett's so dull and boring; I wanted some of what Jerry had.' She looks down, ashamed. 'I was in Manchester for a sales conference and we got blind drunk… I seduced him. It wasn't an affair, it wasn't even a fling. It was a one-night stand.'

My stomach lurches. 'I don't want to hear any more, Lisa,' I say with a trembling voice.

She ignores me. 'I tried to keep it going, gave Jerry a phone just so we could communicate, but he wasn't interested. He tried to end it. I flipped. I threatened to tell Helen everything unless we carried on. Jerry panicked. He was terrified of you finding out, Josie. He loved you so much, he was so proud of you. Compared to that other ghastly girl…'

'Leave Valentina out of it.'

'I pushed him too far, gave him an ultimatum. It's my fault he drove into that tree. Afterwards, I wanted to tell you and Helen, so I left a clue.'

'The roses,' I rasp. 'It was you…'

'Yes… I wanted the boil to burst and… and all the poison to come out, but Brett wanted to cover it up, make it all disappear. He started tracking Valentina's mobile, tried to scare her off with nasty messages, but she wouldn't take any notice.'

My eyes narrow at her. 'Did he try to run her over too?'

'What?'

'Somebody drove at her and knocked over a motorcyclist.'

'Oh God… I don't know… I mean, he never said anything… surely he wouldn't…' she says, her voice breaking up with tears. 'Oh, it's all gone too far. And now Helen's dead… I feel like I killed her myself.'

'She already knew about Sophie and Valentina,' I say.

She shakes her head vehemently. 'No, that's not possible…'

But before I can explain, somebody starts banging loudly on the front door. 'It must be the police,' I say, running into the hallway.

I open up and two smartly dressed women rush in. Behind them, three uniformed officers are blocking the balcony.

'Are you Josie Macauliffe?' says one, who I'm guessing must be a detective.

'Yes… yes, I know what this is about. My mother—'

'Josie Macauliffe, I am arresting you for the murder of Helen Macauliffe. You do not have to say anything, but it may harm your defence if you do not mention when questioned something which you later rely on in court. Anything you do say may be given in evidence. Do you understand?'

'No! What?' I keep protesting as her companion takes out a set of handcuffs and snaps them onto my wrists.

# CHAPTER THIRTY-EIGHT

*Seiðr witchcraft was a solitary art. However, the Norse sagas report that in rare circumstances, seið witches worked together, though they were always kinfolk, usually sisters.*

They take my belongings and ask me to remove my clothes, placing them in large plastic evidence bags. I'm given jogging bottoms and a sweatshirt to wear. Cells are scraped from the inside of my cheek and sent off for DNA identification. I'm asked for my name and date of birth several times, and I sign forms where they point, but I still don't believe this is happening to me.

Everyone's so calm and polite, it's like they're sorry for the inconvenience. I'm in such a daze, I thank them as they explain my rights, accepting their offer of a duty solicitor and making my one permitted phone call so that people know where I am. I call Arun – not because I think he cares, but because I can't think of anyone else. After ringing out a few times, the call is rejected. I leave an incoherent message in a small, flat voice I barely recognise and suspect he might not either.

I have never felt so utterly alone.

The cell door clanks shut behind me and I lie down on the narrow bench bed, hands clasped behind my head, looking up at the ceiling. I'm numb all over. I should be in floods of tears, but there are none left to cry. My insides are dry and stone cold. None of this feels real. It's as if I'm outside my body, looking down at myself.

Mum is dead. I say it over and over again, but I can't seem to perforate this strange, dead shell that's growing over my skin. Questions buzz around me like midges. Why do they think it was murder? How was she killed? Why have they arrested me? How can they possibly think I would kill my own mother?

I soon lose all sense of time. An hour passes, maybe two. The cell is stiflingly warm and smells of previous inhabitants. Their guilt. Their fear. I hear people shouting, doors slamming, loud bursts of laughter, normal chatter. The noises merge as they ricochet off the hard brick walls. Outside, sirens wail, the sound fading and growing, fading and growing.

It's like I'm watching a TV drama. This is the scene where the suspect is waiting in the cell for her solicitor. Soon we'll cut to external shots of people in white suits combing the house, picking things up with tweezers and popping them into bags. Then we'll come back inside the station to a large open-plan incident room. The investigation team is assembled and the lead detective is scrawling 'Josie Macauliffe' on a wipe board, underlining it in red with a large question mark against it. Cut back to the girl in the cell, biting her nails down with anxiety. She knows she's innocent, but the police don't believe her. They've got it horribly wrong. They're wasting valuable time and the real murderer is still out there. But this time the girl in the drama is me, and I can't switch the bloody thing off.

Footsteps are approaching; the door is being unlocked and creaked open. A tall, burly male officer stands just outside the cell and a female uniformed officer walks in. 'Josie? The duty solicitor is here. You can have a short conversation with him, then you'll be interviewed by detectives.'

I roll off the bench and shuffle out in my borrowed socks. The female officer escorts me down the corridor and up a short flight of stairs to the interview rooms. My allocated solicitor, a man in his forties who introduces himself as Jason Mandeville, shakes my hand and we sit down at a desk.

'There's been a mistake,' I tell him straight away. 'I'm completely innocent.'

'Okay…' He takes out a pad and starts making notes. 'There are two ways we can approach this. Either you give your account of what happened and answer their questions as best you can, or you say "no comment" to everything they put to you.'

'"No comment" will make me sound guilty, won't it?' I say. 'I've done nothing wrong, I've got nothing to hide. We need to clear this up so they can get on with finding the person that did it.'

'It's entirely up to you,' he replies. 'But remember, you have a legal right to silence. If you find any of their questions difficult to answer or you don't want to answer them for any reason, then my strong advice would be to say "no comment".'

'I know… I understand that, but surely…' I tail off. What's wrong with him? Doesn't he believe me?

About fifteen minutes later, the two detectives that arrested me enter the room. They sit down and one of them – dark trouser suit, blonde hair and a beaky nose, calls herself DC Collins – inserts a tape. We identify ourselves for the record and Detective Sergeant Brand, who seems to be leading the interview, explains why they're talking to me. She's very quiet and matter-of-fact, as if we're just a group of four people having a chat. The normality of it is freaking me out.

'Josie… I know this must be a very difficult time for you, but we'd like to establish some facts, starting with the last time you saw your mother, Helen Macauliffe. When was that?'

'Last night,' I say quietly. 'She came round to my flat at about… um… nine thirty, ten o'clock. She'd been working at the rehab clinic and she dropped in on her way home.'

'Can you tell us about that visit, please?'

I hesitate. 'Well… I'd asked her to come because I had something I needed to tell her.' I swallow hard. 'It's a long, complicated story…'

'That's all right. We've got time.'

So I go back to the beginning, and soon everything is flooding out of me. I tell them about Dad's death. About finding Valentina and discovering about Sophie. About my sister coming to London and the threats Brett made against her; how he might even have tried to run her over. I tell them about Valentina and Dr Bannister. I even tell them about the rapes.

I don't care what I say any more or how much I expose. My family is dead and on the slab; torso sliced apart, guts on display, the contents of its stomach weighed and picked over, every millimetre of skin put under the microscope. The Macauliffes finally revealed as the corrupt, decaying, deceitful lot they are. We thought we were so marvellous, so clever and successful, but we've been putrefying for years. Now I can smell the rotting flesh, and the stench is overwhelming.

'Can I just be clear before you carry on?' says DS Brand. 'You are an only child, is that right?' I nod. 'Your half-sister Valentina is related to you on your father's side, yes?'

'Yes.'

The sergeant exchanges a quick look with her colleague. 'Thank you… So, if I can take you back to last night. You've had this difficult and traumatic conversation with your mother, then Valentina comes back and tells you about the connection with her past. Then what happens?'

I feel my cheeks reddening as the memory of last night returns. 'We were both very shocked and upset. Valentina was extremely angry; she went crazy – throwing glasses and chairs. She was wasted. I'd drunk too much as well and… I don't know… it all got a bit hysterical. She was working me up into a state, egging me on. I've never felt so angry in my whole life; it was like, really frightening...' A huge wave of emotion suddenly breaks in my throat and I retch. 'Sorry...'

'Are you okay, Josie? If you need a break, just say.'

'No, no, I want to carry on.' I take a sip of water.

'You said you were both feeling shocked and upset, and then you started to feel angry. What happened next?'

'Um... Valentina was being really weird. It was like she was high or something, like she was out of control. She was scaring me. I couldn't take any more, so I ran into my bedroom and locked the door. Just flung myself onto the bed and cried my heart out.'

'And what did Valentina do then?'

'I don't know. I was crying for a long time... I don't know how long, but eventually I calmed down a bit.'

'And Valentina?'

'I don't know. I remember hearing the front door close – I thought she must have gone onto the balcony for a smoke.'

'You didn't see her leave the flat?'

'No, like I said, I'd locked myself in the bedroom. I wanted to get away from her.'

'Did you hear her come back inside?'

'No. She was out there for ages... I fell asleep, so I didn't hear her come back, but in the morning, I woke up really early, about five, and decided to go for a walk. The door to the sitting room was shut; I thought she was asleep on the sofa, but I didn't check in case I woke her. I just left the flat and walked around all day. For hours...'

DS Brand clears her throat. 'Can I take you back to the early hours of this morning? Between the hours of midnight and five a.m. Where were you during that time?'

'Like I just said, I was in bed. Trying to sleep.'

She takes some stapled pages out of her folder and hands them over. 'I'm showing Josie Macauliffe Exhibit JZ12459. These are

CCTV images taken from a property two doors away from 54 Melrose Gardens; you can see the date and time code in the corner. Can you identify the person in those photos?'

My stomach rolls over and over as I flick through the blurry shots. It's dark and rainy, but her face is caught in the lamplight. She's tall and slim. Her hair is tied back. She's wearing flat pumps on her feet, a white shirt, a linen jacket, and, although you can't see it, I know her skirt has embroidery around the hem. These are the clothes I left at the Crossed Keys when we went out dancing; that Valentina wouldn't give back because she claimed they were at the dry cleaner's. The clothes that must have still been in her suitcase…

'This isn't me,' I gasp, my throat feeling strangled. The vile, mad, unthinkable truth starts to take abominable shape. *Valentina killed my mother. She killed her and deliberately tried to make it look like me.*

'Several witnesses have identified you from these images, and these clothes have been found in bins on the ground floor of the block where you live.'

'It isn't me.'

The sergeant takes the sheets away. 'Okay… Can you explain how your debit card was used to make a contactless payment on the number N13 bus at 1.33 a.m. this morning?'

'What? No…' Then I remember. 'I mean… yes, I lent her my card to buy some food.'

'Lent who?'

'Valentina.' My heart is galloping. 'She stole my clothes – she dressed up to look like me… we look a lot alike… Oh my God…'

DS Brand raises her eyebrows, then returns to her notes. 'I'd now like to talk about the initial results of our forensic investigations, Josie. DNA traces have been found at the scene of a person as yet unidentified but who has a 99.9 per cent chance of being a child of the deceased.'

At last, something I can explain. 'I used to live in the house,' I say. 'And I go there all the time.'

'Yes, of course… But these particular traces were found under the victim's fingernails.'

I shudder to a halt. 'What? That's not possible. No, really, this is too much. This is ridiculous, this is wrong, all wrong. You're making a massive mistake here.'

'I don't think so, Josie,' DS Brand says, without any expression. 'But we'll have confirmation when your DNA results come back from the lab.'

'She must have planted my DNA,' I say, realising how crazy the words sound as soon as they leave my mouth. 'I don't know how, but she must have… somehow… She did it, she killed her… My sister… she's trying to frame me… she's evil… she's mad…'

DS Brand watches me dispassionately as I crumple into the chair. 'Do you know something, Josie? I'm starting to wonder if this sister of yours really exists.'

# CHAPTER THIRTY-NINE

*Other terms commonly used for Viking women practising deceiving magic were fjölkunnigr-kona (full-cunning wife) and hamhleypa (skin-changer).*

I've been sent back to the cell to calm down, but it's not working. I'm burning with furious energy, pacing up and down, thumping my fist on the walls.

I suppose I should be grateful to the solicitor for stepping in, but I didn't want a break. I wanted to throw the chair at their smug faces and scream the place down. This whole thing is crazy. I shouldn't be here. It's Valentina they want. They should be out on the streets, searching for her right now, not wasting their time bullying me. That woman is psychotic and extremely dangerous. She could kill again! But no, they think *I'm* the mad one.

I've got to get out of here now. My solicitor should be demanding my immediate release. What's the matter with him – doesn't he believe me either? I've given DS Brand Sophie's details, begged her to contact her. Sophie is the key to getting me out. She knows what Valentina's like, what she's capable of. She'll tell them and then they'll see what a colossal mistake they're making. How can they do this to me when I've just lost my mother? I'm totally innocent, why can't they see that? It's outrageous that they even arrested me. I could lodge a complaint. I *will* lodge a complaint.

And yet…

There's all that evidence against me. I've no alibi, it looks like me on the CCTV footage, and then there's my DNA under Mum's fingernails. I shudder. How the hell did the evil bitch do that? Did she collect it from my dirty clothes? Did she scrape skin cells off me while I was asleep? She must have planned it from the start.

If the police don't work it out, I'm in deep shit. They already think I'm guilty; I can sense it, see their contempt for me in their eyes. They're pretending to be kind but they're just trying to trick me into confessing. I'll never confess, but that won't stop them charging me. Not if they think they can make the evidence stick.

My heart rate starts to speed up again. I just can't get enough air into my lungs. I feel sick. I think I'm having a panic attack. Short, quick breaths groan out of my chest. What if they don't find Valentina? What if she denies it? What if she kills herself and doesn't leave a note?

I'm feeling dizzy; the room is closing in on me. The enormity of the mess I'm in punches me hard and I sink to my knees. My poor mother is dead and I could be charged with her murder! What if the jury don't believe me? I could go to prison for twenty years. I flop onto my side and curl into a ball, sobbing. Thick, wet tears roll off my chin and down my neck, soaking the prison sweatshirt. What if I never get out of here? *Please, please, somebody help me.*

But they tried to help before and I refused. Thought I knew better. I've been such a fool. Other people warned me about Valentina – Sophie, Arun, Brett. Arun knew she was working against me, but I dismissed him. I chose her over him and let him walk out of the door. Even Mum tried. *Do not have* anything *to do with her… Promise me, Josie.* Those were the very last words she ever said to me. Now I understand how real a warning it was. She knew that Valentina was mentally ill, and how she might react if she found out that Dr Bannister was in fact her father's wife. The other woman. *Oh, Mum... Why weren't you honest with me? Why did you persist with all the lies?*

*You were no better*, says a voice inside me. I pull myself in tighter, pounding at my head with angry fists. If I'd told her about Valentina in the beginning, we could have sorted this out, but I was a coward. I'm as bad as Dad, as bad as Mum. Brett and Lisa are to blame too. We've all brought this upon ourselves. Both my parents are dead and Valentina has got her revenge.

The events of the past couple of months flash before my eyes. But this time, I'm seeing them afresh. I let Valentina cast a spell on me – like a naïve kid, I walked right into her web. I wanted to be enchanted. She seemed unreal, like a fantastical experiment. Because she looks so much like me, I saw her as an alternative version of how I might have been. I almost admired her outrageous behaviour, her daring clothes, her constant swearing, how she didn't give a shit about other people's approval. She seemed free. For my whole life, I've been the good girl, the sensible one, the 'easy-care daughter'. Never got into trouble at school, hardly ever rowed with my parents or fell out with friends. Always did my homework on time and revised for my exams. Didn't smoke or get pissed, didn't fake my ID to get into pubs. No piercings, no tattoos. Didn't have sex until I went to uni. I met Arun in Freshers' Week and never even kissed another guy until last...

No, no, I'm not going there. That wasn't my fault. Just thinking about it makes me heave with disgust. Was Valentina behind that too? Oh God... I've been so blind, so fucking stupid... She laid so many traps for me and I walked smiling into them. I can't let her have the last laugh. Can't let her get away with it. She is my sworn enemy. If I ever see her again, I will kill her.

*

Several hours pass before the cell door opens. 'Josie?' says a female voice. 'They're ready to talk to you again.' I look up at her with a grubby, tear-stained face. 'Are you sure you don't want something to eat?' I shake my head vigorously. 'How about a cup of tea?'

'Please.' I know they're just trying to lull me into a false sense of security, but I'm thirsty and need some caffeine. I stand up slowly, pulling down my damp top. She gestures at me to come with her and we go back down the corridor and up to the interview rooms.

The solicitor – Jason something; I've forgotten his surname – is already there. 'How are you?' he asks.

'What's happening?'

'I don't know.'

'Why such a long wait? I've been going demented in that cell, worrying.'

'They'll have been working frantically to pull the case together,' he tells me. 'I imagine they've been hanging on for forensic results.' He checks his watch. 'Time's running out. It's eight o'clock; they've only got two more hours – after that, they have to charge you or let you go.'

Eight o'clock at night? Have I really been here for twenty-two hours? I rub my fists into my eyes. No wonder I feel so wretched.

DS Brand and DC Collins enter the room and we go through the same procedure with the tape, introducing ourselves and recapping why we're all here. I sense a more friendly tone, but that makes me feel worse rather than better. A feeling of dread creeps through my veins as I think about what the solicitor has just said. If they charge me, this could be the start of a new life behind bars. It's so wrong it's absurd, and yet it's starting to feel possible. They could really do this…

'Okay, Josie, let's bring you up to date. First, I'd like to apologise for what I said earlier,' says DS Brand. 'I shouldn't have implied that you'd made up the existence of your half-sister. I was feeling frustrated because I felt that you weren't cooperating – it was the middle of the night and we were all feeling stressed and tired. I'm sorry.' She coughs and looks to DC Collins for approval. 'We've managed to get in touch with Valentina Lane's mother. She's sent through some photos of her daughter and she is indeed very similar-looking to you, although not identical.'

'Thank God,' I say, starting to shake.

'We've had an expert looking at the CCTV footage and we've been examining the other forensic evidence and talking to witnesses. After careful consideration, we've decided not to hold you any longer. For the time being at least, you're free to leave.'

I'm stunned. 'What? *What?* I can go? No charges?' A wave of relief washes over me.

'None at all. I'm sorry for the distress this must have caused you, but I hope you understand that this is a very serious crime, and we have to explore every avenue of investigation.'

As the wave recedes, it leaves something behind on the shore. Anger. Fear. Doubt. 'Have you found Valentina, then? Has she confessed?'

'No, but we are looking for her as a matter of urgency.'

My brow creases. I'm pleased, but I don't understand. If they haven't arrested Valentina, why are they letting me go? It doesn't make sense.

'What about the DNA you found under my mother's fingernails?' DS Brand bites her lip and DC Collins shifts about uncomfortably. 'Well? What is it? Did someone make a mistake?'

'No… there was no mistake,' she replies, her face pinking with embarrassment. 'The results from the swab we took from you yesterday have come back and there's no match with the traces found on the victim. I'm very sorry, we jumped to conclusions there. Understandable in the circumstances…'

'Sorry, I don't get it. You said the DNA you found was 99.9 per cent certain to belong to my mother's child.'

She hesitates, then replies, 'Yes, that is still correct.'

'But… but…' I'm so exhausted, and I've been here so long, I can't compute the information. 'Are you saying that…' No, no, it can't be true. 'That Valentina is my mother's daughter?'

'We can't confirm that,' replies DS Brand carefully, 'not until we can test your half-sister's DNA.'

She's sticking to the rule book here, but we all know Valentina killed my mother, so what's she's saying is…

'We're not half-sisters then,' I gasp. 'We're *full* sisters!'

The detectives exchange an awkward glance. Something's wrong. What is it? What do they know but can't bring themselves to tell me?

DS Brand inhales. 'No, you *are* half-sisters, on your father's side, just as you were told. I don't know how to put this, Josie, but… the DNA tests prove that Helen Macauliffe is not your mother. In fact, the two of you are not related in any way.'

# CHAPTER FORTY

*This year came dreadful fore-warnings over the land of the Northumbrians... These were immense sheets of light rushing through the air, and whirlwinds, and fiery dragons flying across the firmament. (Anglo-Saxon Chronicle, AD 793)*

After seven hours of involuntary eavesdropping on the two women behind me, the coach stops in the centre of Newcastle and several passengers, including them, get off. The driver announces that there'll be a forty-five-minute break, warning us that the coach will leave promptly, whether we are all on board on not. I put my jacket on and descend, joining the back of the queue at the nearest takeaway café.

I haven't eaten properly since Thursday evening, and, although I'm not hungry, I ought to try to force something down. Buying a can of Coke and a packet of tuna sandwiches, I sit down on the kerb and attempt a few mouthfuls. But the edges of the bread are dry and the tuna has a suspicious tang to it, so I throw the second sandwich in the bin and climb back on board.

Sipping at my drink, I stare out of the window at the new passengers assembling with their luggage, waiting for the driver to come back and open up the boot. I expect most of them are going all the way to Edinburgh. I sigh. Only two more hours till we reach my stop. Two more hours to sit quietly and reflect on the last twelve.

I didn't know where I wanted to go at first. Abroad was my first instinct, so I got the coach to Stansted airport and wandered around for a few hours looking at departure boards. Norway, I thought. I could trace my heritage among the fjords. It's a stunningly beautiful country with hundreds of thick, dense forests, perfect for hiding. Not that I'd survive more than a few days in the wilderness. Then I remembered the insane cost of beer and food over there.

I was worried about the cost of a ticket to go further afield, and anxious that my passport would be flagged. The longer I left it, the more likely that would be. Either I had to get on a plane within the next hour or forget the whole idea. So I took the coach back to London and hung around Victoria coach station all night, pretending I was waiting for a friend. There were lots of destinations available to me, coaches heading out in all directions. Where did I want to lose myself – Bournemouth, Barcelona, Berwick-upon-Tweed? The answer came to me in a flash. Of course. If I couldn't go to the land of my ancestors, I would go to the next best place – where it all began.

The driver comes back, loads up and closes the boot. My new fellow passengers climb aboard and take their seats. We crawl out of the city centre and get back on the A1. I curl my knees up and stare out of the window, keeping my eyes peeled for road signs to my destination, counting off the miles.

We must have taken this route on family holidays several times, but the scenery isn't familiar to me. I guess it's been a while, and the car was so tightly packed you could hardly see out of the window. We always took clothes and equipment for every imaginable weather: tents to shelter in on the beach, heavy waterproofs and thin shower capes, a sturdy windbreak, a parasol, a three-pack of disposable barbecues, vacuum flasks, sun hats and shades, wetsuits for me and Dad, buckets and spades, a cricket set.

Thick jumpers and wellies. Flip-flops and swimming costumes. Mum always wanted to go to Spain or Italy, but Dad wouldn't hear of it. Thinking about it now, he probably didn't want to get a telltale tan.

I've no idea what the time is, but it feels elastic and stretched to its limit. The drone of the coach engine forces my eyes to close for a few moments. I see her, legs kicking, arms flailing about. It's like a movie playing on a loop inside my head. The more times I view it, the less shocked I feel, the less it looks or feels like me. If somebody told me I'd imagined the whole thing, I'd probably believe them. Dad and I were always acting out Viking fantasies, some of them quite violent. I think that's what I thought I was doing – working myself into a berserker frenzy, hunting down my enemy and taking her by surprise. But I held the pillow down for too long. I held it until she stopped pretending to be suffocated and it spoilt the game.

I lift my hand to my throat and touch the tiny Thor hammer. What are the limits of its magic power? Can it protect me from the forces of good, as well as evil?

At last the coach pulls into Berwick and several of us get out. Taxis are waiting at the rank, and I'm almost tempted to slip into one and travel the rest of the journey in style. But taxi drivers remember people, and I need anonymity. I drag the suitcase to the bus stop and study the timetable. The next bus is at ten past five. Forty minutes to wait. More time for contemplation. I'm itching to use my phone, but I daren't switch it on. Not until I'm ready.

I wonder what's happening, how far the detectives have got with the investigation. Have they arrested Josie, or have they worked it out? Is my face plastered all over the internet? Are people being advised not to confront me but to call 999 immediately? I adjust the scarf around my scratched neck and hunch my shoulders forward, staring down at the tarmac. I should have bought a cap to hide my hair. I should have sat on the coach with my bright blue eyes firmly closed. I must have been caught on CCTV a hundred times. But I guess you have to know where to look…

The bus chugs into the square and I wrench my case up its steps. 'Single to Beal,' I mumble to the driver, hefting the case into the luggage rack and sitting down in the closest seat. We pull away and I lean against the window, covering the side of my face with my hand. My heart sinks as we start to retrace our steps, heading south and back onto the A1. But after a few miles, the bus turns off and sets me down in the centre of the village.

I watch it drive away, then walk to the crossroads and study the sign. Holy Island is clearly signposted, and so I begin the last stage of my private pilgrimage. I trundle the heavy case behind me – why I've brought so many possessions with me, I don't know; I wasn't thinking straight. Right now, there doesn't seem to be any scenario that would involve even one change of clothes. I should dump the case in a ditch, but I can't seem to let go of the handle. Most of my life is in the case, and it's insisting on coming with me to the very end.

The land around me is flat. Green and brown fields stretch as far as I can see, and the sky above is huge and overwhelming. I'm not entirely alone. Nobody else is walking, but cars drive past, some of them with foreign number plates. A pickup truck hoots, but doesn't stop to offer me a lift. More vehicles are driving away from the island than towards it, which makes me think that the tide is rising. The causeway will be drowned and I probably won't be able to cross tonight.

I continue on the footpath until it comes to a stop just past a farm, where the road bends and narrows. Another, separate walkway is signposted and I take that, still following the thread of the road, but protected by a hedge. My feet and lower back are aching, my palm is sore from gripping the handle of the suitcase.

It is the burden I must pull behind me, like the crucifixes the Christian pilgrims carry across the sands here each Easter. Although I'm not a Christian, I'm a pagan. The enemy in these holy parts.

As I march towards the coast, my eyes are drawn to the island in front of me, its ruins rising out of the cold North Sea. I imagine myself in a Viking longship, thirteen hundred years ago, rowing through the squally waters with the raiding party, armed with iron swords and embossed wooden shields, looking for somewhere to beach; the monks shivering in their priory, clutching their treasure and fearing for their lives.

Our visits to the Lindisfarne Centre were always slightly uncomfortable. Dad would talk too loudly about the corruption of religious faith, and the incredible wealth that the monastery had amassed, making themselves too easy a target. He revelled in the violence of his ancestors, and the stupidity of the monks. And once he made a complaint in the shop because they sold fridge magnets featuring Vikings wearing horned helmets, which as every respectable historian knows is a popular misconception.

Very few vehicles are driving in my direction now, but there's a surge in tourist traffic coming the other way. I reach the shore and the car park that sits at the start of the causeway. It's empty but for a couple of camper vans, no doubt waiting for the return of their owners. A sign depicting a 4x4 car tumbling into the waves warns against venturing further. This is where Dad and I always parted company with Mum. She drove across the causeway, while we walked across the muddy slakes, meeting up on the island two hours later for chicken and chips and a pint of 'mead' in the pub.

I put the suitcase down on its base and sit on it. God knows where I'll sleep tonight. There are no buildings out here, no hotels or B & Bs, no houses or barns. The wind whips across my face, tasting salty, like overseasoned food. Where to go? I look up at the thin strip of raised road, where a small group of tiny figures is approaching. Standing up, I set the case upright and walk with it to the back of the car park. I shove the case in a dip behind some bushes and then crouch down. Several minutes pass before I hear the sound of boots, the murmur of conversation, the opening and closing of car doors. Engines start up and tyres crunch slowly over the gravel, then the sounds fade and all I can make out is the rush of seawater and the cry of birds.

I emerge from my hiding place and take in the desolate but utterly beautiful scene. Time to turn the phone on and pray that there'll be a signal. I need to do this quickly, then turn it off again. The handset springs to life. I swipe into the camera and, turning with my back to the sea and the island, hold it up with an outstretched arm.

My bare face looks pale, my skin blotchy, my eyes rimmed red with tiredness. The wind is tangling my hair into knots and making it dance, threatening to obscure the background. I tuck it behind my ears and stare sternly into the viewfinder. This is not the time for a smile. I capture the picture and immediately click to share, adding a short caption.

*Come and find me.*

# CHAPTER FORTY-ONE

*Vikings would readily fight to the death to defend the honour of their families. Murder was always avenged. As they believed their death was predetermined by the gods, they had no cause to fear it.*

I'm back in my own clothes, waiting at the desk while the custody sergeant fetches my belongings. The last twenty-four hours feel simultaneously like forever and no time at all. It's Saturday evening, or so they tell me – I wouldn't have been able to guess. I haven't slept since I woke up yesterday morning, and the fatigue, coupled with shock and an almost guilty feeling of relief, is taking its toll. I'm shivering to the core, and yet I'm not cold.

'Here we go,' the sergeant says, laying the contents of my bag on the counter. 'Please check everything's there so I can tick them all off.' I survey the familiar items that I carry around every day like a burden: a purse Mum bought me last birthday, my phone, my set of keys, a lipstick and a tin of balm, a small packet of tissues, a comb, hairgrips, a small bottle of deodorant, the photo of Dad and Valentina I stole from Sophie's house. I allow myself a short, ironic laugh. I had evidence of her existence on me all the time, but had forgotten.

I need to burn this photograph, but I can't do it here. I put everything back in the bag and sign the form, refusing their kind offer to call a taxi. The sergeant unlocks the door leading back up to the station reception and wishes me a pleasant evening. *A pleasant evening? What is he talking about?* I walk unsteadily up the stairs, drunk on a heady mix of opposing feelings.

I'm disorientated. I was so shocked when they arrested me, I didn't notice which police station I was being taken to. I don't know where I am, literally and metaphorically. I'm glad to be free, but scared to face the new reality. It's a changed world out there, still full of danger. I'm alone, my parents are both dead and the closest relative I have left is my sworn enemy.

I walk into the foyer with my head bowed, so locked in powerful thought that at first I don't hear my name being called. It's only when he chases after me and puts his hand on my shoulder that I realise he's here.

'Arun!' I turn round, surprised. I'd given up all hope of him hours ago. 'Nobody told me.'

'No? I've been waiting all day. I got your message. I was so worried, but I'm glad you called.' He pulls me towards him and hugs me tightly. 'I'm so sorry about Helen, it's just… just unspeakably awful.' My arms hang limp at my sides. I want to embrace him but I feel too weak.

'Let's go,' I say dully. 'I really need to get out of this place.'

It's already dark outside – the sun has risen and set again without me – and for a moment it feels as if time has stood still. Arun takes my arm as we walk down the steps of the police station. I must seem vulnerable, because he keeps hold of me as we glide through the busy side streets, steering me around lamp posts and between passers-by. The weekend is its usual lively, fun-seeking self. Normally we'd be part of it, but tonight none of it touches me. I feel invisible.

We don't speak. There's so much to say, but the words are shy, the conversations too weighty to hold in the street. We arrive at our car; typically, it has a parking ticket. Arun swears as he removes the plastic bag from under the windscreen wipers and unlocks the doors. He helps me into the passenger seat, then walks around and gets in on the driver's side. He puts the fob into the ignition but doesn't turn the engine on.

'What is it?' I ask.

He screws up his face. 'I don't know where to go.'

'Home?'

'We can't. The police are there, gathering forensic evidence. I don't know why. It's not the crime scene…'

'They're probably looking for Valentina's DNA.' I purse my lips. In some ways, this is over. In others, it's only just begun.

'We could go to my mum and dad's – they want to help.'

'That's very sweet, but I don't think I could cope with them right now.'

'No, I understand. Okay… a hotel then?'

I turn my head towards him. 'Is that where you've been staying? At your parents'?'

He nods. '*And* when I said I was at the stag weekend… I hated lying, but I badly needed some space. I'm sorry.'

'Don't be silly. I should be the one saying sorry to you.'

'No, you shouldn't. You did nothing wrong.'

'Didn't I?' I start making a mental list. I didn't listen to his warnings about Valentina. I was raped and didn't trust in his love enough to tell him. I put stupid loyalty to a stranger before the man I wanted to spend the rest of my life with. I threw away the best relationship I'll probably ever have…

'Josie,' he says gently. 'There's something I need to tell you – about Valentina…'

I hold up my hand. 'Please, no more revelations.'

'But it's important – you need to know. I've been feeling so awful.'

'Please, no… I can't take any more. Not now. You came to the police station. You believed I was innocent, you stood by me. That's all I care about this minute. The rest can wait.'

There's a long pause. 'I don't know what to do...' He blinks back tears.

'Let's go before we get another ticket.'

'But where to?'

'I don't know. Just drive. Get me out of the city.'

He turns on the engine and pulls out of the space. I sit back in my seat, feeling a hard lump forming in my chest. Suddenly I have a desperate urge to escape, to get away from everything and everyone. That's flight, a natural response. But I also feel the urge to fight. I want to track Valentina down and confront her face to face.

We're only a couple of miles from the start of the M1, so Arun takes the road heading north. The traffic is heavy. We crawl to the unwieldy roundabout where everything meets, then pick up speed as we enter the motorway.

'Where to now?' he asks.

'I don't care.'

'I'll keep going until you tell me to stop,' he says. 'Deal?'

'Deal.'

There's something hypnotic about motorways. Thoughts – some of them upsetting and frightening – drift in and out of my head, but none of them stays for long. I feel as if I'm in some kind of suspended state. The emotions I should be feeling have been put out of reach for the time being, like helium balloons stuck in the rafters. I know they're up there, I can see them hovering above me, full and ready to explode. The fullest, largest balloon is the one for Mum. I've not accepted that she's dead yet. For the time being, I'm keeping her alive.

'It was Lisa that left the bouquet and the odd message at the crash scene,' I say, after many miles of strange silence.

'Lisa?' Arun glances at me curiously, then looks back at the road.

'She'd had a fling with Dad. She wanted it to carry on but he wasn't interested. So she threatened to reveal his "darkest secret".' I sigh and stare out of the window at the shrouded black landscape, pierced with distant dots of light. 'She thought the big mystery was the other wife and daughter, but the darkest secret was much darker than that.'

'What do you mean?'

I pause, still not sure I believe what I'm saying. 'Valentina killed her own mother.'

'I'm sorry?'

'It's true. I'm not Helen's daughter, not biologically, but Valentina is.'

Arun turns to gape at me and swerves out of the lane. 'How come?'

I shrug hopelessly. 'I'm still trying to work it out. Did they all know? Was there some kind of arrangement? It's just mind-blowing. God knows who my mother really is…' Tears assemble behind my eyes as one of the helium balloons hanging in the rafters slowly starts to descend. I'm too tired, too mixed up. I have to bat these emotions away again.

'Perhaps it's So—' he ventures.

'Not now. We'll talk about it later.'

He drives on, stacking up the miles. I close my eyes and let the deep hum of the engine take me into a fitful sleep. It's late, and getting colder by the minute. Arun turns up the temperature, and warm stale air flutters across my face. I feel hungry for the first time in two days.

Easing my bum off the seat, I stretch my restless legs. I have no idea how long we've been driving, but we need a break. I open my bag and take out my phone. It's been switched off, so I instinctively press the on button. I don't know why, but I've a really strong feeling that Valentina's trying to get in touch.

Arun turns to me, frowning. 'Don't start looking at that. We're escaping, right?'

'Yeah, let me just do a quick check, then I'll turn it off again.' The handset cranks into action and I stare at the screen impatiently as icons flash excitedly before my eyes. Then it bleeps, telling me I have a message from an unknown number. Even before I open it, I know exactly who it's from. Arun's eyes are fixed on the road, but I angle the screen away from him just in case he tries to look.

She's sent me a selfie. For the first time, I see our differences and none of our similarities. Her eyes, although as bright as mine, are more almond-shaped, and her nose is a little broader. My lips are fuller, my hair less copper red. And there's a hardness behind her stare that I could never impersonate. She's standing in swampy marshland, with a flat grey sea behind her. Long wooden poles are sticking out of the mud, and beyond I can see the unmistakable shape of an island. Beneath the picture is a brief, simple message. I read it and then turn the phone off.

'I've just had an idea,' I say, as casually as I can. 'I know where I want to go.'

'Okay. Where?'

'Lindisfarne.'

'Lindisfarne?' he repeats. 'What, in Northumbria?'

I nod.

'Why?'

But I can't tell him why. If I do, he'll call the police straight away. 'It's a place we went to a lot when I was a child,' I say instead. 'I've lots of happy memories there.'

'Can't you think of somewhere nearer? It's virtually Scotland. It'll take hours to get there.'

'I don't care. I need to go there, now. We keep going until I say, that's what you agreed.'

'Yes, but…'

I put my hand on his thigh. 'If you come with me, it's quits between us, okay? Whatever it is you've done, I forgive you, and we never have to talk about it, not ever.'

'But, Josie, it's not that simple…'

'If you won't come with me, we'll turn off at the next exit and you can make your own way home. I'm going there and you can't stop me.'

# CHAPTER FORTY-TWO

*The worst fate for a Viking was to be declared an outlaw. If convicted of a serious crime, they were banished forever to the wilderness. People were encouraged to hunt them down and kill them.*

It's almost dawn when we arrive at Beal village crossroads and take the narrow road leading to the causeway. I feel cold and wretched with tiredness; the momentousness of the last thirty-six hours, added to the six-hour journey, catching up on me. As we pull into the car park, I almost expect to see Valentina standing there, waving a greeting. But there's nobody about. We park up and get out.

Arun shoves his hands into his pockets, yawning. 'This is a bit desolate.'

'Wait till it gets light. It's really beautiful.'

The shore is a swirling expanse of oozy mudflats, coarse wet sand and shallow rivulets, interspersed with small black rocks and thick, wiry grasses. The smell of salt rises from the marshes. I clutch his arm and we stare out to sea, our eyes adjusting to the chilly blue light as the sun breaks over the low outline of Holy Island. The causeway is still exposed and looks completely passable, but I know the sea moves fast around here and can cover the road in minutes.

Where did Valentina spend the night? I look around furtively. The only place to shelter is the refuge box on the bridge in the middle of the causeway. It's supposed to be for people who get stranded by the incoming tide, but it would be the ideal place to rest and look out at the shoreline.

'I want to walk across,' I say. 'On my own.'

'Fine,' Arun says, still not suspecting anything. 'I'll go and catch some sleep in the car.'

He makes to go and I catch him by the arm, pulling him to me. We kiss. 'I love you,' I say.

'Me too.'

'We'll get through this somehow.'

He swallows. 'Yeah… hope so… Have a good walk. I'll come and meet you later, yeah?' I watch him as he goes back to the car and gets into the back seat.

The metalled road is damp from its previous submersion. On either side, shallow pools shimmer like silver trays, and the muddy slakes have a gunmetal sheen. When I was little, we used to leave the car in the car park and walk along the causeway until we reached the bridge. From there, we stepped off and went barefoot across the sands. I can still remember wading through the mud and getting stuck; Dad pulling me free and carrying me on his back until he grew tired or I asked to be put down.

We always followed the long line of tall, barnacle-encrusted poles that mark the way to the island shore, even though at times it meant sloshing through gullies of freezing water. Other routes look drier and easier to the untrained eye, but they can be treacherous. It was the one time Dad stuck to the rules, reminding us that people had been drowning here for over a thousand years…

Thin eastern sunlight coats the road. I shield my eyes as I look ahead. I can make out a silhouetted figure climbing down from the refuge box. I don't need to see her face to know that it's Valentina. My heart trips over itself. She walks quickly towards me, brandishing a long rough stick. Her head is held defiantly high and there's a warrior air about her. I can feel my knees weakening, but I force myself forward, drawing myself upright and quickening my pace.

We meet face-to-face on the bridge. 'Sis!' she cries. 'You came. I knew you would.'

I stop a few paces away from her. She stands erect, a dark, distorted version of me, a black angel in a halo of cold morning light.

'Shall we get on with it, then? Before everyone wakes up? Not here on the road. On the beach, obviously.' She rests the stick against the railing and starts unlacing her boots. 'Barefoot is best – but you already know that. You've done the Pilgrims' Way dozens of times. Our father duplicated everything. Must have been so tedious for him, but at least he was fair, and it reduced his chances of slipping up – clever bastard.' She whips off her black socks and rolls up the bottom of her jeans. 'Come on.'

I hesitate, looking at the silvery streams snaking between the mudflats. Dare I risk it? The tide is on its way in, and soon the beach will be covered.

'It's safe,' she says, reading my mind. 'I've been watching it from my little tower.'

I bend down and slip off my trainers. I don't know why I'm doing this, but I also know that I can't stop myself. It's as if she's enchanted me. My body is entwined in a magic thread and she's pulling on the end of it.

Valentina picks up her stick again and leads the way. I step down onto the mud and icy black gunge oozes between my toes, shocking them into numbness. The wooden poles line the way like emaciated sentries. We go from one to the next, our feet sliding and squelching as we pick our way over the dull mirrored surface, now sticky, then stony, and all around us the sea quietly encroaching on our space.

'Hurry up, sis!' she shouts, not looking back.

As I follow her, the anger starts to grow inside me. She's so full of herself, so mocking of me. I hate her like I've never hated anyone before. *You killed my mother, you killed my mother*, I chant under my breath, working myself up, letting my feelings propel me into action. I push off the sand and charge at her, leaping like a demon onto her back. The stick flies out of her hand as she screams and falls forward, her knees sinking into the sticky mud. I stay with her, fixing my legs around her waist and tearing at her hair, roaring and calling her every filthy curse I can think of.

She digs at my ankles with her sharp nails, squirming her body until she breaks free. I topple sideways and roll over onto my back. She flings herself on top of me and we wrestle in the mud, scratching and slapping and punching. This is the fight she wanted. That we *both* wanted. Enemy against enemy. Sister against sister. As we roll around, our bodies sinking and squelching into the mud, I pin her down, grabbing the Thor pendant and twisting the leather lace tightly around her neck. It cuts into her skin and she opens her mouth, sucking in air. Her eyes are rolling; she's struggling to breathe.

I look down at her frightened face. I'm on fire with hatred, I could strangle her so easily. But… but do I want to be a killer too? She seizes on my hesitation, raising her arm and punching me in the face. My grip loosens and I fall back into a swirling pool of froth.

She scrambles free and staggers to her feet. The cold North Sea is around her calves and rising rapidly. I lift myself out of the water and stand up. We face each other, soaking wet, black with mud and shivering violently.

'Now what?' she shouts, her hair slapping her face in the bitter wind. 'Shall we fight to the death?'

The tide is coming in fast. The way back to the causeway is already covered with frothy grey water. We'll never make it to land – we're going to drown here, fight or no fight.

'This is fucking insane!' I shout back. She laughs at me maniacally.

I quickly glance behind me. Ten poles or so beyond, I can see another refuge box, its high stilts sticking out of a mudbank. It looks like a tree house in an invisible tree. Using all my strength, I pull my feet out of the mud and start to run towards it.

'Fucking coward!' Valentina cries. 'Stay and fight!' I don't look back, but I hear her feet splashing through the water as she charges after me, roaring a battle cry.

I make it to the box first. Planting my slimy wet feet on the bottom rung of the wooden ladder, I start to climb up. I know I'm backing myself into a corner, but it's better than certain drowning. She's right behind me now, grunting as she claws at the rungs, heaving herself up. As I haul myself onto the platform, she reaches out and grabs me by the ankle. I stumble and fall flat on my face. She clambers after me, and, as I roll away, she leaps on me like a cat, clamping her thighs around my waist. Then, reaching into the back pocket of her jeans, she takes out a jagged shard of bottle glass and holds it against my throat.

I feel the sharp edge against my skin, poised to cut. I can't let her kill me. I have to fight. But I have no weapon. All I have is the truth.

'I need to tell you something…'

'No more talking; I'm *sick* of talking.' She presses down with the glass and I feel it tearing my skin.

'I know the darkest secret.'

'Who fucking cares?' she spits into my face. Her thighs tighten their vice-like grip around me. I'm trapped, but I mustn't seem afraid. One false move and she could slice an artery.

I stare solemnly into her wicked flashing eyes. 'We were… swapped shortly after birth.'

'Oh fuck off!' She pushes the glass in further and I gasp.

'I promise you, it's true. The police proved it with DNA.' Her expression flickers. 'Dr Bannister was your mother, not mine. You should have had my life and I should have had yours.'

'You're lying!' she shouts above the wind. 'You're as bad as the rest of them. Always lying, lying, lying…'

'I swear on my life, I'm not.'

She stares down at me, searching behind my eyes. 'But that's… it's impossible.'

'I promise you, it's true. I don't know why or how… it just is.'

'No… no. They wouldn't… wouldn't do that.' Her voice falters. 'They wouldn't do that to me…'

'They did.'

Her hand starts to tremble as the horror of what she's done sinks in. 'Oh God… Oh God… I killed my real mother… is that what you're saying?'

'Yes, Valentina…'

She takes the glass away and loosens her grip on me. 'But I'm not Valentina, I'm Josie! That's what you said.' She gets off me and stands up. Her thin wet body is shaking like a twig in the wind. 'It's *Josie* that's the nutjob, the crazy girl who gets into trouble, who won't let anyone love her; *Josie* who pushes everyone away before they can abandon her. *Josie* that lives in the darkness and feels all this crushing pain.' She pauses and looks down at me, as if remembering I'm there. 'Funny, isn't it? I hated being Valentina; I so wanted to be you, and now it turns out I am you after all.'

'Yes,' I say gently, getting to my feet. I move slowly towards her, holding out my hand. 'They did terrible things to us. But it's all over now.'

She stands upright, her figure suddenly noble. With one stroke, she slashes the glass across her own throat, drawing a thin red ribbon of blood. I watch, transfixed in horror, as she snaps the Thor pendant from her neck and throws it to the floor.

Her face contorts with pain as the blood starts to run. 'All that… Viking stuff,' she gasps, 'is a load… of… shit.' I move towards her again, but she backs away, hitting the low wall and falling headlong off the platform. There is a cry, and then a loud splash as she somersaults into the water.

For a few seconds, I can't move. Can't breathe. Then I take a few wobbly steps forward to look over the side into the murky, fizzing water. There's no sign of her. Just a thin blue scarf I know to be mine, weaving like a snake through the waves.

I slump to the floor. Above me, grey clouds edged with gold are scudding across the dawn sky. I stay there for a few seconds, panting, my chest swollen with pain.

I see a small red dinghy heading towards me. Flashing blue lights on the mainland. A group of people standing at the shore. Which one is Arun? I can't make him out, but I know he's there. Anxious. Waiting. Wondering which sister has drowned and which has survived.

I hardly know myself.

# EPILOGUE

## August 1992

*A special type of seiðr magic, known as sjónhverfing, was used for the 'deceiving of the sight'. Victims had their minds warped so that they could not see things as they truly were.*

The sun floated behind a cloud and Jerry felt the instant drop in temperature. He looked down at his girls, their flawless skin breaking out in tiny goose bumps. It was time to take them home. He gave them one last adoring look, as if they were presents he longed to keep for himself, then wrapped them up quickly.

He put Josie back in her buggy and lifted Valentina into the sling. It was only a short walk back to Sophie's flat and he wanted to relish these last moments of having them together. 'All babies look the same when they're newborn,' Brett had scoffed when Jerry had told him about the amazing likeness between his daughters. The only way to prove it had been to compare them in the flesh. It had been a risky enterprise, but worth it. Risks were always worth it, in his experience. He was glad he hadn't taken his brother's advice. Thinking about it, he almost never did.

When he got to the flat, he wheeled the buggy down the side alley and left Josie in the back garden, shutting the gate and returning to the front entrance. She would be fine by herself for a few minutes. Sophie knew about Josie, of course, but her emotions were very raw on the subject. He knew she was trying to behave herself because she was scared that he would abandon them, but he didn't want to push it. It was bad enough at home, with Helen being so tired and grumpy and the feeding not working. He suspected post-natal depression. How had he got himself into this extraordinary position of having two new mothers to look after?

'I'm back,' he called, opening the front door with his key. Sophie came out of the kitchen and helped take Valentina out of the sling. 'I'm cooking a chilli,' she said hopefully.

'Sorry, I can't stay.' Her face fell, but he smothered it with kisses. 'I'll try to pop over tomorrow – if I can…'

He hurried away, retrieving Josie from the back garden and almost running down the street, his heart bouncing with the audacity of what he had achieved. He carried the buggy down the steps of the tube station and rode the four stops that separated his two lives.

When he got in, Helen was up and dressed and seemed rested, grateful for having some time to herself. She put Josie in the bath and then laid her on the bed, bundled in a white hooded towel. 'Jerry, come here!' she said. 'Josie's thumbs are stiff. I can't move them. Have you noticed?'

He paused outside the bedroom, his pulse instantly quickening. Valentina had been born with trigger thumbs. It was a sign of Viking genes, apparently, which had selfishly thrilled him, even though it was a slight deformity. Had Josie been born with them too and they hadn't spotted it?

Or had he done something unimaginably awful?

No, surely not. He entered and bent over his daughter, his legs feeling weak beneath his giant frame.

'I've heard of this before,' said Helen. 'It's unusual to have it in both thumbs, but it's a very easy operation; they just release the tendons or something. Poor little thing… how did Mummy miss that?'

He looked on in horror. It was the mischievous god Loki at work – he'd made him mix the girls up to force the secret out into the open. He should have told Helen there and then. Should have confessed about his young student lover who had borne him a daughter just a few days later in the same hospital. Who was compliant and undemanding, who loved him unconditionally and seemed willing – if not delighted – to share. He should have told her.

But he didn't. Instead, he took Valentina – no, she was Josie now – by her tiny hand and wrapped it around his finger. 'No, I didn't notice either,' he said, his words cursing him forever.

When he next saw Sophie, she remarked that Valentina's thumbs had sprung free all by themselves, and how wonderful it was that she'd been spared the operation. He didn't tell her either; just nodded and smiled like the miserable coward he truly was.

After all, he already had so many secrets – what difference could one more make?

# A LETTER FROM JESS

Thank you so much for reading *The Good Sister* – I hope you were gripped by the story and enjoyed following the fortunes of the contrasting characters of Josie and Valentina. You can keep up to date with what I'm writing next by signing up at the link below. Your email address will never be shared and you can unsubscribe at any time.

www.bookouture.com/jess-ryder/

I'd also be really grateful if you could take a little time to post a short review telling other readers why you liked the book. As an avid reader myself, I find reviews really helpful when it comes to deciding what to read next.

One of the great things about being published by Bookouture is that authors are in touch with their readers via social media. Since my debut Jess Ryder novel, *Lie to Me*, was published in April, I've received some fantastic feedback from readers and book bloggers, and I'd like to take this opportunity to thank all of you for taking the time to post your reviews and comments. Writing is a solitary activity, so being able to communicate with readers makes a huge difference. It's easy to get in touch with me via my Facebook page, Goodreads, Twitter or my Jess Ryder website.

Thanks again for reading *The Good Sister*. I hope it will make you want to try my other psychological thriller, *Lie to Me*, too.

I look forward to hearing from you.

Jess Ryder

@jessryderauthor

Website www.jessryder.co.uk

 @jessryderauthor

# ACKNOWLEDGEMENTS

Every time I write a novel, the person that always deserves a huge thank-you is my mother, Brenda Page, and this book is no exception. I'm very grateful for all the research she does – this time particularly into the Vikings – but also for her listening and reading skills.

I would also like to thank my dear friends Karen Drury and Fiona Eldridge for their extremely useful feedback on the first draft, and my youngest son Harry, who as a writer/director himself is a great person to discuss story and structure with.

Thanks also to my literary agent, Rowan Lawton of Furniss Lawton, who has been incredibly supportive throughout this process; and to my editor at Bookouture, Jessie Botterill, who has such a positive energy and enthusiasm for making novels the best they can be. Couldn't have done it without you both.

And finally to my husband David, who always seems to know when to offer helpful suggestions and when to shut up and just listen.

CPSIA information can be obtained
at www.ICGtesting.com
Printed in the USA
LVOW10s1554040917
547475LV00016B/1424/P